LIN FINITY

AND THE

FLIGHTS TO FOREVER

Other Books By Edward Allen Karr

*   *   *   *   *

SERIES: Fringes Of Infinity

Lin Finity And Her Mayhem Rising – Book One

Lin Finity In Holding On
(A Fringes Of Infinity Novella)

Lin Finity And The Words Unspoken – Book Two

Lin Finity And The Islands Of Time – Book Three

*   *   *   *   *

SERIES: Thrills N Kills In The Hills

Dayzee Dazzle And The Kildare Killers – Book One

Dayzee Dazzle And Her Manic Mansion – Book Two

Dayzee Dazzle And The On-Set Onslaught – Book Three

*   *   *   *   *

LIN FINITY

AND THE

FLIGHTS TO FOREVER

Fringes Of Infinity
Book Four

Edward Allen Karr

Lakeside Letters, LLC
30628 Detroit Road, #247
Westlake, OH 44145

Lin Finity And The Flights To Forever
Fringes Of Infinity Book Four

First Edition, 2021
www.lakesideletters.com

Cover design by JD Smith Design
Front Cover Model: Kim Hendrickson as Lin Finity
Back Cover Model: Gloria Ervin as Queen Gloriana
Editing by Preferred Proofreading, LLC

ISBN-13: 978-1-950886-22-7

"And while I'm there, those worlds are as real as this one?"

"Only for you. The choices you make are yours. What happens to you really happens. They are real experiences, but only for you."

"Where are those worlds, Gabby?"

"You might as well ask where this world is. There's no answer to that, Lin. This world and whatever worlds you inhabit on your flights exist in the vast forever our minds can't comprehend."

From Chapter 4 – In The Vast Forever

Dedication

This work is dedicated to the lovely and talented models that grace the covers of the *Fringes Of Infinity* books.

In my imagination, Lin Finity, Queen Gloriana, and Lee Ternity are more memorable and compelling than my meager prose can convey. But those characters made only of words pale and wilt when compared to the real-life women that portray them.

An Infinity of thanks to:

Kim Hendrickson as Lin Finity
Gloria Ervin as Queen Gloriana
Lea Goldsmith as Lee Ternity

Table of Contents

Chapter 1 – They're Finally Home

"Wow, it's freezing out here! I should have kept my coat on."

Jack Madison patted the big dog's head and rubbed his ears.

"Hey, Nomad, don't laugh just because you never leave the house without yours. You aren't cold at all, are you?"

He didn't answer, and after they held each other's gaze for several seconds, both man and dog turned their heads and scanned the cloudless sky in every direction. After sharing a quick look, they studied all around them another time.

"I don't know if I'll ever feel safe back here again."

Jack stood in snow up to his hips in Lin Finity's backyard in frosty Pennsylvania, and he was at the shallowest area near the middle. Closer to the high fence, drifts rose up, broken only by the path he'd shoveled around the perimeter for Nomad earlier that morning. When he examined the snow near them and saw the crusty top surface unspoiled by a single footprint or paw print, he shook his head and laughed.

"Are your paws even touching the ground? Or are you floating?"

The heavy Tibetan Mastiff only looked at him calmly as he rested there with his wide red mane warming the snow, waiting for Jack's word to begin the trip back inside.

Jack glanced up at the roof peak of the house beyond Lin's fence, and in spite of the icy wind, he paused to stare at a spot next to the brick chimney pouring its white smoke into a stream of puffy pearls flowing toward the southeast. He smiled, thinking about the two crows that had studied them from up there only moments earlier, and looked back down at the dog.

"We really should get inside, big boy."

Nomad barked once at the sky, then he panted while looking into Jack's eyes.

"But we have to be a lot more careful, don't you think? Of course, you already know that."

The dog only leaned his head to one side and continued to look into the man's eyes.

"It's still the best New Year's Day ever."

* * *

Jack pulled open the back door leading to Lin's kitchen and kicked his boots against the foundation blocks, casting snow off of them while brushing off his jeans. Nomad shook all over, whipping the long hair of his thick mane in each direction. Then, he kicked each leg, removing some of the snow, but many chunks remained packed in his fur. They both walked inside.

After letting out a deep breath, Jack said, "Let's take it really slow this time, alright?"

Nomad bumped his forehead into Jack's leg, and they both approached the foyer and the entrance to the living room. Before they made it that far, Jack retrieved his coat from a chair at the kitchen table and put it back on.

"Alright, you know we can't just walk in there again. How about if we just look around the corner? Nothing but that, alright? We'll just look."

One step from the corner, they both stopped. In unison, Jack leaned into the opening just enough to see the couch, and Nomad did the same at the level of Jack's waist.

After several seconds, Jack said, in a hushed voice, "Well, we're still here. It's a good start."

They both saw Lin's couch at the far side of the room, and on the middle cushion, a pile of blankets sat motionless. But Jack could see two pairs of eyes, and he knew that Nomad saw them too. Shining green eyes peering out from the darkness of the warm covers and focused only on them.

"Let's just hold up a second, big boy," Jack whispered.

The dog remained silent, and all eyes were locked across the sunny room. Jack saw that the intense green glowing scrutinizing him and the dog from the safe nest of blankets hadn't diminished.

"We have to try again, don't we? I'm hoping for the best. They know who we are, Nomad. They won't hurt us."

He paused, let out a deep breath, and said, "They probably won't hurt us."

He let a minute pass as both of them did nothing but look into Lin's and her daughter Taylor's eyes shrouded under their mountain of blankets.

"One step, big boy, alright? Just one step. You ready?"

Nomad tapped his head against Jack's leg without looking away from the two on the couch.

Jack sighed, chuckled softly, and said, "At least it's sunny outside. Come on."

Each took one step out into the open, and Jack knew that both pairs of eyes, which had flared a blinding green, could see him and Nomad in their entirety.

He was about to suggest to Nomad that they attempt one more step, but in less than a heartbeat, both man and dog found that the snow was far too deep.

* * *

Jack shook his head and laughed as he rubbed Nomad's ears.

"I know, I know. I should have put gloves on too."

They both looked around at the sky in every direction, then they examined Lin's house from their place on the neighbor's side of her fence. Jack turned to glance again at the chimney, still tossing smoke into the air but much nearer than before. All around them, he saw not a sign of the passage of boot or paw in the smooth surface of the previous night's snowfall.

"Here, let me smash some of that snow down to get you started. We'll have to hike around the block this time."

Nomad barked once at the sky and panted.

"Yeah, it is kind of funny, I suppose. Alright, let's get going."

Ten minutes later, they'd trudged around to Kingsbury Court and again stood at Lin's back door, where they cleared snow off of themselves as well as they could before entering the warm house.

Jack kicked off his boots and dropped his coat back onto the chair.

"We need a better plan. Let's just sit awhile and think this through. If she gets mad next time, or even if she just makes a mistake, it could be really, really bad for us."

He hoisted the jumbo bag of dog food out of the pantry and tipped it enough to fill the giant, shiny bowl with chunks. Nomad attacked it before the pouring stopped, and the sound of crunching rang through the otherwise silent house.

Before sitting at the table, Jack peeked around the corner for only a second and saw both pairs of eyes glaring at him. He quickly pulled his head out of their sight and returned to the kitchen.

"At least there aren't any storms, huh, big boy? Thank God Taylor isn't that upset."

Nomad continued to nose his emptying bowl across the floor.

"But they're home, Nomad. They're finally home."

Chapter 2 – Chocolate Chocolate

Late morning sunlight warmed the kitchen table and part of Nomad's back where he lay near Jack's chair. Jack put down the home repair magazine he'd been reading much of the morning and stretched his arms out wide. He let out a deep sigh.

"I need to try talking to them again. That first time, all I said was Lin's name, and she dropped us in the snow. I didn't expect that to happen. I really didn't. And the second time, we didn't get even that far."

Nomad rose up on his thick legs and rested his massive head on Jack's lap. He looked up into his eyes, seldom blinking.

"What if we peek around the corner again, but we go no farther, and we try to talk to them? Well, you can bark, and then—"

A rapping on the back door caused Jack to jump up, sending the dog back a step. When he got to the door and spied through its small window, a smile spread across his face as he opened it.

"Gabriel! You said you'd know if she came back, but I was too upset to even ask you about that. But you did know, and here you are."

"Yes, Jack. The world's a different place when Lin is herself and not part of a flock somewhere. Her presence is unmistakable."

"It's been only a couple of hours since they got back. How . . . how can you—"

"Jack, it's easy. Lin will learn. Taylor too. I could have arrived here a second or two after she and Taylor returned. I stayed in St. Simons until Gloriana and I had secured her gift shop and set Renato up for a little vacation. Then, I made—"

"Renato? I thought he took off?"

"He did, Jack, in a manner of speaking. After Lin and Taylor left, I found him, and he's been working with us in Sunny's Magic Island Gift Shop."

"Should I understand any of that?"

"No, not really, Jack. Anyway, then I made sure Gloriana got to her flight safely before I traveled here in my own way."

A panting Nomad nudged Jack to one side and jumped up to put his wide paws on Gabriel's shoulders.

"My good friend, Nomad. It's wonderful to see you again. Have you been well?"

Nomad barked once at the ceiling, and Gabriel patted his sides before turning to Jack.

"Are they okay, Jack?"

"I don't know. We can't even get close to them. We've tried twice, and each time, we found ourselves out in the snow."

"It will take her a while to feel like herself again. Taylor too. They've been away almost six weeks. I did tell you they'd return, and you waited patiently. You did well, Jack."

"It hasn't been easy, but Nomad's been a big help."

"Yes, he is. It's why he's here."

"Well, where else would he go? Ever since Lin left, he and I—"

"No, Jack. It's why he came here to begin with."

Jack gave the big dog a quick look, then focused again on Gabriel.

"Lin adopted him is why he's here. He showed up on her boss's porch, so she brought him home."

"It was a coincidence, Jack? He appeared out of nowhere, and he's been here to help you for the six weeks that Lin has been gone?"

Jack stared at Gabriel, then looked at Nomad, who was still up on his legs and holding Gabriel's shoulders. He barked once at the ceiling, then he turned his head and panted at Jack.

"You might not have made it on your own. We all have work to do here. Nomad is no different."

"You're right. I'm not sure I could have handled it without him."

Jack took a step closer, and Nomad turned to put his big paws on his shoulders. He looked into Jack's left eye, then his right, then his left again. He opened his mouth and panted, almost like a laugh, then barked once at the ceiling.

"Thanks, Nomad. You sure are a true friend."

He barked once more and dropped to the floor, rattling the nearby table.

"Has Lin or Taylor talked at all?"

"Only when they first got back . . . or became themselves . . . or—"

"Did they seem like the Lin and Taylor that you know?"

"A little, but they're kind of off somehow too. They're acting kind of funny."

"Like crows?"

"Yeah, I guess. They talked a little bit outside, more like chattering, really, but then, that was it. I was just about to try saying something to them, but really, I don't know where I might end up next time."

"Let me try, Jack."

"Sure, maybe you'll have better luck. You've been her friend a lot longer than either of us."

"Yes, more than thirty years."

Jack and Nomad followed Gabriel into the foyer and near the entry to the living room, where Gabriel stepped out into the open. Jack and Nomad stayed behind the wall.

"Lin, I knew you'd make it back. You were gone—"

Jack and Nomad watched from their safe location as Gabriel was silenced mid-sentence and began to twitch.

"Lin, you can stop that. You can't move me around like Jack or Nomad."

Gabriel stopped shaking, let out a deep breath, and immediately started to lean toward Lin and Taylor to resist a wind that looked to be attempting to move nothing else. Jack saw long brown hair almost straight out and clothing flapping, all pointing away from the quiet pair on the couch.

In a voice loud enough to project over the wind, Gabriel said, "Taylor, that's very good that you've learned that. And your control is remarkable, but you can stop now. I won't approach any nearer."

The wind dropped off rapidly and stopped altogether. Gabriel took a quick step to keep from falling forward.

"I'd like you both to consider coming out from under those blankets soon. You're home. You're just Lin and Taylor again. We're all very happy to see you both."

Jack peeked around the corner and saw that their eyes weren't glowing as brightly as before. Then, Nomad looked too. Two pairs of hands appeared and began pulling aside blankets until both women were covered only from their shoulders down.

Jack felt tears building up at being able to gaze upon both of them again. Reaching into his pants pocket, he found the engagement ring and knew that he'd have to leave it there, for how long no one could guess.

"Jack and Nomad won't bother you. Can they stand with me just to look at you? You know, we haven't seen either of you for a long time."

*　*　*

Lin stared at the three figures watching her and Taylor from the doorway, and she was sure that she knew them. Mostly, she knew their names. And she was kind of sure that they meant her no harm. But they were close enough.

"STILL cold STILL cold STILL cold."

Jack said, "I bet, Lin. Stay under those blankets all you want, alright?"

I will, she thought. I will, Jack.

She blinked three times and stared.

"ME too ME too."

"Yes, I'm sure you're cold, too, Taylor," said Gabriel. "Do you think you'd like to get dressed? You can get right back under the blankets."

Lin stared a few seconds before answering. She remembered clothes.

"OH kay OH kay."

Lin turned her head slightly when Jack said to Gabriel, "Taylor's easy to pick for, but what do you think Lin wants to wear? Her old style or the new one?"

"Why not bring both, Jack, and let her choose?"

"Yeah, alright. That makes sense. Be right back."

She watched Jack turn and move out of her sight. The last she saw of Nomad was his fluffy tail as it swished around the corner. And she remembered that he was more than fluffy. He was sweet and fluffy.

Lin watched them leave, then looked all around the room. She knew it was home, and it was good to be home. But inside was odd. So different from the Earth and the sky. So small. So closed.

Several minutes later, she heard Jack returning before she saw him. His arms were full.

"Lin, can you let Jack set all of this right here on the table? He'll only take a few steps into the room. There's no need to put him somewhere else."

Lin nodded and continued to stare. She watched Jack set three piles of clothes on the table—one for Taylor and two for her. He backed himself away, smiling at her the entire time. She observed him without a smile of her own.

Clothes again, thought Lin. I used to wear clothes.

"Jack, why don't the three of us stay in the kitchen for a while? I don't know about you two, but I'm hungry. If Lee didn't finish all that chocolate ice cream, I'll see if I can."

"Chocolate chocolate."

Gabriel turned back toward Lin with a big smile.

"Yes, Lin, chocolate is very good."

Jack shook his head at Gabriel but didn't say anything. His smile left him when he remembered that he was too close to Lin and Taylor. The three of them carefully took steps backward out of the room, and the last Lin saw of them was Nomad's big snout and large, unblinking eyes looking into hers as he backed himself around the corner.

* * *

Jack sat at the table with Nomad standing nearby. He flicked around his ears and rubbed his mane.

"How long, Gabriel? Until they're back to . . . until they're—"

"Themselves again? All we can do is be patient, Jack. For fun, we can try to guess which style she'll choose. Which would you prefer?"

"She's gorgeous in anything, but I'll pick the skirts and heels. I think she likes that the best too."

"We might not find out for a long time. We can't be sure they'll even get dressed soon."

"They can't just sit naked under all those blankets forever. Won't they at least get hungry?"

"It's really only been a short while," Gabriel said and sat across the table with the bucket from Lin's freezer. "Can you imagine how all of this feels to them?"

"No, I sure as hell can't. They turned into crows, Gabriel. Six weeks ago. No one alive, or who has ever been alive, can know what that feels like."

"Exactly so. We'll just have to remain patient with them. In the meantime, this ice cream is quite good. I believe Lin was correct when she stated that chocolate is the best."

They sat in a silent house with only the sound of Gabriel's spoon occasionally scraping around the inside of the plastic container. Nomad lay on the floor beside Jack and turned his eyes up when he spoke.

"Gabriel, what was that wind? I saw it trying to blow you away. Where did that come from?"

"That came from Taylor. You remember that she's a Glyphin now, partly from being born to a mother with power over the magic and partly from whatever powers were mixed in with the Words of God. I believe she might have developed that skill while she was gone. I believe that's another Glyphin power."

"So, let me get this right. Not only can she cause storms and rain and snow, but she can use wind too? Just wind? And she can focus it like that?"

"I believe that might be just her most simple ability, Jack. She might be able to control any amount of air wherever it exists. Even just what either of us have inhaled and hold inside us. We need to be very careful with her too.

"Finding yourself planted in deep snow would be a blessing compared to what else she might be able to do."

* * *

Lin and Taylor peered out from their warm pile at the three neat stacks of folded clothing. They turned to look at each other with their noses almost touching.

"Honey, we really are back."

"Mom, I feel funny."

"Me too, Hon."

They looked again at the clothes Jack had brought them.

"I was a bird. We were birds. I think I'm still a bird."

"I know, Honey. Me too. But we're supposed to wear clothes again."

"That'll be strange."

"Let's try to pretend they're like feathers. Just funny feathers, okay?"

"Sure, Mom."

* * *

"Yeah, you're right, of course. Hey, you hear that?" Jack said very softly. "They're chattering. And I think they're getting dressed!"

Gabriel spoke softly too.

"I think you're right. But they'll probably get right back under their blankets. I intend to sit here awhile and not disturb them."

Gabriel continued digging into the ice cream. Jack glanced at the container with a grin before turning his head to listen again.

"At least as long as there's still ice cream?"

"Exactly right, Jack."

Minutes passed with only the sounds of Gabriel eating and a soft commotion in the living room.

* * *

"COWboy COWboy," Lin said from the doorway. She looked into Jack's eyes and knew that she sounded funny, but she couldn't help it.

Jack held himself in his seat after turning to see her gazing at him and wearing the jeans, sweatshirt, and tall boots that he'd offered as one of her choices.

"Lin, I won't get up. I promise. Damn, it's so good to see you again."

She continued to stare, and Taylor soon stood next to her, wearing the jeans, sweater, and hiking boots that he'd brought for her.

"STILL cold Jack STILL cold Jack."

Jack smiled and wiped at his eyes at the same time as he shook his head and looked from one to the other.

"Welcome home. I'm so happy that you're both home."

They didn't answer, but they did look around at their surroundings and studied the walls and floors and ceiling.

"Are you hungry?" said Gabriel.

Lin nodded and said, "Yeah, Gabby," and Taylor lowered her eyes to gaze at Nomad.

The two women stood shoulder to shoulder and rarely blinked.

"Nomad," Taylor said. "Hi, Nomad."

Nomad's bushy tail swept the floor as he panted and looked up at her, but he didn't go to her.

"Yes," said Jack. "He's been waiting for you. I'm sure he's happy to see you, too, but I think he knows that he should stay put."

Taylor rocked from side to side as she approached the quiet dog and stooped down next to him. She touched the top of his head gently, and they looked into each other's eyes.

"Nomad."

She stood and looked down at him.

"We're home, Nomad."

Nomad panted more, and Lin felt half of her mouth smile at the sight of it.

Taylor took one step closer to Jack and touched his shoulder. She looked into his eyes and said, "Jack."

Jack squinted, and his voice broke when he said, "Yes, it's just me, Taylor. It's so good to see you."

Taylor was too close, Lin knew. Too close. A distraction would help.

"We've been away, Jack," she said from the doorway.

Jack started to rise, then dropped himself back onto the chair. He held the seat with both hands and looked only into her green eyes, which weren't glowing like before.

"Yes, Lin, but you're both home now. Welcome home, Cowgirl."

She stared a few more seconds and said, "Still cold, Jack."

"I know, I know. You can sure get back under those blankets if you want."

Lin's half smile had been replaced with a frown. The brightness of her eyes rose a notch.

"SHE did it, Jack. SHE did it."

"Taylor? Taylor did what? What do you—"

Without another word, Lin and Taylor turned and took short, quick steps out of sight. From the kitchen, sounds of blankets rustling and couch cushions compressing could be heard.

"That's progress, Jack. They'll be fine soon."

"I hope so. What did she mean?"

"I don't know, but I believe she'll tell us eventually. They've had quite the adventure."

Chapter 3 – Two Beautiful Crows

Lin's phone began to chime and vibrate around on the kitchen counter. Jack, Gabriel, and Nomad turned to see it before Gabriel looked back at Jack.

"I haven't moved it, Gabriel. That's where she left it that day she and Taylor walked out into the rain."

The phone continued its panicky performance. Jack glanced at the entryway to the living room.

"She doesn't seem ready for her phone, Jack."

"No, she sure doesn't. Alright, maybe it's just her work again."

He rose from the table, picked up the phone, looked at the number, and shrugged.

"Hello?"

"Oh, you are not Lin."

"No, I'm Jack. Who are you?"

"This is Gloriana. Hello, Jack. Gabriel said that Lin has returned, and I am traveling to her home as quickly as I can."

"Good, maybe you can help. Lin is . . . I don't know. She's not quite herself. Neither is Taylor."

"I was surprised to hear of what they did. Has she said why she made such a drastic decision?"

"No, not yet. We haven't really been able to talk to her yet."

"Perhaps I may be of assistance. I am in a vehicle of some sort drawing near her house. I will be there soon."

"Alright, it'll be good to see you again."

"And you. Goodbye, Jack."

* * *

"That was Gloriana. She said she's almost here. Her being here should help, don't you think?"

Lin had been listening from the living room, and she froze and tipped her head at Jack's mention of Gloriana. She snapped open the blankets, hopped down from the couch, and scurried toward the kitchen.

"I hope so, Jack," said Gabriel. "I believe the more Lin is surrounded by people—"

"No," Lin said from the doorway. "No. NO!"

Jack turned quickly and stared with a smile, then couldn't help himself—he started with a good look at Lin's black boots that rose up over her calves, then her legs barely disguised by the thin denim, then over all the curves he knew so well and had missed so badly for the last six weeks, then into her bright green eyes, which were now glowing in a determined stare.

She saw Jack's happy eyes staring into hers and felt her heart beating slowly, much more slowly than she expected.

"Lin, it's okay," she heard him say, "it's just Gloriana. I mean, Sunny. She—"

"NOT Sunny NOT Sunny."

How could they not understand? she wondered. Gabriel should know. She had to tell Jack.

"Okay, we don't have to call her—"

"SHE did it SHE did it."

Lin turned only her eyes to look at Gabriel.

"HER fault HER fault."

"What did she do, Lin?" said Gabriel.

"She wants power. MY power MY power MY power MY—"

"It's okay, Lin," Gabriel said with both hands raised. "No one is going to take anything from you. I'm here, and I'm still watching out for you. I will for another thirty years if necessary."

"NOT take NOT take."

They don't understand, she knew. Gloriana. What Gloriana did.

"What do you—"

"Trick. Trick. Trick me to give up power."

Lin backed up a step toward the living room, and her eyes darted from Jack to Gabriel and back again. Her eyes fixed on Nomad's calm gaze, and the green fire faded but didn't leave completely.

Gabriel said, "You mean, all those feelings that you were fighting? Those weren't yours?"

"NOT mine NOT mine."

Need to eat, she thought. Gloriana is coming. Will kill soon. Have to eat now.

"She can't hurt you anymore, Lin. She—"

Lin squawked and took quick steps to Nomad's bowl, which still contained a small amount of his chunks. She snatched it up and took rapid steps backward until she was out of sight. The sound of fluffing blankets told them that she and Taylor likely burrowed back into their mound. Muffled crunching sounds found their way to the kitchen.

* * *

"Well, at least they're eating. Gabriel, what was she talking about?"

"Jack, I don't believe Lin ever told you, but those three times Gloriana took her and put her in those make-believe worlds troubled her. She said they changed her, and she and I could only think that some hidden part of her came to life there. She was struggling with it before she left."

"She seemed to want to play around as the Lin from those worlds. She liked it. So did I. But that's not really her? Sunny—I mean, Gloriana—caused all that? Lin was trying to stop it?"

"I believe that's part of why she left us, Jack. She was losing herself to what those worlds had done to her."

"That was only part of the reason? What do you mean?"

"Taylor. Taylor was losing herself, too, from not being able to control her Glyphin powers. It took an enormous amount of strength for Lin to focus her intent on that course of action. She must have known the risk but saw no other choice. Jack, she didn't know if she'd ever be able to return."

"But you knew she would, didn't you?"

"I believed it, yes. But we cannot know such things."

Jack reached up and scratched at the whiskers on his chin and stared at the doorway where Lin had just stood.

"When she first got back—oh, and that was quite an experience— the first thing she said was that she fixed it. And she said Taylor did too. So, being gone like that helped them both? That's what she meant?"

"I believe that's right, Jack. I'll be interested in hearing how that helped."

"Yeah, me too—if she ever really talks to us again."

"She will, Jack. We must give them time. They both got dressed again, didn't they? Is that something two beautiful crows would ever do?"

* * *

A knock on the front door caused Jack to jump up out of his seat.

"She's here. This should be interesting. You said she gave up her powers, though, right? She's just a normal human woman again?"

"That was the deal she made to return here to live again."

Jack passed the doorway to the living room and resisted the urge to look in at Lin and Taylor. But something caught his eye, so after he passed by, he peeked back around the corner. He saw the two sitting with their knees pulled up high and blankets covering all but their heads and shoulders. He noted with a smile that he could see the toes of Lin's boots poking out from under the blanket.

He took a step back and stood gazing at them since he saw that they were both asleep with their heads tipped together and leaning back into the couch cushions. Nomad's bowl lay empty off to one side.

"I'll get the door, Jack," Gabriel said before swinging the door open to reveal Gloriana waiting patiently, dressed in jeans and a sweatshirt with a heavy coat. Jack turned and saw that her eyes were still caramel, and to his great relief, they weren't glowing.

But he was surprised to watch Gabriel step out onto the porch and close the door.

* * *

"Sunny, you made the trip from St. Simons in little time."

She took a step back and said, "Lin is back, yes, Gabriel? Taylor too?"

"Yes, they're both back, but I have to tell you that they're not completely back. They should be fine, but it will take a while."

"May I visit them? Perhaps it will help to see another familiar face."

"Let's talk first. Lin isn't communicating very clearly yet, but some of what she said is alarming. She claimed that those worlds you put her in to learn lessons about herself had bad effects on her. She said it was an attempt to coerce her to give up her powers. Is that true?"

Gloriana stared back a few seconds, then looked down to the concrete.

"Yes."

"And what was your plan? Why would you want her to give up her powers?"

"It is something you know nothing about, Gabriel. It is a practice I learned long, long ago. A person with power can give it up. If their emotions are storming inside, and if they can be convinced that their powers have brought on their distress, they can intend them all away. And in that moment, anyone near that also has power can take what they have voluntarily discarded."

"You would have taken her powers? Do you believe that's a good thing to do?"

"I have lived for many centuries, and at that time, I did not care any longer about good or bad. When the Words of God brought Lin to me, I cared only about power."

"And now?"

"I have lived the life of a woman without powers with you assisting me in that gift shop. I, too, am dismayed by what I tried to do to Lin."

"But you would have left her powerless? You would have done that to her?"

"She would have been happy in the life that was crafted for her. Was she not happy about who she was in those worlds? She was eager to live those feelings."

"She thought so, but it was only because you put her there. Those feelings she felt there . . . those weren't hers, were they?"

"No. I have learned how to put someone in a world and impose on them whatever feelings I choose. I worked hard at taking those feelings as my own. I spent time in brothels and other places that one like you would never visit. It was a hardship to submit to all of that and convince myself that those were my real feelings. I became that woman that Lin believed was her in those worlds."

"You did all of that just to trick Lin?"

"No, Gabriel, I did that many times to many people. Anyone I could find that had any power at all, no matter how small. I was able to convince all of them to give up their power, and I took it as my own."

"That's how you became so powerful?"

"Yes. How else? My powers did not come from my goodness. I am not you."

"But those feelings don't touch you? You're not consumed by them?"

"I have the strength to keep them separate. I put them on as easily as one would wear a coat."

"And you wrapped Lin in that coat? In the feelings you chose for her?"

"Yes. It was not easy. Every other time I did it, it took only one world—one life of living the feelings I gave them—and then their power was mine. Lin is strong. It took three worlds before she considered intending her powers to leave her."

"She has changed herself back. You have failed."

"I am relieved now to know that."

"You're saying that you have changed too?"

"I have changed. I am only a normal human woman now. I seek nothing that can be earned by the use of powers, of which I no longer have any."

"I can't say that Lin will forgive you. The best you can do now is run. She might not be as compassionate as we remember her to be. She's lived as a wild creature for many weeks. Even I could not get near her."

"Then, I will apologize and hope for the best. I wish to go inside now."

"I suggest you leave."

"One like you cannot interfere with me. You know this to be true."

"I can stop you in a normal human way."

"Is that what you will do?"

"Why shouldn't I? That might save your life."

"Perhaps I can be allowed to take that chance? I have information to help her with the Glyphin."

"I don't think Taylor needs any advice from you. She, too, has benefited from her time away. I believe she has more control over things than either of us can imagine."

"Then, I can teach her things of which she still knows nothing— things for which even you cannot offer counsel."

"The numbers? The forgotten numbers?"

"Not completely forgotten if you can so casually speak of them."

"Is that wise? We both know how dangerous that type of power can be."

"I can hope that bestowing that knowledge will save me from Lin's wrath."

"And Taylor's. You arranged for her to become a Glyphin when Lin spoke the Words of God, didn't you?"

"Not her but someone near to Lin. The power I wove into the Words found her daughter. I could not control where it might go."

"Taylor likely knows it was you that caused Lin to take them both away. They both have reason to strike out at you. And I believe they will."

"I cannot run, Gabriel. I wish to continue my life with the gift shop. I would rather not wonder when an angry woman with power over the magic will arrive and destroy me."

"If you go inside, I will not intervene to help you. I'm here only for Lin."

"I understand."

Gabriel opened the door, and they both walked in.

* * *

The wind began the moment that Gloriana rounded the corner and faced the living room couch. Gabriel looked in and saw that Lin only watched with her own glowing eyes as her daughter led the battle, and Taylor's eyes were burning a fiery green.

Gloriana staggered backward to the far wall of the foyer and could not step away. Every part of her—her hair, her arms and legs, her clothing—looked glued to the wall. The wind swirled off of her and tore through the room like a cyclone, lifting and carrying away everything not attached to the floor or a wall.

"Taylor," said Gabriel. "You can let her speak, can't you?"

Then, Gloriana's boots no longer touched the floor. Her head snapped to the left, and her cheek appeared to be grinding a dent into the drywall.

"Taylor, please. You and your mom might want to hear what she has to say about Glyphins."

Taylor quenched her green fire, the wind stopped instantly, and Gloriana slumped to the floor. Lin's head tipped to one side, and the fire in her eyes increased.

"Lin, can you contain your feelings for only a moment or two and listen until—"

Gloriana vanished. The accent table against which she'd been leaning rocked from side to side but didn't fall.

Gabriel smiled and stared at Lin with a shaking head. A tentative knocking on the front door broke the gaze, and the door opened again.

"We can try again if you wish. Come back inside."

Gabriel stood where Lin and Taylor had a clear view, and Jack hid around the corner near the kitchen with Nomad, but Gloriana peeked around the corner to see Lin and Taylor.

"Lin, I—"

"You. I should destroy you where you stand."

"Lin," said Gabriel, "it sounds like that nap has helped you. Do you feel more like yourself?"

"Yeah, Gabby. Take her away before I kill her. I will not say it twice."

Gloriana pulled her head back out of sight and stepped quickly toward the door. Gabriel turned and watched her open it and begin walking out onto the porch.

They heard Taylor from around the corner.

"If Mom doesn't kill her, I will."

A heavy wind forced Gloriana against the far porch rail and blew the door shut. Gabriel went back to face Lin and Taylor on the couch.

"I'm glad you remembered to be kind, Lin. She—"

"I'm not kind, Gabby. What I want to do to her would leave a mess to clean up. I'll kill her later."

"Lin, it's still good to—"

Gabriel stopped at seeing Taylor's eyes blaze a bright green and heard wind howling along the front of the house and rattling the windows.

With another smile, Gabriel rushed to the front door. It took much effort to pry it open to see Gloriana at the far end of the porch, curled up against the wrought iron railing as hurricane winds buffeted her. Gabriel allowed the door to get sucked shut with a boom.

"Taylor, that is truly remarkable. Would it trouble you to wait a short while before you kill her?"

"She's halfway down the block now, Gabriel. Maybe high in a tree."

Gabriel only stared as Taylor's eyes returned to their normal shade of green.

"It would be good for you to try to be kind, too, Taylor."

"I was kind. I wanted to see if she could learn to fly as she fell from the clouds. Instead, I let the wind decide."

Gabriel only stared at her for several silent seconds, then looked at Lin.

"Crows don't think about things, Gabby. We just do them."

"No fear. No doubts," said Taylor.

Gabriel offered them both a smile and a slowly shaking head.

They pulled their blankets up under their chins, their heads tipped together, and they were quickly fast asleep.

Chapter 4 – In The Vast Forever

"Well, that was uncomfortable," said Jack. "I've never heard either of them talking like that before."

"They did live out in the wild for a long time, Jack. They just need time. It's good that they're sleeping."

They both watched the two blondes sleeping under thick layers of blankets.

"Now, about that ice cream."

"What about Gloriana? What happened to her?"

"The wind stopped, so she'll be fine. I think she'll be at the back door soon. She will not risk the front door again."

"Lin would be proud of you, Gabriel, going after the chocolate like that. Hey, next time they're awake, why don't we see if she'll want some of that?"

"There might not be any left."

"Can you save her some? Nomad and I can always run out for more later."

"Okay, Jack. I'll try to save her some. A small amount."

They both laughed quietly as they left the sleeping women and aimed for the kitchen. Gabriel headed straight for the freezer and Jack the back door. He saw Gloriana shivering and waiting, so he opened it, gestured for her to stay quiet, and let her in.

"I have to tell you," said Jack, "I might kill you myself for what you did to Lin."

"Jack, I am sorry. Consider my existence for more centuries than you can imagine. I acted out of desperation."

"Sure, I can see that. But still."

He glared at her, but Gabriel paid them no attention. Jack heard the bucket set on the table and the lid pried off, but he continued to watch Gloriana.

"I do not believe you would kill me. I ask only that all of you give me a chance. You will see soon that I can be a very good friend too. You might soon want me around."

"I can't imagine any reason I'd want you here. Anyway, you look exhausted."

"Yes. I have heard of hurricanes, but I have never been attacked by one. I never allowed any to visit my islands. They are not enjoyable."

"Alright, well, stay quiet, and sneak down to the guest room. Really, don't make a sound. You don't want to wake either of them up now."

"No. Perhaps another time."

*　*　*

"You know, Jack," Gabriel said while rattling a spoon out of a drawer, "if you want to take Nomad for groceries, now might be a good time. My guess is that they're both exhausted from their ordeal."

"I bet. We're mostly stocked up here since I've been keeping up with it. Except for the ice cream. We'll get some of that and maybe some other chocolate stuff too."

"Good, Jack."

At the sight of Jack putting on his coat, Nomad came close and brushed against his leg.

"Yeah, big boy. Me and you. Like always."

The big dog didn't bark, but he did lead them out through the garage.

Minutes later, Gabriel's spoon full of ice cream paused in midair.

*　*　*

"Lin, I'm surprised you're awake already. Are you rested enough?"
"No."

25

"Do you feel more like yourself?"

"A little. Sleep helps."

"And Taylor? She's still sleeping?"

"Yes."

"We're all very happy to have you both back. It's been six weeks, Lin."

"I forgot about weeks. Only sunrise, sunset, and forever in between."

"That's not a bad way to live either. Were your days good?"

"Gabby, there was no good or bad. Only living."

"Were you and Taylor together the whole time?"

"Yes. Always close. Even in the family."

"What family?"

"All around us. So many. But we knew them all. And they knew us."

"What did they know of you?"

"They knew we were special. They knew we could help. And we did."

"Taylor helped with the weather?"

"Yes. She learned starting and stopping rain, snow, storms, wind, and—"

"She learned Windcraft, Lin?"

"Yes, if that's what it's called. She helped the family many times. Hawks can't hunt when the air beneath their wings is taken."

Gabriel stared at her for a moment before continuing.

"And you helped the family too?"

"None of the family was ever hurt by anyone or anything. We stopped every threat. I wasn't Lin, she wasn't Taylor, and we still did it."

"Jack hasn't told me what it was like when you two returned, but he said it was quite an experience."

"They weren't happy to lose us."

"No, I don't suppose they—"

"I had no memory of Lin or Taylor or anyone else. I listened to God's Words every moment."

"How were you able to come back?"

Lin paused to wipe at each eye with a fingertip.

"I heard the Words saying 'I am with you, I am with you,' all the time. Then I heard, 'I am with you, Lin.' I began to remember Lin."

Her eyes squinted, but no tears began trickling down her cheeks.

"God spoke to me, Gabby. I knew I was dying. Why else would God say that name?"

"You felt like you were dying, Lin?"

"Yes, as a crow dies. I knew only that I wanted one last look at something, and I brought Taylor to a roof. We looked down on a man and a dog in the snow. Taylor wanted to go back to the family. I brought her closer. We looked over the edge at the man and dog looking back up at us.

"The family attacked them. The family didn't want us to die. After they'd told their anger to the man and the dog, Taylor and I died."

"Oh, Lin, you didn't really die."

"I died. She died."

Gabriel waited and watched, but she shed no tears.

"Now, Taylor and Lin live."

"We're glad you're alive again as Lin and Taylor."

Lin wiped at her eyes and said, "Don't eat all that chocolate, Gabby."

She didn't smile, but Gabriel did and said, "Jack is out buying more."

She blinked several times and said, "Still cold. Still cold."

Without another word or gesture, she turned and disappeared into the living room and back under the blankets.

*　*　*

Jack parked his truck in the driveway, he and Nomad jumped down and slammed the doors, Jack with a hand and Nomad with a push from his forehead, and they walked past Lin's Temt8tion in the garage. At the entry leading to her laundry room, he hit the switch to lower the garage door. His strong arms were loaded with bags mostly full of chocolate items, and a heavy sack of food for Nomad lay over his shoulder.

"That's good, Jack. Lin wanted me to save her some of this,"— Gabriel held up the empty ice cream bucket—"but I didn't. It's quite good."

"She was awake again? How was she?"

"She's coming back, but it's not quick. I believe the more she and Taylor sleep, the more they return to the Lin and Taylor we know."

Jack set the bags on the table and lowered the dog food into the pantry. Then, he peeked around the corner into the living room and saw both of them covered up to their chins in thick blankets. Their heads were tipped back again, and Taylor snored lightly. Jack dragged the back of his hand across his eyes as he stood and quietly watched them. He took a quick look down the hall and saw the guest room door closed.

"Jack," Gabriel said after Jack had taken a seat in the kitchen, "there is much we must discuss with her, but we shouldn't wake them. Perhaps she—"

"I feel a lot better, Gabby. Hi, Jack."

"Oh, Lin, I can't tell you—"

"Hold me, Jack."

Jack stood quickly but approached her carefully while they looked into each other's eyes. When he stood right in front of her, he reached out to gently hold her arms and pulled her close. She kept her arms straight at her sides but rested her head against his shoulder.

She looked down at the bags on the table and said, "Chocolate things. You found chocolate for me, Jack?"

"Yeah, I sure did. Do you feel like sitting with us and having some?"

She hesitated.

"If you wait too long, maybe Gabriel will eat it all. You know that'll happen."

She let out a short, strange laugh, and he hugged her more tightly. "Okay, Jack. I can sit."

She eased herself down onto a chair and held it with both hands while looking over all the bags. After several seconds of studying her choices, she reached into the nearest bag and dragged out the largest chocolate bar.

"Good choice, Lin," said Gabriel. "The magic of chocolate in an uncomplicated form."

Lin didn't answer, but she did unwrap it, held it with both hands, and took a huge bite. She chewed and turned only her eyes to watch them both. Gabriel waited quietly and let her eat.

Jack said, "Well, I need more than chocolate. Anyone else want a sandwich?"

"No, thanks," said Gabriel. "Chocolate sustains me well enough."

Lin watched him moving around the kitchen, and she'd finished the whole candy bar just as he sat down with his lunch.

"That helped. Eating chocolate—that feels like me."

She closed her eyes and took several deep breaths. When she opened them again, Jack spoke.

"I didn't know if you'd ever come back. If it wasn't for Nomad keeping me company, I'm not sure I would have made it."

"Nomad. Nomad's a good boy. He's my sweet fluffy boy."

At that, the big dog drew near for the first time and laid his massive head on her leg. She reached down and rubbed his head and played with his ears.

"I bet you missed him," said Jack.

"I didn't remember him, Jack. Or you. Even when Taylor and I looked down at you from right above on the roof. You were only a man and Nomad only a dog."

"Somehow, I knew that was you up there. Don't ask me how, but I knew."

"They attacked you and Nomad. I watched them."

"Yeah, I'm not really comfortable in your backyard anymore," Jack said with a laugh.

Lin didn't laugh but turned to Gabriel.

"It's all coming back to me now. I'm mostly Lin again. Gabby, the main thing is that it wasn't me—all those feelings in those worlds Gloriana put me in. She did that to me."

"She admitted it, Lin, before Taylor attacked her with her Windcraft. She said she's learned how to impose feelings on someone, and they become convinced that the feelings are theirs. It was a plan to get you to intend away your powers so she could take them as her own. She said she's done it many times."

"That's how she got so powerful?"

"Yes, I believe so."

"I remember those feelings she gave me. I know they're not mine, but I remember them. I did want to give up my powers. It almost worked."

"And she admitted giving Taylor the powers of a Glyphin. She didn't know who would be affected like that, but it happened to be Taylor."

"She caused all of that to force me, or someone like me, to save her and then give up their powers to her? That's unbelievable, Gabby."

"Her power is matched by her craftiness. She almost succeeded."

"I was so close to giving it all up. I think God showed me an answer, and I listened. I had to save Taylor more than anything. We flew away."

"You did save her. And yourself too."

"I've never felt anything like that. My intent was a giant sun inside me. You saw how many birds came for us."

"It was quite a sight."

"Now, we're back, and I will kill Gloriana."

"Lin, you do have free will again. I only ask that you give it some time and don't commit to an act you might regret."

"I don't feel capable of regret. Like Taylor said: we act."

"I will ask Taylor to be merciful too. It was quite a wind that attacked Gloriana on your porch."

"She *was* kind. She could have started a storm in that vile woman's lungs. Taylor exploded many hawks and owls."

Jack and Gabriel turned and stared at each other for a few seconds.

"I hope she never chooses to do that."

"Okay, we can wait but not for long. What about the hunter thing we trapped when I rescued Gloriana? Where is it? Is it here?"

"I haven't heard or seen anything, Lin," said Jack. "If it's somewhere in the world, it isn't around here."

"I never sensed it anywhere in South Georgia either," said Gabriel.

"You've been in Georgia?"

"Yes, and I suppose I should fill you in on that. We followed through on the arrangements you made last time you were in St. Simons. Do you remember the gift shop? That was purchased and renamed Sunny's Magic Island Gift Shop. I've been there helping her run the place."

"If I would have known her true nature, I never would have wanted that. She never deserved any kindness from me."

"No, we know that now. But at that time, that was a remarkably kind act from you. Renato has helped us, too, and he's still there."

"Renato? How? I thought you—"

"I found a way, Lin. You should see how happy he is now to be alive again."

"Well, good. And Lee? Have you heard from her?"

"No. If she's helping Tayo in some way, we know nothing about it."

"Then, we'll forget about it," she said and continued to play with Nomad's ears.

After unwrapping another chocolate bar and taking a bite, Lin continued.

"I've learned something else, Gabby. I've learned to separate myself from the feelings Gloriana forced on me. No feelings from another world will ever confuse me again. I can go to whatever worlds I want and do whatever I want. I'll still be me when I come back."

"You can find the worlds Gloriana created for you?"

"Probably. I think they still exist out there somewhere. Or I can make my own. I know how to make my own strings of Islands of Time."

Gabriel paused to study Lin before speaking.

"It's like you told me—how it starts with imagination. Then intent. Strong intent."

"If you're going to talk about magic stuff, maybe I'll take Nomad out for a walk. How does that sound?"

"Okay, Jack," said Lin, "that's a good idea."

They waited until Jack had put on a coat and gloves, Nomad had barked once at the ceiling, and they both filed out through the back door.

* * *

"Before we discuss traveling to worlds you create with your intent, there's something else I need to tell you right away."

"No, Gabby, you can't leave. Not after all—"

"Lin, I'm not going anywhere. You've convinced me that I can do good here too. It's about Gloriana."

"Don't try to talk me out of it. Or Taylor."

"I won't. But can you hold off on that for a while? It doesn't have to be today, does it? Or even this week? Can you agree to give it a week and see how you feel then?"

"Sure, but then I'll kill her. What do you need to tell me?"

"Gloriana is in your guest room."

Lin's jaw dropped, and she stared and shook her head. She felt like engaging her intent and viewing the magic all around her, the infinite magic supporting everyone and everything in every instant. From there, it would be easy to go to Gloriana's magic, her spirit, and do any damage she could imagine. The easiest thing would be to bring her completely beneath the concrete floor of her basement and leave her there. Or maybe to allow time to resume right after placing her on the freeway. Or she could—

"Lin?"

Lin shook her head and focused on Gabriel.

"What's she doing there? Taylor got rid of her."

"Almost. She was pinned against your porch railing like a piece of scrap paper. Then, the two of you fell asleep, and we brought her inside."

"Why?"

"She has knowledge that can help Taylor. And you, if you decide to become a Glyphin yourself."

"What knowledge? Oh, you mean those numbers. Those forgotten numbers that have been purged from all memory when they killed anyone that knew about them. That's what you're talking about, isn't it?"

"Yes. It could be of good use."

"You said I can become a Glyphin too?"

"Yes, I believe so."

"Taylor already has control. I watched her many times."

"Can we be sure that, as a human, Taylor still has that much control over the storms she might create? Gloriana could offer techniques that will help if she needs it. That could benefit your Glyphin career,"— Gabriel paused to grin at Lin—"as well."

"Okay, Gabby. You do make sense. We can learn from her before we kill her."

"You said a week, didn't you, Lin?"

"Yeah. Sure."

She stared into Gabriel's big brown eyes without a smile.

"Good. Okay, on to other business. Are you sure those memories Gloriana imposed on you don't still have you in their grip?"

"I'm sure."

"But they still fascinate you?"

"I wouldn't say that. Remembering them is entertaining, nothing more."

"You have been through so much, Lin. Your mayhem erupted not long ago after you'd buried it when you were fifteen. You fought to get control of it, and almost immediately after that, you were pursued by Lancaster Wolfe to read the Words of God. That left you tired and weak, and the Glyphin power put into the Words by Gloriana opened a path to you. She took you three times, each world a lesson for you, or so she said. And that all led to you taking Taylor away for six weeks. And now, you are back."

"It's a lot, Gabby. But I'm stronger now. My life for the last six weeks has made me stronger."

"I know that the worlds Gloriana put you in, and the lives you lived in those worlds, were upsetting. But you also found some enjoyment there. You said you liked being a different Lin for those times, doing things you would never do in your real life."

"Yes, that's true. I didn't expect how those lives would take control of me like they did. It's why I had to leave. Taylor couldn't control her Glyphin powers, so I took her too."

"Now, you feel you're strong enough that if you were in other worlds like that, behaving as a different Lin, you'd be able to keep the lives separate?"

"I won't go back to any world Gloriana created, but I'm strong enough now. I've learned that while I was gone."

"How?"

"There was never a time when feelings mattered more than life. If I felt cold, life continued. If I could not find food, I lived my life. When I killed bobcats and coyotes, there was no fear, and I didn't need anger."

"Yes, I understand. I believe you are that strong, Lin, but there's another danger you must understand if you ever decide to try any of that. You must remember to not dwell in any particular world. Go there once, and if you wish to travel again, go to a different world. If you repeat your visits to a world of your own creation, it will become more real each time. If you were to travel there enough times, I believe you are strong enough to remember that it's still a world of your own creation, but you might not be able to return to this world. And eventually, that world will define you."

"You mean, I'll become whatever I am in that world? For how long?"

"Forever. If you give those worlds enough of your intent, they will attain a reality of their own. When they do, you will become that different Lin, even if you find a way to return here. If you thought it was difficult last time, know that it would be nearly impossible if you took it that far. We're talking about the effect of nearly-real worlds, Lin, not just whatever power Gloriana used."

"And while I'm there, those worlds are as real as this one?"

"Only for you. The choices you make are yours. What happens to you really happens. They are real experiences but only for you.

"You knew before, from the flights Gloriana imposed on you, that there were no consequences to whatever you did there to others. You said you broke most of Ben's bones in one of the worlds. That affected you—you felt bad about that. But Ben didn't. It wasn't really Ben.

"Living with no consequences might be what's attracting you to go again. But at some point, the world you create with your intent will become real and define you. You can't anticipate when that will happen. You might think you have plenty of time, and then you'll feel the door slamming shut. I'd advise you to not take that chance."

"I probably won't."

"Good. But if you do decide to take a little vacation,"—Gabriel paused to give Lin a big smile—"at least try to learn something there."

"What do you mean?"

"Your intent can do many things. And your control over the magic of all things gives you infinite possibilities. A world you create could serve as a place to practice new powers. You might even become a Glyphin in one."

"Really? Huh. I never thought of that. Okay, if I do go to one, I'll try to come back with a new skill to surprise you. I guess it makes sense that I'd have my powers in those worlds too."

"Only if that is your intent. If you intend to be without your powers, you will not be able to find them there—they'll be behind a barrier of your own creation. But the doorway to return can still be found.

Remember, though, that if that door slams shut, you never will find your powers *or* return."

Lin thought back to the desperation she'd felt before she left with Taylor. An image of a whole new life, one without powers, had consumed her. The life she'd craved had her far away from the storms of Taylor's uncontrollable Glyphin powers. Somewhere warm. A dim hotel room . . .

"I don't plan to go anywhere. I've done enough flying lately."

"Good."

"Where are those worlds, Gabby?"

"You might as well ask where this world is. There's no answer to that, Lin. This world and whatever worlds you inhabit on your flights exist in the vast forever our minds can't comprehend."

Chapter 5 – Lin's Flight No. 1

"You deserve to be as tired as you appear, Lin. Maybe you should lie down some more?"

"You're right. I am tired, but I'm hungry too. I don't remember ever going six weeks without chocolate. I just want to sit and eat."

"Chocolate will help you return. Other things will, too, so watch for them."

"Okay, I will."

"I'm going to watch some TV if Taylor will let me. I suspect she will sense that I'm not a threat and will continue to sleep. You won't be needing these chocolate fudge cookies,"—Gabriel grabbed a package out of a bag on the table with a big grin—"but I will. Nomad will appreciate them, too, when he returns."

Gabriel carried the snacks around the corner to the living room, and Lin heard the TV switch on. The zany music and laughing characters of the cartoon careened around the corner into the kitchen, but she barely heard any of it. The moment Gabriel was out of sight, she felt a need to quickly engage her intent.

She noticed that she needed no long deliberations. Just action. Like a crow.

Her intent focused in an instant, and she saw a small dark spot on the refrigerator door. Tears would have trickled out as her eyes locked onto it, but the speeding darkness gave her no time. It rocketed toward her like a black bag pulled over her and blocked out everything she could perceive. It covered her, all thoughts and feelings left her, and her lungs took in no more air. Then, her heart stopped.

Just as quickly, a white dot appeared and surrounded her, returning her beating heart and thoughts and feelings. Her chest expanded with a deep breath of warm ocean air.

*   *   *

Maybe I should have given some thought to my destination, Lin told herself as she looked up and down Mallery Street in St. Simons Island.

But she suspected that it might be where she needed to go: a world like her childhood home in South Georgia but not quite as real. She figured there had to be a reason why her intent had brought her there.

A long look in each direction along the busy street that passed through The Village revealed cars and trucks and bicycles traveling in each direction, and small groups of tourists and locals walked along the sidewalks on both sides of the road.

She took a deep breath and peered at a clear blue sky that was beginning to darken as the sun neared the horizon beyond the buildings behind her. Shadows covered the shops and restaurants on the east side of Mallery, and she marveled at the realization that she'd left her kitchen in early afternoon, but without giving herself a clear goal, she'd arrived in her fake version of the Island in late evening.

A quick look inside revealed her mayhem churning just beneath her surface, and she knew that it would rise up in an instant if needed.

But would it work the same way? she wondered. Could she send out a wave of her magic and take control of someone in this world too?

She remembered doing that in the worlds Gloriana had given her, but what about this one, a world she'd created on her own?

There's only one way to find out, she told herself.

A woman in baggy shorts and a loose t-shirt—a local, Lin guessed— stood close by with a large, shaggy dog on a leash, and she figured she'd be a good test subject.

She found her unbreakable hold on her intent and witnessed infinity spreading out to every horizon, even there. The fake world became a calm, still surface just like in her real world. She felt her eyes glowing a bright green. She gazed upon a familiar scene of unimaginable masses of magic tumbling and crashing in every direction beneath the surface.

She knew that it was only how her mind showed it to her—in a way she could understand—but she still paused to reflect on all the sights and sounds and scents, all the ideas and feelings and memories, all the endless, unknowable possibilities that each wave of magic brought to every infinitely brief Island of Time.

Lin broke her gaze before the magic drew her into it. There would be time for that someday, she told herself. She remembered that she had a purpose and focused on the woman and her dog. She saw that the dog had no narrow space between its body in the world of reality and its spirit in the realm of magic. It was perfectly joined together, and she knew that her wave of magic couldn't invade and take control.

But the woman showed a distinct gap between her body and her magic. Lin remembered Gabriel's explanation weeks before she'd become a bird: that gap was free will, and only humans have that. Her mayhem could invade that space to take away the woman's free will, and she'd have complete control over her. The woman would be a puppet at her command for as long as she wanted because there was no longer any time. Lin was outside of time and in an infinite wave of magic while somehow, in reality, still sitting at her kitchen table.

Not wanting to terrify the woman, which her mayhem would surely do, she allowed the infinity all around her to recede. The world was no longer a flat surface, and all the endless depths of magic below had again become hidden away.

She relaxed and released her intent. She'd learned what she'd wanted to know: her mayhem worked even in a world that she'd conjured up herself. The green glowing of her eyes faded to leave only her normal green, just a bit brighter after the success of finding that she could use her mayhem there.

Then, an amusing realization hit her: she was back in a world where things weren't real, not like in the life that she lived with Jack and Taylor and Gabriel and Nomad. This world had no consequences, at least not yet. It was too new. It was more of a playground—a place where she could try new things, even just for fun. She had all the time she'd ever want because no time would pass for her as she sat at home while Gabriel watched TV.

I need to treat this world for what it is, she thought. It's not real. Nothing matters here. I can do what I want just for the fun of it.

Lin summoned her mayhem again, felt her eyes ignite, and saw the world become a flat surface with boundless, billowing magic below and infinity rolling out in every direction. The swirling magic flowed up into her, bringing her a sweet, unbearable pressure, until her massive wave exploded out from her. She followed her focused wave and invaded the woman. She took her life where she stood on the sidewalk.

She felt the terror the woman felt, and she found that she didn't care because the world wasn't real and neither was the woman. She turned the woman's eyes down so that they could both see the dog frozen to the sidewalk. A bit of his drool leaked down from the side of his snout, but it would never reach the pavement unless Lin let time resume.

Then, she turned the woman's eyes to gaze in her direction, frozen nearby on the sidewalk. She noticed first her long, blond hair and the piercing, burning green eyes above a slight grin. She scanned down farther and saw jeans, a thick, hooded sweatshirt over a t-shirt, and sneakers.

Returning to the testing of her mayhem, she guided the woman's hand to a cup of coffee motionless in the hand of an unmoving man who had been passing by. She took it and drank it, then returned it to the man's hand. Lin felt the warmth of the coffee, just as she felt everything else the woman felt, including the terror.

Satisfied that her powers worked in the intended world, Lin retreated back to herself and let time continue. The dog's slobber splatted on the sidewalk, and Lin waited for what she knew would happen: the woman looked right at her and screamed so loudly that everyone stopped to stare.

An urge for human laughter surprised her, something she hadn't felt since she'd become a crow, as the woman turned and dragged her dog away as quickly as she could run.

* * *

After the nameless passersby had given up their curiosity at the woman's yelling and running for no obvious reason, Lin realized she'd like to sit awhile and enjoy the remaining daylight, so she found a wooden bench still warm from the sun. Only then did she consider again what clothing she wore. A quick peek down only confirmed what she'd seen while she'd held back time and tested her mayhem.

"Yeah, no wonder I feel so warm," she said to two teenage girls walking past. They grinned and giggled when she added, "But I know exactly how to fix that."

I've been a bird for six weeks, wearing nothing but feathers, she thought. And when Jack gave me two choices for getting dressed, I could barely think like a woman, still mostly like a crow, so I picked the practical jeans and sweatshirt.

Back up on her sneakers, she hurried along Mallery, past the familiar bar with the smiling neon sun, and saw across the street the boutique she knew she'd find. A quick look in each direction showed a brief break in the traffic, and she rushed across. The shop was still open, and when she got near the door, a young man walking past stopped to hold it open for her.

"You must be dying in this heat."

"Oh, I sure am but not for long. Thanks."

"Anytime," he said before touching the brim of his ball cap and continuing on his way.

She paused just inside the door, took a deep breath, and let it seep out while scanning the racks. A playful excitement began to brew inside as she walked to a fashionable collection in back. The shop was small and didn't have room for too many racks and shelves, but Lin found what she wanted anyway. She grabbed a few garments, tried them on, and found everything fit just the way she liked.

This is returning me to myself, she realized. What I wear matters. I feel less like a bird when I'm dressed this way. When I fly to other worlds, this will be my style every time. Gabriel was right—I need to watch for ways to return to myself, and there are probably others too.

When she opened her small purse, she grinned at the sight of a wad of crisp bills, marveling at how her intent had set everything up for her. She paid the clerk and stepped out onto the sidewalk.

Right away, she knew that was a missed opportunity. She thought about her new short skirt, heels, and tight blouse and realized that just "walking" wouldn't do.

She turned toward the Atlantic Ocean and began a slow strut, satisfied to feel her hips swaying in the snug skirt and to hear her heels clicking smartly on the concrete. Heads turned, and she remembered that she liked that. Only rarely had any human shown any interest in her as a crow, and it was never in a way she'd wanted.

The blue dome above, all the car engines and laughter, and waves of aromas wafting out of restaurants and coffee shops made her walk down an imaginary Mallery Street feel as authentic as the last time she'd been there. Her goal was the pier, a comforting refuge where she could take a look out over the immense not-quite-real sea.

But when she got to Ocean Boulevard, she paused, looked to her left, and thought of all the hotels cropping up along the shore in that direction. She crossed her arms and thought maybe it was too far to walk or strut, at least for this short visit. She knew that she should probably get back to her kitchen. Staring along Ocean, she tapped out a rhythm with one toe on the concrete as she pondered her return.

"Hey, you need a lift?"

Lin turned and saw a man younger than her at the wheel of a shiny red convertible. He gave her a friendly smile. Before uttering a reflexive "no," Lin reminded herself that none of it was real.

"You know, I think I do. Just a block or two. Thanks."

He looked trustworthy enough to her, and she knew full well that she could leave anytime anyway. Or she could destroy him in a heartbeat. Even if just for fun.

"Good, get in. I'm going that way anyway."

Lin swung open the door, and he tossed two tennis rackets into the back seat. She slipped into the passenger seat and pulled the door shut.

After noting that her skirt had slid up and showed a lot of her thighs, she turned to look at him and saw that he was quite attractive. His curly black hair framed a boyish face with a two-day growth of whiskers, and the tight t-shirt showed that he likely took his sports seriously. His eyes looked up quickly from her bare legs to her eyes.

"How far do you want to go?"

Lin stared and remembered that it was a fake world—just a playground—and she could answer that question any way she wanted. But her life was at home. In the real world. With Jack. She remembered Jack.

She smiled, looked out along Ocean, and said, "Oh, just a block or two."

"Eh, too bad. I'd like to open this thing up and get some wind into all that blond hair."

She caught his eyes darting down to take a look at her breasts in her tight blouse, and she thought about it—thought about taking a longer ride to whatever place the fake world would offer her. She knew that they could race down Interstate 95, and she could even let herself have some fun, peek out above the windshield, and let the wind make a tangled mess of her hair.

Would he risk taking his eyes off the road for that? Could she control what might happen next? Or would it be better to let the world write whatever story it wanted?

"That would be fun, but just a few blocks would be good."

"Okay, whatever you want."

Lin realized that she was free to want anything at all in that world as he piloted his car up Ocean. Taking that speedy ride sounded like fun, but something along this road was drawing her in. There was a reason she'd turned away from the waves that she'd planned to enjoy from the pier.

"Here. Right here. This is good."

He pulled over near the curb, and Lin opened the door.

"Maybe next time?"

She looked at his honest smile and mischievous eyes and laughed inside at the limitless forks in the road she knew she'd find in her flights.

"Yeah, maybe. Thanks for the ride."

She got out and slammed the door.

"Be sure to have some fun," he said and pointed at her as he pulled back out into traffic.

Lin turned and looked at the hotel set back from the road and surrounded by gigantic live oaks. The soft ocean breezes lifted her hair as she gazed at the stately structure and wondered what had guided her there.

She savored a wide view of the building and its giant trees, and despite the urge to venture further in the world she'd assembled, she was sure it was time to return to her kitchen.

She found her intent and got her unbreakable hold on it. A black dot appeared above the hotel entrance, on the clean, sunbaked stucco, and Lin could look nowhere else. It raced to her and swallowed her in a night so dark that not even her heart could beat.

*   *   *

Her death might have endured for lifetimes, but it still came to an end. A point of white appeared, sped toward her, and coated her. Her heartbeat returned, followed by thoughts and feelings, and she took a deep breath that smelled like chocolate.

Before opening her eyes, she heard maniacal music and crazed characters screaming and laughing.

She'd returned home from her flight in a time so brief that no one could ever measure it: the time between one Island of Time and the next.

Chapter 6 – How Glyphins Murder Words

Lin heard the back door slam and Jack laughing as Nomad shook more snow out of his fur.

"You were supposed to do that outside, big boy. Don't get Lin mad at us, alright?"

Nomad barked once softly.

"Come on. You know why."

She opened her eyes in time to see him smiling at her, his big brown eyes appearing happy that she was home again. How could she not have remembered him? Or even Nomad?

Never again will I fly off to live a different life, she told herself. At least not like that, she thought, not as another of life's creatures. But maybe a short trip as herself just for fun.

"Did you two have a good walk?"

"No angry flocks attacked us in your backyard, so yeah, that's enough to make it good."

"Sorry. They just didn't want to let us go."

"I didn't either."

"Oh, come here, Jack."

She stood and reached her arms around his waist before he could take off his coat. She felt Nomad's heavy tail banging into her legs as she gave Jack a deep kiss. His hands gently touching her hair felt like it could cause a tear, but it didn't appear. She pulled herself back from him but stayed in his arms.

"Hey, what's with the beard?"

"Uh, I'm not sure. Just a way of passing the time, I guess, while you were gone."

"Well, I'm back. Mostly. It kind of reminds me that I left you."

He smiled and said, "You're right. Consider it gone."

She gave him a quick kiss.

"Jack, we should try to talk to Taylor. She's been sleeping, so maybe that helped her too. Let's go see."

"Alright."

Hand in hand, they walked into the living room with a curious Nomad close behind.

"Gabby, I'm glad you're already in here. Let's try to wake Taylor up. I want to see if the nap helped her too."

"Okay, Lin." Gabriel muted the TV. "Let's hope for the best."

Lin looked over and saw that somehow, the noise of the TV hadn't awakened Taylor. The blankets still covered all but her head, which was tipped back against the cushion. Lin sat next to her and pushed gently on the mound covering her daughter.

Taylor opened her eyes, and they flared before she recognized Lin. Within seconds, they'd calmed down to their normal shade of green.

"Honey, how are you feeling? Did the nap help?"

"I guess, Mom. I feel more like myself. Still kind of funny, though."

"Me too. But I know I belong here, in this house with those humans and that dog."

Jack and Gabriel turned to look at each other, then back at the couch. Nomad sat and watched Lin and Taylor with no change of expression.

"I guess I feel like I belong here, too, Mom. But not completely. Will I always feel like a bird?"

"I don't know, Hon. I don't think anyone knows."

Taylor shook the blankets down to her lap and stretched her arms out to her sides.

"Mom, now I know what my first book will be about."

"About being a crow, you mean?"

"Yep. Everyone will think it's fiction. I'll have to say it's fiction, won't I?"

"You sure will, Hon. No one would believe your stories anyway. Are you hungry?"

"Yeah, I really am now. But you know what? Even if I get 'hangry,' it'll be fine. I won't destroy your home."

"Our home, Honey. Our home."

*   *   *

"Lin Finity."

Lin hopped to her feet and blocked Taylor from the living room's wide entry, where Gloriana stood in the foyer with Jack beside her. Her eyes flared a dangerous green.

"It was easier to keep from killing you when I didn't see you. Now, I'm looking right at you."

Taylor leaned to one side to look around her mother, and her eyes flashed her own shade of menacing green.

"I see you too."

Jack took a step to block Gloriana from both of them, and Lin shook her head, wondering how Jack thought that could prevent anything.

"Lin, how about if you don't kill her right away, alright?"

"You standing there stops nothing, Jack. Even if it did, you know you'd be out in the snow again. Maybe upside-down this time."

Gabriel still slouched back into the recliner off to the side, out of Lin's and Taylor's line of sight. No effort was made to get up or intervene in any way.

Gabriel said, "Lin, it has not been a week. Time is a real thing here."

Lin's eyes still flamed at Gloriana when she said, "I did say that. Must you hold me to that?"

"I must, Lin."

Lin allowed her eyes to return to their normal green, but her stare never let up. After a few seconds of watching Gloriana staring back with her mouth open, she looked down at Taylor.

"Taylor made no such promise, Gabby."

"I sure didn't."

"Taylor, you are the one who can benefit most from what she could teach you. Will it trouble you to let her live for a while?"

"Yep, that sounds like too much trouble for me. She needs to die."

"I won't stop you if you wait a week, just as your mom has agreed to do. Isn't this moment a great scene for your book? Wouldn't you be seen as a strong, compassionate hero for not killing her right away?"

Lin broke her stare to glance at Gabriel and saw the big smile.

"You're enjoying this."

"Yes, Lin. Everything."

Lin shook her head again, but she didn't smile.

She looked again at Taylor and saw the green of her eyes return to normal, but she still frowned and stared.

"Fine."

Jack let out a big sigh, walked over, and sat at the end of the couch, leaving room for Lin to sit beside Taylor again, who remained beneath the blankets and still warily staring at Gloriana.

"Speak quickly," Taylor said. "I've mostly forgotten what promises are."

Lin had returned her focus to Gloriana, and from the corner of her eye, she saw Jack lean to look past her at Taylor. He sat back into the cushions without a grin.

Gabriel turned toward Gloriana.

"We understand that Taylor is a Glyphin now, and she has indeed learned a great deal of control. But I believe it takes a certain vigilance, isn't that right, Taylor?"

"Now that you mention it, yeah. It's always somewhere in the background. I'm holding it back, even now."

"Holding back the storms?" said Lin.

"Yeah, Mom. They could blow up anytime."

"She's very talented at playing with words now," Gabriel said to Gloriana. "She knows all about combining a known word with an unknown one. More than one of each. I have no doubt that she truly could summon a horrible storm with little effort. Even though she can probably stop it if and when she decides, there must be an easier way. Something she can do that is like hitting a switch to turn it off. Does some technique like that exist?"

"It does," said Gloriana. "It is surprisingly easy, at least for a Glyphin that is calm."

Lin watched Gloriana closely, wondering if she had indeed given up all of her powers. Her eyes should never glow again, she knew. She was only human now—a woman without powers. She posed no threat of any kind, and she could be destroyed with hardly any effort. She decided that she could let her live for a week. Or at least until she'd explained the technique to Taylor.

"The young Glyphin already knows that the key is the word or words that she used to begin the change. Lin, I told you that she must reduce the word down to as low of a level as she can. If she can see only the letters and no longer understand that they form a word, that is very close to the solution."

Gabriel said, "But there's something she can do that's more reliable?"

"Yes."

She paused, and Lin watched her looking from Taylor's eyes up to hers and back again.

That's right, Lin thought. Watch for the green light. From either of us. It will be the last thing you see.

Gloriana continued. "It is sometimes still difficult to see only letters and not a word, especially if the Glyphin is upset. Or even if she is tired. What she must do is imagine the letters far apart. The farther apart she can see them, the more impossible it is for the word to exist."

"You mean, she should put extra spaces between them?" Jack said.

"No. That is not enough."

She focused on Taylor's steady gaze.

"She can leave the first letter on the floor by her boots. She can imagine the second letter on the railing of the pier near the water in St. Simons Island. She can place the third letter on the back of a tiger in a jungle on a faraway continent."

Lin heard the silence in the room and glanced around quickly to see all eyes focused on Gloriana.

"If there is another letter,"—she turned her eyes to lock onto Lin's—"she might choose to banish it to the moon."

Still, the room was silent.

"That is how Glyphins murder words."

Jack said, "Good God."

"Gabby, you didn't know this?"

"No, Lin. I've never met a Glyphin. I've only heard tales passed down through generations. The last known Glyphin lived long ago."

"That is me," said Gloriana. "And I still live."

In that moment, Lin understood that Gloriana should be allowed to live for a week. She'd offered a solution for Taylor that was so simple that it seemed obvious after it had been spoken. What else could she explain? How much knowledge did that woman have?

"I have offered something of value?"

"You have," said Gabriel.

"Perhaps you can offer me food in return?"

Lin turned to Gabriel and saw a huge smile. She gave him a nod and smile of her own, then turned back to Gloriana.

"Pull up a chair. You may live."

*　*　*

"Hey, Taylor, I set up a place for you to write."

From his seat at the kitchen table, Jack pointed at the compact planning desk tucked against the wall near the door to the laundry room.

"What do you think?"

"I don't know, Jack. I might need someplace a little more out of the way."

"Like up in a tree?"

Jack winced, held his breath, and waited. Taylor stared without a hint of a smile for several long seconds.

"You're still a funny guy, Jack. I've missed that. There were no jokes where Mom and I were."

Jack let out his breath and smiled.

"I've missed you too."

He turned to Lin and Gabriel and said, "I'm ready for dinner. How about a pizza? Or two?"

"Yes, Jack," said Gabriel. "Big ones. Maybe make it three."

"What is pizza?" said Gloriana.

Jack turned and saw Gloriana smiling, too, with her caramel eyes looking toward him.

"It's something you'll like. There's hardly anything much better than pizza."

"Then, I am sure that I will like the pizza. It is good to have things one likes, especially in a kitchen."

"Yes, it sure is," said Lin. "Chocolate's pretty good too."

Lin gave Jack a quick smile and a look into her green eyes, but the smile faded quickly, and she turned her eyes to keep a close watch on Gloriana.

Jack stood, took out his phone, and walked a few steps from them. Gabriel turned to Taylor.

"Your mom said you learned to control your Glyphin powers. How much control do you have now?"

"I can show you if—"

"Maybe not now. How did your time away help you?"

Taylor blinked her green eyes three times, and she stared at Gabriel before beginning.

"At first, it didn't. But I wasn't a Glyphin anymore. Or I didn't remember being one. Or the word 'Glyphin' didn't mean anything. I don't know, but I remember our first flight when we flew up into the rain. I felt my wings weighted down by heavy raindrops but only for a second or two. I didn't want it. Then, the rain stopped. We flew away."

"Yes, you sure did fly away. Later on, you found your powers again?"

"I never thought about powers. I just did things. It started with wind. We were in a cornfield, and—"

"Your mom and you?"

"And all the rest, Gabriel. Then, a hawk came. God told me to fly. I stayed. I did something else."

"What did you do?"

"I heard the quick flapping from the others joining the sky to escape. I felt the wind from their wings, and I knew without having words for what I knew. I asked the wind to hit the hawk from below, and that shoved it way up into the sky.

"Everyone else had gone. I was alone, and the hawk slipped to one side of the wind and dove. They're fast, but I was faster. I thought about its life, and I felt the power of all wind as I watched it coming at me. It fell to the ground and didn't move again."

"You killed it."

"The wind killed it."

Gabriel stared for a second, then looked at Lin. She showed no change of expression.

"The wind inside it?"

"There's wind inside everything that breathes. That wind killed the hawk."

Gabriel showed a faint smile and continued watching Taylor.

"Do you know what that's called? What you do?"

"It doesn't matter."

"No, I believe it doesn't. But perhaps you'd like to mention it in your book that you're about to begin?"

"Sure. Okay."

"Windcraft. Isn't that right, Gloriana?"

She nodded.

Gabriel said, "I thought it was only a legend since I'd heard that even many Glyphins have not believed it ever existed. But you've found it."

Taylor nodded and stared, her green eyes calm and unblinking.

"Do you still feel like a bird, Honey?"

Taylor turned to face her mother.

"Yeah, Mom. This feels funny. There's not enough happening. I'm still cold and hungry. I miss the sky too."

Jack walked in with a stack of pizza boxes and set them on the table. Lin and Gabriel each grabbed a slice while Jack took his coat off and left it on Taylor's writing desk chair. He pulled out a chair and joined them at the table, taking a seat between Lin and Gloriana. Gloriana reached into the box at the same time as him, and he laughed when the cheese stuck them together.

"Oh, they are stuck together," said Gloriana. "Probably because they are both so hot."

They each pulled to get them apart, and the cheese started to slide off of Jack's.

"It seems they are becoming good friends," she said as she pinched the cheese on her piece to keep it from falling."

"Yeah, something like that," said Jack.

Taylor put three slices on a plate and stood.

"Thanks for the food, Jack," she said and left for the living room.

They all sat in silence and watched the empty doorway she'd passed through. Jack waited thirty seconds, then rose to peek around the corner. Back at the table, he said, "She's back under the blankets. Is she going to be okay?"

"Oh, I don't know, Jack. How could anyone know? Let's just let her eat and sleep for a while and see how things go."

"She had less to anchor her. Less to assist in her return," said Gabriel.

"Oh, that makes sense," said Lin. "She hasn't been alive as long as me. Is that what you mean?"

"Yes. And you've had several experiences with living the life of another creature. It didn't surprise you to feel like you were dying. This is her first time."

"I'm resisting the urge to get under the blankets with her. I'm making myself finish eating first, then I'll join her. It's not easy, Gabby."

"No, Lin, I'm sure it isn't. But this pizza is excellent."

* * *

Gloriana claimed that she was still tired from traveling and the onslaught of Taylor's Windcraft, and she left for the guest room. Lin picked at the last of the crust in an empty box before she stood up and brought her plate and Gloriana's to the counter next to the sink.

With the fading daylight, the window above the sink became a mirror, and when she glanced up, she saw mostly the baggy sweatshirt she'd put on early that morning. She frowned and tugged at the thick cloth around her shoulders.

This doesn't make sense, she thought. I'm less of a bird with every nap and especially from that flight to St. Simons. Maybe not just the flight itself.

It wasn't even a decision that needed to be made. She turned and walked through the kitchen, past the table, down the hall, and into her bedroom. The other items of clothing that Jack had brought her still sat on the dresser, waiting to be put away.

None of it found their places in drawers and hanging in the closet. But the jeans and sweatshirt she'd been wearing did. And the boots. Lin stood after finishing and putting on her heels and felt further from being a bird. But she knew the blanket was still a safe place.

She didn't notice Jack, Gabriel, and Nomad watching her as she passed them on the way to the living room. There, she found Taylor beneath the warm heap, her eyes a normal green and peering out from a small opening. Her empty plate sat on the table. Lin found the edge of the top blanket, then the edges of the others, and she pulled the thick layers aside.

Taylor sat with her knees pulled up against her and her elbows at her sides. Lin wedged herself in, held her limbs the same way, and closed the protective covering over them.

When she let her head begin to tip to her right, she felt Taylor's had leaned toward hers. With a narrow gap for their eyes to scan the room if needed, they slept.

* * *

A steady stream of conversation and laughter drifted in from the kitchen, but since it posed no threat, Lin knew it best to remain still. The voices were low—Jack and Gabriel—and there was sporadic laughter at a higher pitch—Gloriana.

She slept and listened at the same time. She knew that Taylor did, too, like they'd done for the last six weeks.

When the kitchen noises stopped, Lin's eyes snapped open. She saw Jack standing in the doorway, too cautious, or maybe too afraid—she sensed fear—to approach without an invitation.

"Jack, it's okay."

She watched him take slow steps until he stood near.

"It's getting late, Lin. Do you two plan on staying there all night? A bed would be more comfortable for each of you. With all the blankets you want."

She blinked and stared at him and knew he was right.

"Okay, Jack. Taylor's really tired, though. Maybe she'll let you carry her to bed."

"Um, I'd rather hear her say it's alright first."

Lin elbowed her gently, and Taylor said, "I heard, Mom. Okay, Jack. Thanks, Jack."

They pulled the blankets off of themselves, and Jack took Taylor up into his arms.

"She's still light from being sick, Jack. She needs more pizza."

"And chocolate," Taylor said with her arms around his neck and her head leaning into him.

"That's all you need to do," said Jack. "Eat and sleep until you feel all the way better. Oh, and maybe you could get started writing."

He smiled and waited for a reply, but he got none.

"Alright, I already turned down your blankets. Come on."

Lin watched him carrying her daughter around the corner, heard the door close down the hall, and watched him walk back to her on the couch.

"How about you? You know, I'm happy to carry you too."

"I can walk. Thanks, Jack."

She stood up with all the blankets still around her and began walking toward her bedroom. Jack followed. Near the kitchen, he stopped to say goodnight to Gabriel and Nomad, and Lin kept going.

"Have a good night. I hope the couch is alright, Gabriel. And Nomad, if you need to go out, just let me know, alright?"

"The couch is fine, Jack. I might try an excursion with Nomad, too, if he needs it."

Nomad only panted in Jack's direction.

Jack turned to catch up with Lin and almost tripped over the mound of blankets she'd dropped near the door. He saw her under the bed's blankets with a trail of her clothes and shoes leading to the bed. After getting out of his own clothes, he stood to look at the welcome sight of Lin at home and in her own bed.

He crawled in next to her and didn't say anything when he saw that the commotion of him lying down had caused no reaction. She only lay there with her back to him, the blankets pulled up high.

He dragged the covers up over himself and fell asleep with a smile.

Chapter 7 – Jack's Flight No. 1

The blankets were stuffed with sand. Too heavy and hot and clingy. He kicked them off to the side, where they bunched up against Lin's back.

Jack looked at her blond hair arrayed across the pillow in the dim light. He reached out but stopped just short of running his fingers through it. He frowned and pulled his hand back.

Let her sleep, he thought. Her life has been impossible for a couple of months now, but at least she's back home and in her own bed again.

As his eyes adjusted to the darkness, he let them scan her curves, which couldn't be hidden completely, all the way from her mane to her toes and back again. He let out a deep sigh and rubbed his eyes.

Why on Earth is it so hot in this house? he wondered. It must be that thermostat—somehow, it got cranked up too high. Maybe Taylor decided to mess with it. Couldn't have been Nomad. Did Gabriel ever get cold?

He sat up and brushed back his wavy brown hair before standing and stretching. Even wearing only his boxers, the heat wrapped around him like a thick fur coat.

Was it the whole house? Or just Lin's bedroom?

She's still cold, he thought as he turned to spy her again, but at least she isn't under a mountain of blankets on the couch anymore. That's progress.

He pried his eyes away from her and decided he'd better check outside in the hallway. If the entire house was boiling, he'd turn it down and throw another blanket over Lin.

The doorknob turned easily, and he exited and closed the door softly behind him. He'd walked into a greenhouse on a sunny day. Even the wood flooring beneath his bare feet could have been plucked from a campfire. But what of the rest of the house?

A tiptoe walk through the dark ended with a bump into a chair at the kitchen table, sending a short scraping sound through the quiet house. He hoped Taylor wouldn't hear it in her bedroom or Gloriana in the guest room, but maybe Gabriel and Nomad on the couch in the living room would. He waited a few seconds and heard no one stirring.

He paused for another minute, listening to the silence and wondering if Lin, who'd lived in the wild for six weeks, would be awakened and alarmed at the unexpected sound.

Oh, but she's probably too cold under the blankets to dare investigate it, he reminded himself and walked the few remaining steps to the thermostat.

It sat on a sidewall of the small alcove that contained the modest writing desk that he hoped Taylor would soon begin using. She'd said many times that she wanted to be an author, but Jack suspected that would have to wait—she probably had to chase the crow from her system first.

He found the light switch and turned on the dusty and seldom-used overhead fixture, which held such a low-wattage bulb that even the desktop kept most of its shade.

Still, it seemed bright after the near-total darkness through which he'd just journeyed. He leaned in and waited for his eyes to catch up and squinted at the faint digital readout.

A single sharp shiver spiraled around his spine when something touched his shoulder. Too startled even to scream, he spun around to see Gloriana with her hand still out. Even in the dark night of the kitchen, he saw two eyes glowing with a subtle caramel hue.

She held a finger to her lips, barely blocking a playful grin. Jack forgot to take his next breath, and after studying her smile, he looked up into her eyes and held her gaze. With his eyes unblinking and his heart still beating hard, he heard her voice soft and low.

"We must be very quiet, Jack. Do not speak."

He shook his head while he stared into her eyes, eyes which he knew shouldn't be glowing because she'd given up her powers. He was sure that's what Gabriel had said: she had to give them up to return to life. That was the deal she'd made. He wondered if maybe it was some odd reflection from the light he'd switched on.

Still in shock at seeing her there in the middle of the night, Jack didn't say a word.

"We will let the house cool soon. I chose to make things hot. You felt heat, and you came to me."

Jack started to speak, but she shushed him again.

"I wear my cinnamon gown. Look upon me, Jack."

He still wanted to say something, anything, but he also wanted to see the gown again—the one she'd worn when she'd first arrived at Lin's house. The sight of it the first moment he'd seen her was a memory he'd always keep. He knew that he'd never forget how it had left the dark skin of her shoulders uncovered and her long, dark hair coiled down all over them. The front was cut low and showed much of her breasts, which were straining against the thin cloth. And the high slit had opened as she'd stepped back and forth from the cold, giving a teasing view of her long, shapely legs.

Not waiting for another invitation, he looked at the gown.

It was as he remembered it. If anything, she looked better in it this time, standing in the warm and quiet kitchen under a nightlight as the rest of the household slept.

He looked back up into her eyes, and though he felt an urge to look down again at her body barely hidden by the gown, at the sight of her grin, he also felt the hair on his neck pleading with him to run for his life.

But he'd hesitated too long—Gloriana's eyes flared like boiling pots of caramel, and he would have screamed if he could as his soul was ripped from his body. His arms ignored him, and his legs refused his orders. Speech had become impossible. He couldn't even blink.

Gloriana had taken his life while they stood face-to-face in Lin's kitchen at well past midnight.

Jack could do nothing but watch her take the one step needed to stand so close that he could see the smoldering in her eyes, which were almost even with his. He couldn't stop her arms from reaching around his waist.

"We never got a chance to know each other. But now we are alone. We will know each other better, will we not, Jack?"

Jack felt his head nodding. He hadn't done it, and he couldn't stop it. He felt her hands moving up along the sides of his arms and wanted to turn his eyes to watch them, but they remained locked on hers. All he could do was feel her arms coming to rest on his shoulders and her fingers raking through his hair.

"It is late at night, and I wish to be held."

Feeling like a puppet moved by invisible but all-powerful strings, he reached around her waist, and his palms rested on the small of her back, which was warm against his hands through the silky material. When his arms lifted higher, his hands found the smooth skin of her back. They lingered there and then dropped slowly until he held her behind, one cheek in each hand.

"Yes, Jack. It is good for you to hold me that way."

Still, he could do nothing but look into her shining eyes. With a grim humor, he noted that even though his breathing remained normal—slow and steady when it should have become fast and heavy—his heart had sped up, so he knew that she'd been generous enough to leave that one part of him alone.

He didn't want to do it, but there was no way to fight it. He felt his hands pulling her closer, and she felt both soft and solid in his hands, a captivating blend of feminine and athletic. He drew her in until her gown touched his bare chest, then he pulled her in more tightly until he could feel her breasts waiting just behind the tight fabric and pressing into him.

Why is my head leaning to one side? he wondered. A second later, he got his answer.

Their lips met, and Jack had no way to stop any of it. He couldn't control anything; he'd move only if she desired it.

While she held him there, their lips touching gently in the silent house, he felt his heart rate pick up higher. Her lips against his were soft and smooth and warm and wet. He wondered if she'd use her tongue, but the kiss ended, and she pulled back but remained close. His hands still held her hips tight against his.

She glanced down with a smile and said, "Oh my, Jack. You did like that kiss."

Jack couldn't lie to himself about it—he had reacted to the beautiful woman in his arms. She'd left more than just his heart to respond in whatever ways it would.

She leaned in for another kiss, a longer one, and he couldn't stop either of their mouths from opening so that their tongues could get to know each other too. After a long minute, she pulled away to speak.

"You liked that kiss even more, Jack. I have control of you, but I am not doing that to you," she said, and he felt his hands holding her hips tightly against him.

She kissed him again, a warmer, wetter, deeper, and much longer kiss.

"That is good, Jack. It is about time we become close friends, is it not?"

Jack felt his head nodding.

"I wish to kiss you more."

Her lips found his, and they kissed for many minutes until the sound of a door opening down the hall caught their attention. His hands were still holding her close, and her arms were around his neck, fingers still playing with his hair, as his heart began to pound.

"Oh, Jack, that might be Lin. Or maybe it is the young woman, Taylor. I do not know. Do they travel to the kitchen at night?"

Jack tried to close his eyes, but all he could see was her glowing caramel as her soft lips again touched his. His heart raced as he heard footsteps in the hall and another door. But Gloriana would not let him go, and she wouldn't end their passionate kiss.

She said, "I think it is probably Lin. I made her house hot, and now she is thirsty. Whether crow or woman, she will need water. She will be here soon to drink. She will see us, Jack."

She gave him two quick kisses, each one warm and wet, then she said, "And it seems you are happy about that as well. Is this true, Jack? Do you like how I feel in your arms so much that you do not care if Lin sees us together?"

Jack couldn't stop his head from nodding or his other obvious reaction, but he had a fleeting thought that he might have nodded on his own if he could. She did feel good in his arms. Her kisses were hot and promised so much more, and all of it was happening with an unending view of two shimmering seas of caramel.

"It would be wise to stop, but of course, we will not. We will kiss more and wait for Lin."

He couldn't stop his arms from pulling her body more tightly against his, and he couldn't deny that his enthusiasm only increased as he felt her tongue playing and exploring. It felt like it had a life of its own. A part of her that was warm and wet and slipping around inside his mouth, and he waited for Lin to light up the entire room and see him wearing only his boxers as he held her tightly. And if Gloriana then stepped aside, Lin would have no doubt that he enjoyed the touch of the ancient queen that Lin had brought to her home.

He heard another door, more footsteps, a few quick mumbled words too far down the hall to understand, then another door closing. Silence. Only his and Gloriana's bodies hot in the dark room, pressed together and kissing as if they were alone in the house.

She leaned back and said, "We almost got caught tonight. Lin will surely witness our growing friendship next time."

She kissed him again quickly, his arms released her, and his fingers laced themselves behind his head. Her hands caressed their way down to his hips, and he felt her palms warm against his skin as she slid her hands down inside his boxers until her wrists touched the elastic band at each side.

"We will kiss more. Perhaps without your shorts this time. I believe we would both like that."

She rubbed her hands all the way around and slid them farther down to hold his backside as her lips touched his. And when he felt his mouth open, he wondered if he'd greet her tongue with his own if he could. They kissed for several minutes as they gazed into each other's eyes and her hands held him.

Then, she began slowly moving her hands back around toward the front, her wrists deep enough past the top hem to stretch it open at the top. She held the hard muscles of his thighs and leaned away but never broke her gaze.

Jack still stared at the bright glow when she looked down and said, "Yes, I see that you would like kissing without your shorts much better."

He felt his boxers being pulled down until he was mostly uncovered in back, and the front had met an obstacle and would not easily move any farther.

"You are very happy even at the thought of that. You will be even happier with the lights on and Lin seeing you that way for me. Is that true?"

Jack's head nodded, and he wondered if that really could be true.

She slipped her hands back up and grabbed the top band. She worked it around from front to back several times, pulling the front far up and letting it relax over and over, and Jack felt the cloth lifting and sliding over him, making him all the more happy. Then, she pulled him in close again, pressing him into her while she gave him a big smile.

"Yes, we will be sure to make you more comfortable next time. That will surely lead to the deep friendship we both desire."

With her hands still on his shorts and holding him close, she kissed him for another minute.

"Am I like a dream?"

Jack felt his head nodding several times, and she kissed him again.

"Goodnight, Mr. Jack."

He found that he could turn his eyes, but he could move nothing else. He watched her walk slowly away from him, a vision with long, dark hair draped far down her back, a trim waistline, and a shapely bottom. He heard her heels clicking softly on the wood floor and prayed no one else did.

As he watched her hips swaying enticingly beneath the thin cinnamon gown, all light in the kitchen became a cathedral veil that trailed her obediently across the polished wood floor, leaving only darkness in its wake.

She turned before rounding the corner, snapping her veil of light around her and into the hall, and he saw only two points of glowing caramel in a room now completely dark. They flared for an instant, freezing Jack with his eyes wide open, then they vanished.

Just as his life abruptly returned to him, the night swallowed him whole.

* * *

Lin awoke beneath the thick covers and found that she was comfortable, not freezing and shivering like before. She felt more like herself—like a human woman with a human woman's needs—and she realized that it was from dressing in her favorite wardrobe in her flight to St. Simons Island. And maybe from the chocolate, too, she thought with a smile.

She knew that she didn't want to wait any longer, so she rolled over toward Jack and reached for him.

"Oh, Jack, you're awake?"

"Oh, um, I guess I am. Something must have woke me up. How are you feeling? Are you sleeping alright?"

"I'm feeling a lot more like myself, Jack. Not as much like a bird. Why don't you see how I feel to you?"

She reached over his hips and pulled him close into her.

"Oh, Jack, you really are awake! Were you dreaming about me?"

"Yeah, I must have been. God, you can't imagine how much I've missed you."

She reached around his waist and squeezed tight up against him.

"My goodness, Jack. Keep dreaming that dream."

He smiled as he held her face in both hands, then he gave her a long, deep kiss.

"It's been a long time, Cowboy. Show me how much you've missed me."

Jack only growled and pulled her in for another kiss.

She turned her back to him, and he reached around her waist, his breath hot on the back of her neck. Moments later, they began to make up for lost time, with his hands on her belly and hers over his.

Lin felt her right arm twitching above her, flapping under the covers, and her left elbow struggling to move where it was held into the sheets at her side.

She quickly lost any interest in trying to hold those limbs still, and they continued to flutter as she lost herself in the attention Jack had saved for her for the last six weeks.

Recalling how it had felt when a powerful wind had raised her high into the sky, Lin welcomed the unstoppable pleasure that carried her and her Cowboy to the heaven that she'd never known even once as a crow.

Chapter 8 – Lin's Flight No. 2

"God, I've missed that, Cowgirl," Jack said with his lips brushing Lin's ear.

She rolled over to face him, and they held each other close while they kissed in the dark room.

"Me too, Cowboy. I'm sure I'm even less of a bird now."

"That helps? We should do that as often as possible, then, right?"

"Oh, you might be right about that, Jack," she said and kissed him again. "You must have really missed me, or you really did have a good dream about me. Whatever it was, it's just what I needed."

"Yeah, I always dream about you. It's good you woke up when you did."

"Or else what, Jack?" she said with a soft laugh.

"Oh no, nothing. I mean . . . it's just—"

"Jack, I'm just messing with you. Whatever dream you were having, you should dream it all the time. I'm thrilled to star in your dreams like that and get you all worked up."

"Yeah," he said with a laugh of his own, "I sure was worked up, wasn't I?"

"Yeah, Jack, I insist. Dream about me all you want. You go find that dream every chance you get, okay? Promise me."

"Sure, Lin. Yeah, of course. I promise."

His hands were rough and strong on her back, squeezing her into him, and they continued to kiss until she broke loose and wiped at her eyes.

"Oh, Jack, I really am tired all of a sudden. I guess all that passion kind of woke me up, but I'm still tired from everything."

"I'm not surprised. Let's get some sleep, alright?"

She rolled over and sighed when he again reached around her waist and gently held her close and warm beneath the blankets.

"Okay, Jack. Sweet dreams."

* * *

Before the warmth of Jack and the bed swept her away to her own dreams, Lin stared at the darkness of the wall beneath the window, which let only traces of moonlight sneak past its thick curtains. She remembered again her extreme desires from the feelings Gloriana had forced on her. They'd felt so real. She recalled sitting in her car after returning with Gloriana from the spaces in between the Islands of Time. It had taken only a second for the entire, tempting scene to flash through her mind.

And this time, lying in her dark bedroom next to Jack, who she guessed was probably deep asleep already, she knew that she could take some time to think about it again. And though it was not how a bird would ever behave, that Lin, the one overwhelmed by Gloriana's worlds, had barely resisted racing to find the fantasy: a world where all she wanted was to tease and get attention, and she had no powers and none of the problems they'd brought to her and everyone around her.

It was an alluring affair: a luxurious bath in a hotel somewhere warm, far from the cold of Pennsylvania and the destructive storms brought on by a Glyphin daughter with no control. The bathwater was hot, and the pleasant soaking mixed with anticipation of what would follow.

She imagined the feel of the fluffy towel as she'd pat all of her skin dry. Not a single item of clothing would be needed, just her high heels. Her hair would brush back easily and form a wild mane cascading down over her bare back.

A twitch from Jack as he fell into a deeper sleep broke her reverie. And rather than relive some ridiculous adventure she'd clung to in desperation over six weeks earlier, Lin decided to instead find her intent and take a flight to whatever world it might bring her. There were new powers to learn, she knew, and this time, she'd try something outlandish because where she was traveling, it made no difference to anyone there.

Without a second thought, she found her intent where it always waited: deep in the stillness within her. She knew that she'd be dead beside Jack in a moment, but it wouldn't last. She'd return to the very next Island of Time, and her life would continue right where it had ended.

But to take that journey, however brief, she'd have to die.

She held her intent and watched as a black spot appeared, even in the nearly total darkness of the bedroom. It paused beneath the window as if waiting for her to come to it. When it had decided to move, it tore a path toward her and covered her.

Her lungs locked up first, and she knew that it was because a dead woman needed no oxygen. Her thoughts and feelings vanished, bringing an emptiness and indifference. Her final heartbeat sounded, and she waited there in silence with nothing but the unbreakable hold on her intent.

She died.

But only for an instant. A white point appeared in the darkness, expanded, and wrapped all around her. Her heart began a steady beat. Thoughts and feelings returned. She drew in a deep breath of air that she knew had warmed from traveling many miles between ocean waves and a hot sun.

*   *   *

Before opening her eyes, Lin heard a man's voice.

"Maybe next time? I'd love to take you for a ride."

Oh no, she thought, I'm back here? Gabriel said not to return to the same world!

She opened her eyes and looked at the man's honest smile and playful eyes as he waited in his red convertible. He looked different than the last time, and Lin wondered if her flights would always be sloppy and inconsistent in unimportant ways.

The curly black hair had become short and neat, and his two-day stubble had become a beard fashioned into a sharp point. The polo shirt had become a black sport coat and a crisp white dress shirt that appeared dingy when compared to his blindingly white smile.

She remembered the safe and proper answer she'd given the last time she was there.

But this was a world not to be taken seriously, she reminded herself. This was a world not just for learning but maybe for fun too. And the fun would probably help chase away the last traces of crow, so she'd never twitch her wings for Jack again.

"You can bet I'll take that ride next time. Watch for me."

He paused with a grin, then he said, "Maybe a car ride too."

Lin hesitated for only a moment before she matched his grin.

She shook back her mane and said, "If we can spare the time."

She gave him a big smile and fought her urge to climb in without bothering to open the door.

He shook his head, smiled back, and said, "Forget the car, then, because I'd rather spend all my time,"—his eyes left hers to take in first her tight blouse, then her tight skirt and just the tops of her thighs visible over the car door, then back up to her eyes—"getting to know you."

He waited with a grin, and Lin looked quickly to each side at the unreal world, then she shrugged with a smile.

"Hmm . . . well, you won't need to see this wardrobe again."

He whistled out a long breath and said, "Damn."

He kept smiling, revved the engine, and released the clutch, squealing the tires. Lin made a mental note that she felt a lot less like a crow. Attention to her as a woman helped.

After watching the car speed away, she turned into the ocean breezes and let them carry her hair back over her shoulders. A quick look to the left, then the right, showed the same giant live oaks, their trunks rising thick from the dry ground and their branches twisting together like bony fingers knitted in a knotted tangle.

She stared at the hotel entrance and watched three men walk in only seconds apart.

Probably businessmen here for a convention, she thought.

She looked to the northeast along the sidewalk to see tourists and locals walking past her in each direction. Some held cups of coffee, some held children's hands, and others held both. A few had cameras and phones ready, and two were walking dogs. All chattered and laughed and hurried along, seeming to see everything but her.

She looked back at the hotel and saw two more men enter. She noticed that they all dressed well—no jeans and t-shirts.

Yep, must be a convention today, she thought.

Only then did she think to look at her own wardrobe. She nodded with a slight grin when she looked down and saw the bottom hem of her black skirt high up on her thighs.

Oh, she thought, good thing I didn't try to climb into that car!

Her favorite black heels looked good against the faded gray of the weathered concrete beneath them. She felt the tight blouse and looked down only to confirm its color, which she saw was a delicate pink.

It felt good. It felt right. She knew that every moment she spent dressed that way, whether in a world real or fabricated, led her closer to herself—back to whom she was before any of the bizarre experiences from Gloriana had trapped her. Before she'd escaped with Taylor to become crows.

Another glance at the door revealed one more man, also dressed well but not too much so, walking in with only a paper cup in his hand.

The coffee looked good, and while she wondered if maybe she should get her own, the sun moved behind the thick foliage of a tall tree on the hotel's lot, sending an unwelcome shiver through her.

Oh, I'm still cold, she thought. Even here.

After crossing her arms and rubbing her hands up and down on them, she realized that she should be able to bring back the sunshine. It didn't matter anyway, right? There had to be an easy way to deal with those pesky trees, even though they were graceful and majestic but starting to annoy her.

She remembered the times she'd used the magic of an object or a person. How she'd been able to change it. Rearrange it. Or simply move it.

It had been tiring each time. Traveling to a thing's magic, holding all of that magic and working with it, squeezing it if death was her goal . . . it all took so much energy. There had to be another way . . .

From deep inside her intent, further down in the stillness inside her, the solution percolated up, and she knew how easy it could be.

She thought about the trees. Not all parts of the trees—just their gnarly, rough trunks holding those branches and leaves that blocked the sun from warming her. She felt the magic of each of them. She recognized their magic separate from buildings, people, lamp posts . . . from anything else nearby.

When a green spark ignited in her eyes, she saw infinity sprawl out around her toward every horizon, and she saw the chaotic beauty of the spinning fields of magic below the calm surface of the world.

The magic started rising up into her. She welcomed the sweet pressure of it as it spread to every cell, and she let it pack into her more than she'd ever allowed before. She felt her eyes burning a rich green.

She calmed her excitement and an urge to question it as she felt the magic start to spin. Like a gentle vortex, it swirled around slowly, picking up speed as the pressure increased even more.

When it had reached the speed of a cyclone whirling inside her, Lin focused on the magic of the trees' trunks—only that and nothing else— and her spirit dislodged itself but traveled nowhere. It stayed within her and joined the mad swirling of the magic even as her view never changed.

She couldn't have helped it if she'd tried. From the speed of her rotating spirit, it felt like her arms rose to point straight to each side. She'd become a spinning top of magic, all inside, and her intent focused only on the magic of all the trees, all their thick trunks, as the pressure threatened to explode within her.

Despite the monumental agitation inside, she only gazed calmly at the frozen trees. With a surprising rush of pleasure, a welcome release, she felt the magic shoot out through her extended arms, blasting out through her fingertips to form a thin disk that expanded in every direction.

In an instant, the disk of magic had been sent, and though the spinning inside slowed and stopped, the ecstasy of sending it trailed off slowly. The vast fields and mountains of magic below again hid from her and everyone else. The calm surface of the world returned to its natural state. Infinity pulled back, and the horizon was again as it would always appear in both a real and a fake world. Her eyes were again her normal shade of green, and time resumed.

Lin released her intent and watched the trees for any sign of what she'd done. Nothing had changed. It looked as though her power over the magic, her spinning inside like a top, had had no effect other than entertainment. Leaves still fluttered gently from the touch of the warm breezes. The shade still covered her as tourists and locals continued past her where she stood on the sidewalk in front of the hotel. She still wanted that cup of hot coffee.

A stronger breeze that had traveled inland from the open ocean caused a stir in the last tree to her left. She watched it and saw the topmost branches swaying and pointing themselves away from the sea. She listened, but there was no sound other than the traffic and pedestrians. No creaking or snapping. No sounds of splintering.

Only the slow leaning of a gigantic tree as its trunk opened without a sound at the height of Lin's shoulders.

Its branches couldn't let go of its neighbor's, and that tree began to tip as well. Like a row of giant, beautiful, leafy dominoes, the trees all fell in a wave that traveled from left to right.

She thought of running. She knew that she should, but she didn't. She only watched the devastation her new mayhem had brought.

The tourists screamed and bolted across the street, some dragging kids by their hands and pets by their leashes. Drivers left their cars and trucks running with the doors open. The slow-motion nightmare somehow gave all of them enough time before the falling wall of trees crushed vehicles, bent over light poles, and gouged into the sandy ground.

Lin watched as the branches fell all around her, but none touched her. They all swayed and rattled on the ground like a dying animal with countless legs and arms before they fell silent. So did the crowds huddled and staring on the sidewalk across the street behind her.

Oh, wait till I tell Gabby, she thought, thrilled to not feel even a bit of fatigue from what she'd just done. She'd had no need to travel to a thing's magic. She'd sent an unstoppable force to complete what she'd imagined and then intended.

She knew then what she'd done: she'd sent only a tiny part of each tree's reality back to the magic.

Gabriel will sure be surprised! she thought.

With that unbelievable accomplishment behind her and with a skill she hoped would remain with her in any world, she thought it might be time to return.

Instead, she looked again at the hotel entrance. Another man, dressed well and for some reason oblivious to the destruction she'd brought to the Island, passed through the door, and she watched it close slowly on its own.

A look down revealed a pattern of branches laying over one another and leaving only small patches of pavement on the walk leading to the hotel. Lin stepped one heel into the first open space, then the other into the next opening. She continued until she stood within a few steps of the door.

Another man passed her and turned to take a better look. He smiled as he looked her up and down. She thought she saw him wink before he turned and hurried inside.

Lin felt her heart begin a stronger beat, and she took more steps until she could reach for the door's handle. With her cursory glance down, she saw a tiny black dot on its polished chrome surface. There was no time to consider what it might be because it showed its true nature without hesitation. It rushed toward her, covering her and killing her.

In an eternal darkness, Lin held onto her intent. She could do nothing but wait in silence as centuries might have fled past without her.

Then, a white dot appeared and welcomed her to a world. Her world.

*   *   *

Lin felt Jack finish the twitch he'd started just before she'd left. Before she'd died. She wiggled herself in closer to him and looked again into the darkness coating the wall beneath a window framed by thin lines of moonlight.

Her new ability, the one she'd found in that other world, gave her a smile despite her fatigue. And the thought of opening that hotel door and walking in only made the smile grow. She felt like she might know exactly why she'd been drawn to that world again. And if she were to return, just one more time, maybe—

No, she thought, I'm never going back to that world again.

Like Gabriel had said, that world wouldn't remain safe and phony for very long. How long it would take for it to become real and trap her couldn't be guessed. It would never be worth the risk to go there again.

Still, the thought of what might be waiting beyond those doors invaded and took root in her dreams as her heavy eyelids closed, and she joined Jack in a deep sleep with his strong arms holding her close.

Chapter 9 – Yet Still, They Exist

Lin awoke to an empty bed. She'd reached to Jack's side but found he wasn't there, so she threw the blankets aside, stood up, and stretched. The daylight creeping from the window along the walls convinced her to invite it in, and a sharp snap to the curtains brightened the room.

After a hot shower, she dried off and realized that she wasn't as cold as the day before. She knew her life was returning, and the other life, the one that she'd lived with Taylor for six weeks, had taken another step away.

Without shivering, she found the clothes she'd worn the day before, the ones she remembered discarding on her way to bed. Jack had folded them neatly on the dresser and placed her shoes near. She left it all there and picked a new outfit from her closet.

After slipping it all on, she gave her hair a few quick brushes and ventured down the hall and toward the kitchen, where she found Jack sitting at the table.

"Hey, good morning. Did you sleep alright?"

She managed a tired smile and said, "I sure did."

Nomad rushed over and poked her hand with his big wet snout.

"Oh, my sweet fluffy boy. You're just wonderful, aren't you? I've missed you so much."

She looked back at Jack.

"Yeah, Jack. That's the best way to end the day, don't you think?"

"Oh, yeah. I know I slept like a rock."

"This still feels kind of weird, being back after so long. You just keep having those dreams of me, and that can only help."

She gave him a sleepy grin, and he smiled back.

"Alright, if you insist. Hey, even if a dream seems totally real, it's still just a dream, right?"

"Um, sort of. Gabby could explain it better."

She glanced up to see Gabriel at the counter, which was covered with bowls and gadgets and ingredients, and she walked over to stand behind Jack. She rubbed his shoulders while Nomad bounced his forehead into her leg.

To Gabriel, she said, "Good morning, Gabby. What can you tell Jack about dreams? I know that fake worlds, like where Gloriana stuck me a few times, aren't real. Not like this world. Are dreams the same way?"

"We did talk about that, Lin. If you remember, I said that dreams are just imagination with no intent behind them."

"So, they're not real at all, then, right?" said Jack.

"Yes, you're right. But there's still a possibility for them to have a real effect. Do you remember our discussion, Lin? It's all about the imagination."

"Oh, now I do remember. You said that sometimes, what happens in a dream can get stuck in a person's imagination. Is that it?"

"Yes, and that can cause the dreamer to strive to make it a reality. It takes a strong intent, though, for that to happen."

Jack said, "How about if the dream itself is strong enough? Can that make the difference?"

"I suppose. It would have to be a very strong dream, though. It would have to be so real that you couldn't tell the difference."

"Well, I couldn't always tell if those worlds I visited were real or not," said Lin.

Jack remained silent with Lin's hands on his shoulders, still rubbing them.

"Jack," she said, "go ahead and take that chance. I like your dreams, so you have my permission: go ahead and get hooked on me."

He turned his head to look up at her and gave her a smile.

"More than I already am? Not possible, Cowgirl."

She leaned down, kissed him, and said, "You're the best, Cowboy. Dream all you want."

"I'm not sure I can stop."

Lin turned to focus on Gabriel.

"Gabby, don't tell me. Hotcakes again?"

"Yes. Blueberry. They're the best, and they'll be ready soon, so I hope you're hungry."

"I really am. Is anyone else awake yet?"

"No," said Jack. "They're both still in their rooms."

"Okay, it just sounds a little creepy to talk about Gloriana having her own room."

"I meant the guest room. And it's only for a while, right?"

"Before one of us kills her? Yeah, it's only for a while, that's for sure."

"Please do not kill me, Lin Finity."

Lin felt Jack's shoulders tighten and turned to see Gloriana standing in the hallway. She looked well-rested and strong, her posture perfect in jeans and heels from Lin's closet and a low-cut white sweater a size too small, probably from Taylor's closet, she thought. Her dark hair looked as if it had survived some brushing but not enough to tame it. Her caramel eyes looked first at Lin, then around the room, then to Jack, then back at Lin. Lin was relieved that she didn't see even a hint of glowing.

"Try to understand the desperation I felt in that Godless empty place between the Islands of Time."

Lin shook her head and stared. She felt her mayhem roiling just beneath her surface, ready to rise up and destroy the woman who stood powerless in her home.

"Remember that I gave up powers to return to life. Those powers cannot harm you any longer."

Lin bit her lip, thought of how dreadfully long a week could be, and heard Gabriel say, "Lin, the hotcakes are done. Have a seat, and I'll bring you a plate."

The silence in the room was a thick fog that held everyone in place as Lin glared at Gloriana. She shrugged and took the seat next to Jack. Gabriel set a plate with two big hotcakes in front of her. She didn't look up as she focused only on the meal and thought that one day had already passed. Only six left.

"Gloriana," said Gabriel, "perhaps you'd like some breakfast too?"

"I would like to sit and eat what you have prepared. But I do not wish to die today."

"Lin won't kill you. She's promised. Have a seat."

"Not today," Lin said without looking up.

Gloriana stared at Lin a few seconds, then sat across the table from Jack, leaving one more seat on her side and one at each of the ends. Gabriel delivered another plate of hotcakes, and Gloriana attacked it. In between bites, she met Lin's gaze and held it for only a second before turning her caramel eyes to look at Jack.

"I, uh, I think I'll see if Taylor wants some breakfast. She's probably hungry too."

Jack rose quickly, carried his plate to the sink, and walked down the hallway toward Taylor's room. Lin heard the knocking, then the door opening and Taylor's voice, but she mostly kept her eyes on Gloriana.

Jack returned and leaned against the counter to watch Gabriel cooking.

"She's getting dressed. She'll be here soon. And yes, she said she's hungry."

"I bet she is, Jack," said Gabriel. "She will need a time for mostly eating and resting. Lin too."

Lin returned to her breakfast and listened to the fresh batter sizzling and popping on the griddle. A door down the hallway creaked open, and seconds later, Taylor joined them at the table, taking a seat at the end near Lin.

"Hi, everyone. I'm starving."

"It'll be another minute. Are you feeling more like yourself today?"

"Yeah, Gabriel, but still kind of like a bird. Did you hear that during the night?"

Jack dropped a spoon into the sink, it bounced around noisily, and Lin snapped her head around to look.

"No, I didn't hear anything," said Jack. "What do you mean? What did you hear?"

Lin turned back to her plate with an occasional glance at her daughter.

"Thunder. I started something to try out that new thing."

Taylor turned to Gloriana.

"It worked. I put four of the letters in the exact places you told me yesterday. I put the fifth letter at the bottom of the sea. It all stopped immediately."

"That is very good, Taylor. That technique works well, does it not?"

"Yep. Windcraft is different, though. It doesn't keep going on its own. I do it, and when I'm done, it's done."

After making sure everyone had full cups of coffee and Taylor a hot breakfast plate, Gabriel took a seat at the other end of the table with a tall stack of hotcakes. With cheeks stuffed, the conversation continued.

"Lin, I believe you will become a Glyphin soon yourself. Taylor is already quite an accomplished one. Perhaps it's a good time for a discussion of something I mentioned to you before you left."

"Numbers?"

"Yes, numbers. Knowledge is neither good nor bad, only the choices people make. We could—"

"I've already learned something else, Gabby. I'll tell you about it later."

"Very good, Lin. It's important to keep learning. This will be good for both of you to know," Gabriel said, then turned to Gloriana and waited.

"Learning of the magic truly is a wave of its own kind," Gloriana said between bites. "Not long ago, you did not want to learn any more of the magic."

Lin dropped her fork, and it clattered around on her plate before silence reclaimed the room. She felt her eyes about to burst bright green light.

"Only because of you."

"Yes, I know. I am sorry. It is good that you wish to learn more again."

Lin picked up her fork and took another big bite, but her normal green eyes still bore into Gloriana's.

"Gloriana," said Gabriel, "you know more about the numbers than I. How about a first lesson? Just an introduction would be good for now."

"Very well."

Lin saw Gloriana turn to address Taylor, and she knew why: she was afraid. Of the two, Lin knew that she was more likely to kill her than would be Taylor. And she'd do it in a more gruesome and painful way than Taylor, who would merely eliminate her just like any other threat.

"You are a Glyphin, and soon, your mother might be as well. You use words to focus your Glyphin powers, but you can also use numbers."

"Okay, that still doesn't make sense," Lin said. "I know enough to know that when a Glyphin like Taylor plays with words, she only needs to see one word, then an empty space, then the word again. She reads the one on the left like a normal word, but at the same time, she reads the one on the right backward. She takes the known on the left and the unknown on the right and combines them in the middle."

"That is correct. The words are—"

"How can that be done with numbers? The one on the right will be only a different number, not some unknown thing that gets mixed with the other. They're both still numbers."

Gloriana hurried her gaze back to Taylor.

"Your mother is correct. But that is only for the numbers you know. Gabriel has told your mother that there are other numbers that were used in dangerous ways by Glyphins long ago. Using them is naturally more risky than using words."

Taylor said, "Oh, I've been to school, and I think we know all the numbers. I don't know what you're—"

"You know only of the numbers which remain after the purge."

"What purge?" Taylor said.

"Due to their danger when used by Glyphins, all who knew of them were killed. No record of them was left intact. All knowledge of them was lost."

Lin turned to see that Taylor had been silenced and only sat waiting for Gloriana to continue.

"The numbers you know—every number used and spoken of and written in any form—are all lower case. Capital numbers have been banished. Yet still, they exist."

Lin, Taylor, and Jack might have been statues. Nomad stared from one to the other but didn't make a sound. Gabriel kept eating.

"What? What does that mean?" said Lin.

Gloriana rotated to look at Lin across the table. Her fork had stabbed another heap of hotcakes but rested on the plate as she gave more explanation.

"You use capital letters, do you not? They have a special service that they offer. They carry extra importance, or they can be used to show that a word is not ordinary, like it is a name and not a thing."

"And these capital numbers do the same thing?"

Lin's green eyes stared as she waited for the answer.

"No, not the same thing. A word can be any combination of lower-case and capital letters. When it is read backward, it is nonsense no matter what. When a number is read backward, it is true that it is still a number. But if it begins with a capital number, and it is then read backward by a Glyphin, it has become a chaotic number. The capital is now at its end."

"I still don't get it. Gabby, what's this about?"

"I'll try to explain what I've heard about them. A word read backward is nonsense, and our minds can't understand it. When a number that is all lower-case is read backward, it is still a number, and our minds understand it. This is the important part: it is still a number that we can understand.

"But if a Glyphin uses one that begins with a capital number, the capital number now appears at its end. It should not be at the end. It makes something we can understand instantly become chaotic, and that chaos happens right before the empty space in the middle. You could say that it magnifies the explosion when it all crashes together."

"So, the number still makes sense? That's what makes it so dangerous?"

"Yes, exactly. It's not simply an unknown thought or quantity. It still has a real value, but it becomes unpredictable and destructive. I don't believe there's any way to control the outcome. What do you think, Gloriana?"

"I have had only limited success, and you know that I am—I was— very powerful. The number becomes tangled with whatever the Glyphin might be holding in her thoughts."

All eyes stared at Gloriana except for Nomad's, who looked between Lin and Taylor, and Gabriel's, who focused on a plate that would soon need to be refilled.

"That sounds right, Lin," said Gabriel. "Remember that words and numbers have a connection to our minds. The chaos of proceeding with a number that way draws upon the contents of your thoughts. Well, the Glyphin's thoughts. It might be impossible for a Glyphin to focus her thoughts so completely that the Glyphin power can be controlled when using such a number."

Lin had never looked back at Gabriel. She still stared at Gloriana.

"Now, you wonder if a number can be all capitals. I can tell you this: Glyphins have tried. Not one has survived. For letters, using all capitals is like screaming. You do not wish to hear the scream of a backward number of all capitals."

"But you," said Lin, "you must have—"

"No. I have never tried because I do not wish to die. That must have become clear to you by now."

Lin laughed out loud, something she hadn't done in a normal way since she'd returned.

"Yeah. Oh yeah, that's clear."

The laughter ended as abruptly as did her smile.

"But you only have six days left."

"Lin," Gabriel said while rising with an empty plate, "this is good knowledge, isn't it? Consider making it two weeks. You too, Taylor."

Lin looked at Taylor and saw a calculated excitement in her eyes.

"You want to try it, don't you? Already, you want to try it?"

"Maybe not right now, Mom. These hotcakes are pretty good. And I'm okay with two weeks. But no longer."

"You're letting her off pretty easy. Why is that?"

"Mom, I want to think up a good way to kill her. It's another thing for my book."

Lin shook her head and stared at Taylor, who didn't smile, then turned her eyes back to Gloriana.

"Fine. Two weeks. Just leave me alone before then, or I'll destroy you."

"I will avoid you if you wish. But I cannot prevent you from happening upon me at some point."

Gloriana looked up at Jack, and he quickly looked away.

"I will welcome it as a pleasant surprise. That is, if you do not kill me."

"I'll find you in St. Simons when your two weeks are up."

"Lin," Gabriel said, "if Taylor decides to try that dangerous Glyphin power, she'd benefit from Gloriana's experience, wouldn't she?"

Lin didn't turn to look at Gabriel swishing up a new bowl of batter, but she did look at Taylor.

"Whatever, Mom. As long as she doesn't piss me off either. I'm done eating and should probably just go back to bed."

"Probably, Honey."

Lin nodded to Taylor, who stayed in her seat, and turned back to Gloriana.

"You will live only as long as you have value to us. Do you understand?"

"Yes, Lin. I seek to regain your trust. I wish to be of value in ways that I am able."

Lin's phone chimed and vibrated in tight circles on the counter near the toaster. She heard Jack.

"It's done that a few times since you've been gone. It was Sweet Pets each time, wondering when you'd get back."

"How about that, Jack?" Taylor said. "All that time, Mom and I belonged in a pet shop."

Lin got up to answer her phone.

"That's funny, Taylor," said Jack.

"Oh, this can't be," Lin said while looking at the number. She clicked it off and set it back down.

"I don't work at a pet shop, Hon. Dr. Grayson is a veterinarian. Jack, do I still have a job there?"

"He said you could take as much time as you need. And you should. You still have a pile of that money from The Shield."

"It didn't all go to that gift shop, Jack?"

"Nope. Gabriel took only part of it."

"Good, because I'm not ready for work."

"Who was it?"

"Jack, I don't want to talk to Anna ever again. I almost killed her brat daughter back at the Island. She's lucky I was in a playful mood."

"Could it be about Tayo, Lin?" said Gabriel.

"Oh God, it might be."

The phone resumed its ringing and rattling against the side of the toaster.

Chapter 10 – His Destruction Has Begun

"You'd better have a good reason for calling."

"I believed I would never have reason to call you again. I am sadly wrong."

"Anna, you're done with The Shield. Lancaster Wolfe is gone. Just get on with your life."

"It is something we wish to do, but we cannot. I call today about Tayo. He has sent for Lee, but he does not believe her strength can do more than keep him alive. Maybe not even that."

"Just slow down, okay? What's wrong with Tayo?"

"His destruction has begun. Those were the words he spoke to me before the back of his neck swelled up. He struggles to speak now."

"His neck swelled up, huh? Maybe he's coming down with something. Hold on, okay?"

Lin muted the phone and turned to Gabriel. Jack had turned his chair around, and everyone's eyes stared at her. Even Nomad's.

"Gabby, you were right—something's going on with Tayo. He told Anna that his destruction has begun. Maybe it's not that hunter thing, though. Maybe he's just sick."

"It is here, then," said Gloriana. "We did what we intended, Lin Finity."

"It's still just 'Lin,' okay? And we don't know that for sure. He's just got some swelling—not a big deal."

Gloriana rose from her seat and moved between Jack and the counter, which separated the kitchen area from the table. She reached across for the phone, but Lin only put it on speaker and held it closer to her.

"Your name is Anna? I am Gloriana. Tell me what you see of the man Tayo."

"He is lying down and not moving. He called me and said he needed—"

"But what do you see?"

"His neck behind him is large like a pillow. I am afraid something is growing in there. I touched it once, and his eyes said he would like to scream, but he made no sound. It felt hard. Not soft."

"Is there anything else unusual in his home?"

"I do not know—we have never been here before. We are still in his apartment in Baltimore. I wish he could travel himself, but he cannot. We are packing to come to Lin's house, Daria and I. Ozzy too. I do not wish to be around things that—"

Lin said, "Wait. You were coming to my house? Who said you could do that?"

"Tayo insisted. He required that we bring his hand mirror."

"What are you—"

"And the mirror from his wall. We packed that too."

"You're not making any sense at all. I don't—"

"He said one of his fingers began to peel open on its own. And then—"

"What? What did you say happened to his finger?"

"Perhaps I heard him wrong, but whatever it was, it is gone now."

"What do you mean, it's 'gone?'"

"He used a knife. He placed it in a box. We can hear it scratching around in there. Then, his neck—"

"Oh, you can't be serious. This is some kind of joke, right?"

"No, Lin. When we arrived, he said he felt his neck beginning to grow, and he knew he could not cut that away from his body and confine it in a box. And Lee was still not with him. We have not yet put Tayo in the car because he tried to strangle Ozzy. After that, he—"

"What the hell is going on?"

"I cannot even guess. I should have gone back to Russia. I should take Daria and Ozzy and—"

"Stop already! Look, Lee should get there soon. Tell me where you are, and if I feel like traveling soon, maybe I'll come and help."

"Lin," said Gabriel, and Lin covered the phone. "You don't wish to help him?"

"I'm just not up to it yet. Let Lee handle it. I can't heal him."

Lin pulled the phone back toward her and said, "Tell me his address, just in case."

She began writing and saw Gloriana sit back onto Jack's lap. His eyes stretched open, he smiled, and Gloriana turned her head to say, in no hurry, "Oh, I am sorry, Jack. I should be more careful where I sit."

She stood again, paused with her heels near Jack's boots, straightened the bottom hem of her tight sweater, then took a step.

She found her own seat, and Lin extinguished the green fire that had flared in her eyes, held the phone to her ear while writing Tayo's address, then put down the pen.

* * *

With the address written on Taylor's tablet, Lin clicked off her phone and set it back on the counter. She squinted and stared at Gloriana for several seconds before speaking.

"Okay, so maybe that thing really is here. It doesn't sound like Tayo has what it takes to beat it. I have no idea what to do now. Do you?" she said while still looking at Gloriana.

"I do not know either. If all it has done is to swell the man's neck, and damage his finger, and strangle the Ozzy fellow, then—"

"Ozzy is a dog."

"Another dog in a house? Why? It is likely only a common dog."

"What?" said Lin. "What else could it be?"

"Nothing. The thing attacking Tayo has not figured out how to do its work here yet. It will. It will become much more dangerous."

"So, we need to stop it before that happens? That's what you mean?"

"When it was between the Islands of Time, there were limits on what it could do. It might soon find it has few limits here with us in this world."

"Unless Tayo can stop it?"

"I do not know, Lin. Perhaps Gabriel can share some wisdom."

"Yeah, Gabby, what do you think? All I know is that I don't feel ready to be dealing with any of this."

"First, Lin, it's good that it is here and mostly still trapped. Tayo might not be a match for it when it's as strong as it can be. But now, while it's still adapting, he might have a chance."

"It doesn't sound like it."

"No, Lin, not yet. And we still don't know what form it has taken. Tayo might know. It might help to know how it now appears in this world."

Lin returned and reclaimed her seat between Jack and Taylor.

"Taylor, Honey, are you okay? I hope you're not too worried."

"What, because some *thing* that kills *every* thing is here?"

"Well, it's in Baltimore, and—"

"It's not like Baltimore's all that far away, Mom."

Lin let out a deep breath.

"Hon, it'll probably stay there. I hope they don't need our help, and maybe they won't. Lee is pretty capable."

"You're going to help him? You and Gabriel?"

"I don't want to, but it's my fault. Gloriana's, too, even though Tayo did volunteer for this."

Taylor sighed and brushed her shoulder-length blond hair back.

"It's okay. If you decide to go, I'll go with you, Mom."

"Are you sure, Honey?"

"You might need me. I know a few tricks."

"That's for sure."

"Nomad and I would go too. Maybe we can help somehow."

"Okay, Jack," said Lin, "I know you'd be a big help."

Nomad stood and rested his head on Lin's lap, his big eyes looking up into hers and rarely blinking.

"You too, my sweet fluffy boy. You're the biggest help of all. You know, sometimes, I think you're really an—"

"I gave up powers, Lin, so I would be of little use. I have also seen enough of that thing for many lifetimes."

"You might as well stay here. Maybe you can pitch in and do some chores around the house."

"Yes, I will try that. May I also sample some garments from your closet? Your clothing is so different from what I wore long ago."

"Sure, why not? Take what you want."

"Thank you, Lin, I will."

Gloriana rose from the table and turned to leave.

"Wait," said Lin. "As long as we're all sitting around, what can you tell me about the capital numbers?"

"They do not look odd, if that is what you wonder. They were in common use for many centuries, back before the Glyphins—"

"No, I guess I didn't say that right. Can you show them to me? Can you write them out?"

"Yes, I will."

Jack got up out of his seat and returned with Taylor's tablet that Lin had left on the counter. He handed it to her with a pen.

"Knowing the symbols is only one part of their use, but it is a good start. Here they are."

Lin, Jack, and Taylor leaned over the table to see what Gloriana was marking on the paper. Lin thought that they looked like nonsense, and she believed that they'd still look like nonsense even when not upside-down. Gabriel showed no interest, and Lin figured they weren't a surprise, and there was no need to see them again.

Gloriana finished, clicked the pen, and turned the tablet to face Lin.

"There's ten of them. They start at zero and go to nine?"

"Yes, but do not think of them only as things for counting. They were used for much more than that."

"So, they have some kind of power, is that what you're saying?"

"No, Lin. They are only what you see. They are just markings like the numbers you know."

"Okay, well then, how—"

"They are only receptacles. A Glyphin with even a small strength in her intent can put other things into them. Feelings. Or plans. Thoughts about the meaning of the numbers that follow."

"I don't get it."

"Lin," Gabriel said, "here's what I've heard of them. When you use a number, you usually know what that number refers to. If Taylor, who's a Glyphin, were to say that she flew with a thousand crows, a capital number beginning the number 'one-thousand' might carry how she felt about those crows. Her feeling about them might be caught up in that capital number."

"What good does that do?"

"For an average person, it does nothing. It matters only when used by a Glyphin. When a capital number is used, it's not just a number. It's associated with the Glyphin's feelings or thoughts for the number."

"So, if a Glyphin reads it backward, then—"

"Yes, Lin," said Gloriana, "that brings chaos. It is best avoided."

"Honey, let's not rush into trying that, okay?"

"Sure, Mom. As long as I don't get too 'hangry.' Remember that word, Gabriel? I sure do."

"Yes, I remember. And I like how you can have fun with words now without destroying anything."

"I see something I'll destroy in about two weeks."

She turned her glare toward Gloriana.

"Please do not destroy me. I am harmless. I wish to continue to help."

"Good. Tell us more about the capital numbers," said Lin.

"I also wish to remain useful to you and Taylor. When I am not, I believe you or she will end my life. I will tell you more tomorrow. I will now go where you cannot see me."

Gloriana rose from the table, stood and stretched, looked at each of them, and began a walk toward the guest room.

"I'm going to lie down for a while, Mom. Eat and sleep. That's my motto now."

"That's a good plan, Hon. I feel the same way. I just need to talk to Gabby about something, then I'll probably take a nap myself."

"It's a good time for me to take this big boy outside, then," said Jack.

Nomad's head turned to one side as he looked at Jack, then he barked once at the ceiling and started panting.

"That's a good idea, Jack. Don't be too worried about any flocks attacking you."

"Alright, I won't."

"You too, my sweet fluffy boy."

Nomad barked at the ceiling one more time and followed Jack into Lin's backyard.

Chapter 11 – Why Ocean Boulevard?

"You said you found a new way to use your powers, Lin?"

"Yeah, I sure did, Gabby. I didn't plan to go back to the same world again, but—"

"Your flight brought you to the same world twice? You do remember that that's not a good idea, don't you?"

"Like I said, I didn't plan it. But it worked out fine. Nothing to worry about."

"Perhaps you only got lucky. You won't return a third time?"

"Nope. But while I was there this time, I did something that surprised me. Something that didn't tire me out."

Jack had Nomad out to run and play in the backyard, Taylor had gone off for a nap, and Gloriana had retired to the guest room. The late-morning sun fought its way between the puffy white clouds in the cold Pennsylvania sky, offering through the kitchen window whatever it could of its weak heat.

Gabriel had found the fresh bucket of chocolate ice cream, and Lin had just unwrapped another giant chocolate bar.

"I'm not really hungry at all, but I've become very fond of chocolate ice cream. When you spoke highly of it, you were exactly right."

"I did tell you. And I always have room for chocolate."

"Okay. You used the magic of something—or someone—and it didn't tire you out?"

"That's not exactly how I'd describe it. I did use the magic of some things, but I didn't go there. I didn't travel there. I think the traveling to it is what makes me tired from it."

"I think that's right. So, how did you use its magic? And what thing's magic are we talking about?"

"Trees, Gabby. Big trees in front of a hotel along Ocean Boulevard."

"Why do you suppose you traveled there? Why Ocean Boulevard?"

"I, um . . . I'm not sure. It just kind of happened."

"There must be a reason, but I suppose it doesn't matter since you'll never return. Why were you playing around with trees?"

"I liked standing in the sunshine, but the top branch of one of the trees started blocking the light."

"Was there a reason why you couldn't step back out of the shadow?"

"Well, no, I guess I could have. But these worlds are for fun, remember?"

"Fun and learning."

"And I did both. I cut them all down."

"Not just the one that was irritating you?"

"No, all of them. It felt like a fun thing to try, and Gabby, it worked."

Gabriel pried the lid off and dragged an ice cream scoop over the smooth surface, digging in deep and curling a spiral of the treat into the oversized spoon.

"You're eating with that?"

"Smaller spoons disappoint me when it comes to ice cream. Okay, so what exactly did you do?"

"I intended my mayhem, and it started right up. But I let the magic pack into me more than it ever had before. The pressure was incredible. Then, it felt like all that magic was spinning inside me. Nothing I saw changed—I was still standing there facing the hotel—but I was spinning inside, too, at the same time."

"Why were you at a hotel?"

"Who knows? Maybe I should have been at the ice cream shop?"

"Yes, Lin. Perhaps. That's where I would have gone."

"Okay, I was spinning inside, but maybe the most important thing is what I could sense about the magic of everything around me. I was able to pick out the magic of just the tree trunks. I knew there were people and cars and trash cans and all kinds of stuff around, but my mayhem wouldn't touch it. I knew it wouldn't."

"You're calling this 'mayhem,' too, Lin?"

"I guess I might as well. It's kind of sending out a wave, so yeah. It's just that I don't travel with it. Besides, I like the word 'mayhem.'"

"Maybe you could call it your 'spinning mayhem?'"

"I like that. Good idea."

"What happened?"

"I felt like I was spinning from the magic inside me. That made my arms raise up to each side, but they didn't. Not really. It just felt like it. The pressure got crazy like I couldn't take any more, but still, I could focus just on the tree trunks.

"Gabby, the magic felt like it flew out through my fingertips while I was spinning in circles while I was really standing still. Whatever shot out was thin and formed some kind of disk, and that cut through only the tree trunks just like I intended.

"I knew what it did to them. I felt it or understood it somehow. Whatever part of the trees that it touched stopped being real. It took a thin slice of reality out of each of them. I returned those thin slices back to the magic."

"Then they fell?"

"Not right away. Everything looked normal for a while, then a breeze caught the top of the tree farthest to my left. It took a while, but it started to tip. And you know those live oaks: they're all twisted together. It dragged down its neighbor, and all the rest followed."

"Did you hurt anyone, Lin? Even though it's a fake world, I hope you didn't hurt anyone because for you, hurting them would be real."

"No, no one got hurt. It was like a dream how they fell so slowly that everyone had enough time to get out of the way."

Gabriel said, "You said it didn't tire you at all?" before taking a bite from the scoop.

"Not even a little bit. Every other time I did anything to the magic of something, I did get tired, that's for sure. But not this. I could do this all day long."

"In a fake world, though?"

"Oh, you know? That's a good point. I don't know how it would work here."

"Perhaps you should try it."

"Right now?"

"Why not?"

Lin took a big bite of chocolate and chewed while looking around the room. Gabriel finished the last of what was in the scoop just as Lin's eyes finally rested upon the cold tub of ice cream sitting on the table.

"No, Lin, please pick something else. How about the candle in the centerpiece?"

"You're right, of course. Never take chances with chocolate. Okay, let me give it a try."

"A better test might be the glass that holds the candle. Do you think you could do that, Lin?"

"I did get all those tree trunks and nothing else. Yeah, I think I can."

"You said it felt like you sent some kind of disk out? Did it go in every direction?"

"I think it did, but I was able to target it at the tree trunks and nothing else."

"Were there other trees, the same kind of trees, that you didn't affect?"

"Yeah, probably. Live oaks pop up everywhere down there, but I only hit the ones in front of the hotel."

"All of them? Even though only one small branch blocked your sun?"

Lin watched Gabriel gazing at her with a big grin.

"Yeah, Gabby. It was a fake world, so I figured, why not?"

"Do you remember that it was a fake world, but what you did there was real? For you, it was real?"

"I remember. I have the clear memory of destroying those trees, but I'm glad I didn't really."

"Because the trees weren't real."

"Yes."

"And you won't go there again and maybe make them and everything else there real if only for you?"

"I have no good reason to go there again."

She picked up her chocolate bar, peeled the wrapper down farther, and took a big bite. She looked back up to see Gabriel's head shaking with another grin.

"You did plan to learn something there. You learned something extraordinary, Lin. I've never heard of anyone with that capability."

"Really? It's something new? Huh. I figured out something new on my own. It kind of just happened."

"When you did it, you said your palms were down, and the wave flew out through your fingertips?"

"Yep. Somehow, the magic inside me was spinning, and it felt like my arms were out, but nothing I could see had changed."

"Before you try it on that centerpiece, I'd like you to try it in a different way. Can you turn your hands up and see if you can send out more than one disk?"

"Oh, Gabby, that's brilliant! You're right. I should try that because maybe that'll send out four disks."

"You never know until you try, Lin."

"Okay, I'll do it. You're going to stay there, sitting at the table?"

"Why not? I'm not made of glass," Gabriel said with another grin.

Lin looked at the big plastic tub, and Gabriel said, "And neither is the ice cream."

After nodding a couple of times, Lin turned to face the decorative candleholder on her kitchen table. In an instant, she found her intent where she always finds it: deep within the stillness inside her. She held it with her unbreakable grip, a hold that she knew would never weaken.

Gabriel, the table, and the house all became still, just parts of a frozen surface as infinity spread out to every horizon. Below it all, Lin saw mountains of magic crashing and churning, and it all began to flow into her. She felt the sweet pressure of it as it filled her completely, and still more flowed in.

She let it pack in so tightly that it all started to spin inside her. Her eyes told her that nothing had changed, but it felt like her arms had risen straight out to her sides from the mad rotation inside. Just as she felt like the magic would rush out of her in a sharp, deadly disk, she focused on the glass of the candleholder in front of her.

Then, at the very last moment, she spun her palms up to face forward while they raced around her.

With her eyes blazing a dazzling green, she released the wave, felt it rush up from everywhere inside to cram into her arms. Then, with an explosive rush, it shot out through four fingers of each hand, sending four infinitesimally thin disks out in every direction around her.

In an instant, it was over, and Lin allowed her mayhem to recede, leaving a lingering wave of pleasure. Infinity yielded to a normal view of the world, and she could no longer see the twisting fields of magic below. The green fire in her eyes was quenched, and she let time resume.

"I saw you blink, Lin, and your eyes flashed, but nothing else. Was that it? Did you try it?"

Lin smiled at Gabriel, turned toward the centerpiece, and lifted her hand off of the table and toward the glass surrounding the candle. She reached out and gingerly held it with her fingertips all around it. When she lifted it, most of it remained in its place, and she held only a thin glass ring. With her other hand, she lifted up another ring.

"There should be two more, Gabby."

She put the rings down and picked up the remaining two.

"That's very impressive, Lin. You've expanded your powers much since you first mastered your mayhem."

"Yes, and it makes me wonder what might be next."

"Whatever you learn, it's good to always remind yourself that you have, and can't help but use, free will. It's always your choice."

"Well, I sure won't use any powers unless it's something I choose to do."

"That applies to everything you do, but you already know that."

"Yeah, unless I'm a crow, and I don't have free will."

"Exactly right. Demonstrating your spinning mayhem on that glass item worked out well."

"Better than the ice cream bucket."

"Yes, and I don't believe you harmed any living thing either."

"Oh, you remember that? It seems so long ago, but it really wasn't. I remember thinking that I saw the magic of a rock glowing, and I thought it had to be alive."

"Do you remember how tired you were at that time?"

"Yeah, I was exhausted. I'm still not sure about what I thought I saw."

"You told me that everything was alive. Even a stone."

"But it's not, right? It can't be."

"No, it's not alive like we are. Or like crows, for that matter."

"What did I see, then?"

"Perhaps you only had a higher appreciation of the magic that creates us all and everything else."

"But the trees I cut down were alive."

"Yes, but they lived in a fake world."

"Good. I remember that it's best not to kill anything unless I have to."

"Good, Lin. Let's just eat our chocolate."

"I have another question, Gabby."

"What's that?"

She clinked the four thin rings of glass together in her hands.

"Can I use the magic to put these pieces back together?"

Gabriel's scoop full of chocolate froze above the tub.

"Do you believe there are any limits to the magic?"

"No."

"Good, Lin. I'm beginning to wonder if the magic of chocolate has any limits too."

Lin took a big bite of her chocolate bar, shook her head slowly, and grinned at her impossible friend.

Chapter 12 – Saved My Paint Too

"Oh, I don't believe this."

Lin grabbed her chiming and clattering phone off of the kitchen counter.

"What, Anna?"

"Lin, it is Tayo. He—"

"Yeah, yeah, I know. He's got some kind of neck thing. You need to—"

"No, he is done with that for now. He stabbed it, and it—"

"What do you mean, 'he stabbed it?'"

"With a steak knife. Lin, it did not want to be stabbed. It dodged several times. But Tayo was quick, and the knife found it. He now has stretched skin and several holes with blood. Whatever was in there is now—"

"You know that sounds crazy, don't you?"

"Yes, of course, it does. I did not understand the world any longer after seeing all that you have done. I understand it less now."

"Don't try to understand it—that's the problem. Just accept it. Is Tayo okay?"

"He can speak again. But not much. Here he is."

Lin set her phone to speaker and laid it on the kitchen table. Gabriel kept eating the chocolate ice cream.

"Lin? Are you there?"

"Yes, I'm here, Tayo. What's going on with you?"

"The entity to be hunted, for which you enlisted my help, has officially arrived. I had hoped you were either joking or greatly exaggerating in your description of it. If anything, you painted too pleasant of a picture."

"What is it, Tayo? Where is it?"

"It is with me. It is a part of me now."

"Where? How?"

"It's on my back. Under the skin. I can sense that it is weak. Confused somehow. But it's getting stronger. Every time one of the symbols comes alive and vanishes from my back, the effects are worse."

"You have symbols on your back? What kinds of symbols?"

"They are like nothing I have seen. Before they began their attempts at destroying me, I was able to initiate some research. I can find nothing in any published literature that matches them."

"How many are there?" said Gabriel.

"There were forty. Thirty-six remain. Three have manifested themselves: one damaged my finger; another affected my neck in a deleterious way; and the third brought some level of clinical madness to me—I remember not desiring to attack Anna's dog, but I could not stop myself."

"What happened to the fourth one?"

"I do not know, Gabriel. Fighting to maintain my physical being has been trying. I did not view my back until after my attempts to murder Anna's pet. The fourth symbol could have left in unison with any one of the three, or it might have departed quietly on its own."

"Are you sure that four are missing?"

"Yes, I am fairly certain."

"Okay, and there were forty to begin with?"

"Yes, Gabriel. I cannot anticipate what might happen next. Can we meet? The three of us?"

"I don't think I can help you," said Lin. "I barely feel like Lin right now. I'd try to explain it to you, but I know it sounds crazy."

"I understand, Lin. My hope is that you can witness this adversary of mine, even if you can't help right away. But at least you will know, and perhaps you can devise some way to help or at least provide some advice on how I might prevail against this thing."

"Well, it doesn't sound like it's just one thing. Okay, I'll meet you halfway. Can you drive, or will Anna be able to drive you?"

"The way I feel at the moment, I can surely operate an automobile. But I don't know if or when my face might swell up and make vision impossible. Or perhaps my leg will expand like an aluminum foil pouch as the corn kernels inside are heated, pinning the accelerator pedal to the floor."

Lin and Gabriel paused to look at each other for several quiet seconds.

"So, Anna can drive you, then?"

"She has agreed to chauffeur me as needed. She cannot mask her displeasure at the spectacle I have become, though."

"She'll just have to get over it."

"Your voice is carried by the phone's speaker ability. She can hear you. Daria too."

"It is true, Lin. I will drive Tayo as he needs. I can force myself to be around him, but I do not wish to be near you. I have seen too many frightening things you can do."

"Oh, I've learned some new ones too."

"Like what? What are you—"

"Look, just drive him to French Creek State Park. Get on Route 345, and you'll see my Temt8tion at one of the parking areas. Let's plan for three hours from now."

"Thanks, Lin," said Tayo. "I can't guarantee that I will even be able to speak by then. But it will help my morale to have you involved in some fashion. I'm certain I have little dominion remaining over my physical form, and if my confidence were to crumble any further, I would have no chance. I will see you in three hours."

"See you soon, Tayo."

Lin switched off her phone and left it laying on the kitchen table.

"Gabby, what do you make of all that?"

"It's troubling, Lin. Only three of the forty symbols have taken a shot at him and those around him. There's a lot more yet to come. The fourth symbol, the missing one, is also disturbing."

"Maybe I'm still thinking like a crow, but I have a quick solution to this."

"What's that?"

"If I kill Tayo, that should do it."

"You would kill him, Lin?"

"Yes, I sure would. Even before I kill Gloriana."

"I hope you feel more like Lin soon, then. It's still best to choose good."

"If that would destroy that thing, that hunter, wouldn't that be good?"

"Yes, but it wouldn't erase the bad of killing Tayo. You're not a killer, Lin."

"I was as a crow. I'm still kind of a crow."

"It's different for crows. Crows do not have free will. They just are what God made them. You might feel like a crow still, but you are not. You have free will again."

"I think I'm still part crow."

"Yes, I believe you believe that, but even if you killed him, that might not help. That might serve only to set loose all the rest of it from his back."

"Oh, that's a good point."

"And it might then be thirty-six of them all at once. That might not be the best plan."

"Well, what plan is there anyway? Do you have any advice?"

"No, I don't. Only that we have time yet, and this ice cream is delicious."

"I told you chocolate was the best," Lin said just as Jack and Nomad walked back in, trailing snow and chunks of ice.

*　*　*

"Okay, we should get going soon. Jack, you sure you want to be part of this?"

"Yeah, of course. I always want to help if I can. Nomad does too."

103

Lin rubbed the big dog's ears and looked into his eyes while saying, "I know you do, Jack. It's just that it might be dangerous. I don't want either of you getting hurt."

"What about me, Mom?" Taylor said after walking into the kitchen. "You don't really think I'd get hurt, do you?"

"Oh, Honey, this thing isn't like me moving people around or you starting a storm. We can't predict what this thing might try to do. Or what it might be able to do."

"All the more reason to have me along. I like knowing Windcraft—I'm sure that can help with a lot of stuff."

"Okay, Hon, I believe you're right. Let's just all be careful. We'll go and see Tayo and that's it—we'll come right back home. But in the meantime, if anyone's hungry, now's the time."

* * *

An hour later, Lin grabbed her keys and said, "Well, we should get on the road."

As they filed through the laundry room, they all got on their coats and walked to Lin's Temt8tion in the garage. Gabriel sat up front, and Jack, Taylor, and Nomad filled up the back.

"I don't want to go, Gabby. I haven't got my own life straightened out yet."

"Yes, I believe it will take you some time. Why don't we just see what is afflicting Tayo? We can come back and consider the whole situation from the comfort of your kitchen table."

"And the comfort of that giant bucket in the freezer?" Lin said with a smile.

"Yes, Lin. That can only help."

They both smiled as Lin started the big engine.

* * *

"I recognize Anna's car," Lin said as she pulled into a gravel parking area off of 345. "It's the one with the pesky black dog trying to claw his way through the glass."

Before she reached for her door, she said, "Jack, Taylor, why don't you wait in here? How about if Gabby and I go and see what the deal is?"

"Alright, Lin. If you need us for anything, just let us know."

"Thanks, Jack."

"I'll keep Jack company. But you know I can do more than that, Mom."

"I know you can, Hon."

"I'll wait outside the car, though. I need to feel under the sky."

"I understand. I feel like that too. See you in a few."

Lin, Gabriel, and Taylor got out, and Taylor leaned against the car and looked up at the sky. A glance all around showed Lin a level coating of snow over the large open space hemmed in by dense evergreens far back in each direction. She and Gabriel began the short walk toward the lone man sitting at the distant picnic table.

"Lin, are you feeling enough like yourself to deal with this?"

"Some. I'm still kind of a bird, though. Let's just talk to him and see what's going on."

"Try to remember that your powers might not work on it. Even Lee had problems, didn't she?"

"Yeah, it almost killed her. Okay, we'll just talk."

* * *

Lin saw that they had to pass Anna's car on the way to Tayo, so she stopped nearby, Anna lowered her window, and Lin looked over her sunglasses. She saw the woman's brown hair dropping down to the shoulders of a tight and low-cut sweater. Lin couldn't see it, but she knew the rest of her wardrobe was likely a short skirt and heels.

"Hello, Lin. We meet again."

Lin looked in without any change of expression. She reminded herself that the skirt she usually wore was shorter and her heels higher than anything Anna would dare to wear. Still, she rubbed her mittens on her jeans as she glanced down at her hiking boots, which brought her a slight frown.

"Yeah, wonderful. I can see you don't want to talk to me. That's fine."

"I do not even want you this close to me."

"Oh, Mom," said Daria from the passenger side, "give her a break. She's never hurt you in any way."

Lin leaned over to view in and saw Daria's smile and her thick black hair. She wore a puffy parka, and Lin saw just a bit of a smirk.

"No, but I came close to hurting you."

Lin let the silence drag on as she stared at Daria.

"Still having fun playing with cameras?"

"No. No, I'm done. I swear."

Lin let her eyes flash a blazing green for only an instant and watched with a grin as Daria pushed herself as far from her as she could.

"She will not have fun, Lin. There is no need to destroy either of us."

"I might destroy you just for copying my style."

Anna took a quick peek down at her skirt, then looked back up and out of her window.

"It is a good look, but I do not wish to die for it."

"Don't worry. I won't kill you. Not this time anyway."

"Thank you. Tayo is on that picnic table." She pointed across the field. "Whatever is ailing him belongs far from me and Daria."

"Fine, I'll leave you two alone, then."

"Ozzy too. He has already been strangled."

Lin sighed and looked from face to face to face.

"Just stay out of my way. All three of you."

She stood, and Anna quickly closed the window.

*   *   *

106

"I can see Taylor shivering out there, Nomad, but she still prefers to be outside. How about that?"

Nomad sat on the seat next to Jack with their heads about level. The big dog turned to look at Taylor for a few seconds, then he turned back to Jack.

"I'm curious: does she seem like a person or a bird to you?"

Nomad blinked twice then turned his head to gaze at Taylor. A quiet minute passed.

"Oh, and I never actually thanked you. Gabriel said you've been here mostly to help me. I don't know if that's true or not because how could it be? All I know is that I probably wouldn't have made it without you all that time Lin was gone."

Nomad turned and held Jack's gaze, and he looked first at his left eye, then his right, then back to his left.

"I don't know how much you understand, but thank you, Nomad. Really, you're amazing."

When the big dog began leaning toward him, Jack tilted to meet him halfway, and their foreheads rested against each other's.

The two-hundred-pound Tibetan Mastiff opened his mouth and panted for only a second, then he fell silent again.

"Did you just laugh?"

*　*　*

Lin squinted in the bright light, pushed her sunglasses up, and began walking toward Tayo. The top surface hadn't yet melted any, and her and Gabriel's steps produced a crunching announcement to the shivering man as they drew near.

"Tayo, what's wrong with you?"

Tayo still wore his thick black glasses, and his short dreadlocks fell away from his forehead as he reclined back against the tabletop. His black and white striped long-sleeved shirt was visible beneath his long wool coat. Lin saw that his left hand had sloppy gauze and tape near a

107

void where his little finger should have been. His serious black eyes stared at her through his glasses.

"Lin."

It was a combination of a whisper and a rock dragging across concrete.

"I'm here, Tayo. What happened to you?"

"The thing you told me about. It is here."

"In this world? We really did bring it here?"

"Yes. But *here*," he said in a voice like Ozzy scratching the wood floor of his apartment as he had tried to strangle him.

"I am sorry, but the damage to my neck has rendered speaking a difficult activity."

"I can still understand you. But it's here? With you, you said?"

"Yes. Lin, it is destroying me."

"What exactly do you mean? You said it was in your back?"

"Yes, it resides under the skin of my back."

"But you're leaning on it now, aren't you?"

"It would be a blessing if that could injure it in any way."

"That doesn't hurt you, though?"

Tayo let out a deep breath and closed his eyes.

"I have no sensation that might confirm that I still have a back."

Lin and Gabriel turned to look at each other for a few seconds.

Lin turned back to Tayo and said, "I'd like to know what it looks like."

He opened his eyes and said, "I can show you. It's cold—St. Simons would be preferable—but the enormity of what I've been tasked with accomplishing warrants the discomfort. Still, I'd like to make it brief, so please ready your phone's photography capabilities."

She removed her warm mittens and handed them to Gabriel. With her phone out and ready, Tayo removed his coat and turned to face away. He unbuttoned his shirt, and within seconds, he'd pulled it down over his shoulders and to his waist.

Lin gasped, and Gabriel only looked on calmly as the rows and columns of symbols came into view. Lin saw that there were five columns and eight rows of symbols made up of welts or some deposit of unknown material beneath what should have been the smooth black skin of Tayo's back.

They ran together, overlapping in many places as if some force had deposited them all in a hurry and crowded as many as it could fit under the man's skin. The first four in the top row appeared to have left him, and the skin there looked saggy and scarred.

"Lin, it's exceedingly cold today, especially without benefit of a shirt. Please, take your photo soon."

"Oh, yeah. Sorry, Tayo."

Lin snapped several photos, put her phone away, and slipped back on her mittens. Tayo hastily pulled up and buttoned his shirt and forced his arms through the sleeves of his coat.

"I don't know what that is, Tayo. Gabby, do you?"

"Yes, I have some idea. But we should go and discuss this at your house. Tayo needs to get back to Baltimore soon too."

"Lee will get to your apartment soon, Tayo. Those look like some kind of welts. She might be able to help with them."

"Yes, you are correct. I—"

Lin stared at the man who'd begun to convulse inside his thick coat.

"If you're cold, Tayo, maybe—"

"It is not due to the unfavorable temperature here. It's . . . I think—"

His eyes rolled up, and he fell forward onto his hands and knees in the snow.

"Gabby, do you see that too?"

"Yes, Lin. Something is happening with his back. It might be another symbol reaching out to cause destruction of some sort."

"Tayo, are you okay?"

"No, Lin. The state of being 'okay' is quickly becoming an unrecognizable abstraction."

"Is it trying something else on you?"

"No, I suspect we should all study our surroundings. This feels different. I don't believe it will risk killing me. I am its host, and my estimation is that it wishes only to eradicate my will. It has a different plan."

His eyes closed, and he didn't move, but Lin saw his coat shifting enough to indicate that he was still breathing.

"Gabby, I don't like the sound of that."

Gabriel didn't answer, and they both looked all around them for thirty seconds until Lin saw something approaching from the north.

She pointed and said, "Gabby, there."

Still pointing to the north, she looked to the west.

She tilted her head and said, "And there."

They looked in every direction and saw things too small to recognize creeping over the frozen snow toward them.

She glanced back down at Tayo for a few seconds, then again toward the trees and whatever approached. Finally, Lin recognized their new company.

"Cats, Gabby?"

"I believe these are larger than regular household cats."

"Yeah, they're bobcats."

She turned her head to look quickly in each direction.

"There must be a hundred of them."

"We'd be safe in your car, Lin, but you'd have to use his magic for us to move him in time."

"Or you could carry him. But that still wouldn't save my paint."

"What?"

In a calm voice, Lin said, "My Temt8tion has perfect Oblivion Black paint. I'm not about to let that get all scratched up by a pack of possessed bobcats."

"Lin, it's just paint, and—"

"Besides, moving Tayo like that would tire me out. I'm still not strong enough to be doing that."

"No, not yet, but you will be soon if—"

"I want to try out what I showed you before—that new mayhem of mine."

"You do like calling that mayhem, don't you?"

"Yes, I do. It's spinning mayhem, remember?"

"Lin, there must be a better way than killing all those cats."

They took looks in every direction as the cats continued to approach them.

"Tell me something, Gabby. If they're possessed like that, do they still hear God's voice at every moment?"

"I don't think so."

"And do they wish to do that thing's bidding, that hunter thing?"

"No, they can't. They'd never behave this way."

Lin looked all around again and saw a nearly continuous ring of bobcats staring at them and close enough that their shiny eyes were visible. All of them were crouched down and waiting for some sign of the best time to attack, something that only the cats would know. It seemed to Lin that the hunter had tapped into their natural instincts and didn't propel them blindly. They were still hunting like bobcats would hunt.

"Anyway, we're out of time," she said.

When the first one had just begun to leap up off of the crusty snow, and the rest followed his lead, Lin stopped time. She found her unbreakable hold on her intent and saw that the world had become a calm, flat surface, and beneath it, bottomless mountains of magic wrestled against each other, shifting down and up, crashing left and right, grinding themselves into rivers of magic that flowed in every direction. And infinity revealed itself to every horizon as Lin's senses opened to the endless possibilities of a world built entirely on magic.

She knew the magic of the cats. It was different from the magic of everything else around them. It was as if nothing else was there, only the cats and their magic.

The magic of the world began flowing up into her, rushing to fill her completely and building a tantalizing pressure that carried a profound pleasure as the magic created her anew in every moment.

Then, she felt it begin to spin, slowly at first, then rapidly gaining speed until it seemed as though her arms were raised by the motion to point straight out. She knew that she remained still with her arms at her sides and staring into Gabriel's big brown eyes, who was also frozen by her mayhem.

The vortex within her reached a critical speed. Lin rotated her palms to face forward and extended her fingers, and she felt a massive release, a quick drop in the pressure inside, as the magic shot out from her outstretched fingertips and formed four deadly disks without any measurable thickness. They raced out in every direction, guided by Lin's intent and her focus on only the magic of the attacking cats.

In an instant, it was over except for a telltale trace of ecstasy. Lin watched infinity again hide itself in plain sight all around her. The magic below the reality of the world became obscured to the point that she could barely see it. Then, the world returned to its normal state. Lin let time resume.

She didn't need to look, but she did watch the expression on Gabriel's face as every direction was studied.

"They are in pieces, Lin. You have succeeded. That is quite stunning, but I'm sorry you felt a need to do it this way."

"It's what a crow would do, Gabby. We kill threats if we can. Without regret."

Lin broke her lock on Gabriel's countenance and looked around at what she'd done. Heads had been removed from some and legs from many others. Freezing, staring eyes rested on the icy surface, some pointed toward them, some up at the cold sky. Paws reached up in some places, and others were a pile of parts that lay unrecognizable where they'd slipped and slopped and slimed across the snow.

"Broken hearts or broken bones, Gabby."

"Yes, Lin. You have sent them back to God. You have saved us."

Lin stared without expression.

"Saved my paint too."

Gabriel looked away from the carnage and studied Lin for a few moments.

"Are you okay, Lin?"

"I'm fine, but I think I'm still kind of a bird."

"It will pass. And you have prepared quite a feast for the scavengers on this cold winter day. There is always some good in everything."

"What do you think of my spinning mayhem?"

"I'm very impressed, Lin. I hope if you ever have occasion to use it again, it will be for no more than chopping down more trees."

"Or candleholders."

"Yes, but never chocolate in any form."

"Or any other living things, Gabby. I remember not wanting to kill."

"I know you do, Lin."

*   *   *

Lin looked down at Tayo stirring as he lay in the snow. He opened his eyes and rose to his knees.

"It did not harm me, Lin. I feel as I did before. It's prohibitively cold to check again, but I believe my back contains one less symbol now."

"Each instance is getting stronger, isn't it?" Gabriel said.

"Yes, I believe that's true. How will I survive even the next one, let alone all thirty-five that remain?"

"I don't know," said Lin, "but you need to get back to Baltimore. Lee can help."

Gabriel gave Tayo a hand up, and they walked in silence to Anna's car.

Anna didn't roll down her window, and Lin stood near and glared in at her. She saw that Anna's eyes were stretched wide open as she stared at the red puddles and pieces of cats, some near her car.

Lin rapped on the window, and Anna only looked at Lin for a few seconds before she powered down her window.

"Lin, how . . . what just—"

"It's like everything else: just forget what you saw. You need to get Tayo back to his apartment before Lee gets there."

She leaned over and saw Daria staring back at her.

"Did you like that? It was so quick you didn't even see it. Still feel like taking a photo of me?"

Daria only shook her head as she stared back at Lin without a smirk.

"Good."

Tayo had climbed in the backseat with Ozzy, and Lin looked around past Anna to see him.

"Lee might be able to help you, Tayo. Let her try. Gabby and I will try to figure out what this is all about, okay?"

"I'm not inclined to plead for assistance, but I would indeed treasure your help, Lin. If you had not been here—"

"Maybe none of that would have happened. Maybe that thing was coming after me this time, not you."

"Instead, perhaps my leg would have exploded."

Lin saw the fear in his eyes, but she'd seen the harsh realities of life in so many eyes for the last six weeks. It was part of life.

"Do the best you can, Tayo. I need to find my own life right now."

"I don't understand. Where is your life?"

"Let's just say I only flew back into town yesterday."

Lin left Tayo's pleading eyes to focus again on Anna. From up close, she was able to observe that Anna's skirt covered little of her bare thighs. But it still wasn't as short as most of hers hanging in her closet.

"Anna, he'll be in good hands with Lee. I will never see you or your daughter or your dog again, do you understand?"

"You despise Ozzy as well?"

"All of you. Never again. Got it?"

"Yes, Lin, of course. I want only to be a large amount of miles from you. I did not want to see you this time. But Tayo—"

"Just go. Take him home."

Lin took a step back, and Anna zipped her window shut. The sound of her engine starting joined the cawing of circling birds above the slaughter.

"Gabby, let's go. I need chocolate."

Chapter 13 – A Door Partially Opened

"Mom, I saw what happened out there. It took no time at all. I mean, *no* time. Those cats were just starting to attack, and then every last one was cut up. What the heck did you do?"

Lin and Gabriel had gotten back into the Temt8tion after Anna's car had rolled out of their sight through the forest. Jack and Taylor and Nomad sat quietly in back, with no one fidgeting and all eyes looking forward.

"It's a new form of my mayhem, Honey, except I don't take control—all it does is kill. Well, if the things are alive, that is. It removes a slice—takes away part of its reality."

"How did you learn that? Gabriel, did you teach my mom that?"

"No, she learned that on her own as she has other things as well. Your mom is quite amazing, Taylor."

"Okay, Mom, how did you learn that?"

Lin still hadn't started the engine but only held the wheel in both hands. She watched as the first vultures landed and stood several wing-lengths from a cat corpse, spying all around with discerning eyes.

"Do you remember how Gloriana took me to some other worlds somewhere, back when we were in St. Simons?"

"Yeah, sure."

"Well, I've learned how to create my own worlds if I want. I went to one last night and learned that. I don't know where the idea even came from. I just did it."

"You killed a bunch of bobcats in your dream world?"

"No, Honey, I cut down a bunch of trees."

"Okay, that's not so bad. But you did it the same way?"

"Yeah, just like that. I took a slice out of all of them and nothing else. They just sat there awhile until a breeze got them to start tipping. All of them ended up on the ground."

"I'm a Glyphin, remember? I could have blown them all down for you."

"I know, Hon. You're an amazing Glyphin. Jack, maybe Nomad needs to get some air before we leave? What do you think?"

Nomad barked once at the car's roof and started panting.

"I think that's a yes," Jack said before opening the door.

"I want to go too, okay, Jack?"

"Sure, Taylor, come on."

Both doors slammed shut, and Lin and Gabriel were alone.

"It's been a busy day already, Lin."

"Yeah, and I know you're worried about me, Gabby. I don't blame you. I know I'm not myself. Someday soon, I'll probably cry about all those cats."

"If what I suspect is true, you need not be so hard on yourself."

"What are you talking about this time?"

"Think about it, Lin. We're in Pennsylvania, not some expansive forested wilderness. Is it likely there would be that many bobcats lurking in this park?"

"Oh, you know, that does seem kind of suspicious. What do you think is really going on?"

"We talked earlier about Glyphin powers and the use of numbers. I believe there might have been only one bobcat hiding nearby, minding its own business, when the entity found it and used it to make more."

"You can't be serious, Gabby. That hunter can do that? That's what you're thinking?"

"I don't know everything that is possible, especially when it comes to Glyphin powers. That entity might have the powers of a Glyphin. You saw the symbols on Tayo's back."

"God, Gabby, that makes sense. That thing is all twisted together with symbols and who knows what else. So, maybe I really killed only one cat? One natural cat?"

Lin stared through the windshield and wiped once at each eye.

"That might be the case. Try to remember that none of this has been your fault. You never chose to have the Words of God lead you to Gloriana and all her traps and tricks. If it wasn't for her, Taylor wouldn't have become a Glyphin that couldn't control her power. I know you left to save yourself and the rest of us from the storm Taylor had started and to save yourself from what those worlds did to you."

"Thanks for saying that, but I really don't feel any regret about the cats. Someday, I will but not today. My eyes just felt dry, that's all."

"You'll be fine, Lin. Your strength will carry you through like it always has. As I told you once, 'magic will sort it all out.'"

The doors opened, and they all piled into the backseat.

"Ready to go home, back there?"

"Yeah, Mom. This will make a great chapter in my book."

"Have you thought up a title yet?"

"Sort of. I'm thinking maybe *Magic Is Real.*"

"I like it. No one will believe it, though."

"Maybe that's good, Mom. I hope no one will even ask."

*　*　*

After pulling into her garage, Lin shut down the big motor and closed the garage door. She let out a big sigh before cracking open her door.

"Mom, I feel like playing that game with Nomad at the door. I know he's here with us, so that makes no sense at all. But it's a sign I'm getting more normal. That's a good thing, isn't it?"

"Yeah, Hon. I think we both just need to eat and sleep more. I'm not ashamed to admit I still feel like climbing under a pile of blankets on the couch."

"Me too."

"If you do," said Jack, "just know that I won't bother you. I've learned my lesson. Twice."

"Sorry about that, Jack."

"Hey, I'm just thrilled that you're home again. Dump me wherever you want, thousands of times, as long as you don't mind me coming right back to you."

She held his gaze in the rearview and said, "Oh, Jack, you're the best."

* * *

Lin saw Gloriana waiting in a seat at the kitchen table when they all walked in. She noticed that Nomad didn't go to greet her, something she knew that he'd probably do for anyone else.

As she draped her coat over the back of a chair, she said, "I don't feel like cooking. I'm still used to just finding my food."

"You know," said Gabriel, "ordering pizzas is pretty close to that."

"Oh, it kind of is. That's a great idea."

"I'll take care of it," Jack said before he got up and took out his phone.

"Why are you staring at me, Lin Finity?"

"It's still just 'Lin,' okay? I was just thinking how easily there could be two of you. Or more."

"I do not understand what—"

"You don't want to know," said Taylor. "And I'm not cleaning it up."

Gloriana looked down at her hands in her lap.

Taylor said, "You could easily take a really, really big breath too. The biggest breath ever."

"I do not suppose I wish to know the details of that either."

"Nope."

"I will leave the room if you would all prefer. I could—"

"No, you're fine," said Lin. "You can have some pizza too. Just don't tempt fate."

"If I will do any tempting, it will not be of fate."

* * *

At the pounding on the front door, Jack got up and returned a minute later with a stack of cardboard boxes. Five pairs of eyes focused on the pizzas, and the hot aroma spread all through the house.

"Jack, how about something for Nomad too?"

"You mean, he can't have any of this?" Jack said with a grin.

"Oh, Jack, he shouldn't eat garbage like that."

Jack only laughed and said, "No, he shouldn't. More garbage for us."

He found the heavy bag in the pantry and shook it over the giant metal bowl. The sound of crunching blended with the boxes being ripped open. While Jack was up, he grabbed a stack of paper plates and napkins and passed them around.

With cheeks stuffed with crust and cheese and onions, Gabriel began.

"Lin, I know you need to focus on regaining your own life. But at the same time, perhaps we should consider Tayo's plight."

Gloriana said, "What has happened to that man, Tayo?"

"The hunter thing definitely has him. It's causing all kinds of problems," said Lin. "It could have gotten a lot worse if I wasn't able to do what I did."

"I probably could have handled them, Mom."

"That many? All at once?"

"Oh yeah, maybe not. And I've never tried to turn Windcraft in every direction at the same time."

"Someday, maybe you can try that out, okay?"

"Sure, Mom."

"But what of Tayo?" said Gloriana. "And what of the thing? How does it appear in this world?"

"Oh, that. It's all over his back. There are all these welts—lines of them going in all directions and overlapping. He said he counted forty of them when it first appeared, and they're coming off one at a time and doing some really bad things."

"What of these lines? Can you describe them?"

"I can do better than that. I took pictures of his back."

Lin found her phone, searched for the best of the photos, and held it up for Gloriana to see. She stared at it in silence before looking back at Lin.

"This is not good, Lin. Those are all of the capital numbers."

"You can't be serious. How did that happen?"

"When we trapped the thing from my tower, my intent found those numbers in my memory and gave it that form. Or perhaps it chose them from my memory."

Lin got out the tablet on which Gloriana had written the numbers and compared them to those in the photograph. She was able to pick out a few of them in the tangle, but most of them looked to be rotated or squashed, and some were mirror images.

"Do you not understand the danger of this?"

"Well, yeah, that thing is meant to kill. I already knew that."

"Do you recall me warning you and Taylor about putting all capital numbers together? You said they have been rising from his back one at a time. That is bad enough. If two or more leave together, then—"

"Then Tayo's in big trouble."

"Not just Tayo. It will find the strength to roam this world as it pleases."

"Let's not let that happen. We need to figure something out. You have any ideas?"

"Only this, Lin: it cannot be killed. You must seek a different outcome."

"Was that Lee's mistake when it had Taylor? She almost died herself. That's because she tried to kill it?"

"Perhaps. She must focus on healing Tayo's body, not on any confrontation with the thing."

"But what about Nomad? She was able to help him."

"Nomad is special, Lin," said Gabriel. "You know there's something special about him."

"Well, yeah, he's my sweet fluffy boy, and—"

"It's more than that, Lin. Just accept that he's more special than you know."

Lin stopped and stared into Gabriel's big brown eyes until it became obvious that no more would be revealed.

"Okay,"—she turned back to Gloriana—"Lee won't be able to kill it, but she can still patch Tayo up. That's what you're saying?"

"Yes. He must be kept alive. If he were to die, I believe the thing might leave his body with the chaos of a string of capital numbers."

"Then, why doesn't it just kill him already?" said Taylor.

"Perhaps it is looking at this world as if through a door partially opened," Gloriana said as she turned her eyes toward Jack. "The view might not be what it ever expected to witness."

Gabriel nodded at Gloriana, then turned to Taylor.

"It probably feels lost here, Taylor. It's fighting to try to understand where it's at and what it can do. Or, perhaps Tayo himself is keeping it contained."

No one spoke. Only Nomad's feasting invaded the silence in the house.

"So, even if Lee can keep him alive, we need to hurry up and figure out what to do with it."

"Perhaps it would help if you knew what it is," said Gabriel.

Lin said, "How do we figure that out?"

"I believe the answer will become known, Lin."

More silence. Everyone ate their pizza. Nomad crunched his chunks.

Lin finished her last bite and said, "Maybe that did tire me out some, Gabby. Jack, I'm going to bed."

"I think we're all tired," said Jack. "I know I'd like nothing more than to get a solid night of sleep."

"You're having trouble sleeping?"

"No, I wouldn't say trouble. I think it's just that my dreams are sometimes too real. I'd like to just sleep."

"Jack, your dreams are good. Whatever you dreamed last night . . . dream it again. Taylor, Honey, are you about done for the day?"

"I'm not all that tired, but I'll go to bed anyway. I already know I'll be thinking about what I'm going to write. Magic is pretty cool, Mom."

"Sometimes. As long as we do the right things with it. I'm taking a shower, then it's bedtime for me. Gabby, are you and Nomad still okay with the couch?"

"Yes, of course, Lin. I'll stay up awhile, though, and watch some TV. I think Nomad likes that too."

"I'll take him out first," said Jack.

"I wish everyone to enjoy their night," said Gloriana.

Everyone went in their own directions, and Lin found the bedroom still empty after her shower. So, she slipped on a nightgown and burrowed under the blankets. Sleep found her before Jack was able to join her.

Chapter 14 – Jack's Flight No. 2

"Come on, big boy, let's get back in already. You might be warm out here, but I'm sure not."

Nomad barked once at the cold stars and followed Jack through Lin's back door and into her kitchen. They found the room dark and empty, but TV sounds worked their way in from the living room.

"Go ahead. It's TV time for you. For me? It's bedtime. Tell Gabriel I said goodnight, alright?"

He bumped his head into Jack's thigh and trotted heavily around the corner and into the living room. Jack draped his coat over a chair at the kitchen table, unlaced and kicked off his boots, and walked quietly to Lin's closed bedroom door.

Before turning the knob, memories of his dream about Gloriana in the kitchen raced through his mind.

It had seemed so real, he thought, but it couldn't be. Could it?

He shook his head to chase away any more thoughts of it, grateful to feel the house cool, not warm like during what had to have been just a bizarre dream.

Already imagining Lin cozy beneath the blankets, welcoming him into her arms and kissing him in their quiet, private hideaway, he silently opened the door, stepped inside, and closed it without a sound.

Before taking another step, he unfastened his jeans, dropped them to the floor, and nudged them off to the side. He tossed his shirt to the floor next, then he pulled off his socks, adding them to the pile.

A short walk got him to his side of the bed, where he carefully peeled back the covers. He slipped himself in and pulled the blankets up. With his head resting on the pillow, he closed his eyes and thought the best plan would be to sneak his arm under her, right at her waist, and then he could snuggle up close to her.

Just as he was about to roll toward her, he heard something. Through the closed door came the muffled sounds of deep breathing. Maybe it was more like panting.

Is that Nomad? Jack wondered. Does he need to go out again already?

He took another look at what he could see of Lin tucked in under the heavy blankets, resisted the urge to touch her blond mane, shook his head, and decided that he'd have to wait for that warm embrace.

Another careful turn of the knob allowed him to peek out into the dark hallway, and though it wasn't lit up very well, he was sure he'd see Nomad if he were there. But no Nomad stood panting at him.

He pulled the door open and stepped back out into the hall. After closing the door behind him, he began a cautious, barefoot walk toward the sounds of cartoons. Remembering the unexpected relocation he'd experienced—twice—when first peeking in at Lin, he pushed aside the memory of being dumped into the snow and spied around the corner. On the couch and facing the TV, Gabriel sat with Nomad, both staring and eating cookies that Gabriel alternated feeding to each of them.

Jack withdrew without being seen and retraced his steps back toward the bedroom. He'd just turned the doorknob, pushed the door open while reminding himself to be quiet, then swallowed a sharp scream from the feel of two warm hands on his shoulders.

He froze in the cool air with the door ajar. Still gazing into Lin's dark room, he heard a whisper.

"Jack, why is this house so cold?"

He felt the hands withdraw and turned to face whoever was behind him. The bedroom door remained open.

"Oh, Gloriana, you nearly scared me to death," he said in his own rough whisper.

"I am not frightening. Does the sight of me inspire fear in you?"

Jack observed just a hint of her eyes in the weak light, and while he pondered whether he should fear her or not, her eyes blazed caramel, and she took his life. It felt like his soul had been separated from his body, and a new, unstoppable force—Gloriana—had taken absolute control. It surprised him that it caused no fear because he'd learned from Lin and Gabriel that mayhem always caused terror in those enslaved by it. Why not with Gloriana?

"I have taken you again. You do not mind, do you?"

Jack felt his head shake back and forth.

"Perhaps now you are afraid. Is it fear that you feel, Jack? Or are you feeling something else?"

Jack waited for his head to nod on its own, but it stayed still, and his eyes felt dragged into the caramel glow.

"We are alone again, Jack. We are already friends from our kitchen kissing, but we will become better friends this night. Again, you wear only shorts for me. You may look at what I wear for you. It is not my cinnamon gown of which you have become so fond."

Jack's heart sped up as his eyes lowered from hers, and he saw that Gloriana had taken one of Lin's blouses, a bright pink one. She'd unbuttoned it far down past her breasts, and it barely covered her. When his eyes traveled lower, he saw the bottom of the shirt and only bare legs below it. He couldn't stop his eyes from lingering on Lin's favorite black heels resting on the cold wood floor. He'd just begun to wonder how she'd adapted to the times so quickly by getting a pedicure, but she left him no more time.

His eyes got pried away from the sight of her legs, which in the dim light still showed them to be strong and shapely. She forced his eyes to focus again on hers as they continued to glow.

"I hide very little of myself from you this time. When we kiss, you will more easily touch me."

Jack felt his arms reach around her waist, and his palms felt her warm skin through the thin material. He didn't want to, but he pulled her in so close that she had to step her heels farther apart. Her smooth thighs rubbed against his, and only a few buttons of her blouse touched his skin near his waist. Above that, he felt more of her warm skin only partially covered and soft against the muscles of his bare chest.

"Oh my, Jack. That response is only from you. You cannot deny that you like the touch of my skin."

Wearing Lin's heels gave her enough height that she was even with him. Jack felt his head tip forward only a small amount, and their lips met. His heart began to pound at the feel of her in his hands, squeezed into him from his thighs to his chest, and her lips wet against his. When he felt her lips part, he couldn't stop his tongue from meeting hers, and they kissed quietly for several minutes.

"Oh, Jack. You are very happy to feel so much of my skin. You like me wearing only this small garment."

She'd closed both of his eyes, but Jack knew that his life still belonged to her even without seeing the caramel fire. She kissed him again, and he knew that she was right—he did like how she felt in his arms when held so close. He knew that he couldn't blame himself for that.

She pulled away only enough to speak and commanded his eyes to open.

"We are becoming very good friends, Jack. I hear cartoons. Do you hear them as well?"

Jack felt his head nodding.

"The house dog, which you must know is not a common dog, tends to be inquisitive. It will likely come to visit us soon."

She gave him a quick kiss.

"Gabriel will see too. They will both be disappointed in you. Despite the risk, we will take our time and kiss more."

Jack felt his hands slide down to her bottom, and he held her through the thin fabric. Before she closed his eyes again, he saw her arms reaching up and over his shoulders to pull him in. Her movements lifted the blouse up, and Jack felt his hands on her bare skin.

"That is so much better. You have in your hands a part of me you have watched as I walk around Lin's house."

Their lips met, and they kissed for several more minutes. She broke their deep kiss and moved in closer to whisper in his ear.

"You could not touch me this way with a gown covering that part of my body. This is more enjoyable for us both."

She gave him a quick kiss, then looked past his shoulder.

"You left the bedroom door open. Lin can see us if she awakens. Did you leave the door open on purpose, Jack? Do you wish Lin to see us kissing outside her room?"

Jack fought as hard as he could, but he couldn't stop his head from nodding.

"Oh, Jack, it would be very dangerous for her to see us. She would be angry with us both. Still, you do not care?"

Jack's head shook to each side, then she leaned away enough to kiss him more. He heard the TV turn off and the sounds of blankets rustling in the living room. Gloriana continued to kiss him.

"The dog will go to its bowl in the kitchen soon. It will pass near us."

Jack's heart began to race as he felt her tongue invade his mouth, and his played with it. He heard Lin cough, then the sound of her fluffing the blankets.

"Jack, Lin is surely lying there and watching now. And still, you wish to hold me and kiss me?"

Jack knew that his head would nod, and it did.

"We will allow Lin to see how you touch me after you sneak away from her bed."

Jack felt himself still holding her close but both of them rotating completely around. He looked over Gloriana's shoulder into the mostly dark bedroom, and he could see Lin's blond hair lit by the hallway light leaking in. He fought to release his hold of her, but he couldn't. His arms pulled her tight up against him.

"She would surely be in shock at seeing your hands on me in this way. No matter the danger, we will not be concerned. We will take our time because we are becoming special friends."

Jack found himself locked into another deep kiss with his head tipped to one side. It was enough that he could see Lin's form beneath the blankets, and he felt sure his heart skipped a beat when she sat up and repositioned her pillow before lying back down.

Gloriana lowered her arms, and Jack felt the soft cloth of the blouse cover his hands, which still held her where she'd directed him. She broke the kiss, leaned back, and looked down. He felt her hands at his sides, beginning to pull at the elastic band of his boxers.

"You would be happier without these shorts."

She kissed him and pulled the material forward and back several times, and Jack prayed she wouldn't let it snap back against his skin. She let go of the top and slid her palms under the cloth until he felt her holding him the same way she'd forced him to hold her.

"Can you imagine us touching this way without your shorts, Jack? You would be very happy to have me that way. You would wish to never let me go."

He felt another hot kiss, her hands and skin warm on him in so many places, and he knew it all made him very happy—he couldn't stop it. Still looking past her and into the room, he saw Lin sit up again and pile the pillows behind her before lying back down. Jack knew that all she needed to do was open her eyes, and she'd be looking right at them.

"You feel happier every time Lin moves. You do wish for her to see us. It is so dangerous, Jack, and still, that excites you?"

Jack had to nod. She smiled and let her eyes flash brightly before she spun herself around in his arms so that they both faced the slightly open bedroom door. She reached back to each side and grabbed his shorts. Jack felt his hips squeezed tight against her and looked over her right shoulder into Lin's room. His arms were compelled to reach around her waist and place both palms on her belly.

After she'd reached up and swept her hair off to her left, she said, "You may kiss me where you can now, Jack. We will see if that makes you happier too."

Jack kissed her neck and ear, and he found that he was even happier than before. But his eyes stared into the room and dreaded the possibility of Lin waking up and seeing them.

"That is so good, Jack. I feel how excited you are to be so close to me. Would you like to unbutton my shirt?"

Jack nodded, rubbing his nose along the smooth skin of her neck, and felt his hands reach up until he'd found the highest button that was still fastened. Seconds later, he'd unbuttoned it, and he continued to kiss her and gaze into the room.

"Three more, Jack. Lin might be watching us. She will be angry, but still, you undress me."

He unbuttoned two more, and she turned her head to kiss him. He felt her lips hot and wet against him as her tongue met his. She whispered to him, "Just one more button, Jack," and she turned back toward Lin and pushed the door farther open.

He found the last button and popped it open. He felt his hands hold each edge of Lin's blouse, and she kept him there with his heart racing. She turned back to him for a quick kiss before speaking again.

"Gabriel and the dog are watching from the end of the hallway. Or they soon will be. You must know that Lin is awake now. She is waiting to see what you will do with my blouse. What will you do, Jack?"

Jack knew that he didn't have a choice, and though he wasn't controlling his hands, he wondered if he'd do the same thing if she'd given him back his life. How could he not? He pulled the blouse open, slowly dragging each side across her breasts, causing her to giggle softly, until he'd bared both of them while he still looked in on Lin.

"That is good, Jack. Now, Lin can see what you want so desperately to touch."

His heart spiked when he saw Lin raise her hand up and rub her eyes. She let it drop, and there was no more movement.

"That was close, Jack. She almost awakened to see us."

He felt his hands tugging her blouse to each side and bunching it up between his belly and her lower back, and they were so close that it remained there. His hands reached down to hold her high on her thighs, his fingers extending out to touch as much as he could. She let go of his shorts and placed her hands over his.

"Good, Jack. Keep us close together. You feel very good this close. There is only your thin fabric separating us."

Jack had to hold her even more tightly. She turned her head toward him again, and their lips were almost touching.

"Lin will surely wake up soon. Think about what she will see through the doorway. She will see that you have me mostly undressed and in your arms. My breasts are completely exposed now, and I am wearing her favorite footwear too."

He felt his heart spike again at picturing how they'd appear from the bed.

"You cannot hide that you like that idea. Do you wish for Lin to see us like this, Jack?"

He felt his head nod, then she kissed him for half a minute before speaking again.

"Perhaps I will scream, then Gabriel, the dog, and Lin will all watch us. Taylor, too, will open her door and stare. You would like that, Jack."

She locked him in another deep kiss, and he felt her skin warm in the cool hallway. He realized that he couldn't tell what made his heart pound more: the thought of Lin waking up and seeing them or the feel of her in his arms.

"We have become much better friends tonight. You have undressed me, Jack, and we both like that."

She slowly spun around in his arms, and his hands again held her behind, and when he pulled her in close, he felt her breasts pressing into his chest. Her blouse had slid partway down her arms and back, allowing her long hair to bunch up on her bare shoulders, and when they kissed, he could still see Lin lying under the blankets.

He felt her hands again inside his boxers and holding him from behind when she said, "Next time, I will undress you too. You like Lin in these shoes with high heels, so that will be all I will wear for you. We will become much better friends, Jack."

His hands released her, and he felt hers slide back up out of his shorts. She gave him a quick kiss and moved just one step to the side.

"We were lucky tonight that no one caught us. Our late-night trysts will surely be found out next time. Go to your Lin, but remember how I feel in your arms after you have undressed me."

She kissed him for half a minute in the dim light of the hallway in a quiet house.

"Think of me in the next room, without clothing and waiting for you. Think of where your hands will go next time and all that you will touch. Sleep if you can, Mr. Jack."

Jack was forced to push the door in farther, and he walked to the bed. His heart still pounded as he watched Lin sleeping peacefully, and he wondered if Gloriana would soon release him from her mayhem. After peeling the blankets down, he slipped himself in to lie on his back next to Lin. He felt his head raise and his eyes turn to look at the door.

He didn't remember closing it after him, but he saw that the door was open only wide enough for him to see two glowing caramel eyes. He fought to keep his eyes open as a wave of exhaustion hit him. But he was sure that he saw the door closing slowly, and Gloriana's eyes began to rotate, as if she were leaning to still look in on him with both.

Jack stared as the door closed so far that all he could see was two glowing caramel eyes, one above the other, and as he fought to stay awake and continued to watch, the eyes slowly rose until they were near the top. One eye winked, both rushed upward and were gone, and the darkness of the room took him as his head sank into the pillow.

*   *   *

Lin awoke to a silent room, and she knew that Jack had finally joined her because she was sure that she felt her pillow move. Before opening her eyes, she listened and heard only his slow, steady breathing.

Oh, I must be wrong, she thought. He's already asleep, so he must have crept in here a while ago.

Her thoughts drifted back to the night before, when she'd savored all of Jack's attention, even though she'd wondered if she might still be mostly a bird.

Well, she thought, I'm much less of a bird this time, and I know just how to wake him up.

She rolled to her right onto his left arm, and with her left hand, she reached for him in a place she knew he'd appreciate, even if still asleep. She found that part of him, at least, was wide awake.

"Oh, Lin. You're awake?"

"Yeah, Jack, and so are you. Obviously."

"No, I think I was asleep. I mean . . . maybe I was asleep. I'm not sure. Dreams are funny things sometimes."

"Should I let you sleep?" she said and didn't let go.

"God, no. This is what I want more than anything."

"That's good, Jack. Do you mean more than sleep? Or more than whatever dream you were having?"

She laughed softly and leaned in to kiss his cheek, and when he turned to face her, she felt his lips warm and wet.

"More than sleep, of course. I want you so bad, Cowgirl. More than ever."

"That's good, too, my Cowboy," she said as she fluffed up the blankets and lifted her left leg over him. She giggled once when he grabbed her thigh and pulled her all the way up above him, where she waited up on her knees.

"I'm not as much of a bird anymore, Jack. But maybe you should make sure."

He reached for her thighs with both hands, touching them all over. From there, he held her waist only briefly before finding her breasts. She looked up at the ceiling and sighed from his gentle touching and let the blankets fall behind her.

"Do I feel like a nice dream for you, Cowboy?"

"God, yeah. Better than any dream I could ever imagine."

"This isn't how a girl bird would do it, you know," she said as she sat back in just the right place.

Jack laughed and said, "Thank God you're not a bird anymore. Even when you were, though, you were the hottest bird ever."

"Oh, Jack."

She began a steady motion above him, resting at the bottom each time before rising back up. Her mayhem swirled madly beneath her surface, and she barely gave it a thought as her eyes erupted green fire. She felt Jack calm and content, not flinching a bit as her green light shined down on him.

"I've missed that. Glowing eyes are a real turn-on."

"Really, Jack? Maybe it's just the green color you like?"

He hesitated before saying, "No, it's just because it's you. I love that your eyes glow too."

"Too? What do—"

"No, I just mean that I love everything about you, including your glowing eyes. Maybe it's because I know what you can do with all that power of yours."

"Oh yeah, Jack. The things I can do. Not this time, though. I just feel more like myself with my eyes glowing. It helps."

"Come closer, then. Let me look into those gorgeous, bright eyes of yours."

Lin laid herself down on him but never stopped her motions, and she could see her shiny eyes reflected in his.

"I love you, my Cowgirl. I always will."

"Oh, Cowboy, I love you too."

They kissed, and when she saw Jack's eyes close, she closed her own. She kept her movements slow and steady, a pace that she could maintain forever, as his strong arms wrapped around her, and when the ecstasy began to rise, it rose quickly.

A giant tide of pleasure struck them both, and Lin noticed that her arms didn't want to twitch, and she felt more human than before as wave after crashing wave carried them both away.

Chapter 15 – Lin's Flight No. 3

Hours after they'd both fallen asleep, Jack rolling onto his back woke Lin. She lay under the blankets, keeping still and sensing his breathing slow and steady, and she knew that he'd found a deep sleep. She felt like kissing him again but stopped herself.

As much as I want to, she thought, it's best if I let him sleep awhile. I can always check soon and see if he's dreaming about me again—it'll be obvious, and that's the perfect time to wake him up.

She ran her hands down along her sides under the thick covers and felt her thighs soft beneath the hem of her short nightgown. She knew that she was mostly herself again, but she was stronger than before she'd left with Taylor. Never again would any feelings take control of her, not like the ones Gloriana had forced upon her.

She decided to again find her intent and discover a new world, just another one her intent would spin into existence somewhere out in forever. She'd create a place where she could learn something new, and this time, she decided, it would be the power of a Glyphin. Tonight, her flight would see her return as a Glyphin.

But not yet. There was still time to play with the fun memory of what she'd felt she needed more than anything when she'd wanted to run from her powers and her daughter's destruction.

She felt her hands warm on her thighs and imagined how smooth they'd feel after a hot bath and a layer of lotion. She'd put on her heels next, the ones she'd brought into the hotel's luxurious bath. The dimmed lighting would still provide a clear reflection in the ornately framed mirror, and she'd see the excitement and anticipation in her eyes as she gave her mane long strokes, leaving it all hanging down over her bare back. A last smile at herself would lead to switching off the light, then hesitating only a moment to be sure of her desires to chase that fantasy, accepting that whatever would happen in that room would be real for her, then unlocking and opening the door . . .

No, not there! she thought. It was a good time for another flight, but somewhere else, not the alluring hotel room of her unrealized dream. That could wait for another time. Another flight. Or better yet—never again.

Now, it was time to go. No sense risking falling asleep before flying off to learn something new. Someplace warm, that's all that she required of the world.

Maybe seeing with more than just her eyes, she noticed a dark spot above her, clinging to an almost equally darkened ceiling. She let out a deep breath as its edges melted down around her, taking away even the darkness. Her chest fell still—no air could move in or out. She stared into the emptiness without a single thought or feeling.

Just after her heart had stopped, before she could settle in for what might be centuries of waiting, she saw a pinpoint of white light racing toward her. It blocked out the darkness like milk coating a glass that had imprisoned her on a white tabletop. Her heart pounded, welcoming her back, and her feelings and thoughts crowded their way into her.

She took a deep breath, opened her eyes, and found she was staring at her hand grasping a chrome door handle.

* * *

Not again! she thought. I can't be here! This is the third time!

Lin felt her heart softly pounding a strong and steady beat. She intended a quick return to her own world, the one where she lay beside Jack. The place where she'd be relieved to be back and would go ahead and roll over to him, giving him a dream if he hadn't already found one.

The familiar black dot appeared on the shiny chrome surface. Lin stared at it a few seconds, then she grinned and allowed it to retreat.

135

One more time in this world, she thought, then that's it. I really do want to see what's going on in there.

She let go of the handle, and with both hands, brushed her hair back over her shoulders. She pulled down on her short skirt, but she found it was already as low as it could go, which wasn't very far. Satisfied with her attire and with an eager smile, she opened the door.

But she didn't walk in. She peered around the large room, seeing near her and on the right a young woman at the desk speaking on the phone. Farther past the desk, there were two elevators and a door with a sign marking the route to the stairs.

The left side of the room basked in natural light from an array of skylights three stories above the floor and a wall of glass panes. Plush couches and chairs ringed the large pair of colorful area rugs. Several men sat, looking through papers, and others stood, talking with each other or on their phones. Lin counted ten of them.

Yep, she thought. There must be a convention here today.

"Excuse me, can I get past?"

Lin turned to see a man only a few years younger than her and dressed like the others. Obviously a professional of some kind and here for the convention, she thought.

"Yes, of course. Didn't mean to get in your way."

He smiled and said, "Oh, you can get in my way anytime. In fact, I insist."

Lin held the door for him, and he squeezed by her so close that his tie almost dragged across her clothing. That made her wonder what she was wearing this time.

She looked down with some satisfaction that it was the same color skirt and blouse as the last time. She held one leg out to see and smiled at how high the heel was.

I flew all the way here, so I might as well go in, too, she thought.

She let the door close itself after her and looked around the room again. Before she began walking to the desk, she remembered that strutting was much more fun, especially in a world where nothing mattered. A determined, sultry strut brought her to the desk, where the clerk continued chatting without looking up.

Lin turned her back to the girl and rested both elbows on the high counter. A look to the lounge area showed her that several of the men were looking her way and talking amongst themselves.

Of course, she thought. That's what an outfit like this can do. Oh, and a good strut too.

She turned her head and saw that the elevator on the right had just reached the lobby level. The doors whooshed to each side, and two elderly women exited, engaged in a heated discussion. They passed by her, and she heard one mention breakfast and all the options they had a short walk away in the Village. The other said something about the best coffee, but they'd passed before Lin could hear the rest.

Lin turned back to see the elevators resting patiently. Just to the left, she saw the closed door, and a sign above it said "stairs."

Oh, I did want to become a Glyphin, she thought. Why not now?

She crossed her eyes a small amount, and when she did, one sign became two. One word became two, and there was an empty space between them.

Knowing that the sign had served its purpose, Lin closed her eyes and still saw the two words. She read each one in turn, and both made sense. Then, feeling a rush of excitement, she read from each side back to the middle at the same time—converging on the emptiness in between. One word made sense, and the other didn't.

She felt it right away. She was holding something, something like a bubble or a small balloon. Her left hand felt normal, but when she tried to identify the one on the right, chills climbed up her spine—it could have been anything.

But there was no time to think about any of it. She felt her closed eyes flare into a bright green, felt the explosion between her hand and the other unknown hand thing, and heard thunder boom right above the hotel as the fire left her eyes. She heard the winds howling along every wall of the building and opened her eyes.

Only for a moment did she frown at the sight of not a single man in the lounge looking her way. Instead, all of them had stepped back from the tall windows as barrels of water fought to flood the inside.

Lin remembered then the trees in front—the tall, tangled row of live oaks that she'd cut down in the blink of an eye. She saw that they rose tall and thick above the ground, their branches madly waving as if begging for help.

Beyond the trees, under a sudden nighttime sky, vehicle headlights burned, horns blared, tourists bolted, and she heard the first siren coming from the northeast, farther up Ocean.

She leaned farther back on the counter and closed her eyes. She knew that anyone could see her smiling if they'd look, which she hoped they would again, but she remembered that it didn't matter anyway. None of it made a bit of difference. She closed her eyes to focus on ending the disaster she'd brought.

Recalling Gloriana's instructions, she put the first letter of "stairs" on the clean tile between her heels. The second letter found its place on the railing of the pier at the end of Mallery. She thought of Africa for a moment but decided the third letter would rather take a ride on a gondola in Venice. The fourth letter did go to the moon—she admired the simplicity of it. She painted the fifth letter on the collar of a sled dog in Alaska as it lay warm in a deep snowdrift and sent the last letter to burn on the sun.

She waited and listened. Only silence. She opened her eyes and saw most of the men standing near the windows and looking out. To her left, the trees had given up their pleas to be saved and gave their own leaves a shower from top to bottom as the light ocean breezes danced the branches and twigs about under a brightening sky.

"Did you see that? Where the hell did that come from?"

Lin turned to look over her shoulder and said, "Yeah, that's really something. How could a storm pop up out of nowhere like that?"

"I don't know, but I'm glad it stopped."

"Aw, too bad. Well, if you change your mind, let me know."

When the girl only stared back, Lin turned and saw that three of the men had walked over and were about to pass her on the way to the elevators.

One said, "Hey, looking good."

Another said, "Glad you made it."

All three smiled and continued past. One touched the elevator button, and they talked quietly and waited, each turning once or twice to smile in her direction.

She gave them a smile back when she sensed just then that there probably was no convention in that fake hotel. Those men taking the elevator up, the rest of them waiting near the windows, and the two more that had just walked in, weren't there for any kind of serious, wholesome business. They were likely there for something fun, maybe a huge poker party.

The elevator invited them in with a swish, and the red light took turns on each number as they drew nearer to the top floor. Together, they made a long number, starting at 1 on the left and ending in 8 on the right. Lin sensed that there was an opportunity for more Glyphin magic—a kind even more dangerous than the weather calamity she'd just brought to the Island.

She shook her head when she realized that she couldn't do it. There was no possibility of it because she didn't have a clue how to use capital numbers. Someone would have to show her. Either Gabriel or Gloriana. They'd have to show both her and Taylor. Until then, it would have to be only a quick storm for fun.

The prospect of having fun washed away all her misconceptions, and she knew: those men weren't there for a convention or a poker game and neither was she. She gave her tight skirt one last ineffective tug, shook back her hair, and began her strut toward the elevators.

I'll just go that far, she thought. Just close enough to push the button if I decide to. I won't hit it, though, because I'd better get back. I shouldn't stay here any longer, and I certainly should never return to this same world.

Standing three steps from the closed doors, Lin looked first up at the numbers, the ones she couldn't use as a Glyphin without being sure of how to use a capital number. Then, she stared at the bland cream color painted on the metal, knowing that that was a good place for the spot to appear—the dark spot that would kill her so that she could return to her warm bed beside Jack.

It felt like it was just about to show itself, probably right there where—

"Going up?"

She felt a hand tap on her left shoulder and turned to look. One of the men from the couches had walked up behind her with three other men.

"Oh yeah, I was. Just thinking about the evening ahead of me, that's all."

She turned to look at the door which would soon provide her doorway home. She felt someone touch her right forearm and squeeze it firmly. She turned to look.

He laughed and said, "We're sure thinking of it too. We're really, really glad you're here. Love those heels."

He smiled and looked only into her eyes, and she felt like she might as well smile back.

"I like them too."

And just for fun, since she was leaving in a second or two to never return, she said, "High and spiky—that's what a woman like me wears. I like to wear them all the time, no matter *what* I'm doing."

"Damn, I sure hope you do."

He still grinned at her, but Lin snapped her head back to the door. It was taking too long. She needed to stare at the door and find what she needed. They had to leave her alone!

"The skirt's perfect too. Maybe I'm a dork, but I'm glad I got the chance to see you still wearing that."

Lin didn't even turn toward him. She felt his eyes staring at her, waiting for an answer while she was waiting for her ticket home.

"Right now, I still have to use my imagination. Pretty soon, though? Oh, no. Nope."

She heard continuous talk and laughter behind her as more men joined the small crowd waiting for a ride up. Their words all blended together as they chattered on each side and behind her.

Another storm, she thought. Thunder will shut them up, then maybe enough wind to crack those windows. They'll have to leave her alone, and then she could—

A single point of darkness appeared on the door, and she couldn't look away from it. But she also noticed that the red light above the doors was moving to the left, a steady countdown to the first floor. And when the elevator hit her level, the doors would open, maybe taking the spot away.

That's how she'd get trapped, she realized. She wouldn't be able to focus on the darkness that would take her away!

A bell dinged softly, and the doors had just begun to slide to each side, and—

She died. The spot raced to her and around her, silencing their voices, embracing her in endless night, and sweeping away the lobby, the elevators, and all the eager strangers around her.

Her lungs locked up solid. Her thoughts came to a crashing conclusion. She couldn't feel anything about anything.

When her heart stopped, she held her intent until the light of a world launched itself at her, speeding to envelope her in another world somewhere else in the limitless forever.

Her heart began a calm and steady beat. She could feel again, and she liked feeling her heart. She thought about what she'd just done, what she'd just survived, and welcomed a warm breath of bedroom air.

* * *

Oh, that was too close, Lin thought. I almost didn't make it back. Next time, I'll plan the world I want to visit, and that's the one I'll intend. I can't trust fate as if I'm picking a random card out of a deck!

She heard Jack breathing beside her while her palms still rested on the smooth skin of her thighs. She knew that she could fluff up the blankets, and he'd welcome her into his arms. He'd feel her warm against him, and he'd probably hug her without even waking up. It always felt good in Jack's strong arms.

She reached for the top edge of the blanket and stopped.

The feeling of standing by that elevator, in a world with no consequences at all, demanded some attention, and she knew that there wasn't any real harm in it. Only one of the men had talked about how she was dressed—her shortest skirt and highest heels—but she knew that they'd all seen her attire. Her legs too.

The attention did feel good, she had to admit to herself, even if it was all fake. Then, she realized that even fake attention paid to her as a woman helped restore her and chase away the remaining bird feelings.

And though she knew that she'd never go back to that particular world, she also wondered what sorts of adventures waited on the eighth floor. If she'd had enough time before having to flee, would she have ridden that elevator up?

Chapter 16 – Lin The Glyphin

"No, I'm not at all sorry I woke you," Jack said with a grin. "Did you sleep alright?"

"I sure did, thanks to you."

"Always happy to help, especially like that. Really glad you woke me up last night."

She snuggled next to him under the blankets with her left arm laying across his chest.

"You were kind of already awake, Jack," she said with her own grin.

"Oh, that. That happens sometimes."

"Maybe it's from your dreams. What kinds of dreams are you having anyway?"

"You know, I barely remember. I do remember that it seemed so real, though. But dreams can't be real in any way, can they?"

"No. According to Gabby, they're just imagination, and they don't mean anything."

Her arm rode his chest down as he let out a deep sigh.

"That's mostly what I thought. Imagination can be pretty crazy sometimes."

"Gabby also said that a dream can get fixed in a person's imagination, and then it can sort of pull them in. It can become like a goal for them—they're drawn to it. They might try to change their lives to match."

"Oh, that's not good, not good at all, and that's not something I'd—"

"Jack, don't worry about it. Gabby said that unless there was really strong intent involved, nothing would change."

"Alright, that's good to know."

"Are you ready for some breakfast? As much as I'd like to, we probably shouldn't lie around in bed all day."

"Well, if you insist. You first. I'm not ashamed to admit it: I want to watch you get dressed. Are you wearing a skirt and heels again?"

"Jack, you're silly. Yes, that's what I'm wearing. It might sound crazy, but that style helps me forget about being a bird. I think I'd better dress like that for a while."

"How about longer than a while? Even after you're sure you're not a bird anymore?"

"Aw, come here, Cowboy."

She grabbed his right arm and pulled to get him started, and soon, they were entwined and kissing in the dark room.

"Mm . . . that's nice, Jack. Okay, you can watch me get dressed."

"You don't mind?"

She smiled and said, "Mind?"

She raised her eyebrows twice while smiling at him.

"I insist."

She gave him a quick kiss, rose from the bed, and switched on the lamp on the nightstand. Before reaching for any of her clothes on the dresser, she turned to him and put her hands on her hips.

"What are you doing?"

She reached up with both hands to brush her blond mane back, and she held it there with both hands.

"I don't know exactly why, Jack, but I like standing here with nothing on and being looked at."

"Well, good, because I like it too. Hell of a view. You look damn good with nothing on."

She backed up a step, found her heels, and slipped them on.

"Damn, that's even better. I like that."

"So do I."

"Can you hold your hair up again?"

She let out a short laugh and granted his request.

"How's that?"

"Oh my God."

"I think this helps me forget about being a bird too—standing here just in my heels for no other reason than to be looked at. Does that sound crazy?"

"All I know is that you look like a dream. Oh, and not at all like any kind of bird."

She saw that he was mostly looking into her eyes with a smile.

"Jack, don't I have more than just eyes for you to look at? While you're looking, you should think about how maybe I'll just get back in bed with you. Think about all the fun things you want to do with me."

Lin saw his expression change as he studied her up and down. She saw that his eyes focused mostly on the parts of her that she displayed for his enjoyment, and she smiled and let out a deep sigh.

"I can keep the heels on, too, just so, you know, you're sure I'm not a bird."

Jack laughed and glanced down along her legs again. Finally, he looked back up into her eyes, but she saw that his eyes still showed what he wanted from her.

"I like that look. I like being looked at like that."

"I always will—can't help it. So, I did good? What do I get?" he said with a big grin.

"Anything you want, Cowboy," she said as she let her hair down and leaned over for a long, deep kiss.

"Anything at all."

* * *

After they'd both dressed, Lin took Jack's hand and led him to the kitchen, purposely making sure her hips gave him a compelling sight in her tight skirt. They rounded the corner to see only Gabriel, who was busy with the griddle.

"Oh, Gabby, I don't think I can eat anymore blueberry hotcakes."

"It's what I understand least about you, Lin. I'm cooking these for me anyway."

"That big stack of them? Really?"

"Yes, really. How about some eggs and toast, then? Jack, does that sound good to you?"

"Yeah, it does," said Jack. "How do you know how to do all that cooking?"

"I learned in St. Simons Island. One of us had to see to the meals, and I was sure Gloriana would never—"

"I have many skills and talents, Gabriel," said Gloriana as she swept into the kitchen wearing a long robe and slippers. "I just prefer that others prepare food."

Gabriel smiled at Jack and said, "See? It was me or no one. Even I might have tired of hotcakes every day."

"Really?" said Lin.

"No, not really."

Taylor walked in wearing sweats and socks and rubbing her eyes.

"Good morning, Hon. Did you get enough sleep?"

"Yeah, Mom, but it's weird not hearing night sounds."

"I know, Honey. For me too. Maybe you could leave your window open?"

"I don't like being cold either."

"Good point. Gabby's making more hotcakes, or you could have eggs and toast."

"It doesn't matter. I don't know if I'd ever get tired of eating the same thing all the time."

"Why's that, Hon?" said Lin.

"It's from being a bird, Mom. Food was different then. All that mattered about it was that it kept me alive. You remember that, don't you?"

"Yeah, I sure do, Honey. Still, though, a little variety is a good thing."

"Sure. Gabriel, I'll take whatever you feel like cooking. I'm glad you're a good cook."

"Hey, Taylor," said Jack, "maybe you could add something about food to that book that you're going to write. You could say how you're fine with the same thing, but if all you could find was—"

"Or how about when I couldn't find anything?" said Taylor. "Or not enough, at least? I was so hungry sometimes I thought I'd die."

"I'm glad you didn't, Hon. I felt the same way at times, and even as a crow, I knew it would be sad if I went first and had to wait for you to catch up."

"Not possible," Gabriel said while still facing away and flipping the hotcakes, causing a renewed symphony of sizzling and snapping.

Taylor shrugged at her mother's curious look, and Lin turned to face Gabriel.

"What's not possible? You're not saying that I can't die, are you?"

Gabriel laughed, stacked all of the hotcakes, and placed them on a plate.

"No, of course, you can die, Lin. All living things do. There's no escape from that."

"One can postpone that appointment, though, Gabriel," said Gloriana while taking a seat across from Jack. "I delayed my death for more seasons than can be counted."

"Yes, you did, but you know that you still have only one lifetime, no matter how much time passes in this world while you're between the Islands of Time."

"So, Gabby, what are you talking about?"

Gabriel opened the refrigerator and retrieved a carton of eggs, a loaf of bread, and the butter and jelly. After setting it all on the counter, a few eggs were broken onto the hot griddle and began to cook.

"I'm saying that you wouldn't have to wait for Taylor or anyone else."

"You guys always lose me on this magic talk," said Jack. "I like listening in, I really do, but I never understand any of it."

"This is different, Jack. I'm glad you're here to listen in on this. You won't need power over the magic to see this."

"You have aroused—oh, I am sorry, Jack. I did not mean to kick you."

"It's alright."

"You have aroused my curiosity, Gabriel."

"Mine too," said Taylor.

"Okay, Gabby, you have everyone's attention. What the heck are you talking about?"

Gabriel added four slices of bread to the toaster and pushed down the lever.

"Let's use this as a timer. I'll try to explain before any toast is magically created."

All eyes were on Gabriel. Even Nomad's.

"Lin, you said that if you'd pass before Taylor, then you'd have to wait for her, which would sadden you. First of all, I can't know this for certain, but I do believe you will find yourself in Heaven when your time here is done. Do you believe you could have such a great sadness there?"

"Well, I never thought of that. I mean, to be sad there would be—"

"It would be unlikely. And you also wouldn't want a pretend happiness to mask your real sadness, would you?"

"No, that wouldn't be right. Okay, you said that was the first point. What else?"

Gabriel leaned over the counter and grinned at the browning bread before turning back to the curious faces.

"What else? Here's what else: if you pass before Taylor, you would find that she is already there. Everyone you love is already there. As are you."

"Oh, here we go again," said Lin. "It's always something that doesn't make sense. I know I have to leave sense behind because it doesn't exist in the magic. But, Gabby, I don't know how to understand that."

Gabriel turned when the toast popped up.

"Time's up."

A careful study of the toast showed that none of the slices had browned enough, so another push on the lever sent them back for more.

"We've been given more time."

"That's funny, Gabriel," said Taylor. "There was nothing comical about flying around and pecking at things."

"Humor is a true gift, Taylor," said Gabriel. "Okay, we don't have too much time remaining. Lin," Gabriel said while looking into her big green eyes, "time cannot exist. It cannot be real, even as it appears so during a person's lifetime. Is there any measure of time in eternity? Could any of us exist in Heaven, where there is no time, and somehow believe that time here on Earth is real? It is not. If you've lived well, you are already there. You have never left. Time is part of the experience of our lives, but let's not take it too seriously."

The toast popped up, and since the eggs had scrambled up nicely, Gabriel loaded it up on a plate and said, "Okay, who's the hungriest?"

Everyone stared.

"No takers? Okay, after I finish my hotcakes, then I'll—"

"I will claim a half-measure of that for my first meal," said Gloriana.

"I'll take what's left," said Taylor, "if no one else is starving."

"Of course, Hon. I think Jack and I can wait."

"Yeah, of course," said Jack before glancing down at Nomad's big eyes watching him intently.

"Yeah, you're right, Nomad," he said and rose from his chair.

He found the bag of chunks in the pantry and poured a pile into the polished silver bowl. Nomad's crunching began immediately.

"Remember when you used to weigh everything he ate?" said Jack.

Lin chuckled and said, "Seems like ages ago. God, we've been through so much."

Gabriel cracked more eggs onto the hot surface and got four more slices of bread toasting.

"Gabby," said Lin, "that kind of makes sense as long as I don't think about it."

"Like so many things in this world, there's no way to think and understand."

Jack let out a deep sigh and said, "See? This is why I leave you two alone when you talk about stuff like this."

Gabriel divided the prepared food, set plates in front of Taylor and Gloriana, and they both feasted with abandon. Lin got up, opened the refrigerator, and took out the orange juice.

"All you needed to do was ask, Lin."

"You're already doing so much. I needed to stretch my legs out anyway."

"Oh, I am sorry, Jack. I kicked you again," said Gloriana. "I only wished to stretch my legs out too."

"It's alright. Don't worry about it."

After pouring a glass, Lin leaned against the counter and said, "Gabby, since we're talking about Heaven, there's something else I need to ask about. I've seen so many times how this world we live in is built out of infinite magic, where every possibility exists, both good and evil. I've seen how magic comes in waves, bringing us life, and each time a wave hits, that's an Island of Time. Still, there are spaces in between. You,"—she turned and pointed at Gloriana—"are the expert on that. You've been in those spaces almost forever."

"And it was never pleasant, Lin. I inhabited that empty, vicious space only to survive."

"Well, you sure did that. And here you are. I'm still not sure I can comprehend all of that."

She turned back to Gabriel.

"Okay, here's the question: is there a Hell?"

"Yes, of course, there is, Lin. It is a place of no mercy and no rest. It is filled with unending attacks and pain and regrets and hopelessness. But do not let it trouble you. It takes a conscious embracing of evil to earn passage there."

"And where exactly is 'there?' Maybe I need some breakfast to help think through all this because I still want things to make some kind of sense."

"Heaven and Hell, much like this world, and like any string of Islands of Time that you can construct with your intent, all exist in the vast forever that no breakfast can ever help you understand. There's no other way to speak of it. Forever, Lin."

Lin took a sip of juice then shook her head.

"You've been there," said Gabriel while still facing away. "Several times."

Lin set her glass down hard and stared.

"What? How could I—"

Gabriel turned only enough to hold Lin's questioning gaze.

"You visited your friend Gloriana there. The spaces in between the Islands of Time, Lin. That's Hell."

Even Nomad respected the long moment of silence.

"I suspected as much, Gabriel," said Gloriana. "It is not pleasant there."

"You were strong enough to hold yourself apart from it," said Gabriel. "If you were there without the strength of your intent, the agony would be unbearable. And it would never end."

"First of all, you,"—Lin glared and pointed at Gloriana as she sat back down—"are not my friend. Gabby, you let me go there? You knew?"

"You are strong, Lin. You have an unbreakable hold on your intent, and you always will. I knew you'd be able to return."

Gabriel prepared two more plates of eggs and toast and delivered them to Lin and Jack. With a tall mound of blueberry hotcakes, Gabriel sat at the head of the table.

"Lin, you've been to Hell and back," Jack said with a grin.

"Yeah, I guess I have," she said and leaned closer for a kiss.

"Oh, I am sorry again, Jack. I must be more careful with my feet."

"Yeah, watch your feet," said Lin. "I might deduct a day every time you kick someone."

"Me too," said Taylor with a cheek bulging with toast. "I still don't remember much of what a promise means."

"Well," said Gabriel, "we can all at least enjoy our breakfast. Taylor, is yours good?"

"It's fine. Mom, I can't keep doing nothing but eating and sleeping. This still doesn't feel right."

"I know, Hon. It'll take some time."

"It's boring."

"You're bored being back?" said Jack.

"Like you can't imagine. I miss flying everywhere with the rest of them. Looking for food. Killing hawks and owls. Jack, I miss the sky."

"Looking out the window doesn't help?"

"No. I feel like I still belong in the sky."

Nomad got up, walked over, and put his heavy head on Taylor's lap. Without looking down, she began rubbing his ears and flopping them around.

"Honey, it might take a while, you know? It'll work out. I'm sure it will."

"I want to go back. I know they miss me as much as I miss them. Mom, I want you to come too."

"Oh, Hon, I can't go back to being a crow. We only did that because we had to, remember?"

"Right, because of the storms that I couldn't stop. Maybe I'll just do all of that again, but even more so. How about that? Does that sound like a plan? I bet you'd take me back again. We could just fly—"

"No! Let's not go through that again, okay?"

Taylor set her fork down on her empty plate, crossed her arms, and stared at Lin.

"Hey, Hon," said Lin, "I want to show you something. Come on."

She stood up, looked at Gloriana, and said, "no more footsie under the table. Got it? Unless you're in a hurry to be gone."

"Yes, Lin. Of course."

"Good. Jack, we'll be right back."

* * *

While walking toward the living room, Taylor said, "Mom, I saw what you wrote, or someone wrote, on my tablet. Those are the numbers, right? The capital numbers?"

"Yeah, Hon, but we don't know how to use them yet. Did I tell you I'm a Glyphin now too?"

"Wow, Mom, really? Show me!"

"Sure. Why not?"

Lin knew her eyes had started a faint glow as she thought of the word 'stairs,' saw it in red light above a door, and imagined it repeated with a space in the middle. She read the words, the real one and the fake one, and felt the explosion between her left hand and the other strange hand thing, whatever it was.

One huge boom of thunder right above them shook the house.

"Wow, Mom!"

"Okay, that's all for now."

Lin placed one letter on the tile floor near her heels by the check-in desk in her new favorite hotel, one on the window by the couches, one on the elevator doors, one on a room door on the eighth floor, and one on the mirror in the glamorous bath that she knew waited just for her up there, in a world to which she'd never return. A world where a room full of eager strangers waited only for her. She held the last letter in one hand while the other reached for the doorknob.

Taylor jumped at the sound of three quick thunderclaps. The wind grew wild and buffeted the house from every direction, and a hard, steady rain began.

"Mom, come on. You don't have to show off. Stop it now, alright? I get it—you're already really good at it!"

Lin quickly ran through the letters and sent them all over: Venice, the moon, Alaska . . . anywhere just to get rid of them. She knew that they couldn't possibly form a word anymore. She had no time to laugh, but she realized that she'd never in her life wanted more to murder a word.

The winds quieted, and the rain became a light drizzle before stopping altogether. A few modest rays of sunlight crept in through the window.

"Okay, which one of you two is playing around?" Gabriel said while leaning around the corner with a grin.

"Gabby, it was me. I just wanted to show Taylor, that's all."

"And you figured it best to let it go for a while? Why was that?"

"Oh, I think I just learned something else. That technique that Gloriana taught us—putting the word's letters all over in different places—it doesn't work unless you use real places. I tried scattering them in a different world that I visited, and it didn't work."

"That storm you just created . . . was it in that fake world?"

Lin stared and smiled, and her green eyes carried a natural brightness.

"No, Gabby, it sure wasn't."

"You've learned something valuable, even without trying. Does using your Glyphin powers tire you?"

"Yeah, it sure does."

"It kind of tired me, too, Gabriel. Or maybe I just ate too much."

"Come sit again, the both of you. If that doesn't help, then maybe you both need a nap."

* * *

Lin saw first that Gloriana sat as still as she could, not even moving her eyes, and she and Taylor took their seats.

"Taylor, that was pretty impressive," said Jack. "I hope you're not upset about—"

"It was not Taylor," said Gabriel. "We can thank Lin the Glyphin for adding cold rain to the snow out there."

"You're a Glyphin now too?" said Jack. "God, how did that happen?"

"It just kind of happened, Jack. I created a fake world, just a place where I could go to learn something new. And I did, Jack. Isn't that something?"

"It really is. Amazing. What kind of world was—"

Lin's phone chimed and vibrated around on the countertop, and she jumped up to answer it.

She shook her head with a frown and said, "Not her again!"

Chapter 17 – God Is Not Afraid

"Didn't I make myself clear? Do you wish to die without ever seeing Russia again?"

Lin held the phone to her ear while every pair of eyes around the table, and another pair from Nomad, seated on the floor next to Jack, stared and waited.

"Stop! Hang on, Anna. I want everyone to hear this."

Lin set her phone to speaker and laid it near the center of her kitchen table.

"Okay, go ahead."

"Lin, I am sorry to call with you again. Tayo insists. And while he can still speak, he wishes—"

"You should be sorry. Next time I see you, maybe I'll kill you, and maybe I'll kill your daughter, and then maybe I'll kill that dog of yours too. It won't be pleasant, either, because—"

"Lin," said Gabriel with a gentle touch to her arm, "perhaps we can postpone all that killing for a while. I'm curious how Tayo is."

Lin glared at Gabriel then said, "Fine. Okay, Anna, tell us: what is going on now?"

"Ozzy is a gentle soul, and he would never attack us the way he—"

"Your dog attacked you?"

"Not just me, Lin. He attacked all of us. His eyes turned completely white, and he grew long fangs. He was phoning at his snout, and—"

"'Foaming.'"

"Yes, that is more accurate—I am forgetting English as my mind leaves me. Ozzy was foaming from the snout, and he leapt at Tayo.

Tayo managed to kick him, which only caused him to focus on Daria. His fangs were at her throat, and—"

"Good," said Lin. "She's a brat anyway."

"Yes, well, I grabbed his collar and held him long enough for Tayo to wrestle him into one of his kitchen cabinets. He leaned against the door until Daria and I could arrange his table to block it. He is still in there. The growling has stopped, but we are in no hurry to look inside."

"Hang on."

Lin muted the phone.

"Gabby, it's those symbols on Tayo's back. It's got to be. Another one had to have broken loose, and this time, it took over that stupid dog."

"I believe you are correct, Lin. Gloriana, does this make sense to you?"

"I think the hunter is still confused. It can find much more effective ways to kill than by commanding an ordinary household pet. It will learn."

"Wonderful," Lin said before she unmuted her phone.

"So, you have things under control again, and you can—"

"No, Lin, there are no situations under control. The growling from Ozzy became loud howling, and then it stopped. Lights flickered in Tayo's apartment, then part of his wall began to crack near the entrance. Pieces of wall broke loose and fell, the lamp near the door died, and the end of a wire left the wall. It ripped itself free, making an extensive mess of dust and chips on the floor, and I do not know how we will clean up all the—"

"Anna. Don't worry about cleaning up. What happened next?"

"I am sorry, Lin. I am not thinking in a straight line anymore. You are right. That is not the important idea. The wire continued to free itself until a long length was curling and whipping around, and sparks were exploding from the end of it. I heard more growling, and I still think it came from that wire. It made a lasso—is that a correct term?— around Tayo's neck and started to drag him to—"

"Anna, this is insane. A wire came to life and attacked Tayo?"

"Yes. Yes, that is true. It got him by his throat and pulled him to the wall. It did not strangle him, but it continued to shock him until he lost his consciousness."

"Is he dead? What happened to him?"

"No, he lives still. Daria and I managed to free him. We put him on the couch. I wanted to get a broom because the wall was broken and all over the floor, but Daria—"

"Listen to me: forget about cleaning up the mess. Is Tayo okay?"

"Tayo is a distance from okay. I believe he has mentioned that to you. After we separated him from the wire, the wire became just a wire again. Daria and I managed to wake Tayo, but he is not well."

"Okay, so at least things have settled down. Can you put Tayo—"

"Things did not gain any settling. I am grateful Tayo was awake because Daria was taken next. Her eyes turned black. Lin, they were entirely black. Some oily, slimy sludge oozed from her mouth, and she began to shriek."

"Good God," said Jack.

"There is no God here," said Anna. "I believe He, too, is afraid."

"Hang on, Anna."

Lin muted her phone, and she turned to Gabriel.

Gabriel grinned with a shaking head and said, "God is not afraid, Lin. Anna is understandably caught up in the drama."

"That's what I thought."

She turned the speaker back on and said, "Okay, so your daughter got possessed. Then what?"

"She sat on Tayo as he lay on the couch to recover from electricity, and she began clawing at his face. He held her wrists while I watched from a safe distance and screamed. I thought it wise to keep at least myself safe because someone had to survive to—"

"Anna. What happened to Tayo?"

"He was not as successful as he probably wished, and his face is ripped up like ribbons. He did manage to instruct me to retrieve the wire that had attacked him. I did, and somehow, we managed to wrap

Daria up with it. Tayo pushed her to the floor, and she lay there hissing and snapping at us until she fell asleep."

Lin stared at the phone a few seconds, then looked at Jack. He only shrugged, so she looked at Gabriel.

Before Gabriel could say anything, Gloriana said, "Is the girl still asleep?"

"Yes," said Anna.

"And the dog you call Ozzy. Is he still imprisoned?"

"No, I checked and saw that he was himself again, so I let him out."

"Tayo has survived? He will live?"

"That is a real question. He would say that he will not. I do not know. It can be a tossed coin."

"His back," said Gabriel. "Has he shown you his back?"

"No. I will ask him to reveal it."

Ten seconds later, Anna said, "He has shown it. More of the markings have become absent."

"There are still many more, though?" said Gabriel.

"Yes. There are now thirty-one."

"Wait," said Lin. "By my count, he had thirty-six, then the cats went crazy, so that should leave thirty-five. Now, you just told me about Ozzy, the wire, and your possessed brat daughter. That should leave thirty-two."

"I counted thirty-one, Lin," said Anna. "I will ask him again to—"

"No, don't bother. Leave him be."

"Very well."

"What will you do?" said Lin. "Has Lee arrived yet?"

"No, Lee is not here. What would I like to do? Take my daughter and my dog and flee to Russia. There were no murderous symbols on anyone's back in Russia."

"Can Tayo speak?" said Lin.

"He can only barely focus his eyes. He wishes for your assistance, Lin."

"Hang on."

"Gabby," Lin said with her phone muted, "maybe I should try to help him. At least until Lee gets there."

"That would be very kind of you, Lin. You can at least gather information and come back here, and we can try to form some sort of plan."

"Okay, I'll go, and when Lee shows up, that's it—I'm coming right back."

"Good, Lin."

Lin said into her phone, "Anna, I have to go—we'll see you soon," and hung up.

"Mom, I'm going."

"Oh, Taylor, Honey, I don't know if—"

"I'm bored out of my mind. I can't sit around here."

"You're seriously that unhappy here, Honey?"

"Yeah, Mom. There's just not enough happening. Besides, you might need what I can do anyway."

"You might be right. Okay, Hon, it'll be good to have you with me."

"Oh, I am sorry, Jack. I did not mean to kick you again."

"It's alright. Hey, Lin, I want to go too," he said after a quick glance at Gloriana. "At least to drive, alright? I can even wait in the car if you want."

"Okay, Jack. Sure. Gabby, will you and Nomad be okay?"

"We'll be fine, Lin. We saw that there's a cartoon marathon scheduled for today."

"You both saw?"

Nomad barked once at the ceiling and panted with his big eyes on Lin. She stared at him and shook her head.

"I will be fine too, Lin," said Gloriana.

Lin lost the smile she'd had for Nomad, glared at Gloriana, and said, "Not for long."

"Only twelve more days," said Taylor.

"Eleven, Hon. She just kicked Jack again."

* * *

"Stop right here," said Lin.

Jack jammed the brakes, and Lin's Tempt8tion slid to a stop near the entrance to Tayo's apartment building in Baltimore.

"What the . . ."

"I think that's Anna, Jack."

Anna took hurried steps along the sidewalk, coming toward them as she chased Ozzy. She wore only a thin, low-cut sweater and a tight skirt, and her heels slipped almost continuously on the snowy concrete.

Before reaching the car, she caught up with the dog, scooped him up, and turned to walk back toward the entrance.

"Yeah, that sure is Anna," said Jack. "It's that dog of hers too."

"She's still copying my style," said Lin. "She's irritating."

"She doesn't look anywhere near as good as you," said Jack.

"Aw, thanks, Jack."

"Your skirts are shorter, too, Mom."

"Thanks, Honey."

"I could explode that dog right now, Mom. Do you remember that coyote that thought it was a badass predator? It learned the hard way."

"Oh, Hon. Yes, I remember, but let's not kill Anna's dog, okay? At least not yet. But if she or her daughter aggravate me, who knows?"

Jack said, "Lin, I know you two are joking around."

He glanced at her in the front seat beside him and saw that she was still focused on Anna. A quick look in the rearview showed Taylor also staring at the scene on the sidewalk without a trace of a smile.

"Well, alright, then. Hey, maybe we should go inside and see what's going on?"

Anna rushed back into the building with the dog in her arms and swung the door shut.

"Sure, Jack. But no matter what we see in there, I'm not planning to stay long."

"Good deal. Let's just see how Tayo is, and then—oh, look."

Jack pointed through the windshield, past Tayo's apartment, at Lee Turner, whom Lin had renamed Lee Ternity, approaching. Despite the cold, she wore her short, black leather jacket with no hat. Her long, black hair fell straight down behind her, and though there was little sunlight, she wore mirrored sunglasses. Even from their distance, it was obvious that the faded denim was stretched over the legs of a serious athlete. Her black snakeskin boots crunched the snow with each confident step.

She held the hand of a young girl wearing a long, light gray coat and black boots. The hood was up, and a delicate ring of fake fur framed an angelic face.

"Perfect timing," said Lin. "Good, Lee can handle it. She and her daughter."

"I'm hungry, Mom. We passed a drive-through a couple blocks back. Why don't we just—"

"Hey, you two, shouldn't we at least go take a look? We did just drive for three hours."

Lin didn't answer as she kept watching Lee and the girl approach Tayo's entrance.

"Fine. Taylor, Hon, do you want to come inside or stay out here?"

"I'll come in. I'm curious just how many people can cram into that guy's apartment."

"Me too, Hon. Add that dog to the list too."

Jack said, "Good thing we didn't bring Nomad, right?"

He looked at Lin, who didn't smile, then back over his shoulder at Taylor, who continued to stare intently through the windshield.

"Well, anyway. Are you ready? Let's go."

"Sure," said Lin. "Taylor?"

"Yeah, Mom, let's go."

Chapter 18 – You're Kind Of Peculiar

"I miss St. Simons, Jack," Lin said as she held his arm to keep from slipping. "This cold is—"

"For the birds?" Jack said with a big grin, which he promptly lost when he saw Taylor's unblinking eyes on him.

He sighed when she said, "That's pretty funny, Jack. We didn't like the cold, though, especially when we first got back."

"I remember. You missed your feathers, right?"

"That's right," said Lin. "I think I still do."

"I know I do."

They'd reached the bottom of the three stairs that led to a small porch, and before any of them could take a step, Tayo's door opened, they saw Lee still in her jacket and sunglasses, and she pushed her daughter onto the porch. The door slammed shut with the girl facing it.

Jack looked at Lin, who only shrugged back at him.

"You must be Lee's daughter, right?" he said.

The girl turned only her head to look behind her.

"Yes. I'm Alessa. You're my mom's friends?"

Lin said, "Yes, we are. It's nice to meet you."

Alessa turned back toward the door.

"Nice to meet you too. You are Lin?"

"Yeah, and this is Jack."

Alessa still looked at the door.

"Um, and this is my daughter, Taylor."

Silence.

"Is everything okay in there?"

"Things are often how they're meant to be, Lin, though they might not appear to be okay."

Lin turned to look first at Jack, then at Taylor. Taylor scoffed and looked down the street, in the direction of the fast food, and Jack shook his head with a grin.

"Well, why did your mom put you on the porch?"

"She came to help the man in there. She said his name is Tayo. My mother didn't want me to see the blood, I suppose."

"Uh . . . what blood?" said Jack.

"The blood from Tayo's ankle as the knife in his hand cuts him."

"Mom, let's just get out of here. Like you said, Lee can—"

"Taylor, wait. Alessa, he's in there cutting himself? And your mom didn't want you to see it?"

"She thinks it will upset me. She's often kind and protective."

Jack climbed the stairs and grabbed the doorknob, and Alessa stepped to one side. Lin joined them on the porch, but Taylor stayed on the walkway looking at the sky.

"Alessa, you can wait out here, but Jack and I need to go in. Taylor, Hon, are you coming in?"

"I, um, I . . . changed my mind. You go ahead, Mom."

"Honey, are you—"

"Really, this is good. The porch is good."

A loud peal of thunder rang out, and a light, cold rain began.

"Honey, is that from you?"

Taylor looked at Alessa and said, "Nah, what are you talking about? It's just a freaky storm that came out of nowhere. Go on. I'll just hang with Alessa."

"They'll be fine, Lin," said Jack. "What's a little thunder and rain? Come on."

He turned the knob and pushed in the door. He entered the quiet room first, and Lin followed close behind.

* * *

Alessa turned from the door and gave the sky a quick glance with a hand up to block the first raindrops.

"You're doing that?"

"Maybe."

"Why?"

"I don't know. Who says I need a reason? If I was doing it, I mean."

"I won't. I'm curious about choices people make, that's all."

"Sure. So, why is that Tayo guy cutting himself up?"

"He's not."

"But . . . you said he had a knife, and he was cutting his ankle, right?"

"It does appear that way."

Taylor frowned and shook her head, and another thunderclap echoed off of the buildings all around them.

"How old are you? You're kind of peculiar."

She turned to face the door again.

"I'm eight. My mother tells me I'm creepy sometimes."

"Well, your mom sure would—"

"I'm uncommon. That's how I'd describe myself."

"You're certainly uncommon, I'll give you—"

"You've made larger storms, haven't you?"

"How could you know that?"

"You have strength. Do you consider whether your storms harm any living things?"

Taylor stared at the girl, and the rain lessened and stopped.

"Maybe I do. Why do you care?"

Alessa turned to look at Taylor without a smile.

"I can't help it."

*　*　*

"Wonderful, Jack. Look over there."

"I see them."

They both looked to their left and saw Anna backed into a corner with Daria under one arm and Ozzy in the other. Lin gave a quick look at Anna's legs in black stockings and ending in black heels. Her shoulder-length brown hair was impeccable, in wild contrast to the fear in her eyes.

Lin scoffed, shook her head, and studied Anna's daughter for a brief moment. Daria wore jeans and a sweatshirt, and her thick black hair cascaded down over her shoulders.

Only Ozzy looked their way, and a second later, he looked back at the couch to Lin's right.

Tayo lay on his back with his left hand covering his eyes, his wrist held there by Lee. The bandage over his missing finger appeared to have its own fresh blood, and he held a long kitchen knife. Lee held his other arm close to his side.

Lee strained to keep him down, and then, at the same time, both became still. Her hair hung in front of her on each side of her head, and her eyes were hidden.

"That's his foot?"

"It sure is, Jack. He almost got the other one too."

Blood gushed out from each leg and soaked into the cream-colored couch's fabric, creating sticky brown sponges.

Lin grabbed Jack's arm and walked him over so that they could both stand in front of Anna and her daughter, blocking their view of Lee and Tayo. Anna focused on Lin's eyes, which were green and glowing.

"Don't worry. This just happens. I'm not planning to destroy you."

"Thank you, Lin."

Lin turned only her eyes to peer at Daria and said, "You? I haven't decided yet. We'll see, won't we?"

Daria shrugged, tried to smile, and didn't make a sound.

"Shouldn't we be helping?" said Jack.

He started to turn, and Lin grabbed his arm and kept him looking away, all of them huddled together so none of them could see.

"No, Jack, we can't help with that. Let's just give Lee a second and some privacy."

* * *

"Lin, I'm glad you're here."

Lin let go of Jack and turned around. She saw Lee sitting upright on Tayo's lap and brushing back her hair. She yawned once and rested her palms on his chest.

"Look what she did," said Jack, pointing at Tayo's feet, both of which were attached and without any sign of being cut.

"It's what she does, Jack. Nice work, Lee. And I'm not staying."

"You have saved me again," Tayo said without opening his eyes. One arm hung limply off of the couch. The other still lay across his forehead.

Lee took the knife from his hand, stood up, and looked down on him with a tired smile.

"Check the finger too. I think I patched you up pretty well."

Tayo opened his eyes and unwound the bandage, revealing a replaced little finger that he'd cut off earlier.

"I might never comprehend the skills you possess," Tayo said while wiggling his fingers. "I am in a horrible predicament, and I'm certain more damage will come to me."

"Well, that's why I'm here," said Lee. "Oh, I think I need to sit awhile."

She sat on his lap and slumped back into the cushions. Her head tipped back, and her eyes closed.

"You people are frightening," said Anna. "Normal people cannot do such things. I saw a foot that was alone by itself, and now it is back on its own leg."

"Mom, don't make any trouble, alright? Let's just get out of here."

"Yes, Daria. We are no longer needed. Goodbye, Lin and the rest of you too."

Anna tried to get through between Jack and Lin just when thunder exploded above the apartment building.

*   *   *

"I can do that anytime I want," said Taylor. "How about some rain too?"

A soft drizzle began, soaking into the snow and quickly freezing on railings and steps.

"Isn't that dangerous?" said Alessa.

"Could be, depending on what kind of mood I'm in. Watch this."

They both turned at the sound of a muffled roar to the south. It got louder, and trash of all kinds was swirling in the air from one side of the street to the other as a slender cyclone approached.

"Better hang on."

Taylor and Alessa each grabbed a railing, and Alessa held her hood in place as the vortex of litter swept past them and was gone. The rain stopped too. Another boom sounded directly above them and echoed in both directions down the street.

"That was just for fun. Listen. Here goes another one. Even bigger."

* * *

"Anna, I believe God is indicating that you should remain," said Tayo.

"I do not believe God wishes—"

Taylor's thunder rattled the building.

"That would be a coincidence. Lin, please excuse us, we are—"

A continuous deep rumble above them rolled on for ten seconds, freezing Anna in place as she looked up at the ceiling.

* * *

"At the very least, you are likely scaring people," said Alessa.

"Yeah, maybe. I'm just having fun, though."

Alessa only stared at Taylor from inside a wet, furry ring.

"Fine. No more. Anyone ever tell you you're no fun?"

"Yes."

* * *

"Okay. We will remain," said Anna.

"Not for long, though," said Daria. "I'm not causing any trouble, Lin, and I sure as hell ain't going to go for another photo. But you people scare us. Even you, Lee. What the hell was that? Some kind of voodoo bullshit, except you didn't chant anything, and you're not waving dead chickens around, and you—"

Lin let her eyes flare up a bright green, and she stepped in front of Daria.

"Oh . . . right. Never mind."

Daria shuffled until she stood behind her mother.

"Please, Lin, she means no genuine harm."

Lin tipped her head, let her eyes continue to glow, and said, "I sometimes do."

Anna looked at the floor, but Ozzy continued to stare at Lin and never blinked.

Without looking away, Lin said, "Tayo, can we see your back?"

"Yes, of course, Lin. I no longer feel anything there, but evidence suggests that there is one less symbol."

Jack stayed in the corner near Anna, and Lin approached the couch. Tayo began to roll onto his side, facing the couch back. Lee slept. Jack, Anna, Daria, and Ozzy stared.

"I will need help. I am too weak now."

"Try to get some rest," Lin said as she rolled his t-shirt up.

She saw a patchwork of welts all running together and seeming to overlap. Altogether, they formed a rectangle, and the area nearest to his left shoulder had returned to the smooth, black skin Tayo enjoyed everywhere else.

While Lin studied the symbols, which she now knew were capital numbers, she said, "Do you know why you were cutting off your own feet?"

"I suspect it wants me weak and immobile but still alive. Its attempts still seem random and rather unfocused, though. I dread the likelihood of it applying more intelligence and strategy to its efforts. I will not survive, Lin."

"You'll survive. Lee will keep you going until we can figure this out. Do you mind if I take a photo?"

She turned to look at Daria, who quickly put her hands in the air, shook her head, and grinned.

Lin scoffed and turned back to Tayo.

"No, not at all," said Tayo. "Do you know what these markings represent? Do they have meaning?"

"I know some. They were common long ago, but they were used with a particular type of power to cause great damage. The entity that you are fighting is using those symbols. Let's hope we can defeat it before it learns how to control them more."

Lin snapped a few photos and put her phone away, then she pulled his shirt down. Tayo remained facing the couch back.

"Tayo," she said after glancing at two shattered mirrors on the floor against the wall, "what was the deal with the mirrors? Anna said you wanted to pack those and take them?"

"I might never voluntarily view any reflection again."

"You broke them?"

"Yes."

"Why?"

"I did not relish the sight they offered."

"I don't get it."

He rolled back only enough that he could turn his head and look at Lin.

"One mirror gives one reflection. A second mirror provides a different view. But Lin, I found that if both mirrors are aligned in a specific way, the images multiply to infinity."

"Yeah, I've seen that before, too, but what—"

"It is weak in the near reflections, but it gains strength if one were to focus further into the depth of that infinity."

"What's weak? What did you see?"

"I do not know."

He let out a deep breath so slowly that Lin wondered how he'd breathed it all in.

"Perhaps it was a feeling that I saw with my eyes. Is that possible, Lin? I only knew that what the mirrors revealed was not beneficial to my mental state."

Lin took a quick look at the mirrors, squeezed Tayo's arm, and stood up.

"We have enough to figure out right now. I'd say you shouldn't play with mirrors for a while, okay?"

"I won't."

He buried his face in the couch back and remained still. Lin turned to see Jack shrug again, and Anna only stared with Daria hiding behind her. She looked again down at Tayo.

"I'd help more, Tayo, but I'm not quite myself. Not yet. Lee will keep you going until we know what to do, okay?"

"Yes, Lin. I will do my best, and I take comfort in knowing that I am fighting in service of humanity."

Daria shook her head and said softly, "Oh, gimme a break."

Lin spun around to face Daria and let her eyes light up.

"Fine."

"No! No, no, no—"

Lin stopped time.

She found her intent in a heartbeat, and she held it tight in a grip that she knew would never weaken. Her eyes blazed a blinding green, and she watched infinity spread away from her in every direction, leaving a familiar sight of the world as a calm, flat surface with tumultuous tides of magic flowing and crashing, billowing up and dropping just as quickly back down, with every possible sensation and possibility and thought and memory and feeling twisting into an incomprehensible puzzle.

She turned to face a frozen Daria, her eyes stretched open and her lips forming a circle, as she stood with all the other unmoving lives in the room. Though she felt no doubts as her mayhem raged, she still remembered that there was no need to harm the girl. A lesson was all she needed, and Lin realized that she had an opportunity to learn something new too.

When the magic started to flow up into her, she didn't send it out in a wave to take anyone's life. Instead, she let it build into a sweet, unbearable pressure that filled her completely. Then, the magic started to spin inside, and as the speed increased, Lin felt as if her arms were raising up at her sides, and she was spinning too, although the view never changed.

With a mad top inside her, Lin focused on the magic of Daria's hair. She saw that it had a distinct magic separate from everything else, including even Anna's hair. She knew the magic of Daria's hair in an unmistakable way, and she thought about just the girl's hair at the height of her chin.

Lin's focus caused her fingertips to rise up to point at that height with every revolution, and before she let the magic out, she told herself to send her magic to just one side of the girl's head—that was today's lesson. Just the hair on her left side at the height of her chin.

With a welcome release and a burst of pleasure, Lin let the magic fly out from her in every direction, knowing that it would only affect where she'd directed it. She watched and didn't see any change, but she knew that it was because she'd stopped time.

She allowed the magic to flow back out of her, and quickly, it could no longer be seen. Infinity had hidden itself away again, but the delight trailed away slowly. Leaving her eyes glowing a playful, bright green, Lin watched Daria's hair and permitted time to resume.

The hair on Daria's left side, from the level of her chin downward, fell to the floor.

Everyone came to life as time continued because it had never stopped.

Daria's eyes opened wide when she felt her severed hair tickle across her hand on the way down. She looked at it on the floor, then back up at Lin's green eyes, bright and focused on her like a bird of prey.

"Think of how close that cut came to your throat."

Daria reached up with her right hand to hold her neck. She nodded and looked back at the floor. Anna looked over at her daughter's cut hair.

"Thank you once more, Lin. Thank you for not killing anyone."

"Hey, I'm just here for the photos. Jack, you ready to go?"

* * *

At the door, Lin turned and saw that Lee was still asleep, and Tayo still faced away as he slept too.

Jack said, "Hey, I have an idea, but I'm not sure you'll think it's a good one."

"What's that, Jack?"

"Those photos will help, right? They'll help you and Gabriel and maybe Gloriana, too, figure out what's going on?"

"Well, we hope so. That's just one small part of fighting this thing, though. But yeah, the photos might help. What's your idea?"

"Why not have Daria take photos every time something happens, and she can just send them to you?"

"Oh, you know, Jack? That's a pretty good idea. Hey, you. Daria."

She watched Lin from the corner with her mother between them.

"Yeah, Lin?"

"I need you to keep taking photos of Tayo's back. Every time his back changes, you can—"

"Lin," said Anna, "I do not know much of these things, but I do know that if his back decides to be different, then bad things happen. We truly do wish to be far from all of these happenings."

"Well, now you can't. I need you to stay with Tayo. All I need is photos of his back."

"So," said Daria, "you won't need—"

"No, I won't need videos of him sawing his feet off."

"Ew. No, I mean that you won't need me to write up reports and stuff, right?"

"No. Just the photos. It's your chance to help Tayo serve humanity."

Daria didn't smile and didn't make a sound.

"Good, you're learning. It's the truth. And it's only the photos that I want. Don't be bugging me about how you're having a bad hair day, okay?"

Daria still stared.

"Okay, that was kind of a joke. Look, we have to go. Tell Tayo and Lee we'll figure this out."

Anna and Daria and Ozzy all still gazed at Lin and rarely blinked. Lin smiled, let out a big sigh, and shook her head.

"You know, I could just as easily have trimmed a couple of inches off of that skirt for you, Anna."

Anna looked down then back at Lin and said, "As horribly frightening as that would be, I will try to see it as fashion advice. Thank you, Lin."

She managed a small smile back at Lin.

"Still wouldn't be as short as mine."

Anna lost her smile.

"No. Never, Lin."

Lin laughed and said, "Okay, Jack, now we can go."

Chapter 19 – I Want To Go Too

Jack pulled Tayo's apartment door shut, and he joined Lin on the porch with Taylor and Alessa. The last bit of thunder rolled softly toward the northern horizon, and Lin shook her head at her daughter.

"Honey, how are we getting storms like that? You weren't, I mean, you didn't—"

"What are you talking about? Storms just happen, Mom. You know that."

Lin looked into Alessa's big brown eyes, which looked back at her calmly.

"Alessa, I don't know what Taylor told you, but you really shouldn't think that she caused that weird thunder in January."

The girl paused for several seconds, then she said, "I've learned to believe all sorts of things. I live with my mother."

"I know your mom too. She's a very talented and strong woman, and she—"

"Uses the magic."

Lin stopped and stared. Alessa blinked once and continued her gaze.

"See, Mom? It's alright. She knows all about this stuff."

"Just how much do you know?" said Lin.

"I know that there is good, and there is evil. Healing is good. Storms are not evil, but they can still cause harm."

"Well, lots of things can cause harm. Your mom is here to help Tayo, who's trying to fight something that causes more harm than anyone can know."

"I know."

Lin paused and stared at the child.

"What do you know?"

"How much harm it can cause."

"How? What do you mean?"

Alessa studied Lin for a moment, then turned slightly and faced the closed door.

"I just mean that I know Tayo is a good man. I'm glad my mother is helping to heal his body."

Lin stared a few seconds, then said, "Yeah, well, she does have that ability. So, you understand what she does?"

Alessa turned back to gaze up at Lin, with cheeks red from the chilly Baltimore air.

"No. I can't. Can you?"

Lin gazed at her without blinking.

"Well, maybe I don't actually understand it, but I do know that she—"

"Uses the magic. Is she done in there? I'm getting cold standing out here on the porch."

Lin noticed the girl's rosy cheeks and lack of smile. The fake fur of the hood circled her face, which remained so still that Lin felt she was looking at a photograph. She shook her head and continued.

"Yeah, she's done. She fixed him right up. It was nice meeting you, Alessa. There's no reason you can't go join her now."

"Goodbye, Taylor. Goodbye, Lin."

She reached for the doorknob, and Taylor said, "Wait a second. I'm going with you."

"Taylor, what are you talking about?"

"I told you I was bored, Mom. I'm just going to hang here for a while and see what happens."

"For how long, Honey?"

"I don't know. I'll just fly home when I'm ready."

"I know you're joking. You are joking, aren't you?"

Taylor stared and shook her head.

"I miss it, Mom. I don't even care about learning anything to do with those nonsense numbers. Crows don't need that. I already have all kinds of tricks."

"Oh, that's for sure. Okay, Hon, I guess you know what's best. I'm actually kind of glad you'll be around to help Tayo and Lee."

"I'll try not to kill those Kelgina women and their dog."

"That would be best, Honey. They might be some kind of help anyway. Hey, remember how much Lee always eats? They could be the ones that run out for groceries."

"Right. At least they're good for something."

She gave Taylor a hug and kissed her cheek.

"Bye, Honey."

"Bye, Mom. Come on, Alessa. Let's go see what's going on."

The door closed behind them, and Jack put his arm around Lin, who had begun to shiver.

"Your skirt is definitely shorter, Cowgirl, which I love because I love your legs. But it isn't keeping you very warm."

She kissed him on the lips and said, "That's your job, Cowboy."

The door jerked open, and Taylor rushed out. She frowned and slammed the door shut behind her.

"Honey, did you change your mind?"

"I can't stay here. Just looking at Tayo reminded me of what that thing tried to do to me before. I hate it."

"Well, I'm glad you'll be coming home with us. We can all—"

"Mom, I can't go home either."

"What do you—"

"I don't belong in there. I don't belong at home. I belong—"

"No, Hon. You're wrong. You do belong home. It'll just take more time for you to see that."

"I don't want to see that. I know what I want."

Taylor looked down at the porch floor, and a light rain started up. A weak thunder spread out from directly above Tayo's apartment building.

"Hon, is that you? Are you doing that?"

"I know where I belong, Mom."

"You don't even know how to do that, do you?"

"It's all intent. Isn't that what you always say?"

The rain became heavier and more horizontal, and a louder thunderclap echoed up and down the street lined with brick buildings.

"Can you just give it more time, Honey? Let's go home and stay under those blankets awhile, okay?"

Taylor looked up, and Lin saw that her eyes were glowing a bright green.

"Honey, please don't. Just give it more time, okay?"

"Mom, I wasn't healthy almost my entire life. Lee healed me, and almost right after that, I became a Glyphin. Remember that? Remember how I couldn't control it, and you had to take me away?"

"Yeah, Hon, of course, I remember that."

The wind changed directions, chasing Taylor's hair straight back from her. She turned her glowing eyes to the sky, and the cold rain soaked her short blond hair and ran down her cheeks.

"I felt afraid again."

"When?"

"Now. In there. I don't like feeling afraid."

"No one does, Hon. You don't have to stay here and help."

"I didn't feel fear when we were with the family. I just lived every day. Mom, I had no doubts about anything. No fear either."

"I know, Honey. I felt that too. Still, can you stay, please?"

She gazed up into the rain.

"I miss it too much."

Between the booms of thunder, Lin heard a fluffing and flapping and turned to look up herself. She saw one big crow perched above them on the edge of the three-story building. Another joined it. Then ten more. Seconds later, hundreds were lined up, all peering down on them.

Lin looked back down at her daughter and said, "I understand, Hon. Come back soon, okay? We'll work it out. Promise me you'll come back soon?"

Taylor focused bright green eyes on her mother.

"They're here. It's time."

The chill rain began to resemble buckets being poured from the roof above. An enormous thunderclap caused Lin to wince, and when she opened her eyes, she caught only a flash of black wings racing upward.

She looked up to see, but right above her, crows were racing in each direction so close as to almost brush her with their wings.

As if responding to a signal only they could know, they all sped straight up, not one of them identifiable as Taylor, and every last crow disappeared over the building's roof.

*   *   *

The last traces of thunder simmered away toward every horizon, and the final few drops of rain began to freeze on pavement, handrails, and coats.

Lin stood alone with Jack on the porch, looking up into a quiet and deserted sky. She turned to him, hugged him around his waist, and laid her head on his shoulder.

"Hey," he said as she remained completely still and silent, "she'll be back. This is all really rough on her, I know, but she'll get it out of her system, and then she'll be back."

Lin tipped her head up and wiped at her eyes, though no tears were apparent.

"I know she will. It's not that, Cowboy."

"What then?"

With her eyes casting off a faint green glow, she gazed into Jack's eyes for a second, then she looked at the sky and said, "I want to go too."

She smiled and rested her head on him again, and he reached up to touch her hair as he held her close.

"We still have a lot of blankets back at your house, Cowgirl."

She gave him a tight squeeze and looked into his eyes.

"That sounds good right now, Cowboy. I need some blanket time."
"Just don't send Nomad and me out into the snow again, alright?"
He gave her a smile.
She wiped one last time at her eyes, returned his smile, and said, "No promises."

Chapter 20 – A Murderous Monster Appears

Lin pulled her Temt8tion into the garage and clicked to close the door.

"Thanks for the company, Jack. I miss Taylor."

"I know. Me too. I really believe she'll be back soon."

"I hope you're right. I hope she stays safe."

"The girl that can explode anything that might come after her?" Jack said with a laugh. "Oh, I think she'll be fine."

"You make a good point. Okay, that was all pretty weird, especially for Tayo, but maybe Gabby can help us figure out a plan."

"Sure. That would be good, but what about eating? I can finally almost get the image of Tayo's foot laying on the floor out of my head. Still, that's not as incredible as Lee putting it back on him. Anyway, now I'm hungry."

"I like your appetites, Jack," she said with a faint grin. "We'll have to talk about that more later. Right now, I need to remind Nomad how to play our game."

She got out and slammed her door much harder than was needed. She stomped her way to the door that led into her laundry room and beyond that, the kitchen. With an ear held close, she watched Jack and waited.

A quiet minute passed, and she shook her head and reached for the knob. But she stopped herself and continued the vigil.

Seconds later, a single, loud bark vibrated the door, and Lin smiled and cracked it open. As soon as it was open wide enough for a big, wet Tibetan Mastiff nose, Nomad wedged his big snout through, and with his thick red mane, he shoved the door open.

"Nomad, my sweet fluffy boy."

He barked once at the ceiling and jumped up to put his paws on Lin's shoulders. He panted for only a second with his big eyes staring at her, then he began to lick her cheeks.

"Oh, my big boy. I missed you too. I bet you're hungry, though, aren't you?"

He stopped only long enough to look up and bark once.

"Okay, okay. Enough exercise for my legs."

She took his paws and helped him drop to the floor.

"Okay, Jack, we can go in now. We really do have to play this game, you know."

"Hey, maybe I should try that sometime too. I never even thought of it the last six weeks, though."

"I think he'd like that. I'm not sure you'd ever beat him, though. He's really stubborn. Come on. Let's see what Gabby's up to."

* * *

Nomad led them inside, then he promptly disappeared around the corner and toward the sound of cartoons cackling from the TV. Jack hooked his coat on the chair of Taylor's writing desk, and Lin left hers in the laundry.

"Oh, Gloriana," Lin said at the sight of her sitting at the kitchen table. "It's always an unpleasant surprise to see you in my house. How many days do you have left?"

"Lin, I do not wish to die. You know that. As for counting days, that could involve lower case or capital numbers—you may choose."

"That's funny. I do want to show you what's left on Tayo's back. I took a photo, and there are more missing."

"I wish to see what you have found. Has your daughter remained in the car's room?"

"No, she won't be home for a while."

Gloriana let out a deep sigh and said, "Well, I will not say that I am grateful, yet I *am* grateful. She appears closer to annihilating me than do you."

"You might be right about that. Don't get too comfortable, though. She could be back any second. I'm never that far from wiping you out either."

"Yes. I understand. I must be careful in all I do."

Lin sat at one end of the table, with Jack near her and across the table from Gloriana.

"Hello, Jack. I trust your journey was safe and beneficial."

"Mixed reviews. It was good that—"

"Oh, I am sorry, Jack. I am becoming clumsier as time continues."

"Not a problem. It's not like you're trying to kick me."

"Here's an idea," said Lin. "No more joking around—let's really take a day off of your remaining lifetime for every time you kick my boyfriend."

"Oh, Lin," said Jack. "I don't think that's necessary."

"It is not necessary, Lin. I will be more careful."

"Good. Just remember how close you always are to the end."

Gloriana looked down at the table and said, "I will remember."

Seconds after the cartoons came to an abrupt end, Gabriel entered the kitchen with a hand on Nomad's head.

"Good, Gabby," said Lin. "I have some photos of Tayo to look at. Wow, that was a weird experience."

"Tayo is okay, though, Lin?"

"He is now. Lee showed up and put him back together."

"Do you mean that literally?"

"She does," said Jack. "He'd cut off one of his feet just before we got there. He was close to hacking off the other one too."

"And Lee saved him," said Gabriel. "She is quite remarkable."

"She sure is," said Lin. "It exhausted her, though. We didn't wait for her to wake up before heading back."

Gabriel nodded and looked around the room, then listened intently for a few seconds.

"Taylor didn't return with you?"

"Oh, Gabby, she's back to being a crow. I didn't think she knew how to do that."

"She learned much in the last six weeks."

"Yeah, that's for sure. She said she couldn't take being human again. I believe she meant to promise that she'd come back soon just before she left, but she was already too far gone."

"It's much more difficult for her. She'll find her way, Lin. She'll return to you soon."

"I hope so. Most of all, though, I want her to be happy."

"I believe she is. What of Tayo?"

"He's struggling," said Lin. "I can't imagine what he's going through. Lee was able to restore the finger he'd cut off too. How is he going to keep fighting this thing? That can't be fun to suffer all kinds of damage, even if Lee is able to patch him up."

"No, that can't be easy," said Gabriel. "We should seek a solution as quickly as we can."

"I believe the numbers on the man's back are key," said Gloriana. "That hunter became born into this world with the ability to use them. Perhaps they can be its downfall as well."

"Perhaps. Perhaps they'll be your downfall instead," said Lin. "Still, you'll have to take that chance and teach me what you can."

"I will, Lin Finity. I—"

"It's just 'Lin,' remember?"

"Yes, Lin. I am not accustomed to the fear of imminent death, that is all. Except for my time between the Islands of Time. I will teach you. You say you have photographs of the man's affliction?"

Lin took out her phone, tapped it a couple of times, then turned it so Gloriana could see.

"Oh, that is not good," said Gloriana.

"What isn't? There are less of them on his back—that's good, isn't it?"

"That much is encouraging, but it is startling how much more clearly defined they have become. They have migrated apart and now more closely exist as individual capital numbers."

"I don't get it. Why would—"

"Think of them as being more in focus."

"I suspect that means that the entity is gaining more control over them," said Gabriel.

"Gabriel is correct. This is troubling."

"So, the clock's ticking?"

Gabriel laughed and said, "Only until you stop time, Lin."

She shook her head and grinned at Gabriel.

"After all we've been through, you're still testing me? I know that I can't stop time—it's just that I'm outside of time."

"That's exactly right. Still, you will surely attempt to enlarge your Glyphin powers soon with the capability of capital numbers. Do you feel ready for that?"

"Yeah, why not? You were sure right about one thing, Gloriana, when you said that learning of the magic is a wave of its own kind."

"Yes, it will tow you along, and you must find the strength and judgment on your own to deal with it."

"Okay, I get it. What's first?"

"Control of capital numbers for a Glyphin is more about control of your own mind. The numbers are of secondary importance."

"That doesn't sound too difficult," said Lin. "It's like that every time I use my mayhem and when I use the magic of things. Even that new thing I just learned."

Lin turned to smile at Gabriel, who nodded back at her.

"What new thing is that?"

"Oh, just a fun little thing I can do now. I'd say, watch your step."

"I will. And I will strive to not kick Jack anymore."

"Good."

"But it is not as simple as you think. The controlling thought might be buried somewhere beneath your more obvious thoughts. You might think it is insignificant, but it is not. A minor thought, barely noticed by you, could unleash your Glyphin power in an unexpected way."

"Okay, so how do I make it work?"

"I have said this before, and it has not led to your happiness: you must practice. Allow yourself to make mistakes, and if you are wise in your attempts, you will be less likely to destroy anyone you care about."

Lin stared at Gloriana, then she turned to look at Gabriel. Gabriel only shrugged.

"Are you sure you still wish to learn of this deadly use of the magic, Lin?"

"Yeah, Gabby. I'll just try it, um, somewhere else, if you know what I mean."

"I do know."

"I do not know," said Gloriana.

"You don't need to know," said Lin.

"That is true. Very well. You now know that a clear focus, one with which you are not yet proficient, is necessary. Beyond that, you proceed as with the Glyphin power of using a word except that you use a number. When you see the entire number, you change the first one to its capital relative. Then, go about your usual Glyphin method."

"Well, that seems easy enough."

"It is not."

"But if it works the same way, then—"

"You will find that it is new and strange. It will be violent and unpredictable. It is like expecting a meek mouse, and instead, a murderous monster appears as if it screamed itself into existence."

Lin shook her head and gazed at Gloriana. Nomad was near, and he set his massive head on her lap, so she began to scratch his head and flop his ears around. She looked down at him with a grin.

"Oh, my sweet fluffy boy. Don't worry, Nomad, I won't ever try any of that with you."

"Or with me, Lin Finity."

"How many times have I—"

"I am sorry. The thought startled me."

"Fine. I won't use that on you. I don't have to. There's still lots I can do."

"Yes, I know."

Gabriel said, "Gloriana, is there any way to start out in a modest way?"

"Yes. The longer the number, the more likely it is to produce chaotic results. If you use a short collection of numbers, even if it brings horror, you can take comfort in knowing that it could have been much worse."

"Seems easy enough. I'll learn. I do appreciate you sharing your knowledge. If I find that you haven't been truthful about any of this, dreadful things will happen to you."

"Yes, I know, Lin. I have been honest. Believe me that the actions of a Glyphin using capital numbers are dangerous enough. I have no need to set traps for you."

"Good. How do you like my guest room?"

"Oh, I was just going to retire there. I will go now."

"Gabby and I will whip up some dinner. I'll call you."

"Thank you, Lin."

Gloriana left, and Lin waited until she heard the bedroom door close.

"Jack, what do you think about all of this?"

"I kind of wish you wouldn't try any of that. You don't really need to, do you?"

"Who knows? Maybe someday I'll need to use that power for something?"

"Well, since you put it that way . . . yeah, you might. Hey, instead of you two doing all that cooking, why don't we order pizzas again?"

"Very good idea, Jack," said Gabriel. "Onions and green peppers for me. Cheese too. Lots of cheese."

Jack smiled and said, "Coming right up."

∗　∗　∗

187

"I am gaining an appreciation for foods known only in this time period," said Gloriana.

"No pizzas back on that island of yours?" said Jack.

"No, but fish practically jumped into our nets. Sometimes even without my commands."

She pulled her second slice out of the box and plopped it onto her plate.

"There certainly wasn't any in those spaces in between the Islands of Time," said Lin. "There wasn't anything. Only what you intended."

"That is true. I intended many things when we spoke there."

"Hey, I've wondered about something: how were your eyes glowing there if none of that was real?"

"That is easy to explain: I intended my eyes to glow. It brought a meager amount of comfort, but it was worth the effort."

"Lin," said Gabriel, "remember that your eyes don't need to glow in this world we call real either. Do you remember that talk we had?"

"Oh yeah, I sure do. You said I could have horns or a halo instead. That made me realize that I do like the glowing eyes. You know, if I were trapped in that awful place, and if I lured some unsuspecting, innocent victim in there, then—"

"Lin, you are about to become angry. I will likely not survive that."

"Okay, you're right. I'm just saying that I'd make my eyes glow too. There's something else that was strange, too, about your behavior. When you were there, everything you said was in the present tense. You never spoke of a future or past."

"Yes, because those ideas no longer existed. There was only an eternity and my survival in that moment. After being imprisoned there, I lost any sense of time."

"I believe that was a shrewd strategy, Lin," said Gabriel, "even if she hadn't planned it. Faced with an eternity of suffering, with no escape in sight, it would be disheartening to focus on anything but the moment."

Jack chewed his last bite and wiped his hands with a napkin. He looked around and said, "I'll gather up these dishes, then I bet Nomad needs some air. This is too much magic talk for us."

"Well, it's getting late," said Lin. "I'm off to bed. See you later."

"I'll be on the couch," said Gabriel.

"I will retire, too," said Gloriana, "though I do not need sleep. Getting air sounds good, but it is too cold to walk, and I cannot operate a vehicle."

"It's not like we'd let you anyway," said Lin.

"Well, okay, then," said Jack. "It's out in the cold and snow for me and this big boy."

Nomad barked once at the ceiling and looked into Jack's eyes.

Chapter 21 – Jack's Flight No. 3

Jack had brought Nomad back inside, asked him not to shake so he could pick more snow and ice chunks out of his thick fur, and led him to the couch to sit with Gabriel. He handed Gabriel a box of crackers, then he crept into Lin's bedroom, undressed down to his boxers, and got in under the covers. He saw that she lay facing away from him, and even in the dim light, he saw her long blond hair spilling out over the blanket she'd pulled up to her chin.

After snuggling his back up against hers, he thought of how easy it would be to roll over and hug her. He believed that she'd like to be awakened to help catch up on all of the times they'd lost while she was gone. But he also knew that she needed sleep, and so did he.

Maybe next time, he thought and closed his eyes.

It felt like only seconds later that they snapped open again.

He carefully climbed out of the bed, put on his jeans, boots, and flannel shirt, and walked to the door. Not questioning his actions but knowing to stay quiet, he closed it gently behind him, found his keys in the kitchen, and left through the front door, surprising himself at not waking Gabriel or Nomad, whose paws protruded from under the blanket, twitching.

An elongated smear of moonlight reflected off of his truck's windshield, and he watched how it began to crawl across the glass as he approached. It moved enough to uncover the passenger side, and beside the pale moonlight were two distinct points of caramel shining through the glass.

Jack froze halfway down the icy walkway. He knew that he should turn and run, but he didn't. He hesitated there just a moment too long.

The white light from the moon held constant, but the caramel flashed, and he felt Gloriana's will replace his own as she invaded the narrow gap between his body and his spirit. Running was no longer an option. He knew that no options were left for him. Once again, his life belonged to the woman whose own life had begun countless centuries ago.

His legs unlocked and began carrying him toward his truck. He felt his jeans brush against the cold chrome bumper as he stepped into the snow on his way to the driver's side door. His eyes looked down, and he appreciated that she'd allowed him to be careful and not bang up his leg.

After his eyes had focused on the door handle, she paused him there to cause him to look through the tinted glass. The moon lit his face, creating a clear reflection, and beyond the glass, he saw her eyes shining a compelling caramel and replacing his own in the mirror between them.

How appropriate, he thought without any amusement but ample dread.

His hand lifted the handle and swung the door open, then she halted him there to listen to her first words.

"You are mine again, Jack. We will become much better friends this night. No, I will speak only truth for you. We will become lovers this night. You will desire that."

Jack didn't feel his head nod to her comments, but his body sat behind the wheel, and he yanked the door shut.

For a moment, he forgot his predicament when his head turned to his right and his eyes focused on Gloriana's legs. He saw that they were long and bare and hardly covered at all by one of Lin's short skirts. She smiled as she lifted one knee up high so that he could see the heels that she wore.

His eyes continued farther up, and he saw that she wore only a white tank top stretched tight, probably also Lin's, despite the cold of early January in Pennsylvania.

She turned her shoulders toward him and gave him a more complete view of both of what he suspected she'd soon offer him. He felt his eyes move left and right several times, causing his heart rate to climb as the sight reminded him of the cold air in his truck. Then, his vision traveled higher, and he looked into two caramel pools that seemed to bubble and churn with heat and passion.

"You like what you see. You will soon see with no clothing covering me. You will do more than just see."

His eyes were snapped back up to hers as she turned to face forward.

"It is good to get out in the air. We will go now."

Jack's eyes turned to look out through the windshield.

"Let us go somewhere, Jack. Would you like to spend time with me away from nosy interruptions? Yes, I believe you would."

It was a quiet drive to a motel three towns away. She made him park then compelled him to walk beside her, and he heard her heels striking the concrete of the parking lot.

Minutes later, she had a key, and he could do nothing but trail her into their room. She closed and bolted the door, caused him to take off his coat, and walked his legs across the small room to stand him beside the bed.

He watched her stride over and stand in front of him, and he felt himself removing his shirt.

"Twice we kissed when you wore only shorts. It was obvious that you liked that. We will kiss that way again."

He finished unbuttoning and dropped the shirt onto the worn motel carpeting.

"You look very strong, yet you are powerless for me. We will start with only shorts, Jack, for now."

Jack felt himself reaching down to untie his boots, which he kicked aside. Next, he removed his jeans and stood before her wearing only his boxers. He found no way to stop, or even decrease, the excitement he felt.

"Very good, Jack. I see that you are so very happy to be here with me. Do you like me taking control of you?"

Jack felt his head nodding, and he felt himself growing even happier.

She looked down at his boxers and said, "I really am not doing that to you. Let us see if you will be happier yet. I believe you will. I give back your eyes, but only your eyes, for a short while. Still, you will look on your own at what you will soon enjoy."

Jack could again control the direction of his sight, and he focused on Gloriana's hands as she reached down to the bottom of her shirt and began pulling it up. She used it to lift and lower her breasts several times while grinning at him, then she stretched it away and let them bounce back down as she took it off over her head. Her long, wild dark hair spilled down far past her shoulders. His eyes focused on her breasts, and he couldn't look away from them. He had a fleeting moment of doubt, wondering if she had truly given him back his eyes.

She glanced down.

"You like what you now see that I have bared for you. You are happier all the time, are you not?"

Jack felt himself nodding again. When she pushed against his chest, he couldn't resist, fell onto the bed with arms out to each side, and continued to stare up at her.

"I am going to remove all of my clothes, Jack. You enjoyed undressing me when last we touched. This time, I undress for you to watch. I will leave on only Lin's high heels because you like me that way."

She grabbed the top band of her skirt and worked it halfway down her thighs and left it there, showing Jack that she wore nothing under it.

"I'm very warm and smooth all over," she said as she rubbed her fingertips everywhere she could reach, all while looking into his eyes.

"You cannot hide that you like what you see. It grows more evident every second."

She wiggled until her skirt dropped to the floor, and she kicked it aside.

"Oh my, Jack, I really am not doing that to you. You know that to be true. You are very happy that I am naked for you in this room where Lin cannot interrupt us."

She leaned over him and grabbed the top band of his boxers with both hands.

"We kissed in the kitchen and hallway while you wore only shorts. Would you like to kiss me without your clothing this time?"

To his relief, he didn't feel his head being forced to nod. And he didn't try to nod on his own.

Her eyes tracked down across his chest and farther, and she said, "A part of you has answered my question. That part of you is eager to know me."

Jack couldn't deny it, even to himself.

"We will kiss, and soon, you will choose to be without any clothing."

She climbed up on the bed and knelt over him, and Jack felt her knees tight against his sides.

"You know what we are about to do in this rented room. It is something you do not wish to escape."

She leaned forward, placed her hands on the blanket at each side of his head, and looked into his eyes.

"You are my prisoner, and I can force you to do as I wish. Look at how close I am. It is only your thin garment which separates us."

Jack's eyes were jerked down to see that she waited very near, and only his shorts prevented it.

"You are already imagining how it will feel. You must know that it will be better than your imagination can tell you."

He felt his heart beating hard in his chest.

"I wish that we become lovers this night. Do you wish the same, Jack?"

He fought to hold his head still, but he couldn't.

"I knew you would. You see a naked woman above you, and you are about to have her. No one would expect you to deny yourself this natural pleasure."

Jack's eyes snapped first to her breasts then back up to the hot caramel. His head agreed with her.

"Lovers are willing partners, Jack, and you will be my lover beginning tonight in this room so far from Lin."

He stared helplessly.

"I wear nothing, and I will rest upon you, and you will wish for me to remove your shorts."

She sat on his lap and wiggled around until she let out a deep sigh.

"Oh, Jack, we are so close to being lovers. Can you imagine it?"

He had to nod.

"You must learn something first. Hold my waist."

His hands reached up to each side of her waist, and he felt her skin warm and smooth.

"If you were free and also without clothing, you could pull me down onto you. Can you imagine how that would feel, Jack? Would you like to force me to be your lover?"

Jack could only stare as his head nodded.

"Now, touch my thighs."

His palms pressed against the sides of her thighs. His hands confirmed what his eyes had known from the day she'd arrived: her legs were strong and muscular while also soft and feminine.

"Rub my skin. Enjoy my smooth skin, Jack."

He had no choice. His hands glided over her skin, up and down her thighs, caressing the sides and the tops, briefly touching the backs with his fingertips while he stared into her glowing eyes.

"Imagine how it would feel to have these legs working for you, bringing you pleasure with every movement. Can you imagine touching my legs as we enjoy being lovers, Jack?"

He nodded; he couldn't stop it.

"Now, take my heels in your hands."

He reached down and held a sharp spike in each hand. Each heel jutted out between his thumb and forefinger, and his hands wrapped around the warm leather.

"Here is what you now must learn. My heels are sharp and hard, and they remind you of the power I have over you. They tell you that I control everything you do, except for the excitement you feel. That comes only from you."

Jack felt his heart thumping as he held the powerful, naked woman's heels in the still room. He knew that she was right—her heels felt hard and unyielding in his hands.

"When you touched my thighs, you learned that I am also soft and smooth. Your hands felt much, but you will also feel in another way, as lovers do, how warm and inviting I am for you."

He knew that he'd reacted to her words as he imagined exactly what she'd suggested.

"Oh my, Jack," she said as she glanced down. "Even the thought of being my lover is becoming overpowering for you."

Jack nodded three times and stared up into her eyes.

"This is how we will begin our love affair. My heels remind you that I have power over you, and at the same time, you will know that I also touch you and hold you in ways that bring you nothing but pleasure."

He wished that he could close his eyes, but all of his strength couldn't make it happen.

She rose straight up above him and brushed her hair back.

"Soon, I will have you. Look at all that you will soon enjoy, Jack."

She forced his eyes to look first at her mouth, and she slowly slid her tongue across her top lip before puckering up as in a kiss. He looked lower until he found her breasts, and he looked from one to the other before his gaze drifted down across her flat belly and past her navel.

"Yes, Jack. Let your imagination tell you what is waiting for you."

Jack stared before looking back to her eyes.

"It is all for you. You may take me any way that pleases you. Are there fantasies you wish to demand of me, Jack?"

He nodded, and it didn't surprise him.

"You may enjoy me as you wish. All I ask is that you do it by your choice. Do you understand?"

Jack fought to stop and think, and he realized that she might soon set him free—to tempt him into submitting of his own free will. But he didn't have the strength to delay his response any longer, and his head nodded.

"You know that all you dream of will be in your hands soon, do you not?"

He knew that he might soon have an opportunity—he had no need to wonder about it again—and he didn't resist nodding his head.

"I will free you. You will choose to enjoy any fantasy you can imagine right here, right now, with the undressed woman that you will claim as your lover."

Jack continued to look up into her glowing, caramel eyes, and he fought to not consider the naked woman so close. Instead, he struggled to hold an image of Lin, and not just her physical beauty. He sought to cling to the closeness they felt for each other and all the experiences they'd had together.

"You will need only to guide me to where you most want me to be. Your hands are strong, and I cannot resist. You will force me to pleasure you."

While still staring, Jack found his love for Lin, a love so deep that it seemed to be an unchangeable part of his very soul.

"I release you now. Make me your fantasy lover, Jack."

Then, Jack felt his soul returned to him in an instant. And in that moment, while holding her heels, he held a vision of Lin above him instead, the woman he'd loved since the day they'd met, her green eyes looking down on him as she smiled and called him her—"

With a loud groan, he let go of Gloriana's heels and squeezed her waist hard, and she gasped and stared in disbelief. Just as he began lifting her up off of him, her eyes flared a blinding caramel, and the free will he'd experienced for only a second evaporated, leaving him again her captive.

"Oh, you are a strong-willed man, Jack. I know you want what I can give you, but I suspect you have some misplaced loyalty for Lin. You will lose that soon. Hold my heels. Take one in each hand."

His hands reached for her heels and held them tightly like before.

"Good, Jack. You feel them hard and sharp in your hands, and another part of you knows that I am soft and smooth. Hard and sharp remind you that I have powers. Soon, soft and smooth will be the power you cannot resist."

Jack's head nodded.

"Now, look into my eyes."

He looked into the caramel that maintained a stronger glow than he'd seen before.

"This is your greatest pleasure: to gaze into these eyes as you allow me to take you."

Jack could barely remember Lin, and he stared into her burning eyes and imagined what it would be like.

"You can feel true ecstasy only this way—when holding my heels and looking up into my eyes."

He fought against her power and tried to resist her, but all he did was nod.

"Lin cannot give you this, can she?"

Jack felt his head shake slowly, and he couldn't find the strength to even blink.

"When you want pleasure, you will think only of me."

He had to nod.

"When you see me, you will think only of pleasure."

Jack struggled to hold his memories of Lin, but still, he nodded again.

"You no longer desire Lin in any way. You will choose to become my lover, is that true?"

He struggled to hold his head still, but he couldn't. He felt himself nodding enthusiastically.

"Good, Jack. And you have never really loved her. Is that true?"

Somehow, using a strength that surprised him, he was able to close his eyes. But he nodded too.

"That is good."

Jack stared into the eyes of the woman above him as she placed her palms near his head on the bedspread, and her hair hung down on both sides, offering them a private space filled with caramel light.

"We will become lovers soon, will we not?"

He couldn't help it—he nodded again.

"When you see my eyes, this is all you will want. When you see my body hidden by clothing, you will feel anguish until you can undress me. You will want only to have me above you while you look into my eyes."

She leaned down to kiss him. He couldn't resist, and when she laid herself out on him, straightening out her legs, he had no choice but to kiss her for several quiet minutes.

"You are tired, Jack. Lin must surely wonder where you are, but still, we will not hurry."

She rolled to his left side, laid up against him, and rested her left arm across his chest. He felt the soft weight of it with every breath as his eyelids got heavier and began to close.

Then, with his eyes closed, he felt that she'd switched sides.

He took a deep breath, let it out, and felt her pressed in close under his left arm again.

"Rest now, Mr. Jack."

With his heart slowing again, he knew that he had to get back to Lin before she awoke and found him gone. There might still be time to sneak back into the house and get under the covers next to her.

But all he could feel was his still-strong anticipation of the pleasure she'd offered him, her skin warm and smooth and pressing up against him on his right side, then his left, then his right again.

Hearing only the silence of a motel room where he lay wearing just his boxers with a completely undressed Gloriana, paralyzed and helpless from her power and many miles from Lin, sleep was the next force to take him captive.

* * *

Jack opened his eyes to a darkened room. He pushed away the arm on his chest, stood, and switched on a lamp.

"What's wrong, Jack?"

He looked down at Lin beneath the covers, rubbing her eyes and frowning.

"Did you have a bad dream or something?"

"Oh Lin, I . . . I was . . . I mean—"

"Jack, just come back to bed. It was only a dream. Come on," she said with a smile, "I want to get back to my dreams too."

"Lin, it felt so real. Too real. Are you sure dreams can't be real somehow? I'd never want to get trapped in a dream. I mean, if there was a way to escape one, you know, to get away from it, could a person—"

"Jack, relax. Your dreams don't have that kind of power. Let's talk to Gabby about it in the morning, okay? It really was just a dream. Try to get some sleep."

"Alright. Yeah, you're right—just a dream."

He turned the lamp off and lay beside her, and they snugged the blankets up tight. When Lin laid her arm across his chest, Jack stared into the dark and refused to close his eyes until they finally closed themselves.

Chapter 22 – Lin's Flight No. 4

Warm under the blankets, Lin heard Jack's breaths finally slow and deepen, and when he rolled onto his back, dragging his arm off of her, she knew that he'd fallen asleep.

The curtains shut out most of the weak moonlight, transforming her bedroom into a dark and quiet retreat. She felt the sheet cool and soft against her bare skin, and she gave it a gentle tug to rest it up under her chin.

Even though fatigued from using her new Glyphin powers, she resisted sleep and felt her skin warm and smooth. She let her hands find their own paths down over her until they rested on her thighs. It felt so good to lie still, naked under the blankets, almost too tired to move, and it reminded her of what else she'd fantasized about before leaving with Taylor: being without her powers. Giving them up. It had seemed so appealing at the time to be naked and helpless for the strangers that she'd been teasing.

It surprised her that she felt a subtle spike of excitement at recalling that.

But a fantasy of being helpless was nonsense, she knew. She'd learned as a crow that there's nothing fun about being helpless. Her powers had saved all of them countless times, even while she was a bird. No, that could never be good in a real world. The stakes were too high.

But in a fake world? Just for fun?

She realized that she should explore that sometime, to try leaving her powers behind in a flight to a made-up world. Perhaps it was time to know for sure and either reject or accept that desire. If it felt too vulnerable, she could fly right back.

She decided that this wasn't the time. Maybe on her next flight. But it was a perfect time to learn a new power, like using the Glyphin capital numbers power, in a safer fake world, one that wasn't threatening to become real.

Faint fingers of timid light held themselves tight against the ceiling after sneaking above the curtains to invade the room. The strongest of them reached past the still blades of the ceiling fan above the bed as if readying itself to grab her and take her away.

She knew that would never happen. But that tiny smudge of black that had appeared in one of the bright strips—that would do it. Like so many other times, she couldn't look away.

* * *

Lin heard nothing at first, but she knew that she was standing and no longer lying in her bed. The skirt that she'd laid neatly on the dresser felt snug around her hips. She stood on the heels that she'd kicked aside to get comfortable under the warm covers.

Unable to wait any longer to discover what place and time, what fake world her intent had created for her, she opened her eyes. She saw only a bland, metallic cream color, and when she heard a bell chime, her view expanded, and she saw closed elevator doors.

Oh no, not again! she thought. I barely got out of here last time!

She looked above the doors and saw that the elevator was on the third floor, then the second, then the doors opened to an inviting space lined with rich wood panels and illuminated more like a lounge during happy hour.

I'll just stand here and wait for the doors to close, she told herself. I'll wait for that black spot, or start a storm if I need to, and get back home quick—back to the real world.

Then, she heard the talking and calm laughter around her, felt a strong hand on each arm, and had to take short steps on her heels through the doors and into the cab.

"The lobby's not where you belong," said a voice to her right. She turned and looked up into the eyes of a good-looking man with short dark hair and a pleasant smile.

"I know where you're headed. Allow me," said a voice to her left, and Lin turned to see another stranger with wavy black hair and a short beard peppered with gray. His eyes showed his intensity and eagerness, and she watched him hit the button for the eighth floor.

Neither one had let go of her arms. Two more men had entered after them and still faced her. They smiled too.

No, thought Lin, I can't go up there. Where's that dark dot? Where will it appear? I need to get back!

"Eighth floor for you, Honey."

Lin knew that she'd better muster an answer, and with a reminder to herself that it was all fake, she said, "Oh yeah, that's where I want to be."

She looked from face to face and found it impossible to focus long enough to find her way home. She glanced again at the panel and saw that they'd just passed the fourth floor.

"We're early, we know," said the man to her right. "There's just no way in hell any of us wanted to miss your entrance."

A man in front of her said, "We needed to get here early anyway—we're drawing lots."

She didn't know why, but what they'd just said had given her heart a slight boost. His smile only added to it. She began to feel more curiosity about what waited all the way up in that penthouse suite.

It wasn't really all that difficult to get back the last time, she thought. I could have started a storm and hurried right back, and I didn't even need to. It had all worked out well anyway.

Surrounded by men that she didn't know and remembering others had already gone up and more waited in the lobby, Lin thought of Jack. Her first thought was that he seemed to want her more than ever, maybe because of those dreams. She felt their closeness every time he was near, but she also felt the wildness and harshness of the last six weeks of her life as a crow and a need to do whatever it took to get back to herself. A quick thought of how Taylor had flown off on her own, and the sadness and disappointment of it, made her realize that some entertainment could only help keep her from returning to the life of a crow.

These men obviously didn't think that she was a crow. They'd already complimented her, and there was no doubt that they liked what they saw. So, why not enjoy a bit more attention? It's harmless. It's a fake world.

When the bell chimed, Lin spied the lit-up 8. The door opened, and the two men in front of her turned and walked into the hallway. She felt the two men still holding her elbows, and they coaxed her into taking more careful steps until they all stood on the clean tile floor of a dim and quiet hallway. To her right, past the door to the stairs, Lin saw only three other doors on each side, each with its own flickering light fixture, giving an impression of another time.

They led her to the first door across the hall on the left.

"Don't take too long to make your entrance. I don't think I could stand to wait much longer."

She saw in his eyes the honest attraction that he felt, much like what she'd seen in Jack's eyes when she'd stood naked in front of him, inviting him to enjoy the sight. This man had that same look, maybe even more so, and in this world, he wasn't the only one.

What if she stayed here long enough and stood naked in front of him and all the rest like she'd done for Jack? What would that invitation bring? Since doing that for Jack had helped her restore herself, wouldn't she make quicker progress with many more appreciative eyes on her?

She reminded herself that if she'd ever take it that far, which she never would, of course, that it would be even better without her powers too. She'd be sending that invitation with no control over what it would bring.

For the fun of it, she said, "Oh, I'm positive I'll make it worth the wait."

She watched him look her up and down with a big smile. She knew that her bare legs looked good with only a tiny, short skirt covering her.

"I'll make damn sure it is," he said. "We all will. We know what you want."

When his smile changed to something only a hint more serious, Lin knew what he meant—he planned to make sure she was helpless. The excitement rose higher, and she decided to play along just one more time because she was leaving soon anyway, never to return.

"It's not like you'll leave me any choice, is it?"

"No, ma'am. This is going to happen just the way you said you wanted it. Every sexy little detail."

She wondered just what details she'd supposedly told them, but she also said, "Oh yeah, that's how I like it."

He gave her another grin, and they all left for the next door, which Lin guessed must lead to an adjoining room. The same man was the last to enter, and he paused to gaze at her a moment. She had time to see that his casual and tasteful clothing did little to conceal the muscles beneath. He appeared strong in a modest way, a man who could surely take what he wanted. And she saw him looking right at her. He entered the room with the others and closed the door.

Alone in the hallway, she turned to face her own door, knowing without any doubt that the luxurious bath of her imaginings waited inside. She reached out and held the door handle, thinking about the hot bath that she could take and also the stranger's strong arms. She knew that if she didn't have any powers, she'd probably never be able to fight her way free. She was sure it wouldn't be a gentle, romantic embrace.

She noticed that she was holding her breath, and her heart had picked up its pace as she realized that he'd hold her in ways that left her no options but to do as she was told. That was the fantasy that she'd imagined before she'd joined the flock. That man, and probably all the others, too, would make sure that she'd have no choice—she'd have no chance of escape.

She focused again on the handle, gave it a turn, and found it to be locked. Only then did she notice the key card in her hand. But she didn't use it. Instead, she stared at the room number just above the peephole.

Just an eight and a zero and a one. A simple number . . . harmless in its current form. She knew that it was a perfect time and place to try a capital number. Just swap out the first one to begin the number. Just one capital number . . . easy.

A commotion to her right caused her to turn to see a different man had stepped back into the hallway. He looked at least as strong as the other one, but his smile looked more determined. Maybe more impatient too.

"Any problems? Can you get in okay?"

She held the key up with a smile.

"Yeah, it's fine."

She looked at his arms and imagined them wrapped around her, maybe one of his strong hands covering her mouth, too, before she turned back to the number she'd created, one for her Glyphin powers to use.

She crossed her eyes like before and saw the number repeated with an empty space between them. Then, for each of them, she replaced the first number with its capital counterpart.

It was too late, she knew, but she remembered that the capital number needed a feeling or a focus, something supplied by whoever wrote it. She knew that she hadn't done that—she wasn't even sure how. She'd forgotten to try to control her thoughts!

But it was a fake world that she'd be leaving soon, so it wouldn't matter. Not there.

Instead of feeling some strange balloon thing squeezed between her left hand and some other kind of thing, she felt dozens of left hands and just as many right-hand things, whether they were hands or paws or machines, she couldn't tell, and not a single one of either belonged to her.

Feeling caught in a collapsing mountainside while at the same time shot skyward out of a volcano, Lin felt all of the hands and other unknown machine paw things vibrate violently, then quickly crush a captive, squealing, and squirming thing in the middle as it both howled and laughed hysterically.

It had lasted less than a blink of her green eyes, and there was only silence.

Then, the screaming began.

She turned and saw the man struggling to stand as each side of his body grew more arms, ripping his shirt open. There were five on each side, and the man shrieked like he'd been stabbed as he looked down at what he'd become.

Another arm snapped out on each side. Then another. He fell to the tile and had arms sprouting everywhere, on every side, down to his waist, all flexing and making fists and obscene gestures, waving around and slapping against each other from being packed in so tightly. He'd become a bristling, nightmarish sea creature fighting for its life.

The screams stopped, replaced by deathly gurgling, but the arms never slowed, and there were so many that they smothered and blocked any view of his head.

The door opened, and Lin saw two men reach for the monster, but they stayed inside the room and out of its reach. A hand fumbled outside along the wall, pulled the alarm, and sirens and flashing lights filled the hallway.

Lin's heart pounded as she turned back to her door and stared at a clearly defined black spot. In a panicky silence, amid a storm she'd created, she waited.

"Oh God," she said out loud after two seconds, "that's just the peephole!"

She moved her eyes up to see the door above it, at a place where she could find what she needed.

But without her wanting it, her eyes snapped back down to where they were—back to the tiny lens.

"Oh, no. Come on!"

She heard footsteps approaching from her right. Angry voices. Scared voices. Doors opening and people running in both directions.

She fought to look to the left at the plain paint finish of the door. She felt a different door closing: the escape route that would take her home. She stared and waited and tried to focus as her heart raced.

Again, with a will of their own, her eyes snapped back to the peephole.

"God, will you just hold still for—"

She felt her right arm grabbed tightly and someone trying to pull her down the hall, away from what she needed more than anything.

"Come on, it's not safe for a lady out here!" said the man holding her.

"What the hell happened to him?" said another.

She had to take a step, grinding one pointy heel into the tile, but her eyes remained where they'd been focused. She forced them to look at a place lower on the door, an open area that she was sure would welcome the appearance of the black spot that would kill her. Strong hands dragged her another step away.

"Let's get you inside with the boys. They won't even care about that freak once they see you!"

"Oh, I don't—"

She saw the tiniest of black dots against the gray surface, so small that it could have been a gnat or piece of lint. She felt the hand yank her farther down the hall, but she kept staring at it.

"Hey, let's strip her down before we toss her in there!"

A strong hand grabbed her blouse above her breasts, ripped it open, and sent buttons to the floor, and she got pulled farther away. She felt dozens of hands grasping at her ankles and calves, some getting a solid hold of her and trying to pull her to the floor.

The sea creature had her!

Then, the dot expanded into a black dome that grew in an instant large enough to cover her. She felt no hands, heard no screaming, and saw no hallway. The hotel and the entire fake world had sunk into a bottomless pit of black oil.

She died and waited in silence, holding on to her intent. She couldn't think about it, but still, she knew that centuries might be rushing past, and everyone that knew her might already be long gone. But for her, there was only the quiet of her intent without even a beating heart for company.

* * *

A white spot appeared against the black emptiness. It hesitated, and Lin waited, unable to feel or think anything about it. Without a sound, it rushed toward her, dragging another world behind it. When all darkness had been chased away, she felt her heart begin a normal, healthy beating. Thoughts returned to her along with her feelings. She took a deep breath and opened her eyes.

The ceiling fan still tried to hide narrow streaks of moonlight clinging to the ceiling. The soft coverings above her and the sheet below her felt as cool as when she'd left, which she knew had been only one Island of Time earlier, a time so fleeting that no one would ever be able to measure it.

Her heart beat a bit harder than normal as she recalled almost remaining trapped in another world, especially one where her Glyphin powers had destroyed a man in such a merciless manner.

But part of her heartbeat came from the excitement of it all. She had to face that what she'd told Gabriel earlier wasn't true. She *did* still have some fascination for the fantasy that had consumed her.

But it was a fascination that would never become reality—she couldn't ever take that chance again.

She knew that she'd never return to that world of hotels, and lobbies, and elevators, and admiring strangers, and clothes being torn off. Her intent would never let that happen again.

Drifting off to a well-deserved sleep with the sounds of Jack's slow, contented snores, Lin enjoyed the memory of her hand on the doorknob, trying to guess every delicious detail of what the man had said that she'd planned for herself within the penthouse of her fantasy.

Chapter 23 – A Forbidden Thought

"I swear, Jack, I'm so hungry I'll eat as many blueberry hotcakes as Gabby this morning."

"I doubt that, but it'll be fun to watch you try. Did you sleep alright?"

"Yes, I really did. I did that imaginary world thing for a second, even though it seemed longer, and I got to mess around with the capital numbers Glyphin power."

"Wow, really? How was it? What did you do?"

"Oh, it was exciting, Jack, but only because it was a disaster. I'm glad none of that was real because some innocent guy grew more arms than I could count."

"Sounds horrible. Don't ever try that on me, alright?"

He reached around her waist and pulled her closer under the blankets.

After a quick kiss, he said, "What unlucky guy got that nightmare treatment?"

"It was just some guy down the hallway. I started playing with a number like a Glyphin would, and—"

"What hallway was that? This one?"

He pointed toward the bedroom door.

"Oh, um, no. You know, I don't know exactly. It was a big building, that's for sure, and Gloriana was right about it being unpredictable."

"Why his arms? That's a weird kind of random, isn't it?"

"Oh, I did notice his arms before all that happened, but I sure didn't aim anything at that guy. Somehow, he just got in the way, maybe?"

"What about his arms? Did he already have extras?"

He smiled and gave her another kiss.

"You're silly, Cowboy. No, he didn't. Not until the Glyphin business got him."

"So . . . tell me about the hallway. What was going on there? Any idea why you were there?"

"You know, Jack, I'm still learning about this fake world thing, and I'm not completely sure what that world was all about. Anyway, it was over in a second or two."

"One last question: he's dead, right? Can't grow a bunch of extra limbs and still live, I bet."

"I don't really know, Jack. I left right after that. I know none of that's real, but still, I kind of hope that didn't kill him."

"Why, you hoping to see him again?"

"Oh, Jack," she said and leaned in to kiss him.

When she pulled away, he smiled, but he still waited for an answer.

"No, Jack. He's nobody I know or ever will know. Just some stranger in a fake world."

"Well, then, I say you get some hotcakes in you. You seem to be busy all night."

"Jack, it really takes less than a second. Like no time, really."

"I've been listening when you talk with Gabriel, and I think that means no time here, but maybe a lot of time there?"

"Oh, um, I suppose it could be, but that guy sprouted arms right after I read the number, so I—"

"Hey, what number?"

"Just a number on a door, that's all."

"Sounds like a hotel. Do you think it was a hotel?"

"Now that you mention it, you might be right, Jack. This whole business is weird, uncontrollable, and unpredictable. Maybe it was a hotel."

"Alright, enough questions from me. You're hungry? I bet we can get Gabriel to whip up a few stacks for us."

"In a second, Jack," she said as she slipped out from the blankets and stood next to the bed.

She switched on the weak lamp and turned to face him. With a grin, she reached up and held her hair back with both hands.

"Damn, I never get tired of a sight like this. You like doing that, don't you, Cowgirl?"

"Oh, yeah, Cowboy. Attention is good."

"The heels. How about the heels too?"

"Mm-hmm. I like it better with my heels. I like this kind of attention."

"I think we might be late for breakfast," he said while not looking into her eyes.

"Hope so. I'm in no hurry."

*   *   *

"Finally, Lin, you're developing an appreciation for these hotcakes. I've been telling you ever since I became real again that they're the best."

Lin and Jack sat at the kitchen table, grinning at each other, each with a cup of coffee. Lin had traded her heels for slippers, and Jack had only socks, and their feet played under the table.

Lin turned her head toward Gabriel, who was busy at the griddle, and said, "I'll never like them as much as you, Gabby, except maybe for today. I'm starving."

"Very good. These will be ready in a minute or two. Has anyone seen Gloriana yet?"

"No, and I don't want to," said Lin. "I really do want to kill her."

"I won't stop you," said Jack.

Lin snapped her head back around, looked at Jack, and said, "Really, Jack? You don't care if I kill her?"

"Oh, I just . . . I sometimes wonder if she's as nice as she's acting. Maybe she's just pretending. Hey, are we sure she doesn't have any powers anymore?"

"I can't tell for sure. Gabby, can you? Do you know?"

"I can cook for you, Lin, and if you have to face demons again, I will definitely help. But I cannot interfere in any special way. You know that."

"But she shouldn't have any powers left, should she?"

Gabriel set a plate of hotcakes in front of each of them and stood at the table with hands in oven mitts.

"Okay, that's just a bizarre sight," said Lin. "Gabby, I know what you are, and look at you. How does this make any kind of sense?"

"Ah . . . 'sense.' No, it doesn't make any of that. Still, you'll look past all of that and enjoy your breakfast, won't you?"

"Well, yeah, of course. I'm just saying."

"Gloriana made a deal to give up her powers to return to life on the Islands of Time," said Gabriel. "That was a deal between her and God. I hope she wasn't foolish enough to try to cheat Him. That never ends well."

"Wait a minute," said Jack. "So, maybe she does have powers?"

"It's doubtful, Jack," said Gabriel. "It's more likely that she retained a great deal of strength in her intent, but she likely has no power over the magic."

"Oh, Jack," said Lin, "she probably just—"

"No, wait," said Jack. "What can someone do with strong intent but none of that magic stuff?"

"Probably nothing," said Lin. "Jack, what are you so worried about?"

"Oh, I'm not worried, um, except maybe for you. You know, because she wasn't exactly your friend, you remember?"

"Yeah, I sure do remember. Thanks for watching out for me, Cowboy, but I'm sure I can handle her. She's no match for me anymore."

Jack let out a big sigh and focused on stabbing a forkful of hotcakes.

"You still look worried. Jack, I swear, if she were stupid enough to—"

Lin's phone rang out and vibrated around on the kitchen table where she'd set it. She tilted it up enough to see the calling number.

"Gabby, I can't keep dealing with them."

"Perhaps they have news of Taylor, Lin?"

Lin bit her lip and looked at Jack, who shrugged and smiled.

"Fine."

She picked it up, tapped it, and put it on speaker. She set it back down and said, "What now, Anna? Did Tayo fill with helium and float out through a window?"

"That's a good one," Jack whispered, and she gave him a quick smile.

"No, he is not a balloon, at least not yet. No, Tayo is—oh, did you hear that? That is the fourth one. He—"

"Fourth what? I didn't hear anything."

"Fourth bone breaking inside Tayo's body. That was a big one, and I thought you surely would have heard when it—"

"This can't be happening. His bones are breaking now?"

"Not all of them, Lin."

"Not yet!" Daria said from a distance.

"Has his neck been broken yet?" said Gabriel.

"No," said Anna. "It seems that his less consequential bones are considered, well, less consequential. They are snapping within him."

"Uh-oh, that's gotta hurt!" said Daria after they all heard a loud crack.

"Oh, Lin, this is not pleasant. A leg bone sticks out as if someone stabbed it into him. I thought that there would be more blood, but no, it is white. Just white. It is whiter than I would have—"

"Anna, slow down. Stop talking a second and just answer me. Is Lee still there?"

"She is sleeping with him."

"What?"

"Mom!" said Daria. "She means that Lee is doing whatever voodoo she does, and she—"

"It's not voodoo," said Lin. "You know, I think I can have some fun even from way over here at home. Want me to try?"

"Sorry. No, don't try. I just mean that Lee is sitting on him, and they're both unconscious. That's what my mom meant. Oh, but *that's* not good."

"What now, Daria?"

"I just heard another bone crack apart, and God, I can see it almost jabbing through his skin. But the bad part is that Lee is getting more pale every second. What if she can't help him? What then?"

"I will have to call emergency vehicles, Lin," said Anna. "They can reset his bones, and if they have smelly salts, they can—"

"Smelling. Smelling salts."

"Yes, well, they can wake up Lee, and then—"

"Then, you'll all go to jail or an asylum. Do NOT call anyone, do you understand?"

"Okay, but—oh, Lee has opened her eyes. How is this possible? Daria, do you see?"

"I see it, but I don't—"

"See what?" said Lin.

"His bone has returned to his body, and it is moving around in there. That is good because—Lee is becoming pale again! Tayo's bones are again outside of his skin!"

"Daria," said Lin, "take a photo."

"Yuck! No way do I want—"

"Can you see how green my eyes are? Do it!"

"Okay, okay! There, it's on its way."

"Lin," said Anna, "Lee is again waking herself up, and Tayo is healing. It is a miracle, and I maybe should have waited before calling."

"That's okay. Don't worry about it, Anna. Make sure that daughter of yours, the one with the weird haircut, sends a photo of Tayo's back. Got it?"

"Yes. Yes, of course, Lin. I will say goodbye now."

"Bye."

Lin clicked off the phone and said, "Gabby, this is kind of too much. I kind of don't care anymore if that thing gets loose and roams the planet."

"That might be unavoidable anyway," said Gabriel. "Still, if we can find a safer path, it is worth our effort."

"Jack, are you okay?"

"Yeah. Yeah, I think so. It's just a lot of unbelievable stuff."

"It's just part of the deal with me, Cowboy."

She leaned over and gave him a kiss.

"I accept that deal. I welcome it. What's next?"

"We finish breakfast," said Gabriel. "What else?"

Lin turned toward Gabriel with a big grin and said, "You're more wise than even I suspected."

* * *

"Well, I didn't eat nearly as many hotcakes as I thought I would."

"Which is very good," said Gabriel, "because we're running dangerously low on ingredients."

"Yeah, I see it, Nomad," said Jack. "I'll get the bag."

Jack got up, went to the pantry, and brought out the big bag of chunks.

"Nomad told you to get that, Jack?"

"Uh, sort of, I guess. He gets his message across."

Lin nodded and sipped her coffee. She set the mug down and turned around in her seat to face Gabriel at the kitchen sink.

"Hey, Gabby, do you suppose I could use capital numbers and Glyphin powers to fill up Nomad's bowl?"

Gabriel turned off the water and said, "That's a very good question, Lin. If you did, do you believe the food you provided for him would be just as tasty and nutritious as what's in the bag?"

"Oh, I don't really know. That sure is a good question. What do you think?"

Gabriel got a big smile while shaking wet hands toward the sink and said, "Worked with loaves and fishes."

"No, you can't be serious. That was Glyphin magic? He knew that too?"

"Oh, Lin, of course, he knew. Don't ever doubt that."

"Good, then maybe I'll try it sometime. I truly don't want to see her anymore, but I need more instruction from Gloriana before I dare try that again."

"For sure," said Jack. "Don't try it in a hotel again either."

"Hotel, Lin?"

"Oh, Gabby, I just gave it a try in a fake world, that's all. It was a disaster, and I was so relieved to vanish out of there."

"I agree: more advice from Gloriana would be of great benefit."

"Hey, remember when we all called her Sunny?" said Jack.

"Yeah, Jack, but no more. Nothing sunny about her."

"No, there sure isn't."

"Now that breakfast is over," said Gabriel, "I'm ready for some ice cream. Anyone else?"

"Gabby, you can't possibly—"

Lin's phone again danced around on the table and rattled against the centerpiece.

"I swear, if this is Anna, I'm really going to try to—"

She looked down at the phone.

"Oh, it's Lee."

She set it to speaker.

"Hi, Lee. Are you okay?"

"Hi, Lin. I'm exhausted, but yeah, I'm okay."

"How's Tayo?"

"Good as new. Well, except for the trauma. That poor man is going through a lot. I can fix his bones and stuff, but if he's terrorized by all this, that's on him."

"You're doing enough by healing him. That really is amazing."

"It tires me out, but it's not as horrible as you might think. I do what I can to make it fun for both of us."

"What? How?"

"Remember when I first healed his leg at that restaurant in Allentown?"

"Oh, okay. I get it. Yeah, I remember. I'll never forget that smile on his face."

"Good, because you won't see any more. I make it as good as I can for us, but really, Lin, he's being destroyed. He's not smiling anymore."

"That hunter thing isn't killing you like when you tried to heal Taylor?"

"Not anymore. I've learned to not think about the hunter. I sense it there, like something lurking in the weeds around my clearing. Something really nasty. But all I do is focus on Tayo. Don't ask me to try to destroy that thing. Lin, I don't think anything can."

"You are probably correct," said Gabriel. "It is wise to not even try. We will try to figure something out here."

"Gabby's right, Lee. We'll keep working on it, and you keep helping Tayo. Can you get that brat Daria to send a photo of Tayo's back?"

"Yeah, sure. Did you do that to her hair?"

"Pretty neat, huh?"

"I'm guessing it could have been worse."

"Oh, yeah. Hey, could you fix her hair if you wanted to?"

"I don't know. Maybe. Do you want me to try?"

"Nope. It's a good reminder for her."

"Alright. Look, I'm really tired, Lin, but I wanted to let you know that I'm doing alright at keeping him alive. Figure something out soon, alright?"

"We'll try. Good luck, Lee."

* * *

"Yes," Lin typed into her phone, "I got the photos of Tayo's broken bones and his back. Thank you."

She set the phone down and said, "That girl's a brat, but she is pretty useful. Thanks, Jack. That was a good idea."

"You know what else is a good idea?" said Jack. "Groceries. I should run out and get some."

"Take Nomad with you? He likes getting out."

"Yeah, of course."

Jack looked at Nomad and raised his eyebrows twice, causing the big dog to bark once at the ceiling and begin panting.

"Hey," said Lin. "That's how you ask him? By copying my thing with the eyebrows?"

Jack laughed and said, "We have all kinds of ways to talk. I did that hoping you'd notice. It's a compliment."

"Well, it's cute, Jack. I bet Nomad thinks so too."

Jack rose up, and Nomad immediately bumped his forehead into his leg, then followed him toward the exit to the garage.

"Have a safe trip, Cowboy."

"We will."

Lin smiled in Jack's direction until she heard the door close, then she picked up her phone and clicked a few buttons.

"Gabby, take a look. There's one less symbol on Tayo's back, but more importantly, look how neat and evenly spaced the rest of them are."

"It's quite noticeable," said Gabriel. "And that can't be a good thing. The hunter seems to be getting more organized. It will only get worse for Tayo unless we can devise a strategy to help him."

Lin shook her head slowly and said, "It'll get worse for all of humanity. Isn't that what we're really talking about here?"

"Yes, that's exactly right. It's a shame that Tayo will be destroyed in the process. But if that happens, try to remember that he will have died in selfless service to all of us. None of us can do any better than that."

"How about the people that make ice cream? Especially chocolate?"

Gabriel smiled and said, "They're a close second."

"Do you know what exactly that hunter thing is, Gabby?"

"Maybe. I do know that its role, and the work of others like it, is to destroy us. Everything that lives is subject to their work. Countless times in every moment, when we or any other thing, alive or not, pass between the Islands of Time, those hunters do the task assigned to them. They bring us our deaths."

"Some quicker than others."

"Yes."

"There's no escape?"

"No permanent escape. Recall that Gloriana sensed her own death was near, and she chose to flee to that horrible space where—"

"Hell?"

"Yes, she chose to exist in Hell for as long as her strength would last."

"Or until someone like me came along."

"Yes. We don't have to like her, Lin, but we can respect her strength."

"Is she still strong?"

"She might be stronger than she lets on. I don't believe she has power over the magic anymore, though."

"Good. She's caused enough trouble. It's bad enough she's even in my house."

"Yes, but I also admire your strength in allowing her to live. Besides, you and Taylor have already learned much from her. Do you wish to know more about the capital numbers and how to use them?"

"Well, yeah, I can't help it—I do want to learn more."

"She might be the only one that can help. And if she's dead, then there's no way—"

Lin's phone rattled and rang its way across the table.

"I can't hear any more about Tayo, Gabby. This is all my fault."

Before Gabriel could respond, Lin picked up the phone, saw that Daria had sent a text, and clicked to view it.

"Oh, this is getting even more cruel. Gabby, look."

Gabriel looked quickly at the photo, then back up at Lin.

"It's not your fault, Lin. It is the fault of the hunter and no one else."

"But, Gabby, his arm is on fire! Why doesn't that thing just kill him if that's what it wants? Heck, it could just explode him if it wanted to. Even Taylor could do that."

"It doesn't want to kill him."

"What? Why not?"

"I believe it only wants him to give up. It's not Tayo's body that stands in its way."

Lin met Gabriel's calm gaze, and after a few seconds, she nodded and said, "His spirit. His pure heart. That's what's in its way?"

"Yes, Lin. For now, it needs Tayo's body because that's where it is trapped. It cannot kill the body—and neither should you—because it can't be sure it will survive that."

"You mean, it might not?"

"Yes, perhaps. Killing Tayo might send it back to Hell. Or it might turn it loose to wreak destruction on all of the living. We don't know and neither does it."

"But if it breaks Tayo's spirit, then—"

"Yes, then it can take its time in a body with no resistance. It can focus and strengthen until it knows how to travel in this realm."

"We can't let that happen."

"No, we can't, Lin. Should we assume that the fire is out?"

"I think so. That brat would be in the corner crying instead of sending a photo if Tayo was still burning."

"Would it help to know for sure?"

"I suppose. Okay."

She keyed Anna's number.

"Anna, is the fire out?"

"Yes. The fire on Tayo is out. Lee is attempting to heal him."

"Good. So, everything is back to normal."

"No. Ozzy tried to help and was burned badly. Daria and I placed him in the kitchen sink and ran water to end his flames. He is still there. He is not happy. Neither am I. Or Daria."

"Can Lee help the dog too?"

"I hope so. He will never last for the journey back to Russia. We will go soon. When Ozzy is cured, if he can be."

"No, not yet, you won't. I need updates from your daughter. In fact, tell her she owes me a new one of Tayo's back. It must have changed after he played with fire."

"He did no playing. I will tell Daria to send something after Lee is done. Then, when Ozzy is himself, we will all—"

"Oh, Anna, I'm too tired from all of this to argue with you. If you leave, I'll destroy all of you. We need your help until we can fix this."

There was a long moment of silence.

"Fine, Lin. I believe you could locate us in Russia, so I will stay."

"Smart. Get going on that photo."

Lin clicked off her phone and set it down.

"This is starting to feel like when Taylor's Glyphin powers were wrecking all of Pennsylvania. That was my fault too."

"You are not to blame, Lin. Gloriana has free will, and she chose to attack you. She turned Taylor into a Glyphin."

"What about this hunter thing? Does it have free will?"

"No. It is doing only as it is instructed."

"It sounds like you know what it is. You do, don't you?"

"Yes. But knowing that will only make things more difficult for you."

"So, you're not going to tell me?"

"No. I still want that ice cream, though."

Lin smiled, shook her head, and stood up from the table.

"Let me wait on you for a change."

"I thought you'd never offer."

Lin smiled and said, "You're really something, you know that?"

"Yes. I've heard that several times over the centuries."

* * *

Lin set the bucket on the table, handed Gabriel a scoop, and took her seat. She looked up to see Gloriana walking into the kitchen, stretching her arms and yawning.

"I tried to forget you were in this house."

"I am sorry to intrude. I smelled breakfast long ago, and I resisted the hunger and tried to remain in my room. But after—"

"It's not your room."

"Yes, that is true. I am only saying that I am hungry. Of all the ways you can kill me, Lin Finity, starvation seems lacking in creativity."

"You make a good point. I don't even mind you calling me by my full name when you're making sense like that. Fine. Have some breakfast."

"Hotcakes?" said Gabriel.

"Please."

"Oh, I just remembered that we used up all the ingredients. Perhaps you could—"

The door from the garage opened, and a loud bark told them that Jack and Nomad had returned. Jack walked in with his arms full of bags, and Gabriel walked over and looked through them before he could set them down.

"In a hurry?" Jack said with a laugh.

"Not me. Gloriana. Ah, here we go."

Gabriel left for the griddle with all that was needed. Jack emptied the bags on the counter and began putting everything away.

"You found Taylor's closet?" Lin said while glaring at Gloriana.

"Yes, I hope no one minds since she is . . . well—"

"No, it's fine. Just don't get syrup on anything. She'll be back."

"Yes, of course, she will."

Lin focused on her coffee and Nomad's head on her lap. The griddle began snapping and sizzling, and Jack joined them at the table.

"Look, Jack," Lin said as she showed him Tayo's arm on fire.

"Good God! Is he okay?"

"Probably by now, yeah. Lee is good at what she does."

"That's just crazy. I'd go nuts if all that was happening to me."

"No, you'd be fine," said Lin. "I know you. You're really strong, Jack."

"Let's not test that, alright?"

"You are wise to not wish to play with things too hot," said Gloriana.

Jack turned to her and said, "Um, yeah, for sure. Not my thing."

"No, of course not. Thank you for going outside for supplies while others remained inside."

Jack squinted, scratched his chin, and said, "Well, it's for all of us, but you're welcome."

"You know," said Lin, "speaking of food: what else can you tell me about capital numbers? I tried it once, and it was a real mess."

"I am very distracted by hunger. Perhaps after—"

"Perhaps now."

"Yes. Okay. I can tell you something else that is obvious, an understanding you would likely find on your own."

"Sure, let's hear it."

"I told you before that some thought held by a Glyphin, one that she thinks is insignificant, can be the one that guides the power when using a capital number."

"Yeah, I remember that."

"Well, Lin, that short thought, which is not a large focus for the Glyphin, can be emphasized—made special—if it is a thought that is uncommon to the Glyphin."

"What does that mean? Uncommon how?"

"It must be a thought that does not align with her typical thoughts. It might be a thought that seems out of place. It can be because there is some emotion attached to it."

"I don't get it. Try to give me an example. Like just a while ago, I wondered if I could fill Nomad's bowl with chunks using a capital number. How would I do that?"

"I fear I will anger you with the idea that first came to my mind."

"You're already on my schedule to be finished off soon. Go ahead and tell me."

"Very well. This is just one possible path. Your intention could be to multiply the pieces of dog food in the bowl, but you must add a twist to mark the thought. One way could be that you know you are making the food because you love the dog. To mark the thought in an unusual way, you could think of your daughter and how much you love her. Then, for only a short time, you cast aside your feelings for her and entertain the idea of loving the dog more. Then, you reject that because it is not true. You have marked your intention of providing for the dog."

"That's crazy," said Lin.

"If you think about it, no, you will not convince yourself that it is valid."

"So, it's about having a thought I ordinarily wouldn't?"

"Yes. It could be considered like a forbidden thought. Gabriel," said Gloriana, "you do not doubt this, do you?"

"No. That makes sense."

"That's funny, Gabby," said Lin. "Right. It makes sense."

"I mean, it's believable. It's an old power, Lin, and the practices will seem odd, but that doesn't mean they don't work."

"Hey," said Jack, "what about all those arms? You know, that time you tried it? How does that fit?"

"Oh, um, I don't know, Jack. That was just some random thing, I think."

"You don't remember what you were thinking?"

"Jack, it was a weird fake world, and it all happened so fast, and then I was back home."

She turned to Gloriana and said, "And that's not the only way, right? A Glyphin can 'mark' a thought in other ways, even if she isn't trying to?"

"Yes, but that is the most reliable way."

"See, Jack? It probably wasn't anything I thought or did."

"Hey, I'm just trying to keep up. It's a lot to figure out."

"That's for sure."

"Well, that's enough magic talk for me," said Jack. "I need to get some supplies for the house work tomorrow. I'll be back soon."

"Okay, Jack. Are you taking Nomad?"
"Wouldn't leave without him."
Nomad barked once at the ceiling and panted.
Jack grinned and said, "No, you can't drive this time."
When he looked at Lin, he saw her squinting at him.
"It's a joke. We like to joke, that's all."

Chapter 24 – Jack's Flight No. 4

"I'm glad you're back, Jack. I need to run out real quick. Everything okay at your house?"

"Yeah, it's holding up fine. I dropped off the supplies, which are mostly just for cleaning and some masking for when I paint."

"Was Nomad any help?"

"He always is. You know that."

Jack reached down and patted the big furry head that was bumping into his leg, and he fluffed up the thick, red mane.

"You need to run out? For what?"

"Mostly just to get out of the house. I think I'll put some gas in the Temt8tion. I just didn't feel like leaving Gloriana alone here with Gabby."

"What do you think might happen? She's off in her room anyway, isn't she?"

"It's *not* her room. Yeah, that's where she is."

"So, what's wrong?"

"I still don't trust her, Jack, but there are things she can teach me and Taylor, too, when she comes back. Things about Glyphin powers that I'd probably never figure out on my own. She's had centuries to learn all of it."

"Well, it's probably good to be kind, like Gabriel always says. Not long ago, you said you didn't want to hurt anyone again, even if they deserved it."

"That's not how birds think, Jack. We just . . . I mean, *they* just do what has to be done. I might not have to kill her myself anyway. I can wait around for Taylor to come back and do it."

"Yeah, Taylor will be back soon, but there's probably no reason to kill her, is there?"

"You like her, Jack? You sound like you like her."

"No, um, it's not like that. I just can't decide if I think she still has powers or not. Besides, Taylor will be back soon, and she can't mess with either of you like before."

"That's true. She doesn't have powers anymore."

Jack looked at the floor, nodded, and said, "Nope, probably not."

"Gabby's watching TV, and I think Gloriana's probably taking a nap. How about if I run out and get some gas in the car? I'll only be gone a few minutes. I'll put Nomad out back. He'll be fine back there for a while."

"You don't want to take him?"

"Not this time. I could use a little bit of alone time. See you soon, okay?"

"Sure. I wouldn't mind some alone time too. I'll probably lie down myself as soon as you leave."

She gave him a quick kiss and left for the garage. When he heard the garage close shut, he went to Lin's bedroom and lay down above the blankets. As soon as his head rested on the cool covers, a deep sleep overpowered him.

*　*　*

A dream of Lin offering him more enticing views had only just begun, then he snapped open his eyes when he felt someone shaking his arm.

"We are alone. You will become my lover here and now."

Jack stared and tried to speak, but he couldn't, though he knew she hadn't used her powers on him yet.

"You will have no choice but to be quiet. I will take you with Taylor in the next room."

He wondered when Taylor had returned, but he quickly forgot that mystery when Gloriana's normal caramel eyes burst with a bright glow.

She'd snatched his soul away from him again, and he lay there paralyzed and staring into her eyes.

"I told you we would have another chance to become lovers. As for Taylor, perhaps I will make noise to wake her. Would it not be an extra excitement to have Lin's daughter watch us? She would witness the moment we become lovers."

Jack couldn't move a muscle as he lay there helpless.

"We do not have as much time as I would like. Only undo enough to free yourself for me."

Jack felt his hands moving toward his zipper as she forced his eyes to look at more than just hers. He saw that she wore only his long-sleeved white dress shirt, the one that he couldn't find in Lin's closet where he'd left it days earlier. Her long, wild dark hair coiled down far past her shoulders, and she swept it all behind her. When she stepped one leg up onto the bed, he saw that she wore a pair of Lin's spiky heels too.

He finished undoing things, pulled his jeans partway down his thighs, and felt his arms straighten themselves at his sides.

She smiled and said, "Good, Jack. You are happy. You are very happy already."

He tried again to move and found that he couldn't. She'd taken complete control of him after he'd followed her orders.

"You are happy because you want what Lin cannot give you. You wish to become my lover today."

He breathed deeply and couldn't stop his reaction.

"You will learn that your greatest ecstasy is to lie beneath me and look into my eyes. You will always crave it."

She knelt on the bed and swung one leg over him. When she lifted the shirt, Jack saw nothing but her with not even a tiny garment covering her.

"Once again, I control all but your natural reaction. I can force you to become my lover. You would witness us knowing each other in intimate ways, whether you choose it or not. However, I wish for you to choose."

He could only stare helplessly into her caramel eyes, and his heart jumped when he remembered that Lin could be home any minute.

"I urge you to stop your useless resistance and enjoy the pleasure of my touch. Know that my patience with this will expire, and I will force you if I must. You cannot escape being my lover. You know this to be true?"

Jack had to nod. He had no choice.

When his arms moved, he knew that he'd soon feel her sharp heels in his hands. He held them tightly while she let her shirt drop over his hands and unbuttoned it all the way. She flicked her hair back on each side and pulled the shirt wide open to expose herself, and Jack couldn't help but stare.

"For now, you may use your arms. Touch me as you wish. You cannot deny that you have wanted that."

The use of his arms had returned, but he resisted the urge to reach for her, and instead, he forced them to stay down at his sides.

"Your hands will be happy touching me. Let them find soft places, Jack, which your eyes already enjoy."

He refused, and after her eyes flashed, he had no choice. His hands each found a place, and Gloriana said, "That is better, Jack. Even as you resist, I am teaching you how pleasurable it is to enjoy me. You will weaken."

He felt his fingers gain even more enthusiasm as he explored every detail.

"You are a happier man when you touch me this way. I wish to touch you in another way. It will not involve your hands."

He felt his eyes driven lower to view her as she waited so close above him.

"Do you see, Jack? Imagine how I will feel when I hold you in a way you will learn to crave. Your excitement grows. I will not rush to make you my lover—we will take time, and perhaps Lin will soon find us."

She'll be home any minute, Jack thought. You need to get out of her bedroom!

"I can use my power to enjoy you as I see fit. Perhaps I want her to see us. You could not stop that, could you?"

No, he thought, you can't be serious, as he felt his head shaking from side to side.

"No, of course, you cannot. Did you hear that? I just heard a vehicle door close."

He'd heard it, too, and his heart pounded.

"Lin is home, but I still wish for you to submit. We will take that chance as lovers so often do. You do not mind because you are close to accepting my offer."

Jack had a quick moment of wondering if he'd nod on his own if he could because his imagination couldn't be controlled either.

"Do I feel good in your hands? Am I not much more enjoyable to touch than Lin could ever be? You can nod on your own now if you wish."

Jack felt a regained control and ability to nod, and though he wanted to, he wouldn't. Within seconds, bright caramel left him no choice.

"I am patient, Jack. You will learn, and we will take our time."

She kept her caramel eyes fixed on his as she smiled and looked down on him.

"Did you hear the large door to the car's room close? I am sure that is what I just heard. She will be inside the house any second."

He'd heard the door, too, and Gloriana grinned and shook her head.

"Lin is so close, but I am closer. Hold my heels, and remember that you cannot resist me."

He felt his hands move to hold her heels, and she brushed her hair back over both shoulders. With both hands, she held herself and forced him to focus on the sight.

"You do not care if Lin finds us because you know how good it would be with me?"

He nodded and wished he hadn't.

"It would be better with me than it ever was with Lin?"

All he could do was nod.

"Yes, you will want only me. You will not ever want Lin again. Only me. Only like this."

Still holding her heels, his staring eyes moved from her glowing eyes to what her hands held for him to view.

"You are strong, but I can wait for you to weaken. Already, a part of you wishes to choose me as your lover. We will not hide, and we will accept whatever happens."

She placed her warm palms on his chest, and when her hair cascaded down on either side, it framed the mesmerizing caramel lights.

God, he thought, I just heard the door to the garage. She's in the house!

"She is inside the house now. But she does not know that we will soon be lovers, here in her bed."

Jack felt his heart pounding and looked back into her bright caramel eyes.

"You are very happy here. I know now how much you like us together in Lin's bed. We will enjoy each other here many more times."

He nodded.

"Lin is very near now, and you know you do not want her. She can never make you as happy as I can. You do not wish to ever touch her again."

Jack had to shake his head, and he expected a knocking on the bedroom door at any second.

"Jack, I'm home."

He heard her in the kitchen when her keys rattled on the countertop.

"She will walk in and see us now. Let us make it memorable for her. I know you want that too."

She rose up on her knees, and with one hand, she twisted her shirt tight up around her waist, high enough to uncover herself.

Jack knew that Gloriana's back faced Lin's bedroom door, and he could imagine the view from the doorway.

"Lin will open the door soon. She will be surprised to see you with me in her bed. She will see that you have undressed me."

He couldn't speak, and he couldn't fight himself free of her.

"She will see that you demand me to be naked for you in her bed."

He stared into her eyes, knowing that the door would soon open.

"She will see your enthusiasm while I hold this shirt out of our way. I know you are very happy this way, Jack."

He only stared into her lit-up eyes as his heart thumped in his chest.

"Lin will know that she left only for a moment, and now we are together in her bed."

There were more sounds in the kitchen.

"Feel the warmth of my skin against your legs. Look into my glowing eyes as your heart pounds and you know the door will open any second. These are feelings you can never have with Lin. Only with me. Only like this."

His hands were forced to move up to hold her waist while she gazed down at him with her shirt held out of the way.

"And when she screams your name, you will agree to be my lover, and her screaming will only make it feel good for us both."

He waited for his head to nod, but it didn't.

Gloriana said, "When she opens the door, you will realize it is already too late—Lin will banish you. Then, you will know that accepting me is all you have left."

He heard Lin's heels clicking on the wood floor as she approached her bedroom.

Jack watched Gloriana twist her shirt tighter to make sure that she was uncovered from her waist down.

"She draws near. There is nothing to block her view of how you remove my clothing when she is gone."

Lin's heels fell silent in the hallway. Gloriana spoke very softly.

"Lin is right outside the door now. Her hand will be on the doorknob in seconds. After she sees us, you will submit, then I will take you very, very slowly. You will not care that she stares at us in shock."

The footsteps stopped.

"Jack, I'm going to see Nomad in the backyard. See you in a second."

"I'll come with you, Mom."

Oh God, Jack thought. Taylor's awake too? She's right outside Lin's bedroom door! Taylor might open the door and see me in Lin's bed beneath Gloriana?

Seconds later, Jack heard the back door slam shut.

"There, you see? We are alone in Lin's house. Now, I will pretend that they will stay outside for an hour."

She continued smiling down at a silenced, helpless Jack.

"I will take a lot of time with you now. We both know that we do not have an hour, but I will pretend that we do. They will come inside soon, but still, we will not hurry. And when they both look in, this is what they will see."

She held her shirt tightly around her waist with one hand, and with the other, she brushed her wild mane over her shoulders.

"I will wait as long as it takes, Jack. I like how happy you are when I play with you like this. Soon, that door will open."

He wished that he could push her aside and run out of the room, but his hands kept holding her waist as she looked down on him with burning caramel eyes.

Nomad began barking in the backyard.

Thank God the window's too high for any of them to see in, Jack thought.

"They want you outside with them, and you are here with me. You will soon be my lover while they play outside the window. They do not know that you are playing too. With me."

He stared helplessly into her eyes. He heard a rapping on the window, and Taylor said, "Jack, come out and join us!"

And Lin said, "Honey, let him sleep. We'll wake him up soon. Come on, let's chase Nomad!"

"See? We do have time. But surely they will surprise us before I am done with you. They would not guess that they would ever see you like this."

Jack's heart raced as he had to nod and keep touching the soft skin of her waist.

"Perhaps at the moment she turns the doorknob, I will not wait for you to choose. I will force you to be my lover."

His hands squeezed harder.

"Oh, I think you like that idea. You want Lin and Taylor to see us. You want them to know what we do in Lin's bed."

He tried again to close his eyes, but he couldn't. All he did was nod and try to focus on Lin.

"Good, Jack. Now I will free you, and you will choose to be my lover, no matter what might happen."

Jack felt control of his body return to him, and he knew that he could throw her off of the bed, but she felt good in his hands. And her skin was soft, at least as soft as Lin's, and the way she shed her caramel light down on him, just the thought that Lin and Taylor would open the door and see that, seeing how happy he was with her kneeling above him, and—

"No!"

He tightened his grip on her waist and was instantly recaptured by two caramel explosions.

"Oh, Jack, that was better. It took you a second or two. Soon, you will be mine."

He felt his head nodding.

"If Lin and Taylor were about to open the door to see us, if you had just enough time to hide in the closet, would you want me to let you run?"

His head shook from side to side.

"Good. We will not leave Lin's bed. I do not wish to hurry."

He heard more rapping on the window and Taylor's voice.

"Mom, boost me up. Let me peek in there."

"Okay, Honey. Step in my hands."

Nomad barked.

Jack's heart raced.

"Now, Taylor will surely see, and this is what she will see."

Gloriana slid her shirt down over her shoulders, shook it loose behind her, and tossed it to the floor. Jack's head turned to look at the window, and he saw both of Taylor's hands. He turned back to look at how excited Gloriana had become as she knelt high above him.

"Hold onto the sill, Taylor. Try to pull yourself up there."

"I'm almost there, Mom. Just a little bit higher!"

"Jack! Jack, Taylor wants you to wake up!"

Nomad barked.

Jack's heart pounded.

"Taylor will see us soon. She will never forget the sight."

"Higher, Mom!"

"She will scream, and they will rush into the house. It will all happen in seconds. Think about what they will see from the doorway, Jack."

Jack knew what they'd see and heard Lin calling his name and Nomad barking.

"The door will open in seconds, Jack. Taylor will watch us. I want her to see you holding my heels."

His hands reached down to hold both of her spikes, and he heard Lin calling his name again in the backyard. Taylor, too, as she pulled herself higher, trying to look into Lin's bedroom window. And Nomad barking. All at the same time.

"Mom, it's too high. Let me down."

"Okay, Hon."

"I'm going inside to wake him up, Mom. Right now!"

"Choose the pleasure that I will bring to you. Be my lover, Jack."

Jack stared, held Gloriana's heels, and fought to hold an image of Lin in his mind while also imagining the ecstasy Gloriana could give him right there in that moment if he'd only agree.

"No, Honey, let's let him sleep. Come on and chase Nomad with me!"

"Okay, Mom."

Nomad barked.

As the voices outside faded, Gloriana shook her head and smiled down at him.

"They did not see us, but I know that you almost chose to be my lover. When you do, we will be lovers many times in Lin's bed while they are home too. We will be reckless lovers, and we will not care, Jack."

Maintaining total control, she smiled and lay down over him, forcing his hands to reach up and hold her behind. He felt her lips hot and wet, and her tongue deep in his mouth, and she was so close he could see nothing but shiny caramel.

She broke the kiss and said, "Good, Jack. We will try this again soon. In Lin's bed."

She stood beside the bed, put on her shirt, and walked to the door. Jack breathed deeply and listened to the sound of her heels on the cold wood floor of Lin's bedroom and the distant voices through the glass.

"It is best if they find you here. You were only asleep and did not hear them. That is your plan."

He nodded.

"Sweet dreams, Mr. Jack."

She smoothed down her cinnamon gown and gave him a quick smile.

Jack blinked and stared at her.

Then, she tightened the belt in her jeans, pulled up her sweatshirt hood, and laughed at the ceiling.

Jack blinked twice.

After buttoning the very last button of Jack's white shirt all the way up to the collar, her smile left her, and she saluted once with each hand. Her eyes flashed, she blew him a kiss, the door opened on its own, she backed herself through it, and it closed by itself.

Jack's life returned to him, his eyes snapped shut, and he felt the lingering reaction of their encounter with every pound of his heart, and though his agitation nearly shook him off of Lin's bed, sleep wrestled him into its darkness.

*　*　*

"Jack. Jack, wake up."

He opened his eyes to see Lin's bright green eyes looking down at him. She blinked three times and stared.

"Did you have a good nap, Jack? It took a while to wake you up."

"I guess. I must have been more tired than I knew. Did you just get home?"

"I returned about ten minutes ago. We went to the outside to play with the dog for a while."

"Taylor's back?"

She frowned and said, "Where did she go, Jack?"

"Oh, I, uh . . . I don't—"

"She tried to peek in the window, but I could not lift her up that high."

"Well, that's good."

"And why is that good?"

"Um . . . she wouldn't have seen anything. It wouldn't be worth the trouble."

"She wanted to rush in and wake you up too."

"Oh, probably just best to let me sleep. Hey, why don't you join me?"

He hooked the pocket of her jeans and pulled her closer.

"Jack, I think maybe you had better just rest."

"I can rest later. It's you I need most."

"Well, you will just have to move beyond that, will you not?"

"Uh, what do you mean?"

"I like you just fine, but I do not see us ever doing that again."

"You mean—"

"Yes. Come on, Jack. We have had some good times, but they were not all that good, and they were long ago. I am done."

Jack stared up at her with his mouth moving, unable to form words.

"You said you were having strange dreams, did you not? I bet they were about someone else, were they not?"

"I . . . uh, I mean—"

"You do not have to admit it. I can tell. Here is the deal: whoever she is, she is lucky to have you."

"What? How could—"

"Is she a real, live woman, Jack? I bet she is. Is she attractive? Does she look good when she is naked for you? Do not resist her. Take her every chance you get. You might as well because I will never be your lover again."

Jack could only stare up at her calm eyes.

"Really, Jack. You can have her right in this bed if you want. I just do not care anymore. You know what? I am not sure I ever did."

She patted the top of his head, walked back to the door, and said, "I will come get you when dinner is ready. It will be about a half of an hour. Sweet dreams, Jack."

"You know, maybe it's better if I don't sleep. I should probably—"

"You look very tired. Maybe more sleep will help. Go back to your dream lover, Jack."

She left, closed the door behind her, and though Jack fought to stay awake, he could not.

* * *

Jack awoke to the clamor of conversation and pans banging in the kitchen. The sound of a hushed voice rode along with warm breath in his ear.

"Jack, I heard Lin. She said we have a half of an hour before dinner is complete."

He opened his eyes and found that Gloriana lay beside him, and his arm was around her. Her lips were against his ear as she whispered to him.

"But you must know that there is no real risk of us being caught. She will not care if she sees us together."

She rubbed his chest with her left hand.

"They have all left us alone, even the dog, because they know we belong together. They all want us to be lovers. Must I take control of you, or will you stop denying your feelings?"

Jack hesitated and stared.

239

He never saw the flash, but he did feel his soul stolen from his body. Then, he felt her gently turn his head to face hers, and their lips met. He didn't want to, but he lost himself in her warm, wet lips and her tongue darting playfully into his mouth.

"Do I kiss better than Lin? Do my kisses excite you more than hers ever could?"

He'd run out of patience with the constant nodding, but still, he nodded to answer her.

"Enjoy my kisses. Lin will never willingly kiss you again."

She pressed her lips into his, and he didn't want to believe her. But he couldn't stop himself from passionately returning her kiss.

"If Lin saw us only kissing as I lay naked with you, she would tell you herself that you should do much more. Can you deny that you wish to do more?"

He fought and lost: his head shook from side to side.

She gave him a quick kiss, then pulled away only enough to say, "Next time, Jack, my beauty will control you. Your desire for me will control you. Is that correct?"

He nodded.

"I will not always need to take your life. Be my lover, and you will not want Lin anymore. When you want pleasure, you will want me. Only me."

He didn't have time to nod.

"Lin and Taylor are both only steps away. Neither one cares what you do."

She kissed him more.

"I undressed in my room and put on only Lin's heels. I passed Taylor in the hall on my way to you, and she only smiled and nodded."

Jack felt his excitement growing as he stared up at her. Could that really be true? he wondered.

"Before I opened the door, Lin approached me. She stood behind me and swept all of my hair back for me. When she had finished making sure I looked good for you, she left for the kitchen, unconcerned about what we would soon do."

Her wild mane dragged across his face as she rolled on top of him. Her eyes glowed into his and allowed him no freedom. She placed her hands on his chest and pushed herself up to sit on his lap.

"I wear Lin's heels for your enjoyment. You are happiest when you hold them."

His hands reached down to hold her sharp heels, and he nodded.

"It is the only choice left for you, Jack. Do not reject what your feelings tell you."

She put her hands on her hips and shook her hair back as her caramel light shone down on him.

"They might both leave us alone, or they might both come to see. We will take our time. I will remain naked with you as lovers often do."

When they heard Lin's heels approaching, Gloriana turned her head back toward the door and grinned.

"That must be Lin. Listen to her steps. She will surely find amusement that you allow a naked and willing woman so close, yet you do not take her."

Jack wondered if it was true before his head nodded.

"Taylor will see too. Would you rather they see us doing what lovers do?"

Jack imagined being Gloriana's lover as the door opened. His head nodded before he could consider nodding it himself.

The clicking of Lin's heels retreated back toward the kitchen.

"That was a missed opportunity. I would enjoy providing such a display for them. Now, you must know that we are meant to become lovers. Enjoy all that I offer. Whatever fantasy you can imagine, Jack."

His hands were forced to touch her thighs, and they began touching them all over.

"You have never felt this much excitement with Lin. You know that to be true."

Her skin looked smooth and soft, and Jack wished he could run out of the room, plead with Lin to take him back, but he could only caress her thighs.

"This will be your best ecstasy. You will never want to touch Lin again. She will never let you anyway."

He stared into brightly glowing caramel pools.

"She dresses very sexy, and she has done many things for you, but you know that I will do more. There are no limits to the ways I will pleasure you."

He watched her smiling down on him with her eyes glowing.

"Imagine the pleasure of becoming my lover as you hold Lin's heels as we lie in Lin's bed, yet I am not Lin. You are already forgetting her."

He fought her hold on him, but he was powerless.

"Admit it: you have never loved her?"

He felt the order to shake his head, but he fought it just long enough to pause and remember all the times they'd spent together, all the closeness and special moments. They'd been through so much together. He knew that he loved Lin and wanted to get her back, no matter what it might be like with Gloriana.

He saw her eyes brighten, and when the command came again to shake his head, he couldn't resist.

"Good, Jack. I knew that you have never loved her. We are making progress."

She squirmed herself around on his lap, grinning down at him the entire time.

"You will soon be my lover, Jack. You already feel that we are very close, do you not?"

His head nodded, and he knew that it was the correct answer even though he hadn't given it. She wiggled around more and became still before sighing.

"There, Jack. We are very close. You will remember the sweet agony you now feel when next I am naked for you."

He stared up at her and believed that she was right: the agony *was* sweet.

"You do not need to answer. I know that your resistance is becoming weak. Lin does not want you. I do. I will be naked again, and so will you. We will become lovers next time, Mr. Jack, whether you resist me or not."

She lay down over him, and he felt every soft curve of her body warm against him and saw her bright eyes near to his. It came as no surprise when his hands again found her hard and sharp heels.

Barely able to prop open his eyes, he saw only two points of caramel, which had fallen far back to glow in the boundless night. They drew nearer and became four, arranged like a square.

He blinked twice, but they only doubled again. Then again. And they began racing toward him.

After three more blinks, he saw countless caramel lights flying toward him, and before they struck, they became an unbroken ocean of caramel. Her skin caressed him everywhere, and he couldn't help but imagine how only a thin layer of cloth had separated them as he sank into the smoldering depths, down to where only darkness survived.

* * *

"Jack. Jack, dinner's ready. Time to get up."

He opened his eyes and reached to each side as he forced all of his breath out in a single blast.

He inhaled and said, "Oh, Lin, I did fall asleep again."

"Still with the crazy dreams, Jack?"

"I'm afraid so. I even dreamed that Taylor was home. She's not, right?"

"Jack, you really are silly. If she came back, I'd wake you up, that's for sure."

Jack sighed and said, "Lin, I need you to get in bed, even just for a minute, alright? I mean . . . if you still want to."

Lin stared for a few seconds, saw the pleading in his eyes, then said, "Sure, Jack. Okay, I can do that. I'll always want to."

She lay down next to him, and he pulled her in close. He didn't kiss her. He just held her tight.

"Oh, Jack. Don't worry about those zany dreams of yours. Everything is okay."

She closed her eyes and enjoyed the innocent embrace for several minutes.

"Okay, Jack, things will be burning soon. I better go."

She kissed him and stood up.

"You still look tired. Maybe you're coming down with something."

"Yeah, Lin. I love you. That's what it is."

"Jack, whatever you're dreaming, don't stop."

She blew him a kiss and turned toward the door.

"No, wait! Wait for me, alright?"

"Sure, Jack."

He hurried himself out of the bed, never taking his eyes off of her, and took her outstretched hand. When she left for the kitchen, so did he.

Chapter 25 – Lin's Flight No. 5

"Dinner was excellent," said Jack. "And if no one needs me, I should get in a few quick hours at my house."

"We'll be fine," said Lin. "What's going on this time?"

"I just want to get the first coat of paint on the walls in the living room. It won't take long."

"Are you bringing Nomad?"

The big dog's head rested on his lap, and Jack flopped his ears around and said, "Maybe not this time. I'm not sure any buyer would want paint textured with Tibetan Mastiff hair."

"Oh, good point."

"He can keep you and Gabriel company. Oh, and what's-her-name too."

"Now, you're just being silly again. You remember her name."

"It sure isn't 'Sunny.'"

"No, it sure as hell isn't. Have a good trip. I think I'm just going to lie down for a while. If you're late, don't think that you can't wake me, okay?"

He pulled her in tight and gave her a kiss.

"Plan on it."

He kissed her again and left through the front door.

*　*　*

"If you don't mind," said Gabriel, "I'm going to enjoy one of this time's greatest luxuries: falling asleep on a couch to the sound of cartoons."

"Well, I don't know if everyone agrees about the cartoons, but the couch thing sounds about right. Have a good nap, Gabby."

Gabriel left for the living room, and Nomad followed, offering the sight of his bushy, swishing tail to her as he rounded the corner.

Lin thought it through, let out a deep breath, and came to a conclusion. She stood looking out through the kitchen window at the deep snow marred only by a trampled area where she'd planted Jack and Nomad and their tracks to the house. She crossed her arms and couldn't stop herself from smiling, recalling the world she'd already visited three times too many.

With a quick analysis, she concluded that it had only become impossible to find her way back from that world she'd visited a few times because she'd used her powers. Things had gone crazy after she'd tried the new Glyphin technique—using a capital number even though she didn't understand enough about it.

Without her powers, she figured, that world would stay normal. No matter how intriguing it became, she'd only have to stare long enough to see her escape path, the single black dot that would expand, cover her, and end her life. The key was obviously to leave her powers behind on her next flight.

Jack was off doing some necessary work on his project house, and she promised herself that she'd think about him and how much he loved her later.

Gabriel and Nomad were eating and watching TV. The sounds of the cartoons sometimes sneaked into the quiet room. And, of course, Taylor still hadn't returned. Gloriana had learned how to use the laundry room and was putting a load into the washer. And even though she'd given more instruction on using capital numbers, Lin knew that wouldn't matter. Not this time. Not for her to visit as a woman with no powers.

Inside her large walk-in closet, even the cartoons had given up. Only silence surrounded her. And clothing. Jeans, t-shirts, and sweaters on one side along with all manner of sneakers and boots. And on the other side, the clothes that she liked better, and Jack liked better, and a whole lot of others waiting for her to rejoin their fake world liked much better.

Oh, this is kind of silly, she thought as she reached for her choices on the fun side of the closet. I don't need to get dressed here first. My intent will set me up just how I want to be dressed as soon as I arrive.

Still, she scoffed and hung the skirt and blouse up near her mirror and got undressed, catching her reflected smile several times. The skirt slipped on easily—the first garment she put on. Heels followed, her highest, and she sat to fasten the straps around her ankles. She took from its hanger a thin, sheer blouse that she knew fit tightly and wouldn't hide the details that she'd want to be seen in that dim hallway.

Sheer and white always worked, she told herself with a grin.

Dressed just how she wanted, she closed the closet door from the inside and held its handle. She let out a deep breath and intended a flight back to the hotel but this time, with no powers at all. She suspected they'd still be part of her, but somehow, they wouldn't work there. She wouldn't be able to find her mayhem waiting just beneath her surface. No Glyphin powers would be at her command. And she couldn't find the magic of anything if she'd seek it.

Her heart sped up at the thought of being powerless, even in an imaginary world where nothing she did mattered.

She visualized each of those two strangers using their strong arms to hold her and prevent any escape. Then, she added the feeling of knowing she'd have no powers to resist any of it, and she felt her knees get weak. She knew that she had to go one more time. Just one more time to the world of that fantasy but only to come closer to, but never to live through, its conclusion and see if it really had a hold on her.

A brief pang of guilt hit her, so slight and distant that it could have been part of the cartoon in the living room, and she thought of Jack. But Jack's love for her was true and would be waiting for her when she returned. It could only help for her to work through these questions and doubts and put them behind her. It really would be just kind of like a dream. Besides, all that attention seemed necessary for her recovery.

When a tiny black spot appeared on the closet door, she remembered Gabriel saying that it was real for her—what she experienced there really did happen to her, no matter how intense, physical, and personal. If she dwelt there long enough, without the power she'd need to resist whatever was planned for her—or that she'd planned for herself—that would really be her doing it. Every little detail of it.

She bit her lip and felt she stood on a precipice, and when the uncertainty of being back in that hotel without her mayhem began to evolve into anticipation that replaced the fear, she intended that her powers not be part of the flight.

Already feeling weaker and more helpless, perhaps about to become an unwilling victim in a world of her own creation, she intended for her powers to be unreachable in the world that her intent had built just as a dark smudge appeared on her door. Her eyes could not look away.

With one last faint, far-off spike of panic clamoring to get her in its grip, the night covered her. Immediately, a white dot appeared and coated her entirely, returning her as a powerless woman to the world she'd intended, leaving her subject to the whims and desires and demands of those she knew waited there only for her.

* * *

The first thing Lin saw was the peephole she'd stared at so desperately the last time she'd visited. No sirens wailed, and no lights flashed. She looked down with a smile at the clothes from her closet, short and tight and looking just the way she'd wanted.

She flicked back her blond mane, looked to her right, and saw with relief that no abomination of a man struggled on the floor. But two men were walking toward her, one whom she'd seen before in the elevator and one other that looked somewhat familiar. Both looked strong and determined and focused on her alone.

"It's too late to change your mind," said the familiar one with a smile as he grabbed her right arm.

"Hey, don't I know you?"

"Maybe. Lots of people know me."

The other man took a step to her left side, where he grabbed her left arm.

"Nice outfit. Really hot. Don't forget how you said you'd make your appearance, though."

"I was just—"

"Save it. Let's get on with this already," said the man to her right as he swiped a key and pushed the door in.

Both men forced her into the room, and she took quick, careful steps in her heels to keep up. One hit the light switch, which lit up the foyer but left the rest of the spacious suite barely illuminated. She saw a plush couch and several upholstered chairs with ottomans. A door on the left was opened, and there was just enough light to see a large bed covered in pillows and fine art on the walls.

"I'm not sure if—"

The man to her right spun her around and pressed her back into the wall next to the bathroom doorway. He held her by her shoulders, and though he still smiled, showing perfectly white teeth, Lin didn't see much humor in his eyes.

Okay, she thought, maybe this isn't so amusing anymore.

She looked for her mayhem and found what she feared she'd find: nothing. Looking as deeply into the stillness inside as she could, she found that every last trace of her powers was gone. She was in a hotel room with two men who had no reason to let her go, and she had no powers to resist them.

She tried to pull each arm free, but all that did was confirm how weak she was compared to them. She remembered the beginning of mild panic that had come for her back in her closet, but there, in the fake reality she'd created, she mostly felt her heart beating strong and a mild electricity beginning to flow through her.

"Get ready in there," he said and gestured toward the bathroom. "Don't take too much time, or you can bet we'll come in and drag you out."

Lin turned only enough to glance into the bathroom.

"Okay, okay, but you'll have to let me go."

"Oh, you know what, Honey? I don't feel like letting you go. Maybe you should give me a little appetizer right now."

Lin felt his hands move to her shoulders and push down hard, and though she knew that her legs were strong, she found that she didn't want to resist too much, and she ended up on her knees on the plush carpeting.

"Hey, what the—"

"Just like that," he said to his partner, "she's right there where she belongs."

"Damn right. Talk about room service."

The man in front of her held her head in both hands, and the man behind her gathered up her hair. Lin felt her heart pounding and looked again for her mayhem. She found nothing at all except for an urge to flee, which yielded to excitement.

She looked straight ahead at the man's trousers, visible through his opened jacket, then up into his eyes. He grinned down at her.

"Is that what you want, Beautiful? How about if the two of us get a little sample before the rest of them go crazy on you?"

With her heart pounding and her powers nowhere in sight, Lin studied the man again, and she was sure that she'd seen him before. But she couldn't have, she knew, because she'd fabricated all of this, including him.

"Well, you're not leaving me any choice, are you?"

She figured a smile could only help.

From behind her, the man said, "No, Honey. We know that's the way you like it."

The grip on her hair tightened, and she couldn't turn her head to either side. She had one last thought of Jack, but she reminded herself that it was only a fake world, and none of these men were real. Feeling no powers inside and no way to get to them, and a strange and growing exhilaration like she'd imagined she'd feel, she said, "Sure. Like you said: There's always time for room service, right?"

She looked up and held his gaze, promised herself that she'd find a way to deal with any feelings of guilt later, and reminded herself that it was all fake. Kind of like a dream. She could do what they wanted her to do, and she could even allow herself to enjoy it. Kind of like an amusement park. Besides, she had no choice.

His friendly smile returned with a loud laugh. She felt her hair released, and the man who'd forced her to kneel for him reached down for her arms and helped her up. She felt her hands instinctively smoothing down her skirt.

"Hey, just kidding. We can wait. We know you won't disappoint us. Not any of us."

Still trying to identify the stranger, and with her heart still beating a strong rhythm, she said, "Do I look like a woman who'd disappoint you?"

He looked her up and down and said, "No, you sure as hell don't. Now, get yourself ready. The plan was for us to wait in the next room, but word got out, and now there are too many. When you come out of that bathroom, you damn well better be ready."

Lin nodded, and knowing that she'd never take her flight that far, said, "Oh yeah, I'll be ready. Just how many of you are there?"

"Honey, I lost count. There are more showing up all the time."

She felt like her heart had skipped a beat.

"All for you. Every last one. You won't mind a few extras, will you?"

"Um, no, of course not."

The man behind her said, "And don't think of saying no to anything. Got it?"

Lin cleared her throat, felt her heart beating, and said, "I never do."

He took the bottom hem of her skirt in his right hand and began lifting it. Lin fought the urge to swat his hand away but only for a second. Then, it surprised her that she started to wish that he'd pull it up high enough to see the delicate, lacy garment underneath—just to observe his reaction.

That would be only like standing there for Jack, she told herself as she held still and looked into his eyes.

But he held it up only an inch or two while he stared at more of her exposed thighs and grinned, and she felt his hand rough against her skin.

"I bet you always wear short skirts, don't you?"

Lin again saw something familiar in his eyes, but all she did was say, "I do like showing off these legs."

"Yeah, you sure do. But you won't be needing any of this. Understand?"

"Oh, I understand. It'll be just me and these heels. Think that's a sight you might all like?"

His smile grew.

"Yeah, that's just the way I've imagined you. Don't take too long."

"I won't."

"My name's Luke, and this is Mack."

No, that can't be! Lin thought. Those are the names of Jack's two best friends!

"Pleasure to meet you."

"Pleasure for us, for sure."

Obeying a voice inside that told her to play along, she said, "Mm-hmm. Are you sure we haven't met?"

He laughed while rubbing her skirt down over her thighs and said, "Well, that would be a surprise, wouldn't it?"

Lin still felt her heart beating as she watched them walk toward the door to the adjoining room. When it was opened, she saw it packed with other men and heard their laughter and conversations. He pulled the door closed, and she was alone in her half of the suite.

She waited for her heart to calm and knew that it was time to return. That was too close, she realized, and it was probably a bad idea to come there without her powers.

But she couldn't deny that it had been exciting, just like she'd imagined it would be. It wasn't just the rough treatment—it was the unchangeable reality of her being powerless to stop them. That had fueled the thrill higher than she would have guessed.

Knowing that she could find that black dot anytime she wanted, especially since they'd left her alone and without distractions, she decided that it wouldn't hurt to take a look in the bath if only to see if it lived up to her expectations.

She reached around the door jamb, found the switch, and lit up the large room. Her eyes were drawn first to the bathtub, which was large, clean, and inviting. She saw several thick, fluffy white towels hanging on the rack and everything she'd need to get ready lined up on the vanity.

Another glance around her half of the suite revealed the luxury and comfort of all the furnishings. Lamps on end tables now cast a subtle light about the room, and the door to the other side let in not a single sound. It would have been easy to believe that there was nothing beyond that door. There was no evidence that so many men had gathered there for her and for all they'd expected her to do. Even if she were to end up screaming and pleading, changing her mind about the whole deal, no one would hear. No one would come to her rescue.

I've been here really only a few moments, she thought, and since it's so quiet and peaceful, maybe hurrying back isn't necessary at all.

She walked into the bathroom and looked down into the tub. She saw that there were ports for jets, and in one corner near the wall sat a bucket of ice with a bottle of champagne. One delicate glass sat nearby on a white cloth napkin.

Oh my, she thought. That does look good. I haven't had a drink since coming back from the flock. And what's wrong with taking a quick bath in a dream world? Especially if I leave right after that?

A couple of turns of the knobs began to fill it up with water at just the temperature Lin liked. She watched it flow in for a moment before she began unbuttoning her blouse. A glance behind the door revealed a decorative hook with a padded hanger. She hung up the blouse before stooping down to loosen the straps around her ankles. With the shoes sitting side-by-side against the door that she'd closed and locked, she slipped out of her skirt, folded it neatly, and laid it on the vanity top. Her underwear was next, and everything found a place above her skirt.

Somehow, she knew she'd find it there, and she did: a dimmer switch for the lights. She turned it down to a comfortable level and saw that the water had filled to a generous depth. The porcelain knobs didn't make a sound as she stopped the flow, lifted one leg over the edge, and watched her painted toenails disappear beneath the surface. She stepped in and sat, and with a towel folded behind her, she leaned back and felt the heat soaking into her, relaxing every muscle and calming her heart after the tense encounter with Luke and Mack only moments earlier.

Maybe some champagne, she thought. Just a sip or two, then back to my own closet and Jack.

A loud pop sent the cork bouncing across the floor before it rested near her heels. The bottle tipped more than she'd planned, and she held a full glass. After putting the bottle back on ice, she took a sip. It tasted good, so she allowed herself a good swallow before setting the glass down.

She slipped farther down into the water. It felt better than real water—different, somehow—and she wondered how that could be. She also wondered if everything would have a different feel in this world. She knew that she'd find out if she rode the fantasy to its conclusion, something she knew that she would never allow herself to do.

She reached up for another sip and intrigued with the taste, decided to empty the glass. She set it down, let her hands dip into the hot water, and rubbed her thighs several times, savoring the luxury of it all. But she knew it had to end—she needed to return.

Soon, she told herself. She poured another glass and downed half of it. She noticed a small dial near the faucet and realized that the tub had a heater too. Warmer would be good, she thought and turned up the heat.

Heating the water will take some time, she told herself, finished the glass, and poured some more. After another sip, she could tell the water had warmed.

With eyes closed, she felt like she was melting there in that tub of hot water, in a hotel that didn't exist, in a world that only seemed real somewhere in the vast forever that no one could describe or comprehend. A magical place where absolutely anything could happen.

When her hands again found her thighs, she let them go wherever and do whatever they wanted. One decided to reach out for the glass, and the other chose to stay beneath the hot water. A pleasant thought of Jack and their times together occupied her for a moment, but the memory of being on her knees for two strangers nudged him off to the side. She didn't fight to get him back—she'd see him in no time anyway.

Instead, she finished her drink, set the glass down, and closed her eyes. What had started as imaginary water with the illusion of heat became as real as anything that she could remember. The alcohol sure was real, she thought as her thoughts lazily drifted back to moments earlier, wondering what might have happened if Luke hadn't changed his mind—if they'd kept her on her knees, helpless with her hair held tight, no powers to save her, no one to rescue her, just having to do what they wanted . . . do what she—

Oh God, she thought and snapped her eyes open. I almost fell asleep here!

What would that do? she wondered. Is it even safe to sleep in an imaginary world?

She sat up quickly and stepped out onto the floor, her wet skin warm and clean and dripping everywhere. A thirsty towel sat waiting, so she took it and began carefully blotting off all of the warm beads clinging to her skin. All over she used the towel, touching herself everywhere until she was completely dry. She dropped the damp towel to the floor, and with her toes, spread it out for a comfortable place to stand.

All I need to do now, she told herself, is to look somewhere, anywhere, and find that black spot, the one that will race toward me and take me home.

She delayed that for a moment to study herself in the mirror and saw that her hair could use a brushing. She almost laughed out loud, thinking that she didn't want to have to do it at home—it was much more fun to do it there.

So, she brushed it all back over her shoulders, taking her time and feeling the champagne, and she noted the glorious mane that fell far down her back. Realizing that a mirror wouldn't be the best place for the dark spot to appear, and knowing that she really did need to depart, she turned to face the closed bathroom door.

Her blouse hung there, reminding her that if she stayed, she wouldn't be wearing it. It was solid white, and she knew that that would work much better for finding some kind of spot. It amused her to realize that she didn't mind showing up naked in her closet, even though none of that made a bit of sense.

Her eyes were drawn down to her heels, and without any deliberations, she reached for them. Can't leave those here, she thought.

It took only seconds to get them in place, and she stood up to look again in the mirror. Considering how many eyes would soon be on her if she were to stay, which she wouldn't even if she wanted to, she made an effort to hold herself in the best posture she could. All the smooth skin and curves brought out a satisfied grin, and she knew that Luke and Mack and all the rest would like the sight, too, even though that would never happen. Those two and the rest of them would never, ever see her without any clothes. With just her heels. Fresh out of a hot bath. Like she was now. With all of them just beyond that one door, just waiting for her to turn that knob and walk out there for them.

She shook those pointless thoughts aside and wondered how she'd look naked with her hair brushed back and holding a full champagne glass. The chilled bottle rattled the ice in the bucket when she lifted it out, and she set the bottle and glass on the counter.

Oh, that's not good, she thought when she saw she'd already emptied half of the bottle, and it was a big bottle. But it sure was tasty.

Thinking it would be a dramatic entrance if she were to open the door and share the sight, and since it was only for the fun of it, she poured another glass so full that some spilled over the edge. She carefully held it up and turned to look at her reflection, and without thinking about it, she lifted the glass to her lips and welcomed half of it, enjoying the rush of bubbles.

Well, she thought, that does look good—I certainly look ready to give them all some entertainment. No, that's not right, she realized with a chuckle—I look ready for all of them to *take* whatever entertainment they want. She shook her head at her own grin in the mirror, knowing that none of that would ever happen.

But what about holding it in my left hand? How would that look to all of those strangers waiting for me?

She passed the glass to her left and looked again in the mirror. She smiled back at herself, thought that a view of her naked and drinking the champagne would generate some comments and cheers, and held her own gaze as she brought the glass up and finished it.

I sure didn't plan that! she thought with a bigger grin. But this whole world seems so much more relaxed now. It's just a fun place to visit, and even the alcohol has a surprising new intensity.

She set the glass down and wondered if she had time for a nap. Could she sneak out, lock the door to the adjoining room, crawl into that luxurious bed, and take a short nap? Probably not, she realized, not with all those strangers waiting for her because maybe they had a key anyway! Maybe they'd like to find her naked in that bed, though . . .

No, the nap would have to wait because it was time to go back.

Okay, she thought with a big smile, wearing only her heels and maybe a little drunk, too, was a good way to appear back at home. And who knows, maybe somehow, Jack would be waiting in the closet when she arrived. He wouldn't even ask her where she'd been or why her kisses tasted like champagne. He'd take her in his arms. They'd have a quick, passionate reunion there before anyone could discover them, and maybe she'd close her eyes and remember this sexy flight world, imagine herself still there while Jack took her, and maybe he'd overpower her just for the fun of it, just like those strangers soon would, then they'd—

A pounding on the bathroom door jerked her back to her fake reality.

"Hey! You're taking too long!"

"Oh, Luke. I, um . . . I'm almost ready. Just give me a minute, okay?"

"Just open the door. You're ready. God knows, all of us are."

Lin drilled her eyes into the white blouse hanging on the door. The spot. She had to find that darned black spot.

"I said, now!"

Lin knew that she couldn't answer. She couldn't break her concentration, even though it wobbled around a little after all of that champagne. Maybe more than a little. All she saw was white.

"I was thinking of watching out for you with all of them. Some of them, I think, plan to get rough. Now, you're on your own."

He pounded again.

Lin fought to clear her mind and saw a black dot so small that she could barely believe that was it. But she stared at it anyway. Until it moved. Her eyes followed it, but it rested there only a second and shifted again.

It must be that champagne! she thought.

"Mack, there's a key in the other room. Go get it."

"Gladly."

More pounding—each hit bouncing the black dot around. Lin's heart began to race.

"Hey, don't think you can change your mind now. We'll drag you out of there if we have to."

Lin stared. Luke pounded. The dot danced. She felt like belching from the champagne.

"Good man. Give me that key."

Lin heard metal striking metal and saw the doorknob begin to turn.

Her heart pounded, and the black dot finally held still. As it raced toward her, she felt only how thrilling it would be for the two men to force her out of there wearing only her heels, her skin still hot from the bath and her hair brushed back. She knew that they'd hold her arms tightly and drag her toward the bedroom, where there would be more strangers waiting. And through it all, she'd be powerless, and a little drunk, and helpless to whatever they wanted from her. She'd have no choice but to—

Lin died. Her lungs froze, and her feelings and thoughts left her. She had no heart and no memory of one.

She had only her intent and her unbreakable hold on it for whatever amount of time might pass in her real world before she'd return. If she could return.

A racing white light pulled a different world around her. Her life restarted, and she felt her heart still beating a strong rhythm as she held tightly the doorknob of her closet door.

That world was again lost somewhere in the unknowable forever, but the feelings remained with her. The memories stayed strong. She craved another glass of champagne.

Lin left the closet and stood in front of the mirror above her dresser to get undressed. She moved slowly, removing each garment and placing them on the dresser, wondering how it would be received if she'd do that in the suite she'd just left. Maybe a little strip show would be fun, she thought, knowing that she'd never recreate that alluring world again.

She kicked off her heels last and looked one more time at her smile in the mirror before donning a modest nightgown and climbing into bed.

I won't even think about that phony world again, she told herself. Except maybe to figure out who Luke was. Or maybe what might happen right after they open that door. Or five minutes after that. Or fifteen . . .

Chapter 26 – Jack's Flight No. 5

Jack crept into the bedroom and kept his eyes on the bed as he closed the door behind him. A few careful steps brought him to his side, where he quietly stripped down and snuck in under the covers. He watched Lin sleeping for several minutes, shook his head with a grin, and tried to wiggle his arm under her waist.

"Oh, Jack, you're back. Everything okay at the house?"

"Yeah, sure. It's all good. You know, I'm not sorry I woke you, in case you're wondering."

"I'm not sorry either," she said as she grabbed his other arm and pulled him close for a kiss.

"Damn, you feel good," he said and held her waist with both hands.

"Do I, Jack? How do I look, though?"

"Well," he said with a grin, "you're all covered up, so I really have no idea. No idea at all."

She kissed him and said, "Let's see what we can do about that, okay?"

"Oh, yeah. Get out from under these blankets. Maybe hit that lamp too?"

"Ooh, good idea."

Lin swung her legs out and stood, pulling her nightshirt down with one hand while switching on the dim nightstand lamp. She turned and stood facing him.

"You look good in white," he said with a big smile. "You look good in my arms too. Come here."

She smiled and said, "Not so fast. Just look at me."

She put her hands on her hips, pulled the material back to tighten it up, and shook her hair back.

"Tell me if you think you could overpower me."

"What? You're joking, right? With all the powers you have?"

"No, Jack. I mean, what if I didn't have those powers? And how about if we were fighting about something?"

"Like what?"

Lin paused to look at the ceiling before answering.

"Like, I don't know, maybe if I thought you liked Gloriana kicking you all the time."

"Oh, well, uh, I don't, so you—"

"But what if? What if I got mad and said you had to choose between us. What then?"

"Well, of course, I'd choose you, because you . . . you're—"

"Jack," she said with a grin, "I'm just playing. I don't think you like her. I'm just saying that if I was mad at you, and you wanted to, but I didn't, could I stop you?"

Jack shook his head and let out a deep sigh.

"I'm not sure where you're going with this, but you do look damn hot, and that's really all I can think about," he said with a grin.

She fought to keep her eyes from glowing, but she did hope they twinkled when she said, "I'm going to take a second and change. When I come back, maybe I won't even want you to touch me. How about that, Jack?" she said and raised her eyebrows twice.

"You wouldn't have a chance," he said with a grin. "I'd get ahold of you, and you'd never get away. You'll find out."

"Well, then I think I'll just slip on something else. Be right back."

She looked back over her shoulder on her way to the closet and saw that his eyes didn't meet hers—they were enjoying a different part of her altogether.

* * *

Jack tipped his head on his pillow to listen to Lin finish brushing her teeth and rustling clothing on the rack behind the bathroom door. He crossed his arms as he lay above the blankets and stared at the door.

When she'd switched out the light and stepped into the mostly dark bedroom, he saw that she'd put on a lacy white nightie so short he could see her thin white underwear. She wore a pair of heels, and he looked all the way up her long, bare legs and past the hem of her lingerie, where he saw the loose, sheer cloth held out from her by two noticeable features.

She stood beside the bed and said, "See anything you like?"

"Oh yeah, but mostly I see things I crave and adore," he said as he looked only up into her eyes.

"My Cowboy, you're being especially sweet lately. I'm not complaining, that's for sure. And you won't have to fight me."

"Right, because I'd take you too easily, my Cowgirl. God, you look good."

"Aw, thanks, Jack. Any room in that bed for me?"

"Hell, yeah. You're my favorite kind of dream."

"Oh, not like all those other ones that have been bugging you?"

"The only ones I want are when you're the star."

She climbed up and sat on his lap, facing him, and said, "I feel like being a star for you right now. How does that sound?"

She smiled and raised her eyebrows a few times.

"Like heaven? No . . . better."

He reached around her waist and leaned her down toward him for a long, deep kiss.

"Oh my, Jack, you're not so sleepy this time. We'll have to talk about those dreams of yours some other time. Right now,"—she rose to her knees with her hands still on his pillow—"I need help with some silly little thing."

Jack smiled only until her lips pressed against his, and while kissing her, he reached with both hands for her. He found a thin strand of elastic hugging her hips, and he began slipping it down over her skin, taking his time.

"I'm glad you're such a big help, Cowboy."

She rolled onto her side next to him and helped him reach his goal, then she reclaimed her seat.

"Are you watching, Jack?"

"Oh, yeah."

As she lifted her lingerie up over her head and tossed it over her shoulder, she said, "I kind of like the view up here. Do you like what you see?"

"Oh my God, yeah. Come here."

He held both of her wrists and tried to pull her down for a kiss, but she resisted. He pulled harder, and she fought him while seeing that he watched her bouncing and swaying from the effort.

"You like that?"

He still didn't look into her eyes and said, "Oh, God yeah."

She squirmed around on his lap, and he still held her wrists.

"I like that look in your eye. I like being looked at like that."

She sighed and leaned forward over and past him, held the headboard, and said, "Like your view now?"

Jack didn't answer, at least not with words, although she did feel him nodding.

"Let's just make sure I don't slip off your lap."

She shifted her hips around with Jack lending a hand.

"Mm . . . just like a dreamworld."

*   *   *

Jack awoke to a warm fingertip against his lips. He resisted the urge to speak but dared to look. He found that Gloriana's caramel eyes were inches from his.

"We are not alone, but we will act as if we are."

She touched his chin and turned his head to his left, and he saw Lin still facing away from him and sleeping.

"You have seen Lin. Now, look upon me."

He turned to his right, and Gloriana stood up so that he could see her wearing a white nightie just like Lin's. Hers was short, too, and Jack saw that she wore nothing else, causing his heart to jump despite Lin lying beside him. He looked up higher and saw her squeezed tight into the sheer material cut so low that it barely covered her.

"What . . . I mean, what are you—"

"I gave her a drug. I put it in her water glass. She might still respond, but she is mostly unconscious and will not remember anything."

"Is she going to be alright? You shouldn't have—"

"She is in no danger. While she sleeps beside you, we will, at long last, become lovers. Must I take control of you, or do you see that I am who you truly desire?"

Jack frowned and said, "There's no way I'll ever—"

Two blazing caramel eruptions silenced him and captured his life.

"We will try to return your freedom in a moment. And if you resist at any time, I will scream, and Taylor will run in here. Do not tempt me. I would enjoy her witnessing us as lovers, especially with her mother here too."

She looked down at Jack.

"Good, Jack. This situation arouses happiness in you. I see that you have grown very happy already. You may speak."

Jack felt something unlock, and he cleared his throat with a cough.

"Why don't you just leave me alone? What do you think—"

"I will offer myself to you while you lie beside Lin. She might awaken at any moment. I really do not know. We will find out together."

Jack turned only his eyes to try to look at Lin again, and Gloriana said, "Your eyes enjoy me more than her, do they not, Jack?"

She turned them back to herself, and he gazed into her bottomless lakes of caramel. Then, she reached past him and rolled Lin onto her back.

"Kiss her, Jack."

"What? Why?"

"I want to watch you kiss her. I will free you enough for that but no more. Do not test me. I will certainly bring Taylor into this room. I desire a display such as that."

"Didn't she go back to being a crow?"

"That is nonsense. You are confused. She can walk in at any time."

Jack felt some control return to him, and he got up on one elbow, leaned over, and brushed his lips against Lin's. She sighed and began kissing him back, but her eyes never opened.

"Show more enthusiasm. See if she responds to the passion the kiss promises."

Jack pressed his lips harder into hers and touched her lips with his tongue. He felt her mouth relax and open, and her tongue played with his until he pulled away.

"She is mostly unconscious, Jack. She does not know who is kissing her. Did she willingly respond to the stranger that was kissing her?"

"Well, no—she knew it was me. She must have."

"No, she does not know. Has she told you of the worlds she visits, where she can do anything she wishes because they are not real? That is the kind of woman she has become from her travels to her make-believe worlds. She is becoming the kind of woman that will kiss a stranger for the anonymous pleasure of it."

"You're crazy. I don't believe you."

"It is true, Jack."

She grabbed his shoulder and shoved him down onto his back again. Her eyes flashed, and his will was taken, leaving him with only his heart and one other thing.

"Soon, I will be above you as you hold my heels and look into my eyes. We might see Lin begin to stir because she can awaken at any moment. She will awaken right here to see us together."

Jack imagined Gloriana above him again and felt his enthusiasm growing, despite his efforts to hold it back.

"We will now see if you wear any clothes, Jack."

She peeled the covers off of him and Lin, and Jack lay frozen, wearing only his boxers.

"Shorts again? Soon, you will do without."

She walked around to Lin's side of the bed, and from there, she rolled Lin up against him until his left arm was around her and her cheek rested on his chest. Lin licked her lips a few times and remained still.

"You will now have your last chance to willingly be my lover, Jack. Oh my, you are really happy, are you not?"

He fought it, but he still had to nod.

"She will never remember kissing you. But she surely might awaken soon. When we become lovers, Lin will be here to witness it."

Gloriana walked back around the bed to Jack's side. She climbed up and straddled him with her hands near his waistline. She sat back onto his thighs, and he felt her skin warm and smooth on his legs.

"There, Jack. We are again very close to being lovers. It will be the only way you will find true happiness. Any second now, Lin will see that too."

Jack felt himself take a deep breath, and he sighed, knowing neither were by choice, but his eyes never left hers.

"She will awaken, and the first thing she will see is that we are lovers. Imagine the excitement, Jack, of you enjoying me as lovers do and knowing that Lin can wake up at any second."

She smiled and nodded at him. He imagined the possibility, and he was surprised that it did seem exciting.

"She might become very angry. You should hope she does not wake up."

Jack realized that was true—he couldn't guess how Lin would react to seeing Gloriana sitting there on him. He caught his breath when Lin laid her left arm across his chest and sighed deeply.

"Hold my heel with your free hand and Lin with the other."

Jack hugged Lin close with his left arm and held Gloriana's sharp heel with his right.

"You can have either of us now. It is your choice."

He only stared; it was all he could do.

"I can roll her onto you, and she will not resist, even though she does not know you. Even in her drugged sleep, she will sense your enthusiasm. Do you wish to have her? She will likely behave just how you want. You may gesture your response."

He shook his head to tell her no.

"She really is beautiful, Jack. Are you sure? You must understand what she has allowed herself to become. In her pretend worlds, she would offer herself to any stranger now without a thought. If you wish, I will watch her satisfy you as she would anyone there. I will even kiss you while she gives herself to you, not knowing or caring who you are. You may speak now."

He felt a gentle release, like a thin rubber band snapping.

"I . . . I don't know. She—"

"Would you not enjoy her touch, Jack? You can imagine that you are one of them that she concocts in her fake worlds, and you will see how she behaves there."

Jack tipped his head back and closed his eyes.

"No, she'd never . . . I mean, I—"

"You might find that she offers them more passion than she does you. Take her, Jack. See that I speak truth."

He remembered all of the times he and Lin had been together. All of the lovemaking, even the hugging and kissing. All of the closeness.

"I can't. Not like this."

"Is she enjoyed by all the strangers she meets in her worlds?"

Jack glanced at the ceiling and let out a heavy breath. His eyes were snapped back to the caramel.

He fought to raise his hands to Gloriana's throat, but all he could do was say, "No, she doesn't do any of that."

"She is friendly with them all, Jack. In whatever ways they want. You must know that she travels there for the adventure."

"I don't believe you."

He turned his eyes to look at Lin with a slight frown, and he tried but failed to hold her more tightly because his arm was no longer his.

"You will ask her yourself if you still care. I do not believe you will care much longer."

She reached down to the floor, retrieved his jeans, and laid them across his chest.

"There is something in your pocket. Take it out."

Jack knew exactly what she meant, and though it didn't feel right, he knew that he couldn't deny her. His hand reached in and took out the engagement ring that he'd been trying to give to Lin since weeks before she'd flown away with Taylor. He held it up and looked at it while he hugged Lin close and Gloriana sat on his lap.

"What would you like to do with that, Jack?"

He hesitated and stared into eyes that burst like starlight.

"Where do you most want to place that?"

She held her left hand out. Jack looked away from her eyes just long enough to slide the ring onto her finger. He felt a tear close to the surface, but it, too, was under her control and went nowhere.

"There, Jack. Now you are completely mine and never again for Lin. Is that right?"

All he could see was caramel, and he nodded his head as she forced his right hand back to her heel.

"Good. When Lin is awakening, we will test you again."

While looking only into Gloriana's eyes, he saw Lin reach up and rub her face. She mumbled something then fell silent again.

"Good, she is waking up. But we will pretend that she is not. We will be patient and pretend we have much time."

Jack's heart pounded as Lin shifted her head around on his chest before resting still again. Gloriana watched with a smile as Lin twitched and rubbed her eyes before dropping her arm back across Jack's chest.

He stared up at Gloriana and felt his heart racing. He held Lin and the pointy heel more tightly.

"We are still pretending we have time, but it is not true. We both know she will be awake soon. She will not be happy with you, but you will not care."

He wondered if Lin would ever take him back if she were to see Gloriana sitting on him and wearing so little.

"She is very near this time, not standing across a room in a doorway. The first thing she will see is us together."

He felt Lin twitch again, and she reached up to flick some of her hair back, sending a few long strands across his face.

"We are still pretending we have time, Jack, but we both know she is almost awake. You know she will see us. Do you wish me to leave?"

Jack's heart raced as his head shook. Lin rubbed her cheek into his chest and coughed.

"She is about to wake up. She will never love you again. Consider that and feel how close I am to you. We are so close to being lovers."

She shifted around, rubbing herself on him, then came to a stop with a grin.

"So close. Imagine agreeing to be my lover, Jack, and we will both wonder when Lin will see us. You will always crave excitement like that."

Gloriana reached down with her left hand to touch Lin's hair. The diamond he'd placed on her finger sparkled in the dim light. She played with Lin's hair, repeatedly smoothing it back gently.

"With this ring," Gloriana said as she continued to touch Lin's hair, "I have you, and Lin has given us her blessing."

She touched Lin's cheek with the diamond ring still visible.

"I like pretending that we have time. It is enjoyable to know that there really is no time. She will not wear anything from you on her left hand."

As if on cue, Lin dragged her left hand across her eyes several times and stretched her arm out to the side with a deep yawn.

Jack held his breath, and Gloriana smiled down on them both with glowing eyes.

"When the time is nearly upon us, I will dig a nail into Lin's hand, the one that will never wear your ring, and that will awaken her. She will have quite the view, Jack."

Caught in a flood of anger, he found that he could clench his jaw on his own, but only for a brief moment. He focused on it, tried to increase it, and realized that he still couldn't move his eyes away from the ring on Gloriana's hand.

He also realized that he didn't want to look away from it. He knew that he needed to focus on it even more. He had to see that ring, at least in his mind, where it belonged—on Lin's finger.

"Lin is dangerous, but she will not injure us. She will accept that you are mine and that you are happy."

Jack tested his sight and was able to glance briefly at Lin's blond hair, then he quickly focused again on the ring. He began to grind his teeth together weakly.

"Jack, I know you are very close now to being my lover. You will forever want only me and never Lin. Now, I set you free. Do as your strongest feelings direct you. We are so close . . ."

Jack's life returned to him in a rush. He thrust his right hand out and got a crushing grip on Gloriana's left wrist. He began trying to drag his left arm out from under Lin.

"Jack! You are a foolish man!"

Without thinking, he looked up to see her eyes, and the light was so overwhelming he had to close his own. He felt a thousand hands grabbing at every nerve in his body, clamping tightly, forcing him to comply.

But he did not. Through a pain like being burned from the inside out, he fought to keep his grip on Gloriana's left wrist, and with his freed left hand, he roughly tore the ring from her finger.

"You will never have me!" he said and dared to stare into her piercing eyes.

He released her wrist and shoved her to the side and off of the bed.

She stood quickly, with eyes blasting a blinding caramel and her fists on her hips. Jack held the ring in his right hand and looked up at her with his chest heaving.

The force that had invaded every part of him, and the pain from fighting it, began to weaken, and he saw a faint smile growing beneath

Gloriana's still-glowing eyes. When the glow had ended, so had the pain.

"I underestimated you, Jack. You have a love stronger than I have ever seen, deeper even than the love held for me by one named Marco long ago."

He fought to catch his breath, and the tears that had been blocked began two thin, trickling paths down his cheeks.

"I cannot take you by force. So, I will ask you: be mine of your own free will, and I will show you eternity. We will share a love that spans millennia. Only say that you wish that too."

Jack shook his head and said, "I've already seen eternity."

He pulled Lin back up close under his arm, held up her left hand, and placed the ring on her finger.

"Eternity, for me, will always be in Lin's eyes. Hell, they don't even have to glow."

Gloriana still wore a smile.

"Then, she is a lucky woman."

She lost her smile.

"I must tell you, Jack, that still I have tried to deceive you. I do not care about you at all. I only want to destroy any happiness Lin has. And I still might."

Jack stared with a frown and his head shaking slowly, and he said, "Why?"

"Because she has happiness, and I do not, Mr. Jack."

She turned and walked toward the door, and though her lingerie was so short that it covered nothing below her waist, Jack never looked at anything but her hair.

When she'd reached the door, she turned to face him with softly glowing eyes, took a step backward, then another. With her back against the closed door, she took yet another step back, and the last Jack saw was two once-bright caramel suns fading and spiraling away in opposite directions into the blackest of nights.

* * *

271

Jack awoke with a start and found Lin lying close under his left arm. He tried to sit up, but the motion woke her, so he lay back down.

"Jack, is everything okay? I sure fell asleep quick."

"Things are better than I can tell you."

"Huh?" she said and sat up.

She reached up quickly with her left hand to flick back her hair, and Jack grabbed her wrist, pulled it close, and stared at it. She didn't wear the ring.

"Oh, you're feeling playful. That rest did you some good, Cowboy."

"No, that's just . . . I mean, I, uh—"

"More crazy dreams, Jack? You know, you're going to have to tell me about those sometime soon."

"I can tell you that I won't be having any more, at least not at night. When I'm awake, though? That's what you're for."

He pulled her back down, hugged her tightly, and locked her in a long, deep kiss.

"Really? How can you be so sure?"

"I just know. Trust me. They're over."

"Well, then . . . let me give you something better than any dream."

Chapter 27 – A Self-Serving Soul

"This is day five," Lin said as her bright green eyes focused across the breakfast table at Gloriana.

Gloriana set her coffee mug down and looked at it for several seconds before meeting Lin's gaze.

"Yes. My time is drawing near. I beseech you to reconsider. I have value. You have not mastered your new Glyphin powers, and I can help you with that but not if I am dead."

Lin picked up her own coffee, held it up, and inhaled its strong scent as she calmly peered over the mug and said, "Which do you believe has more value to me?"

"Lin," said Gabriel, "breakfast is almost ready. Perhaps you should postpone the planning stages of your annihilation of Gloriana and take a moment to wake up Jack."

"Fine. It's not like I need to plan any of that. I can intend it, and it'll be done in less than a heartbeat."

"A crow's heartbeat?" Gabriel said with a grin.

"Yeah, Gabby. A really short one."

"Jack is sleeping better today than before?" said Gloriana.

"Yes, he is," said Lin. "Whatever was bugging him in his dreams is over. He said so."

"Perhaps he has but traded one misery for a looming new one."

"You act nice sometimes," said Lin, "but I'm still not convinced that you're anything but evil."

"Gabriel," Gloriana said as she turned toward the sound of kitchen utensils clattering into the sink, "you do not believe that I am evil, do you?"

Gabriel paused before turning to hold Lin's gaze.

"Time's running out, Gabby," she said. "Might as well be open about what you think. I say, breakfast can wait."

"Yes, it can. I'll finish it up when Jack joins us."

Gabriel sat at the table, let out a deep breath, and looked at Gloriana with a shrug.

"Very well. Gloriana, I have heard accounts of how you have spent most of your days, whether in the current time or long ago. I have also lived and worked with you and Renato in St. Simons for several weeks while Lin and her daughter were crows. Which, we all know, became necessary only because of your selfish interventions in Lin's life."

Gloriana's expression never changed, but she looked down at her placemat.

"You have done some good here by helping Lin and Taylor with certain new aspects of Glyphin powers, mainly the use of capital numbers. How to dismantle the word used to bring havoc too. But you've done that under threat of Lin destroying you. You have merely bargained for your survival."

"And that bargain is just about up," said Lin.

"Not yet, though," said Gabriel. "What I see when I look at you,"— Gabriel paused and focused intently on her—"is a powerful woman but a self-serving soul that firstly and eagerly resorts to evil when it brings her an advantage."

"There it is," said Lin. "Try to deny it."

"I cannot. Gabriel speaks truth and cannot do otherwise. I told you before, Lin Finity, that—"

"It's still just 'Lin,' okay? Even if I am about to kill you."

"Yes, of course. Lin, I told you before that learning of the magic is a wave of its own kind. You know now that I spoke truth. That wave will carry you along, and it will shape you if you are not vigilant. As you gain power over the magic, it can be used to satisfy any dark and nefarious tendencies you might have, and we all have them."

"She's right, Lin," said Gabriel. "Do you recall when you'd first gained control of your mayhem, and you were headed for a confrontation with Ben?"

"Oh, God yeah, Gabby. I wanted only to destroy him. I was convinced that he deserved it, and—"

"Were you right about him deserving it?"

Lin stared without blinking, her eyes big and green.

"Did he?"

"Yes, Lin, you can say that he did. Do bad acts not have consequences? Shouldn't they?"

"Well, yeah, but you later told me that if I'd chosen evil over good, if I *had* destroyed him, then you would have had to destroy me too."

"That's all true because you were already too powerful to be allowed to choose evil."

"I don't get what you're—"

"Here's what I'm saying, Lin. It applied then with Ben just as it applies now with Gloriana. Even if you're entirely sure that someone has earned your wrath, and even if you're exactly right about their actions being based in evil to some level, that vengeance is not yours to deliver."

"But Ben *did* deserve it, just like she,"—Lin tipped her head and hooked a thumb toward Gloriana—"deserves it."

"They don't deserve the vengeance and retaliation that is driven by anger. When you destroyed the army that Lancaster Wolfe had assembled and that had surrounded all of us in your cabin, did you act out of anger?"

"No. I only wanted to protect Taylor and the rest of us."

"And still, didn't you regret it? It brought you no satisfaction?"

"Yeah, Gabby. Right now, I even feel bad about all those bobcats, even if only one of them was real."

"I don't believe any of them were real, Lin."

"But I thought you said—"

"I did say that one *might* have been real. It was best that you didn't close the door on that action—I wanted you to still consider it, which you have."

Lin's eyes shined brightly above a growing smile as she gazed at her best friend and slowly shook her head. She scoffed and wiped at one eye then the other.

"You're still guiding me and watching out for me, Gabby. It's been over thirty years, and still, where would I be without you?"

"You would be me, Lin Finity," said Gloriana before she covered her face with both hands.

Lin shook her head and took a breath, but before she could issue a correction, Gabriel touched her arm softly. They both watched as Gloriana shook quietly.

"Gabby, what the hell?"

"Hell exists for a reason, Lin."

"I do not wish to go to Hell, Gabriel," said Gloriana from behind her hands.

"'Back.' You do not wish to go back."

She lowered her hands and stared at Gabriel, who only returned her gaze calmly.

"Your intent was strong, so you survived. You felt that strength about to vanish, though, didn't you?"

"Yes. I could no longer maintain the tower or the sea. I could make only enough of a world to talk with Lin Finity."

Lin started to speak, but Gabriel again touched her arm, and she closed her eyes and let out a deep breath before speaking.

"I remember. We ended up standing on one single block, and there was only emptiness around us. Somehow, though, we were still alive. Gabby, I don't get how we could be alive in Hell. I felt my heart beating."

"I created the illusion of being alive," said Gloriana. "None of that was real. It was all from my intent."

Gabriel stood and said, "And what do you both think of this world? The time we spend on the Islands of Time?"

"It isn't Hell," said Lin.

"She is correct," said Gloriana.

"Do you see traces of it, though?"

"Oh, I remember you saying that we—all of us—pass through those spaces countless times in the smallest of moments, so short of a time that it can't possibly be measured. We're passing through Hell, Gabby?"

"Yes, Lin. You must have felt that. Isn't there always a hint of agony and foreboding lurking nearby, no matter how much happiness visits your life? We learn to not dwell on it, but it's like gravity—constantly pulling us down and working to destroy us and everything we've done or ever will do. That is the nature of our lives."

"I do not wish to dwell in Hell for eternity, Gabriel."

"I do not wish that for you."

"But you believe it is my fate?"

"Perhaps. There's mercy in creation too. There is hope."

"What must I do?"

"Talking is good. Accepting our shortcomings—"

"You mean, accepting that I am evil."

"You are not evil. You resort to evil. You choose it."

"And if I stop?"

"It would be a good change, of course."

"You can start," said Lin, "by telling us how all of this got started. How did you figure out how to mess with people and take their power?"

"Are we not feeling an urgency for that breakfast that is almost complete?"

Lin shook her head and grinned.

"Let's see: sorting out Heaven and Hell or stuffing our faces. What do you think?"

Gloriana managed a weak smile, closed her eyes, and said, "It was long ago . . ."

* * *

"Before you go any further," Lin said with a quick eye roll, "let me guess: your life was impossible, but you never gave up. You fought hard to—"

"No, Lin Finity, my life was a feckless float down a river of riches. I was the youngest in the household of the wealthiest warlord in the land. Servants fought to their deaths for the privilege of suffering my scorn and indifference while fulfilling my every whim. I was rarely expected to walk on my own. Food and drink were brought to me before I knew I wanted them. I was decorated with the most valuable gems and metals that could be stolen. I wanted for nothing. Nothing except power.

"There was only one in the house who had the truest power I could see. If I wished something to be, he caused it. That angered me. It should have been me that ruled over the lands."

"Wait," said Lin. "You didn't have any powers? None at all?"

"I know now that I had a strong intent. How I was in possession of that, I cannot say, yet it was there.

"I had heard tales of characters in stories told by my attendants as they sought to entertain me or lull me to sleep. They spoke of individuals that could do impossible things, like vanish and appear elsewhere or cause rain to commence. I knew I wanted to be such a person. No, I knew I deserved to be.

"I sought out our palace healer, an old, withered man with skin burnt too often by the sun. I hid my snarl as I approached him, thinking that if he had real power, he would not look as he did.

"As I was quite young, he felt he could be friendly with me and not treat me with the deference I was due. I let him continue with his jokes and compliments, even though I had no respect for him.

"I did not expect it—our separation and differences were pronounced—and I was shocked when he touched me. It was a gentle touch, perhaps even kindly and innocent, but he was too far out of his place, and his face showed the fear he had earned for himself.

"He asked aloud for forgiveness, which I did not give. He pleaded that no one ever find out, but I offered no such generosity. He said he knew he deserved to die, and when I only stared at him silently, he fell to his hands and knees and sobbed.

"Even then, I enjoyed his repentance and humiliation, and I wished for it to continue. I had no need to tolerate him—any sounds I made would have called the guard to remove his head and his limbs in whatever order the court would enjoy the most, but still, I wondered what had possessed him to act in such a way."

"Let me guess," said Lin. "He said you were just so attractive that he—"

"No, he did not profess anything of the sort. He blamed it on his power. He said out loud that it gave him too much confidence. He said it was a tide running through him that brought courage while it swept away all fear and doubts. He begged for his life and swore he wished to never again use his power because it had led to his death as surely as if he had jumped from the highest tower.

"I believed he spoke the truth. He knew his head would soon be on the end of a spear unless he could rid himself of his evil power."

"You didn't really think it was evil, did you?"

"No, I did not, but I was having more fun at that moment than all the rest of my days combined. It was difficult to keep from jumping up and down. He shook and wailed when I only stared at him calmly. He kept his head near the floor, and he struck it many times on the stone while renouncing his power as evil.

"I knew I was smiling at his display, and I did not wish it to end. I wished for him to know that his head would be removed and catapulted from the tower and out to where the sea grows very deep. And if he did not reject his evil power, his eyes would still function, and he would still feel fear, as his head sunk beneath the waves and the sharks drew near for their next meal."

"Good God," said Jack from the doorway where he'd been listening and had heard most of Gloriana's story.

"Oh, good morning, Jack," said Lin. "Have a seat. It's story time."

"Yeah, I see that."

Jack sat, and Gloriana took a sip of her coffee.

"Was that all true?" said Jack.

"I do not know. Perhaps. None of the heads retrieved in our nets were willing to respond to interrogations."

Jack stared and so did Lin and Gabriel.

"That is an attempt at humor."

Jack let out a huge sigh, and Lin shook her head with a grin.

"That was pretty good, actually. Continue."

"Thank you. After the healer understood what type of Hell he faced, he began a low wail like an outcast dog dying in a distant dungeon."

Lin looked at Nomad, who slept near her feet, then back at Gloriana and said, "Hey."

"Oh, I am sorry. Not that dog. The healer's moaning had increased, and when it reached a high pitch, I felt as if lightning had struck me at my head and the bottom of each leg. It all raced through me, and it crashed together in the middle. That crash remained inside me."

Lin, Jack, Gabriel, and Nomad all remained silent.

Finally, Lin said, "Lightning, huh?"

"Yes, Lin Finity. It felt that way, but I learned later that it was not. When I first felt the pleasure of another's touch, I learned that taking power from another was similar."

"No, you can't be serious. Really?"

"Yes, but it is more than just a feeling. In some ways, they *are* the same. If an encounter is planned and executed in the correct way, it can result in the theft of a small amount of the other's power. It is so small that they do not notice."

"That doesn't sound possible. That's a source of power too?"

"Yes. It is why some are drawn to vulgar attention and excessive wanton activity. They know without knowing, and they seek to take power. Few succeed. It requires a clear intent."

Lin glanced at Jack quickly, then down at the table.

"I stood taller than ever before and looked down upon the healer with a new confidence and strength. I felt power, a power I knew was different and more potent than possessed by anyone in the land. Taking his strength had changed me in a profound way. In observable ways too.

"I was about to test my power by attempting to kill the weak man on the floor. I nudged him with a foot so that I could look into his eyes, but he fell over dead."

Lin frowned, shook her head, and said, "Wait. Forget about that for a second. When you tried to take my power, you didn't care if it killed me?"

"No, Lin Finity, you were in no danger of dying. The healer was one of only two who died when losing power. I believe I was like a sea sponge that had dried in the sun, and I took all that he had. For all the others, and there have been many, I left enough that they could continue their lives in a normal fashion."

"Gloriana," said Gabriel, "perhaps you could share how you learned to impose feelings on others."

"I would rather not."

"You're just about out of days anyway," said Lin. "You have nothing to lose."

"Very well. I looked down upon the dead healer, and I considered the impulses that drove him to touch me. I found that I could feel what he felt, the impulse to have physical contact with me.

"He had witnessed me becoming a very attractive young woman, and—"

"I hate to admit it, but you still look good. Doesn't she, Jack?"

Jack looked only at Lin and said, "Oh, I don't know. I guess."

"Thank you. Anyway, I imagined seeing myself through his eyes. I let the feelings grow until I knew that I would touch me too if I were him. I intended to save that feeling, mostly as a reminder of the day.

"The guard outside the door had been instructed to check on me at regular intervals, and he looked in at the scene. Though his eyes grew wide, he knew to not react to anything he saw, including the healer's body growing cold on the stone floor. Still, he could not hide his fright. Perhaps his greatest fear was what I had become.

"I did not want to see his weak fear, and I wished that he would instead feel what the healer had felt. Where the lightning had crashed and remained inside me became . . . aroused."

"Wait," said Lin. "How did you even think to try that?"

"It is a wave of its own kind, Lin Finity. It leads us and will compel us."

"Yeah, I get that. Go on. What happened next?"

"He approached me, stood close, and touched my cheek.

"While I smiled at his advances, I wondered if he had any power that I could add to what I'd taken from the healer. Instantly, I felt the meager force of his ordinary life as thin strands of faint light that raced through me, collected in the middle, and remained.

"He fell over dead."

Lin turned to see Gabriel looking at the floor. She turned to Jack and saw that he stared with his mouth open. She turned her gaze back to Gloriana.

"You seem to like to kill. How many people have you murdered?"

"Only those two, Lin Finity. I have taken power from countless others, but only those two have forfeited their lives."

Gabriel looked up and said, "Why did you create your own islands far out in the ocean?"

Gloriana closed her eyes and said, "I grew very powerful, and the people could not understand how I had changed so dramatically. They could not forget what I had been before. I performed what they considered to be miracles—healing injuries and making small objects disappear. But when I howled with blazing caramel eyes, pointed to the mountaintop, and it erupted fire, people became afraid.

"They backed away and let me return to my palace. Later, they—"

"Wait," Lin said with her head shaking, "'your' palace?"

"Yes. Most accepted me as their rightful ruler. Those that resisted were driven deep into the jungle, never to be seen again."

"Your father too?" said Jack.

"The warlord was the first to face exile. I had him taken to a region that is frequented by hyenas. They are always hungry."

Lin looked over at Gabriel, who looked down with a shaking head. "So, you killed him too?"

"No. I did not join whatever pack visited him."

"Good God," said Jack.

"After I blew up the mountaintop, the people gathered around my palace with swords and torches. They had come to kill me."

"And you could have killed all of them?" said Gabriel.

"Yes. In a single eye blink. But I had killed enough, so I left."

"You made your own islands?" said Lin. "Far out in the ocean, right?"

"Yes. It tired me greatly, and when I intended my tower, one higher than any in any land anywhere, I felt I might not recover. It had to be tall—I will always choose to view the world from as high as possible. I learned that at the moment I first took power, and it changed me."

"You do like wearing high heels, don't you?"

"Yes, Lin Finity. As for the tower, you have observed its construction in detail many times. It had become an obsession to make it appear impossible to build. But I regained my strength, and those islands became my home."

"Your intent," said Gabriel, "maintained all that you had created, never letting any of it falter?"

"Yes. With enough strength, one can set their intent in a direction of their choosing and not need to attend to it ever again."

"Well, until you were about to die," said Lin, "so you left for the emptiness between the Islands of Time after you set your trap for me."

"Or someone like you. You are rare, Lin Finity."

"That's when you created the Scroll, which used to be Renato, and—"

"We cannot create. I have told you this."

"Well, yeah, but you know what I mean. Then, you concocted those Words of God with all that Glyphin magic to trap me."

"Yes."

"You are not a good person," said Lin.

"I am a person that has killed only two."

"And your father."

"I did not kill the warlord."

"Maybe not technically, but you drained the power out of countless others."

Gloriana looked down at the table and sighed.

"Yes. Whatever becomes of me, I have lived an interesting life with a multitude of accomplishments."

Gabriel stood and said, "We are not here only to amuse ourselves and impress others."

"Why exactly are we here, Gabby? When I read the Words of God, we talked about how our lives were about choosing good—about us making that choice. That's it? Why does that matter?"

"I might not be good," said Gloriana, "yet still I am hungry."

"It can wait," said Lin.

Gabriel sat back down, sighed, and looked at everyone waiting for the answer.

"We can't know for sure, Lin, but here is what I have determined from the life I've lead.

"Consider your own life. Think of one tiny moment, the shortest you can imagine—just one single Island of Time. In that brief moment of your life, there are countless things on which you can focus any or all of your senses. Most often, you can handle only one at a time, especially in that shortest of moments. It might be the color of the sky seen through a thin sliver between leaves and branches of a close-by tree. It might be the touch of a single raindrop that had fallen from high above you and landed on your cheek. Or it might be a sadness that consumes you and prevents you from noticing anything around you.

"Now, Lin, think of all you have experienced in your life—all of those moments added together and all you will ever experience. It's an overwhelming amount, isn't it? It's too much for any of us to comprehend.

"You're at a time, now, where you will know this is true. Jack, I'm glad you're listening too. Gloriana, you might already know this, and it might rightly lead you to more regrets for how you have chosen to live.

"The entirety of your life's experiences—everything you've ever sensed, your every thought and feeling and hope and dream—those are to God as that single, tiny moment of your life is to you.

"You and everyone and everything are all part of God. God lives in every moment of our lives."

No one spoke. They only stared until Nomad began to pant. Lin looked down at him and smiled.

"Are you laughing about all that, my sweet fluffy boy?"

"Maybe he's just relieved that Gabriel told us," said Jack. "I think he already knew."

Lin tilted her head and gazed at Jack for a second, then she looked back at Gabriel.

"Gabby, we're God's eyes and ears and everything else?"

"God is much more than that, but it's good that you now know how your choices in life are felt by God. He always wants good to triumph. When any of us choose a different path, of course, He isn't happy about that."

Gabriel turned to look at Gloriana, who still studied the tabletop.

"I have done much to displease not only people and animals but God Himself. Perhaps I do belong in those dreadful spaces between the Islands of Time."

"Are you sure you originally traveled there of your own volition?"

She looked up and held Gabriel's gaze.

"I did believe so at the time, Gabriel."

"Perhaps you were sent there, but you retained some strength in your intent?"

"It felt like my choice at that time."

"We often believe ideas which bring us comfort."

"Have I chosen the wrong path too many times?"

Lin and Jack watched Gabriel intently, and Gloriana listened with wide eyes for whatever Gabriel would say next.

"You have been given a second chance but only from the strength and kindness of Lin. You, like everyone else, will come to a crossroads, a time when it will be decided for you which way you will travel.

"You will be a dry, lifeless leaf whose days have all been spent, tossed into the sky and lingering there for your last time on Earth. The sum of all of your choices and what you have carried in your heart will determine in which direction your final wind will gust."

Chapter 28 – A Man Named Nomad

"Well, that sure is quite a life story," said Lin. "I'm impressed, even though I don't like you or approve of all you've done, especially to Taylor and me. You messed Taylor up so bad that she's gone back to being a crow. How do you feel about that?"

"I am not pleased with that outcome. I do not have those powers any longer. That should give you some satisfaction."

"Yeah, some. Don't you feel like you should atone for all you've done, though?"

Gloriana shrugged and looked back down at the table.

"She will," said Gabriel. "As will all of us."

"Well, whatever happens to you," said Lin, "you can try to be happy that you've lasted so long."

"Without a strong intent, I would not have lasted any time—"

"Time," Lin said with an eye roll.

"Yes, no time at all in those dreadful spaces."

"Well," said Lin, "you're not going to last much longer anyway."

Gloriana looked down at the table and stayed silent.

"Okay, Jack," said Lin, "I'm going to ask more about stuff that you usually don't want to listen to. Would you rather take Nomad out back for a while?"

Nomad stood at Lin's side and looked up at her while she rubbed his ears.

"No, he doesn't want to go right now. And besides, I kind of like listening in sometimes. I might even have some questions of my own."

Lin gave him a grin and said, "That's wonderful, Jack. You can appreciate this stuff probably as well as anyone else anyway."

He leaned over and gave her a quick kiss, and she said, "Thanks, I really need that sometimes."

"There's an endless supply just waiting for you."

"Oh, I am sorry. Lin, I truly did not mean to bump Jack with my clumsy foot. It was not the result of any intent on my part."

Lin frowned at her and said, "Too bad. One less day for you."

She turned to Gabriel and said, "Speaking of intent, Gabby, what exactly is it? I think of it as willpower, or determination, or something like that."

Lin had stopped giving attention to the big dog, so he'd moved over to Gabriel's side, who flopped his ears around and scratched his head.

"It's quite simple, Lin. It's what most people call their soul."

"Like everything else, that doesn't make sense. I thought a soul just existed inside us, something that stayed the same no matter what we go through in life. You're saying that my soul somehow became stronger than the average person?"

"Much stronger. As has Gloriana's. Even though she was forced to let go of her powers, her soul—her intent—is still strong."

"But most people just have what . . . an ordinary amount of strength in their intent? In their souls?"

"Yes, that's usually the case. We are all delivered here with a fixed amount of power in our souls, which is enough for whatever our purpose might be. Some people have only enough that they can touch those closest to them and live on in their memories, leading them onward in their own work. Others have more power that is bestowed for more extensive acts, and many of them squander that power on distractions and choices that weaken them. Still others, such as you and Gloriana, are given—"

"You too, Gabby?"

"Yes. I, too, squandered some before I found my path. It is our nature. But we all chose paths that challenged us but increased our strength. None of it is given easily. If it is, it is likely from a source best avoided."

"When I was between the Islands of Time—in Hell—all I had was the power of my intent," said Lin. "Same thing with Gloriana. Does that mean that we keep our intent—our souls—if we end up in Hell?"

"Yes, of course. It's not a good place for your soul, Lin. You've experienced the pain and anguish of the place. You have too,"—Gabriel looked at Gloriana and nodded at her—"but you were strong enough to insulate yourselves. Few can do that. Most only suffer."

"You said before that you believed I came into the world with an uncommon strength and that I added to it. How?"

Gabriel smiled and said, "How about if I get a fresh pot of coffee going for everyone first?"

* * *

Jack had answered Nomad's single bark at the ceiling to go outside, and Gloriana had scoured Lin's closet for a different outfit, causing Lin to sneer at the short skirt, heels, and tight sweater. Lin had remained at the table lost in thought, mostly about taking another flight and trying to guess every nuance of what might transpire in her fake hotel's penthouse. Gabriel had eaten a candy bar and waited patiently for the coffee pot to finish its work.

Everyone had returned to the table, and hot coffee waited for each, except for Nomad, who'd been nosing his bowl around the room until Gabriel began, and he returned to place his massive head on Lin's lap.

"Okay, let's see what we can figure out about why some are brought here with more strength than others.

"We cannot say for sure how or why some of us have more or less strength as we begin our lives. Perhaps it's because we each have roles, or maybe missions, that are before us if we accept them. In your case, Lin, you might have needed more strength to face what you have faced and come away from it even stronger."

"For some specific reason, you mean? Like what?"

"You'll likely never know that for sure. It might be something insignificant to you—something you'd never notice—that has a far-reaching effect long after you're gone."

"How about an example?"

"Here's one possibility: all of the events of your life led you to become a crow for a period of time. While living a crow's life, you said that you saved the flock from predators and other threats many times. Let's think about just one of those times.

"One of your crow friends might have felt weak and despondent, maybe even close to death, but also on the verge of something that she couldn't explain to herself. She might have been waging an additional struggle within herself as she felt that mystery, besides the day-to-day strife every crow must face.

"When the predator drew near, she came to a fork in the road of her existence. She found herself facing imminent death, and she also had a vague sense that another path could open in front of her. But she had no idea how to follow that new path or where it might lead.

"When you eliminated the threat, she witnessed your compassion and caring, and she caught a brief glimpse of something above and beyond her daily trials and challenges. She witnessed the use of a power greater than she'd ever seen before. She saw a miracle, Lin. That sparked something inside her. It allowed her to sort of take a leap in a new direction.

"Remember that only humans have imagination, and she, as a crow, could not, on her own, conceive of anything but life as a bird.

"Can you imagine how that felt in her heart? A new path beckoned her, and your actions showed her that a new life was possible for her. Your selfless act of safeguarding her allowed her to take that leap, and she made a big change, one not even remotely possible for her just moments earlier."

Lin knew that her green eyes weren't glowing, but she couldn't bring herself to look away from Gabriel's calm brown eyes. Gabriel remained still and held her gaze.

Finally, she looked at Jack and saw that he, too, seemed hypnotized. She looked at Gloriana and found that she'd had no reaction as if she understood it already. She turned back toward Gabriel.

"She leaped? What kind of change are you talking about?"

"You became a crow when your circumstances nudged you in that direction. Is it so hard to believe that—"

"Wait a second, Gabby. We didn't become crows. Taylor and I only tagged along with two of them, right?"

Gabriel smiled and said, "Is that easier for your mind to accept?"

Lin could only stare with her mouth moving slowly and not saying a word.

"Jack and I," Lin finally said with her eyes wide, "really became baby birds in a nest somewhere? And you and I . . . that was just us swimming in that ocean?"

"The mysteries and possibilities are without end in this world built upon infinite layers of magic."

Gabriel took a long drink of coffee and looked around the room before resting eyes again on Lin.

"So, is it so hard to believe that a crow could also make such a change? A very special crow that had managed to stockpile enough strength?"

Lin shook her head without a smile and said, "Gabby, you think that crow turned into a human somewhere?"

"It does happen, Lin. Remember, this is just one possibility that we're discussing. Just know that one crow, out of the many that you knew, might have been affected by your actions after the entirety of your life led you to that moment. In that moment, she might have found the strength and courage—the *imagination*—to make a transition such as that. She might be walking around nearby, even now, trying to find her bearings in an unfamiliar life."

"Alright, maybe I should take Nomad outside again," said Jack.

Lin didn't look at him, but she said, "Gabby, can we find her? Is there some way to know that she used to be a crow?"

"No, you will never know for sure. There could be hints, though. Think about the lingering feelings you still have after returning."

"I still kind of feel like a bird. Not as much as before, but it's still there. She'd be the same way?"

"Have you known people in your life that have seemed more heartless and cold-blooded in their dealings than others? Have you read about people that display a ruthless savagery that seems foreign to you? Consider that being a human might be new to them and that they are trying to learn something that was completely unknown to them just a short time earlier."

"Sure, there are plenty of people like that. They all used to be something else?"

"No, probably very few of them. Maybe none of them. Too many people choose evil over good, or they are too weak to follow a noble path. But you cannot be sure which is which. Treat all people with compassion and fairness. Protect yourself and others from their actions, but do not act out of vengeance. And remember in your heart that the person you might rush to condemn could have been a crow only moments ago, and she is doing the absolute best she can with something entirely new to her that we call free will."

After a length of silence from them all, Jack said, "Good God. See, Lin? This is a lot to try to absorb."

"Yeah, it really is, Jack. Gloriana, you don't look surprised by any of that."

"No, I am not. I have seen such transformations first-hand. I have even brought them."

Lin's mouth hung open, and she turned to look at Gabriel, who sat quietly and nodded.

"Oh, you can't be serious. You've turned crows into people?"

Gloriana grinned and shook her head slowly.

"No, Lin Finity, I have never bothered with insignificant birds. Lions, though, were often quite useful to me."

"Wait. You've turned lions into people? How?"

"You wish to learn more of Glyphin powers? Consider allowing me to live into this land's warmer seasons and beyond."

Lin turned to Gabriel and said, "Gabby, is she for real? What do you know about that?"

"I know nothing about that, Lin, but the mysteries of this world and all of its magic go on forever. I have heard stories of Windcraft, but this? No, this is new to me."

"That can't be a good thing," said Lin. "Can it?"

Gabriel looked down at the coffee before taking a sip and said, "Just because something *can* be done with the magic doesn't mean that it ever *should*. Free will, Lin, is not license to do anything that we might learn is possible."

Lin snapped her head to face Gloriana, but before she could speak, Gloriana said, "I will say no more about it except that it involves the use of the capital numbers. If you think, as you should, that the common Glyphin use of those numbers is dangerous, know that such a transformation carries with it more risk than you might imagine."

"I don't know. I have a pretty good imagination."

"Then, Lin Finity, imagine a man that is mostly still a lion. A ravenous lion. You are, to that starving and merciless new man eager to exercise his free will, no more than his next meal."

Lin could only stare.

"And your mayhem would not work with him. You would need to be quick with another plan."

* * *

"Just when I think I might be understanding even a little bit, then there's something like that."

"Oh, Jack," said Lin, "I think this is like everything else: just don't try to understand it. Our minds can take us only so far."

"She's right," said Gabriel. "Once you accept one fundamental truth—that this world, everything you can perceive, is nothing but magic—then you won't require it to make sense."

"Alright, I'll try that. Wish me well," he said with a smile.

"We do, Jack. You're further on your way than you might realize."

"I don't know how, Gabriel, but alright."

"So," said Lin, "why would you turn a lion into a man?"

"I am not the same person I once was. Please remember that."

"Fine. Why, though?"

"An army of men who are mostly still lions is a formidable force. They are fearless and will vanquish any foolish enough to threaten you."

"That's not so bad," said Lin. "Just defending yourself."

"There is more, isn't there?" said Gabriel.

"Yes. I allowed them to do as lions would naturally do with the soldiers they had killed."

"Your army ate their army?"

"Every army must eat," she said.

"Good God. Again," said Jack.

"And there is still more?" said Gabriel before sipping the hot coffee.

"Yes, Gabriel."

"It might help if you told us. We cannot correct our past actions, but speaking of them might invite a measure of mercy."

"Very well. I worked transformations for entertainment as well."

"My God," said Jack, "what did you do?"

"I pitted lion against tiger, both as men. Or as women. Snake fought mongoose as men. Most times, neither survived. They fought to their deaths without a thought."

Lin and Jack stared, and Gabriel said, "Do you feel that was a good use of your power?"

Gloriana looked down and said, "No. But you are right, Gabriel. It does feel beneficial to speak of those acts."

"Yes, it does. Is there more?"

Gloriana didn't look up, but she said, "Yes. Many times, as the transformed human beast lay dying, I hastened its death by taking what power still remained."

"So, it wasn't just that you tricked people out of their power. You also played with their lives and led them to their deaths."

"I am not proud of my past. I wish to be judged by my present day. You know that I no longer have any of those powers."

"Yes," said Gabriel. "You made that deal to return to—"

"Hey, Gabriel, there's something I want to ask you about."

"Sure, Jack," Gabriel said and took a drink of hot coffee.

"Um, Gloriana," Jack said after turning to her, "how about giving us some privacy for this?"

"Yes, Jack. As you wish."

She stood and paused to wipe her lips with the napkin while holding his gaze. She pushed her chair under the table, tried to pull down her skirt, then stood holding the chair back.

"I am not evil. If you wish to discuss that, remember that I have left my powers behind. It is a new life that I seek."

"Who said we're even going to talk about you?" said Jack.

"No one need say it. I see much in people's eyes."

She turned to face Lin and said, "You wish to learn more of Glyphin power. I wish to live. We can find agreement."

Before Lin could respond, Gabriel said, "I will talk to Lin about allowing your life to continue."

"Yes, please do. She might wish to experience friendship with a man named Nomad, even if only for one hour."

In a completely silenced room, Gloriana looked once at Lin, turned, and left for her guest room with her high heels offering a steady, confident cadence.

*   *   *

"The reason I wanted her to leave is that—"

"Wait a second, Jack," said Lin. "Gabby, tell me she's making up all that transformation business."

"I can tell you that, but it would not be true. Yes, Lin, such things can be done."

"To take a lion and turn it into a man? Really?"

"Yes. Or one can take a girl named Taylor and make her a crow."

"But that was different: all we really did was tag along with two of the crows that came for us. We didn't actually become crows."

"Perhaps you are right. How would we ever check to be sure? Either way, you both ended up feeling like crows yourselves."

"Well, yeah. We did. Still, that took an enormous amount of strength to make that happen."

"And the next step," said Gabriel, "beyond that, is a true transformation."

"That just doesn't seem possible."

"Lin, what you are questioning is all a matter of how much strength you possess. At that time, you were desperate, and you were able to summon enough strength that you and Taylor joined with those crows' lives, or perhaps you did more. It's all a matter of strength."

Lin shook her head and let a deep breath escape slowly.

"Alright, like I was saying," said Jack. "Lin, it's about those dreams I've been having."

"Oh yeah, those dreams about me. What about them? You can't stop dreaming about me?"

"Um, yeah, I'm always dreaming about you, but there were some that bothered me too. I need to hear again how dreams don't mean anything—that they can't become real somehow."

"Gabby, maybe this is a good one for you."

"I think we'll need more coffee. Hang on."

Gabriel got up and returned with the coffee pot, which was set on a placemat after all mugs were topped off.

"Okay, now we're ready. Jack, about dreams: they really are just imagination, and they stay that way—just harmless distractions—unless the dreamer is powerful and focusing their intent. You are very strong in your own ways, but I don't believe you're able to—"

"But it's not just me. I mean, what if there's someone else causing the dream? And what if they do have that kind of power?"

"Jack," said Lin, "maybe you should tell us about the dreams, okay?"

Jack cleared his throat and drank half of his cup. He set it down with a rattle and looked first at Gabriel then at Lin.

"It's Gloriana. I've had these crazy dreams with her in them. I've never had dreams that have seemed so real."

"What exactly are you dreaming about her, Jack?"

"Oh, um, it's kind of weird, but it's like she's trying to get me to like her."

Lin frowned and said, "What, like so you could be buddies? Is that it?"

"Well, no, I mean, she—"

"Is she trying to seduce you, Jack? Is that what you're dreaming about?"

"No, Lin, I swear. I don't think they're my dreams. It's even worse than that."

Gabriel sat quietly and listened. Lin's frown intensified.

"She succeeds, Jack? Are you off in your dreams having a wild time with her?"

"No, Lin, she has mayhem in the dreams, and her eyes are glowing that bright, brownish—"

"Caramel."

"Yeah, caramel. Her eyes are glowing. But she doesn't have that power anymore, does she?"

"No," said Gabriel, "I don't believe she does. Recall that Taylor nearly killed her with Windcraft, and Lin has been promising to kill her every chance she gets."

Gabriel turned to Lin with a barely concealed grin. She continued to stare only at Jack.

"I will surely kill her, Gabby. I have even more reason now."

She turned to face Gabriel and said, "Can she be doing this? I thought she didn't have powers anymore."

"She does still have a strong intent, Lin, but I don't know if she can accomplish what Jack is describing."

Lin turned back to Jack, but before she could speak, he said, "The dreams are over, though. I'm sure of it. She tried that caramel mayhem of hers, and I still found the strength to reject her. I made it clear, even in those insane dreams, that I love only you. It's true, Cowgirl: I love only you."

Lin's frown softened but didn't become a smile, and she wiped at an eye that showed no sign of tearing.

"I knew she shouldn't have been kicking you all the time. Remember when she sat on your lap too? Remember that? I think she was trying to get you to think of her, that's all."

"That sounds about right, Lin," said Gabriel. "If the dreams don't return, we can assume Jack's imagination took him down an unexpected path. It's not surprising, is it? With all the outlandish things we've been living through?"

"Oh, that's for sure, Gabby. Jack, whatever it was, I'm glad it's done. Actually, I'm quite flattered. Even in a dream where it seemed like Gloriana had her mayhem again, you still chose me. I love you, my Cowboy."

"And I love you, Cowgirl. Hey, what about those dreamworlds of yours? I never picked anything that happened in mine. How about yours? Do you set those up how you want?"

"Oh, um, not really, Jack. Maybe if I had more control, then I could, but, um, it's kind of a surprise the things that happen, you know?"

Jack scratched at his chin and gazed at her, then he shook his head and said, "I'll never figure this stuff out."

"Me neither, Cowboy."

They leaned in for a quick kiss, which was interrupted by the angry yelling and dancing of Lin's phone.

Chapter 29 – Busy Assembling Something

"This better be good, Anna."

"It is anything but good, Lin. I do not wish to see you or even speak at you again."

"Okay, what's going on this time? Tayo's ear fell off?"

"I wish it were only that simple. Tayo is no longer injured. Lee has healed him. I do not even want to know how she can do such things. What kind of person could—"

"Anna, get to the point."

"Yes, well, as I was saying, everyone is fine now, thanks to Lee. She was even so generous as to repair Daria's hair. Do you remember her hair? How could someone make another person's hair fall off in just one—"

"Last chance, Anna, and then I swear, there will be no way for you to ever see me again because you won't be around. Neither will your brat daughter or your brat dog."

"Of the two, Ozzy is less of—"

"Anna!"

"Oh, I am sorry, Lin. My mind is being lost. I am calling because Tayo wishes you to visit again."

"Why? If everyone is okay, what's the point? Do you think we like driving for three hours each way just so I can disappoint myself by not finishing you off? Your wardrobe is really irritating. You must know that."

"It really is a good look, Lin, and if your offer is still good about shortening—"

"Forget your stupid skirt. Why does Tayo want me there?"

"He said there is something growing inside the walls. I have never seen him so scared. I have heard it too. Ozzy has noticed."

"What do you mean? What's in the walls?"

"Tayo is awake now. He can tell you."

Lin held the phone down on her lap and said, "Gabby, I think I'm ready to fight this thing. I'm still a crow, I think, but maybe that's good—that hunter is an obstacle that I want to eliminate. Here, listen in."

Lin switched the phone to speaker mode and set it on the kitchen table.

"Lin? Are you there?"

The words came slowly, and Lin could imagine Tayo's black eyes darting about the room as he spoke.

"Yes, Tayo, I'm here. What's the problem this time?"

"I did not wish to render Anna unconscious. I had no time to think before I struck her, and she fell to the floor. I also did not have the desire to try to assault Daria. At that moment, it became overpowering."

"You beat up Daria too?"

"No, Lin. I will use the word 'assault' and allow your own mind to supply details."

"Well, a good slap would have been enough because she's a brat, and—"

"I know you are trying to be amusing, Lin, but I cannot laugh. I can barely find the will to continue."

"So, I'm guessing you didn't get too far with her?"

"No, I did not. The dog distracted me with its surprisingly strong little jaw gouging into an ankle."

"The one where Lee just stuck your foot back on?"

"No, the other one."

"Okay, what else?"

"Lee awoke from her fatigue and convinced me to stop."

"Convinced you?"

"She is surprisingly strong, Lin. With one casual slap, she broke my neck."

"Good God," said Jack. "It's a nightmare over there."

"What about the kid?"

"Daria is fine. She—"

"No, the other one—Alessa."

"Her. That one is unusual. She watched me calmly, even as my neck was snapped. As I lay there dying, I saw her studying the walls of this room. Lin, something gathers in there."

"What are you talking about? What do you think is in there?"

"I prefer to not learn that. It is coming from the numbers, I believe. Extra symbols are missing for which I cannot account. They don't seem to be correlated with the attacks. The entity appears to be busy assembling something."

"Hang on."

Lin muted the phone.

"Let's hope it's just shooting blanks," said Jack.

"That's funny, Jack. Thanks."

"Hey, it might be true."

"Yeah, maybe it does misfire sometimes."

To Tayo, she said, "Hang on, Tayo. We'll see you soon."

"Thank you, Lin."

She ended the call.

"Gabby, whatever's going on, it seems to be speeding up. I have no idea what might be lurking in Tayo's walls. How do we fight this thing?"

"I'm glad you're back in the battle, Lin. I held back my recommendation until you were. There is an action you can take that is dangerous and will lead to either your immediate destruction, along with the rest of humanity, or it will destroy the entity. There can be no changing course once you begin."

"Wonderful. Just gets better all the time."

* * *

"Okay, Gabby, we raced out of the house with the leftover pizza and some chunks for Nomad, and we're well on our way. Maybe now you can tell me?"

Lin's Temt8tion purred like a content beast as it flew over the cold surface of Route 22. Gabriel rode up front, mostly watching the roadway approaching at high speeds as Lin passed car after car.

She glanced in the rearview and saw Nomad's panting face in the middle of the backseat. She leaned one way and saw Gloriana looking out her window. When she leaned the other way, she saw Jack smiling at her, so she blew him a kiss.

"Yes, we sure are on our way, Lin. Quickly too."

"You know I drive fast. Always have and always will. So, what is this thing I can do that will help?"

"Right now, the entity, the hunter as we've been calling it, is trapped in the capital numbers on Tayo's back. If it knew how to free itself all at once, it probably would."

"Which wouldn't be good for anyone, would it?"

"No, I don't think so. It would quickly gain experience in this world and begin slaughtering wholesale."

"Instead of just tormenting poor Tayo."

"Yes."

"So, what are you thinking?"

"Lin, you will have to summon it. Lure it. Get it to focus on you. I believe that it will sense your strength, and it will be drawn to you. It will know that using your strength will magnify its capabilities."

"And then, what? Why would I do that?"

"It's the only way. Remember that it's mostly Tayo's will and desire to serve humanity that is keeping the hunter in check. It is trying to break him, and if it succeeds, it will free itself quickly. From what we are hearing, it may very well succeed. Tayo is a good man, but every one of us has a breaking point."

"Oh, not you, Gabby."

"Recall my fondness for breakfast."

"Oh, and you wanted to be a rock star. I remember that."

"That hasn't changed. Each of us has a limit."

"Killing Tayo won't help?"

Gabriel turned to gaze at Lin, but she only watched the highway.

"Besides killing an innocent man being a bad thing to do,"—Gabriel looked out through the windshield again—"let's remember that it hasn't figured out how to stand on its own. It would have to inhabit someone else nearby."

"Like Anna or Daria? That doesn't sound so bad."

"Lin, that still wouldn't solve the problem. The ideal outcome is to save Tayo and everyone else while destroying the hunter."

Lin scoffed and shook her head, then she said, "I know you're right, Gabby, but if I lure that thing toward me, won't it just pile up under my skin somewhere?"

"That is a risk, but you have great strength in your intent. You must intend to hold it off by itself before it can take you. It will be angry and confused, if such a thing can have actual feelings, and it still will not have learned how to manage its power here."

"Fine. How do I lure it?"

"Oh, that's simple. You simply send an invitation. You tell Tayo that you will take the hunter from him. He will protest because he's a good man, but he's so weakened from his battles that he will agree.

"The hunter will hear that, and it will sense your power. It will be drawn to it. It really won't have any choice, Lin."

Jack leaned forward and said, "I don't like it. That doesn't sound safe at all. I like Tayo, I really do, but Lin, maybe you should just kill him and hope for the best."

Gabriel turned to look at Jack and said, "Jack, you have witnessed the enormous strength Lin possesses, haven't you? I believe she can do this, and no one, not even Tayo, will have to die."

To Jack, Lin said, "I know you're just worried about me, but don't be. I think I can do this."

"You can accomplish this, Lin Finity," said Gloriana while still peering out her side window. "If you need my assistance, even though I have no powers, I will try to help."

"Right. Cram in some good deeds before that death wind carries you away."

"Yes. Perhaps it is not too late."

"This isn't going to be a fun afternoon, that's for sure."

* * *

"No strange kid on the porch and no Anna in a short skirt, chasing that dog of hers. I guess they're all inside."

Lin parked her Temt8tion along the road, and they all sat a moment as she held the steering wheel and looked out through the windshield.

She looked up at the roof edge of Tayo's building, then she scanned in every direction she could along the street. Gabriel watched her eyes moving from roof to roof.

"She will return when you least expect her, Lin. She'll find her way."

Lin turned to Gabriel and wiped once at each of her eyes. She sighed and looked back out at the road.

"I hope so. Okay, let's get this over with. Jack, can you stay out here with Nomad? I know both of you would die in a heartbeat to protect me, but you might be rushing in when you don't need to. There might be some scary times, and there's no point in either of you being in danger."

"Alright, Lin, if that's what you want. Just be safe, alright?"

"Oh, I will, Jack."

"Do you wish me to remain in the car too?"

Lin turned to glare at Gloriana and said, "There's no way in hell. You're coming inside too."

"Because I can help?"

"No, because you can give up your life anytime you want."

"I promise I would not kick him again."

Lin flared her eyes bright green and focused them on Gloriana in the mirror.

"You are so right about that. Let's go."

* * *

Lin knocked softly and waited, but no one answered. She looked at Gabriel, who only shrugged.

"Lin Finity, perhaps you—"

"Shh. You're here and still alive only in case we need you," said Lin. "Stay quiet and out of my way."

She pushed the door into a room held in darkness despite a cold January sun high above lighting up the street.

"Anyone home?"

"Oh, it is you," said Anna from behind the door. She leaned around it and said, "We are in shock, and we fear every sight and sound."

"That's why the lights are out? You're too afraid of what you might see?"

"No, Lin. The electricity has left. We think whatever is in the wall is causing damage there."

"This still sounds crazy. You know that, right?"

"It is surely crazy, yet we are living it. This would never happen in Russia. Soon, I will take—"

"Yeah, right. I know. Let us in, okay?"

Anna stepped aside and pulled the door in, allowing Lin to enter the room, followed by Gabriel then Gloriana. Lin stopped and first took a glance at Anna's attire, which consisted of the same skirt, heels, and sweater she'd worn the last time they were there.

She scoffed and tried to look around the room, but the outside light lit a path only to the couch, which was empty except for Alessa sitting up on the back with her boots on the seat cushions. She turned to Lin without any change of expression.

"Nice," said Lin. "Anna, is there a flashlight in here?"

"Daria found one, but Tayo pleaded that it be left off."

"Why?"

"I do not know, but I did not debate."

Lin called into the darkness, "Daria, I know you're in here somewhere. Get that flashlight going, okay?"

305

The bright light shined into Lin's face, causing her to squint and hold up her hand to block it.

"That's great, Daria. Really helpful. Point that at Tayo a second, will you?"

"Only if you say—"

"Don't. I don't need to see you to teach you a lesson you'll never forget."

The beam of light moved to the floor, where Tayo lay on his back with Lee sitting next to him.

"Tayo, are you okay?"

"Yes. For the moment, Lin."

"Hi," said Lee. "Just so you know, I'm exhausted. I'm keeping up with the damage, but it isn't easy."

"You're still amazing, Lee. Lee Ternity—that's you. Daria, keep that light on. Maybe point it at the ceiling, okay?"

The flashlight illuminated the white plaster, brightening the room enough for Lin to see everyone.

"Everyone's okay?"

"Lee repaired me, and Daria needed no attention," said Anna.

"My neck has been restored, but I choose to remain still, Lin. I suspect some critical part of my anatomy will explode soon. It's very likely that I might grow a second head, and an additional one after that wouldn't surprise any of my other heads at that point. If the hunter were to invade my digestive system, I fear that—"

"Whoa. Hold up, okay? Let's take things as they are right now. You said there are symbols missing from your back."

"Yes. By my count—which is a formidable task when one is being annihilated, I can assure you—there are now five that have left my body with no corresponding calamity."

"And you think they're in the walls? Doing what?"

"You wish for me to engage my imagination?"

Tayo cackled while raising his head off of the floor and stretching his eyes open wide. Daria pointed the beam at his face.

"The ceiling, Daria, okay? I don't think the man needs a spotlight right now."

"I surely do not," he said and let his head clunk on the wood floor.

"We have a plan," said Lin, "but first, let's all just listen."

Lin gave a sideways glance at Alessa, who sat calmly in the near darkness. She turned her eyes to hold Lin's gaze and once again convinced Lin that she might be a photograph.

A squeal and three scratching sounds came from the wall separating Tayo's modest living room from his kitchen. Daria trained the flashlight on it.

"I really don't want to have to tell you again."

The ceiling lit up again.

"Was that it? That mousy kind of sound?"

Tayo laughed and said, "A mouse? There isn't a hint of hope that that's a mouse. Not an iota of optimism, or even a microscopic molecule of—"

"Okay, okay. Let's listen some more."

Twenty seconds of silence passed, then Gloriana said, "I believe that was only a mouse."

"It was NOT a mouse!" said Tayo. "Lin, I know what it will do to me next. It will move my eyes inside my intestines. I will have to watch as—"

A loud screech rang out from the wall behind Alessa. She only turned her head for a moment, then she faced the room again.

"Lin," said Gabriel from close to her ear, "Tayo can't hang on much longer. I don't recommend we try to wait for what lurks in the wall to make an appearance."

"You might be right. Hey, Gabby, isn't this bizarre enough that you can, you know, help out?"

"No. I am truly sorry, Lin. My mission is to safeguard you, and that involves me acting like anyone else."

"You can't use,"—Lin turned to look around the room at everyone listening—"any special talents?"

"No. Lancaster Wolfe was different. He was evil. This hunter is not."

"Not evil," said Tayo as his head rolled to one side and his chest heaved with his silent cackling.

"Fine."

Lin gestured for Gabriel and Gloriana to remain by the door with Anna, and she held a finger to her lips when she looked at Alessa. Alessa only nodded back. She pointed her finger at Daria and frowned, causing the light in her hand to shake.

"Keep that light where it is, and keep that dog of yours out of the way."

Daria nodded, and Lin said, "Wait. Point that at your hair."

She did.

"No. Come on. Don't be stupid. The other side."

She moved the light, and Lin chuckled at the restored thick black hair. She looked down at Lee.

"Nice work."

Lin looked back up.

"Daria, we're done with your hair."

The ceiling got bright, adding light to the room. Lin walked over and stood beside Tayo.

In a loud, steady voice, Lin said, "Tayo, I wish to take from you that which has invaded you."

Screeching and scratching erupted from every wall. The light on the ceiling danced around, and Tayo began to wail.

"Oh, here we go," said Lin, and she allowed her eyes to erupt with fiery green light that dwarfed the flashlight's weak beam.

Chapter 30 – Go To God

Lin's blazing green eyes switched off, and she collapsed to lie beside Tayo. In the flashlight's direct beam, he turned only his head to glance at her, then he looked straight up at the ceiling.

"Easy come, easy go!" he said and kept shaking his head slowly with a toothy grin.

Lee reached over Tayo to shake Lin by her arm, which only flopped her head to one side.

"Lin, what happened? Are you alright?"

Gloriana took two steps closer and looked down on them.

"It has taken her to a place I know all too well, Gabriel. My time is nearing its end, whether from natural forces or from Lin's promise. I will go and assist if I can."

"How?" said Gabriel. "You still have that kind of power?"

"No, I have only strong intent. I will display it like a tasty morsel in a trap. That hunter has tried for centuries to destroy me. It will rejoice at the opportunity to take me again."

"Will you be able to return?"

Gloriana turned to hold Gabriel's gaze and said, "Am I meant to?"

Gabriel didn't answer, only nodded, and Lee narrowly escaped Gloriana crumpling to lie on Tayo's other side.

"I can't really help them, can I?" said Lee.

"No, not this time."

"What was she talking about? Where are they?"

Gabriel said, "I believe she's in the fight, Lee. The hunter has indeed taken her. They're in a place where it is at its strongest."

"Is Lin going to be alright?"

"She's very strong. I believe she will."

Gabriel turned to the corner where Anna stared with her arm around Daria, who held a silent Ozzy.

"Daria is your name?" Gabriel said, holding one hand up to block the light, "Lin's idea for the flashlight was wise, don't you think?"

"Oh yeah, I just . . . with all the stuff going on . . ."

The room brightened with the beam directed up again.

Gabriel turned toward the couch.

"None of this surprises or scares you, does it?"

Alessa looked calmly at Gabriel and said, "This is hopeful, and it's nothing I need to fear. Do you?"

Gabriel only smiled with a shaking head.

* * *

"Oh, I can't believe I'm here again!"

Lin looked to her right and saw Gloriana staring out over a churning ocean with waves capped in white, and beyond her, a fiery sun tried to set itself, burning a hot pit into the water. Her cinnamon gown flapped around her legs from the steady wind whipping at them from across the waves.

"You stole my shoes?"

Gloriana turned to her slowly and smiled.

"No, Lin Finity. They are not real, but you know that. None of this is real."

"This is where it began with us."

"Yes. It is also where it ends. You do not feel anything, do you?"

"I feel the wind and some crazy heat from your sun."

She looked down at the intricate stone shapes all fit together with an impossible precision, and she also saw that she still wore her skirt and heels.

"I feel the stone beneath my high heels too. You intended this outfit for me?"

"Yes, Lin Finity. It is a gesture of kindness."

"Thank you. What else should I feel?"

"There are teeth in my throat but not yours. The hunter is here, and my strength sustains me, but it stops as I weaken."

"You're doing it again, aren't you? No past or future?"

Gloriana shook her head and looked down.

"I am with you too long on the Islands of Time. I must accept the nature of this place."

"Hell, you mean."

"Yes."

Lin gazed out over the ocean and the darkening sky. The wind whistled directly at them and lifted both of their manes up and back.

"I know why I'm here. I volunteered for this to save Tayo. Oh, and the rest of humanity, I suppose."

"I, too, am a volunteer."

Lin turned to look at her, but Gloriana kept looking out over the low wall of her tower.

"Why? Why would you do that?"

She turned to face Lin, and her caramel eyes glowed weakly.

"I do much to deserve my fate, and I cannot argue with the judgment I receive. The clothing you wear is not my only gesture."

She looked out to the horizon and raised her arms to each side. Her chest expanded with a deep breath of the not-real air.

"This tower . . . the ocean and sky . . . these I offer to you while you are here and not on the Islands."

"You're protecting me too?"

"Yes, but it does not last. You are meant to live."

"What about you? You're not returning?"

"I cannot."

She closed her eyes.

"She does not let me."

Lin leaned out farther to try to look into Gloriana's eyes.

"Who? Who won't let you?"

Gloriana remained silent and still and again gazed far out across the sea. With her wild, dark hair blown back, Lin wondered if that's how

Hell would take her: she'd become a statue on an imaginary tower, never to move again.

* * *

A loud squeak threatened to rip open the wall behind the couch, followed by scratching that traced a path from floor to ceiling as it circled the room, shaking anything clinging to the walls. Alessa continued to gaze at Gabriel with no change in expression.

"Mr. Gabriel, we really must go, Daria and I. Ozzy too. This crazy story must come to an end."

Gabriel gave Alessa another smile and turned to Anna.

"I won't stop you. But after all we've been through, wouldn't you like to see what happens next? Aren't you curious?"

Anna shook her head and said, "No, I am not at all. I do not know why, but you ring louder alarms than even Lin. You are too calm as a giant mouse attacks us all."

"Mouse!" said Tayo.

She turned to look at Alessa and said, "As are you. Do you not hear the scratch and squeak all around you?"

"Mom, don't start pissing off the creepy kid too. Let's just—"

"Your hearts are good," said Alessa. "Your souls are safe."

Anna stared silently with her mouth moving, then she said, "There are things in the walls that are about to kill us all, and you sit on that furniture like you are eating ice cream in a park. Who are you people?"

Alessa offered only a smile and said, "You do know that something will eventually end your life, don't you?"

Anna froze, and Daria stepped behind her and peeked over her shoulder.

"Mom," she said in a shaky voice, "let's get the hell out of here. She's creepy as hell, and these people—"

"People!" Tayo said, followed by a weak cackle. "Do *not* be afraid of people. What inhabits the simple walls of the simple home of a simple man who's simply insane? Oh, yeah, go ahead and fear *that!*"

Lee held his arm, and Tayo closed his eyes and laughed as the squeaking erupted from the wall across the room, causing her to look.

"Gabriel, it's all over the place in here. Any advice?"

"My hope is that Lin, or Lin and Gloriana together, can finish their task quickly. The wall won't resist it much longer."

"Why can it not break through these flimsy walls?" said Anna. "I have seen it do just that. It made a mess, and we wanted to clean it, but—"

"Mom," said Daria. "Lin was right—forget about cleaning, alright?"

"I do not mean these walls," Gabriel said while pointing all around the room and looking from face to face.

Gabriel looked down at Tayo, who still grinned but had picked his head up off of the floor and opened his eyes to look at Gabriel.

Gabriel pointed down at him and said, "*He* is the wall."

* * *

The scratching and squeaking came from behind every wall in Tayo's apartment at the same time. Daria held Ozzy and hid behind Anna, and Lee remained near Tayo and holding one of his hands while he muttered to himself and shook his head, occasionally saying words like "explosions" and "dismemberment."

Lin and Gloriana still lay unconscious on either side of Tayo, and Gabriel stood quietly watching the scene before turning to look at Alessa.

"You have a message, don't you?"

Alessa nodded.

"I have a message, and I have a mission."

The squeaking diminished, but the scratching continued.

With a tilted head and a smile, Gabriel said, "I think it might be listening."

Alessa managed a barely noticeable smile.

"We can start with the message, if you'd like. It's more of an explanation, isn't it?"

"Yes."

Lee still held Tayo's hand, but she stared at her daughter with a confused frown.

"About the hunter?" said Gabriel.

"Yes. 'It' is really 'they.'"

"I have suspected as much."

"I haven't," said Lee. "Lessa, baby, what are you talking about?"

Alessa looked down at her and said, "If I seem odd, Mom, it's because I am not like so many others. I'm more . . . like Gabriel."

Lee stared and waited for her daughter to continue, but Alessa looked back at Gabriel and said, "I believe you understand this already, Gabriel, so this message is for everyone else here. And Lin too."

"Not Gloriana?"

"No. Tell Lin that what she calls the hunter is a vast collection of damned souls. They have earned their places in Hell, and they have been given a job, one which they embrace because they have no other purpose left. Their work is to devour the living. They hunt in packs.

"It lessens their pain and suffering but only by a small amount. Still, they have nothing else, so they pursue their work with a desperate enthusiasm."

Gabriel nodded and said, "This hunter, this particular entity, was a collection of forty damned souls?"

"Yes."

"Lin and Gloriana are battling—"

"A different one. There are too many to count."

She looked at the floor and shook her head slowly, and Gabriel said, "Yes, it is very much a waste of souls."

She looked back up.

"Some from Tayo have launched themselves, causing havoc for him, then returning to Hell. Others wait in the walls, not understanding their actions or having any plan, but still, they are attempting to find some solution."

Anna and Daria looked all around the room as the scratching continued.

"And others remain embedded in Tayo."

"And your mission?" said Gabriel.

"First, to stop the attack from those that remain. They can't return on their own until they act as their lot compels them."

"That's likely to destroy Tayo. We believed it could be vanquished here, and that would help free mankind from the disease and destruction that they bring."

Alessa shook her head slowly while gazing at Gabriel and said, "That's not the plan. This world isn't meant to be easy. Even if it were, don't we all want to return to God eventually?"

Gabriel nodded and looked down at Tayo.

"Yes. These damned souls are what send us home."

"Yes, Gabriel."

The scratching increased, and the squeaking started up again.

"Perhaps we could talk more about this when you're done," said Gabriel. "It might be best if you fulfill your mission sooner rather than later."

"I agree. Mom, can we see Tayo's back?"

"Sure."

Lee grabbed Tayo's shoulders, and with one strong snap like he was a tablecloth, she lifted and rotated him to face down, carefully holding his head so it wouldn't clunk on the floor. He never resisted, and he continued to cackle softly. She pulled his shirt up to reveal twenty-four symbols still intact.

"God, they're moving," said Lee. "Whatever's in there is moving around."

The squeaking inside the walls increased, as did the scratching.

"It's okay, Mom. They'll be gone soon."

* * *

"What? Who won't let you return?"

Gloriana turned to meet Lin's gaze.

"The girl who is not just a girl. She is empowered to resolve this situation, and I accept what that brings to me."

"Lee's daughter? She's kind of odd, but how could—"

"Yes, she is odd. As is Gabriel. I choose those words. Do you understand, Lin Finity?"

"How could that be? How could she be an—"

"Do we understand any of this? Any of it at all?"

Lin looked back out at the horizon and saw that there wasn't enough water in the ocean to reach that far. A glance to her right revealed an orange sun fainter by several shades.

"No. No, we really don't. That thing. That hunter. It has its teeth in you?"

"It does, and I cannot fight it. Already, this world is too much for me to hold. My islands are let go because I become weak. My people there, too, as I lose strength."

"And this is where you came. You escaped."

"I escape nothing. Your strong intent gives me only few days on the Islands of Time, and I cannot make up for my life if I try."

"It almost sounds like you're saying you're sorry for everything you've done."

"That is not likely. If more time is granted, I try to atone to save my life, nothing more."

"You didn't even try before, though. You invaded Jack's dreams, didn't you?"

"I cannot be blamed if Jack dreams of me."

"You didn't cause any of that?"

Gloriana looked out over the ocean as the glow of her eyes continued to dwindle.

"Even now, as my tower sinks into the emptiness, I still cannot change. The answer I give is no."

"Lying right now won't help you, that's for sure. This might be your last chance. Did you mess with Jack's dreams?"

Gloriana sighed and closed her eyes.

"I live as this woman for countless centuries, and even with what I face . . . I cannot change."

"I'll ask you again: did you cause those dreams with Jack?"

Gloriana opened her eyes and focused on the ragged edge of the ocean drawing nearer as the wind died entirely, and her long, dark hair hung still upon her shoulders and down her back.

"No."

* * *

"What will you do?" said Gabriel.

"I will not let these souls harm anyone else."

Tayo still shook with his silent laughter, and Lee held his hand. Anna and Daria cowered in the corner, and Alessa looked down on Tayo's back.

Gabriel looked up at the ceiling, then at Daria.

"Daria, try switching off that light."

Daria clicked the flashlight, taking away the bright spot from the ceiling, and the room remained lit.

"What the—"

"Mom, don't say another word. I want to survive this, alright?"

Alessa had become the light source for the room. Her dark clothing and boots appeared almost white, and it was as if she reflected light off of herself from unknown sources aimed at her from every direction.

Gabriel watched silently as Alessa leaned over to look at the remaining symbols. She waited there as her light increased. When she spoke, all scratching and squeaking stopped.

"Any one of you could have killed this man, yet you did not. It's not because you knew that I would arrive.

"You also knew that you could have set yourselves free to rampage across the Earth if only you had ended his life. Still, you didn't."

She paused but never broke her gaze upon his back.

"You have suffered so long that you can't even form the question anymore."

Alessa looked up at Gabriel, who smiled and nodded. She glanced at each of the silent walls, then she looked back down on the symbols beneath Tayo's skin.

"So, I will answer the question that you have given up all hope of even asking."

* * *

Gloriana's body shook, and she closed her eyes.

"It's taking you, isn't it?"

"Yes. You should return. You should live."

"How much longer do you have?"

Gloriana was wracked again by a tremor, and a large portion of the ocean all around vanished, leaving only a gray void. She let out a short laugh.

"Time?"

"I don't know how else to talk about it."

"Because you do not belong in Hell."

"You're really not going to try to get back?"

She shook her head slowly and bit her lip as another tremor ripped through her.

"No. I am the dead leaf of which Gabriel speaks. I am tossed into the air, and I know which direction my last wind follows."

"Which way?"

She took in a deep breath and let it out slowly.

"My wind stops because I am already here."

Lin groaned and wiped at one eye.

"God, I can't believe I even care about you."

"Though I try, I do not care about you. I cannot find a way. And though I try to resist it, I still wish to ruin you and take your power so that I may live. No other path presents itself."

"That sure sounded like some kind of confession."

Gloriana didn't respond.

Noticing a change, Lin snapped her head to face out at where the horizon should be just as a black spot appeared. It waited there, and she couldn't look away from it again.

"Well, you can't take my power. My hold on my intent is unbreakable."

"I know this," Gloriana said in almost a whisper. "I cannot take your life. Still . . . I cannot help but try to diminish it."

"You just can't choose good, can you, even at the end?"

"No, Lin Finity. In none of my days do I make *that* leap."

Lin felt a shiver chatter up her spine, and she fought to turn her eyes, not just her head, to see who remained beside her. But she couldn't look directly at the figure that appeared to be on its hands and knees, raising one arm to reach out through the gap in the low wall.

The figure let out a raspy, forlorn wail and cried, "Free will!"

"What about it?"

"It brings me here."

"No. You should have chosen good."

"Though I gather great power, I still cannot. I should stay for all my days what God makes me."

"What? No, you can't mean that—"

"It is my . . . moment, Lin Finity. Perhaps we meet again. Tell Mr. Jack I say goodbye."

Lin still couldn't break her gaze at the spot which had begun its race toward her, expanding itself to cover sky and ocean, but she did perceive enough to know that she stood alone on the tower.

"No, not yet! Come back!"

Just as she felt the first sharp claws find her neck, and as the hungry jaws found her flesh and ground into her bones, empty blackness covered the last surviving patches of incomplete sky and fractured ocean and then swallowed every block of the tower. She felt one small stone solid beneath her favorite heels.

Pushing aside the silent scream gathering inside her, she called out to the emptiness, "Wait! Gloriana, what did God make you?"

The stone beneath her vanished, but there was nowhere for her to fall.

"Why did you call him Mr.—"

Lin's lungs turned to ice. Every thought was erased, and all feelings boiled away, leaving her alone with a drum for a heart.

Until it stopped.

* * *

Anna held a hand out to block the light coming from Alessa, and Daria buried her face in her mom's hair. Only Ozzy continued to study the scene.

Gabriel still smiled and watched Alessa, and Lee only looked down on Tayo as she held both of his hands while he whimpered and shook.

"You, and those that have acted and returned to Hell,"—Alessa held both of her palms over Tayo's back—"have all chosen good despite your lot. Know that there is mercy in creation, and there is hope, even for you that have none."

She paused as her splendor flared.

"You forty are forgiven. Go to God."

In a brightly lit room, Anna turned around and embraced Daria, blocking even Ozzy's view. Gabriel and Lee watched Tayo's back.

One symbol at a time vanished from beneath his skin, drawing a laugh from him each time as if he'd been tickled. The scratching and squeaking in the walls had started up again, and it increased with each new symbol that joined the others. When the last symbol had departed, the walls offered only silence.

Under Alessa's illumination, the perfect, smooth black skin of Tayo's back moved with his gentle, deep breaths.

Lee looked up with a smile just as Alessa's sublime radiance left her, and the room went dark.

Silent seconds passed before Gabriel said, "Daria, would you mind?"

After some fumbling sounds and a click, the flashlight beam found the ceiling, and the room brightened.

Lee was standing with an unconscious Alessa in her arms. Lin still lay on one side of Tayo, but Gloriana was gone.

"She collapsed," said Lee, "but I caught her. Is she going to be alright, Gabriel? Should I try to heal her, or what?"

"There's no need. She will be—"

Gabriel stopped at the sight of Lin dragging a hand across her face and coughing. She sat up and looked around.

"Lin, I'm glad to see you back," said Gabriel. "You were safer than you thought. We all were, thanks to Alessa."

"I'm glad to be back. What happened to the hunter?"

"Alessa took care of that," said Gabriel.

"She killed it? How? Who is she?"

"She's a very special being, Lin. No, she didn't destroy them."

"'Them?' Okay, then, where are they?"

"She brought them a message of forgiveness."

Lin turned to look at Lee, who met her gaze and shrugged.

"We figured something must have happened to her, Lee. Do you remember that talk we had?"

"Oh, yeah. She was just beginning her life inside me when I found that power of mine, the one that healed me."

"Healed you and a lot of other people. Is she going to be okay?"

"Like anyone could know," said Lee, and she looked back at her daughter in her arms.

Lin looked up at Gabriel.

"Gloriana won't be joining us. She's lost there."

"Yes, she departed a moment ago. That might have been her final act with the last of her strength: she took her physical form with her."

"Is that possible?"

Gabriel smiled and shrugged.

"What isn't, Lin?"

She shook her head and stood with a hand up from Gabriel.

"Gabby, she wasn't completely bad. She spent what strength she had left protecting me. She created the tower, the ocean, sky, and sun. She could have used that power to keep herself insulated for a while."

"Very few are completely bad, Lin. It seems she had a reason to want you to live."

"She did say she wanted to diminish my life. Even at the very end, that's what she said."

"I believe you will find out how eventually."

"She said some other things too. Things I almost don't dare to think about. I need to ask you about that later."

"There will be time for that."

"Lee," said Lin, "I guess your work here is done. You're heading back to Jacksonville?"

"Yep. Back to a normal life," she said with a laugh. "I hope we meet up again sometime, Lin, maybe for fun instead of whatever all this was."

"I look forward to it."

"Maybe with another bottle of wine."

"Oh, that's for sure."

She turned to face Anna, Daria, and Ozzy in the corner.

"Can you guess what I'm going to say?"

They continued to stare.

"No? You've heard it before. It's simple: forget everything you've seen the last couple of days. Get back to your lives. Go to Russia. I don't ever, ever want to see any of you again."

"We are mostly happy you have not destroyed us, Lin. You are very generous. We will go."

Anna took the lead, stepping around Tayo, still face-down on the floor, and led her daughter to the door. She pulled it in, and Daria and Ozzy hurried onto the porch while Anna turned to face the room.

Before Anna could speak, Daria leaned into the open doorway, viewed Lin through fingers resembling a camera lens, winked, and fled out of sight.

"God, she never stops, does she?"

"You might be right about her, Lin."

"That's for sure."

"I will not forget everything about you. I will continue to remember your sense of fashion. That is one thing about you that is not frightening. But I do not wish to see you again. Goodbye."

She stepped out and slammed the door shut.

Lin let out a deep sigh and said, "I feel better already. Gabby, we should get out to the car and head home. Do you feel like cooking when we get back? I'll even eat those hotcakes of yours if that's what you want."

"Yes, I'll cook. And yes, I always want the hotcakes."

They walked to the door, and Lin turned and said, "Tayo, you're going to be fine. You've served humanity in an impossible way like probably no one ever has before. Take a vacation. Go somewhere warm and relax."

In a low, strained voice, Tayo said, "Thank you, Lin. If I willfully shield myself from all recent recollections, a recovery of some type seems possible. I will try."

"I'll stay with him awhile," said Lee. "I might even give him a tune-up just to be sure."

Lin smiled and said, "That's a great idea, Lee Ternity. Until we meet again."

Lin stepped outside with Gabriel and shut the door. She looked down the street and saw Jack and Nomad standing near her Temt8tion. Jack waved, and Nomad barked once at the sky.

"Why does he bark at the sky like that?"

They both stared for a second, then Gabriel said, "Perhaps he's laughing to Heaven."

Lin turned to Gabriel with a frown, but Gabriel only smiled in Nomad's direction. After a moment, Lin looked there too.

"Well, it's been some kind of a week, huh, Gabby?"

"Yes, it sure has. You deserve some rest and relaxation."

"Maybe some recreation too," she said, thinking of her secret destination and its next episode. "Enough with this life and death stuff."

"Fresh blueberry hotcakes will be a good start, don't you think?"

"Oh yeah, Gabby. That's for sure."

* * *

Before Jack could say anything, Lin said, "Jack, everyone is fine. Everyone except Gloriana, that is."

"God, that's good to hear. You killed that thing?"

"No, that's not at all what happened. It's a long story, Jack, so maybe we should get back on the road, okay?"

"Yeah, sure. I can drive if you want to take a break."

"Oh, you know what? Gabby, do you feel like driving? I bet Nomad would make a good copilot for you."

"Yes, I do like driving, but we won't get to your house as quickly."

"Nope."

"And you're exactly right about Nomad. He's a big help."

Gabriel and Nomad sat up front, and Lin and Jack took the back seats. Gabriel started the engine, and Nomad turned around and panted as Jack put an arm around Lin. She snuggled in close, and the big dog studied Jack's eyes for a moment, then he turned to look out through the windshield.

"Oh, Jack, now I really feel how tired I am. That hunter, and then being on that windy phantom tower, and . . . and then . . ."

Jack held her tight in the quiet car all the way back to her hometown in Pennsylvania.

Chapter 31 – This Might Be Goodbye

"I'm still glad you're a good cook," Jack said as Gabriel rattled around in the kitchen, cleaning up after dinner.

"Happy to pitch in, Jack. Lin, it's good that you let me feed a couple of scrambled eggs to Nomad too. Do you remember when you were concerned with his weight?"

"Hmm . . . maybe I still should be," she said with his big head on her lap as she flopped his ears around. "He's a big boy. My sweet fluffy boy."

"Speaking of that big boy," said Jack, "I'm ready to go out if he is."

Nomad picked his head up, barked once at the ceiling, and panted and stared at Jack.

"How is it that he understands you when you talk about him?"

"Oh, it's not just then," said Jack. "We just got to be better friends while you were off flying around. We're both glad you're done flying."

Lin glanced at Gabriel before turning back to Jack.

"I'm sure done being a crow. And you know what? I don't miss Gloriana at all. Do you want to know one of the last things she said to me?"

"Where, up on that tower of yours?"

"Yep, up there. She basically said she wanted to ruin my life. Whatever else she was, she wasn't a good woman, Jack."

"No, not at all. Nothing sunny about her."

"You know what else, Jack? Just before Hell took her away, she told me to say goodbye to 'Mr. Jack.'"

Jack bumped his cup over, forming a hot puddle of coffee that dripped over the table's edge.

"Jack, are you okay? What's wrong?"

"What did she call me?"

"Mr. Jack. I thought that was odd because she—"

"Oh God, Lin. This can't be happening."

"I don't understand. What are you talking about?"

"Mr. Jack. Lin, do you remember those dreams that I had of Gloriana?"

"Well, I don't really know what happened in them, but I remember you—"

"Lin, in the dreams, that's what she called me. When the dream was ending, *each time*, she called me Mr. Jack."

Lin stared, and Nomad put his head back down on her lap.

"What exactly did you two do in those dreams?"

"Nothing. I mean, she wanted all kinds of things to happen, but I—"

"You said they seemed real. Were they real? She made them real? Just how much happened?"

"Alright, she was trying to seduce me. She wanted me to want her, not you. God, she really tried. But you know what? I rejected her. She had mayhem in those dreams. I couldn't run away. I couldn't throw her through a window. She—"

"So, how much did she make you do? Did you sleep with her, Jack?"

"No. No, I never did. When she made me put your engagement ring on her finger, then I—"

"You did what? You gave her my ring?"

"She had mayhem! Her eyes were glowing! But, Lin, I fought through it and took the ring back. I ripped it off her finger. That ended it. She knew she'd lost. I swear. I chose you. I never wanted her."

Lin looked down at Nomad, allowed the room to stay in silence for many moments, and said, "Do you need to go out, my big boy?"

Nomad didn't bark at the ceiling or pant at Jack. He only walked over and bumped his head into Jack's leg, and he held it there.

Lin aimed a steady stare at Jack, and he stood, paused to hold her gaze, then walked toward the door. Nomad followed him. They left for the backyard, and Jack pulled the door shut.

Lin turned to Gabriel.

"Gabby, those dreams were real? She really made Jack dream of her?"

"I wouldn't call them real, Lin. Her intent was still very strong, but she didn't have mayhem. All she could do was create the illusion in a dream."

"But you told me that if there was enough intent, then it was real. Was it real for Jack? Whatever happened, did he really do whatever they did?"

"No, it wasn't real at all for him, but it was somewhat real for Gloriana. Lin, Jack resisted her onslaught and chose you. You know how overpowering your mayhem is. Could anyone fight through that?"

"No, there's no way."

"Exactly. That's what Jack experienced in those dreams. And still, he *did* fight against it and triumph. He did that with the strength of his love for you."

"How could he beat that?"

"I told you something once, but you were distracted by so much else. I believe Taylor was causing storms in St. Simons, and I don't think you gave it much thought. But I said that perhaps love is a type of magic too. Do you remember that?"

"Yeah, I do."

"Jack is very strong, isn't he?"

"That's for sure. He must be to keep up with me."

"Yes, exactly. His love for you has passed a test like no one has ever faced before. He passed that test, Lin."

Lin exhaled all of her breath and looked up at the ceiling. She looked back down at Gabriel's kind eyes just as the back door opened, Nomad ran in, shaking off snow and whipping his mane around, and Jack said, "Um, I'm going to run to the hardware store. Be back soon."

He closed the door, and Nomad returned to Lin's side.

"It's just one thing after another, you know? Now, I have to try to stop imagining everything that happened in those dreams of theirs."

"Not theirs, Lin. Gloriana's. Jack is innocent."

"Then, why do I feel like I need a break?"

"I believe you do. You've been through a lot. What kind of break?"

"A flight to forever. It'll only take a second."

"Were Gloriana's flights for Jack somewhere in forever, too, Lin?"

Lin held Gabriel's gaze for a moment, then she looked at her hands in her lap.

"At least, I'm trying to learn new things when I go."

"Every time?"

She looked back up into Gabriel's steady gaze.

"Well, maybe not every single—"

"You must always do what you think is best, Lin."

Lin hesitated, then said, "I'm going."

"I won't try to convince you otherwise."

Gabriel got up to clear the table, and Lin left for the living room.

* * *

Gabriel sat at the far end of the couch, gazing calmly while playing with Nomad's ears, whose heavy head rested on a pillow. Lin sat at the other end, occasionally taking hits from Nomad's bushy, swishing tail.

"I've thought about it, and I'm not mad at Jack, but still, it's best if I go one more time."

"Good. Jack was only a victim of her strong intent. Where will you go, Lin?"

"I have to go back to the same place. I'm going to that hotel in St. Simons, even though I barely made it back last time."

"How many times have you been to the same world?"

"Only five times, and the last one—"

"That is four too many. You've already taken a very large risk. I'd advise that you don't even consider trying that again."

"I am thinking about just one more time."

"Why? What's drawing you back there?"

"Well, it's not to learn a new power. You once asked if I had a fascination with the feelings Gloriana imposed on me. I told you I didn't. I didn't lie, but I don't think I understood how maybe I really did. Could some of that just be me? Maybe those are mostly my feelings like we thought, and Gloriana's worlds only brought them out into the open."

"It's more likely that Gloriana's influence is still lingering in you."

"Could be. It might be from her, or maybe it's just me."

"Whichever it is, what's your plan?"

"I need to go back to take that world further and see if it's what I really want. I have to recreate the right conditions."

"Does that mean that you'll go without your powers?"

Lin squirmed into the cushion and said, "Yeah, that's the only way. I already tried that once, and it worked because there came a time when I needed, or at least wanted, those powers, and I couldn't—"

"You've already gone once without your powers."

Gabriel looked up at the ceiling and paused for a few moments before showing a smile and facing Lin again.

"Tell me: on that particular flight, did you happen to look out a window?"

"What? No. Why would I? I was focused on more exciting things."

"If you try a flight like that again, which I still advise you to forgo, then I ask you to try it. Just look, and if you do make it back to us, you can tell me if you noticed anything."

"You're not even going to give me a hint, are you?"

"No, because it's not about what you might see. It's about what might notice you."

"That sounds kind of ominous."

"It's not."

Lin only stared at her unbelievable best friend and shook her head.

"So, Lin, you will be there again without your powers?"

"Yes, it's the only way. That's the fantasy—to be the cheap and easy Lin with no magic powers. For that kind of flight, being helpless seems to be the biggest attraction."

"Do you understand why that is?"

"We talked about it once. I think it's kind of an escape from my mayhem and powers over the magic. It's like a vacation from my powers."

"This will be your sixth visit to the same world. I'm surprised that door hasn't closed already."

"It felt like it was about to close that last time. It kept stringing me along even after I wanted to leave."

"Yes, that's part of it becoming real: you're becoming a part of it. Your feelings are being shaped as that world grows more real."

"Well, I'm not worried. I'll just let myself enjoy those feelings— that's the whole point. I'll still be able to come back when I want."

"That's just it, Lin. Part of those feelings will be that you will not want to come back. You'll always find a reason to stay just a moment longer."

"I have to take that risk. I need to at least go far enough to experience part of what was waiting for me there."

"What exactly is waiting for you?"

Lin stared at Gabriel a moment, then shook her head.

"Let's just say I'm the center of attention. I do like attention."

"And if the door slams shut the next time you're there?"

"Well, it's just in St. Simons, right? Couldn't I just find my way back here?"

She gave Gabriel a hopeful smile.

"By then, you won't want to. You won't remember anything about your life here. Not Jack or Taylor or Nomad. Not even me."

Nomad picked his head up and stared at Lin, both big eyes unblinking. She only stared at Gabriel and shook her head, then she met Nomad's gaze.

"You might not come back, Lin."

Nomad swallowed hard enough that Lin and Gabriel heard it, and he tipped his head to one side while still staring at her. She shook her head gently and closed her eyes.

Then, she relived for just a second the moment the door was about to get pushed in, and the strangers, including the one that seemed oddly familiar, would roughly drag her out. Out into the dim room for the enjoyment of more strangers than she could count. She felt the hunger inside her, the craving to live that experience. The audacity of it gave her a chill.

She again felt like if that world kept her, if she were to become that Lin with no way back, that it wouldn't be so bad. Taylor would be fine—if she were to come back. Gabriel would return to the fight against evil. And Jack would probably get over her eventually. He'd find someone new and get on with his life. If there was some way that Gloriana could escape Hell again, maybe they could be a couple and not just in his dreams.

She knew that Jack didn't want Gloriana, only her, but so did all of those strangers. The things they'd expect of her. The things she couldn't stop them from doing to her. And if she *could* find a way to guarantee a safe passage back home, it wouldn't have to be the last time. That could be something she'd arrange for herself many times—anytime she needed a break for some fun. With many strangers in many hotels. All of them wanting—

"Lin?"

"Gabby, I have to go. I'll leave from my room. If I make it back, it'll be like I walked in there and back out. I'll be back on the couch before Jack gets home. Wish me luck, okay?"

"This might be goodbye, Lin. I wish you well in all your travels."

"Let's hope for the best," she said as she leaned forward to pat Nomad's head and rub his ears. She held his chin and said, "See you soon, my sweet fluffy boy."

He pulled his head from her hand to bark once at the ceiling, then he panted while holding her gaze.

"Nomad thinks I'll be fine. I think that's his way of smiling."

"If he says you will, then you probably will."

"How would he know?"

"He knows much."

She rubbed his ears again.

"When you come back, you should consider looking at him."

"I'm looking at him right now."

"No, Lin. His spirit. Have you ever looked at that?"

"Only that one time when I tried to take control of him. But all I really did was look for that gap, and my only plan was to take him with my mayhem."

"Maybe you should just see what you can see sometime. After you come back."

"I could look right now."

"I'd rather you wait."

"Oh, I get it. It's one more reason to come back, right?"

Gabriel only smiled.

"You're really something, Gabby."

Lin gazed at Gabriel, shaking her head slowly, then said to Nomad, "Okay, it's a date, my sweet fluffy boy."

* * *

Lin stepped lightly to her bedroom, her walking becoming a determined strutting, and closed and locked the door. Standing in front of her dresser mirror, she faced the danger of what she was determined to do. And still, she saw a smile along with the bright green eyes looking back at her. All she could think about was learning what might happen in that world after the locked door opened to her fantasy's finale.

She sighed and unbuttoned her blouse, watched as she pulled the tight shirt open, and tossed it onto the bed. She shimmied out of her skirt, kicked it aside, and picked up her brush. Standing in only her heels, she brushed back her hair and felt her heart beating strong inside her, whether from fear or excitement, she couldn't be sure. Maybe both, she thought.

Satisfied that her hair was ready and knowing that it probably wouldn't carry through to where she was going, she ran her hands up her sides, over her breasts, and up into her hair. She held it back with both hands and looked at all of her exposed skin, imagining how many hands that she might soon feel all over her. How completely helpless and unable to stop them she'd soon be.

With one last smile to the soon-to-be powerless woman with excited eyes in the mirror, she turned and walked to her bathroom. Inside, she closed the door and took a deep breath. She intended a return to the exact time and place she'd left, and she intended that she'd be only a woman with no powers, with rooms full of eager strangers waiting for her while two of them forced their way in to take her.

She caught herself with a reminder: she intended that whatever awaited her in the suite would follow the plan the two strangers had said she'd outlined herself. Would it match how she'd visualized it? Or would it be even more extreme, something she couldn't imagine while standing safe in her real world? Was some hidden, wanton slice of her imagination spinning some surprising plot for her?

Waiting there naked except for her heels, she felt even more undressed at the certainty that her powers would soon be dwindling. She waited for the final flare of panic, and when it struck, she embraced it as what it would be during her flight: the excitement of being helpless with no escape.

The black dot found her quickly. It seemed to be in on the plot like it didn't want to give her any chance to back out. Without waiting, it rushed toward her and engulfed her. In the tiniest of moments, she felt herself die, and another world took her—a tempting but treacherous world that could trap her in a heartbeat with no powers and no warning.

Chapter 32 – Lin's Flight No. 6

Lin's eyes still focused on the bathroom door, but this door held her white blouse and rattled from the pounding. And on the other side of the fake door, an angry and very real-sounding Luke called to her.

"Hey! Let's go already!"

She heard her heart echoing inside her, and the champagne still chased all of the dangers of the world closer to some horizon somewhere.

I'll think about that in a second, she told herself. This is so nice here in this plush bathroom, and that bathwater was so hot and comfortable, and since I only swilled about half of that big bottle of champagne, maybe I'll pour some more, then for sure I won't just be naked—I'll be ready and willing to—

"I'm not joking here. Mack, hand me that key."

Wait a second, Lin thought. I need to forget about Luke for a second. And Mack. Didn't Gabby tell me to look for something? Oh, a window!

She turned away from the door, looked above the tub, and saw a window covered with curtains that lofted inward from a steady breeze.

That wasn't here before, she thought. How odd. Did Gabby somehow convince me to add that?

She carefully took one step up onto the tub's edge, paused to admire the height of her heel, then she stepped up with the other while leaning against the far wall. With one hand, she spread the curtains apart, felt the hot, humid air of South Georgia touching her cheeks, and leaned closer to get a good view.

It's just St. Simons Island, she observed. I see the sky, which is a pretty blue with a bright sun close to the horizon. Oh, and there are those live oaks, still looking healthy and strong. Glad I didn't kill them! There are roads and sidewalks, landscaped areas and neatly trimmed lawns, and of course, people walking and driving all over the place. What the heck is Gabby—

She stopped and turned her head, pointing an ear to the breeze that carried a faint sound. It was softer than traffic sounds, but still, it found its way past the rumble of engines far below and through the window. Maybe it was a higher pitch than—

No, wait, she realized . . . it didn't have any pitch. It didn't sound like anything. How could that be? Is that what Gabby meant? Did that strange sound somehow notice her? How could that make any sense? Why would that matter in a make-believe world far away from—

"You think you can hide in there? Get your sweet naked ass out here!"

Lin hurried to the floor, looked down, and saw that she sure was completely naked. She found her underwear and slid it on just as she heard the key scraping the lock, and her heart pounded.

"This ain't the one," said Luke. "Go get the other one."

Why did I do that? she wondered. Isn't naked better?

"Come on. Hurry up, Mack."

She saw her white blouse hanging on the door, and she wondered if there might be a dark spot on it somewhere. Then, she realized she wasn't ready to leave—not yet—and needed to push the flight further. No, she corrected herself: she *wanted* to push the flight further. Her fantasy waited right outside that door, and she wasn't going anywhere.

Still, she grabbed the shirt, put it on, and buttoned part-way up just as the door pounded again.

"Now, you're coming out. Thanks, Mack."

The fake world had changed. Luke, who she still thought she'd seen before, didn't sound playful anymore. No, he sounded more aggressive. Was more antagonism something that she'd wanted too?

She was glad that she'd stayed two steps inside the room because a violent shove snapped the door inward, and the hanger fell to the floor.

Luke stepped in, and even in her heels, Lin had to look up into his eyes. He shook his head slowly as he scanned every inch of her.

"Well, you do look good, but I gotta tell you—these boys are gonna get rough."

"Oh, I'll be fine. How rough do you think?"

She gave him a smile.

"Rougher than you're gonna want. Too late. I told you to hurry."

"I did hurry, but—"

"You were supposed to be naked too. What's with this?"

He pinched her blouse between her breasts and shook them up and down a few times. She looked down at the black sleeve of his jacket, then back up at his gleaming smile.

"I told you that I needed more—"

"Look, it doesn't matter. That's all getting ripped off of you anyway. They're really going to use you and abuse you. Probably more ways than you want."

Lin felt her heart pounding as her imagination gave her some startling possibilities.

"No, I take that back. I think you *do* want," he said with a laugh.

He's right, she thought after considering those possibilities. Maybe I do want.

Mack crowded in beside Luke, and each grabbed a wrist. Lin felt her arms pulled behind her, and she tried to fight them, but she couldn't. Mack crossed her wrists and wound a belt tight around them.

"Hey, that's not necessary. I'll do whatever—"

A quick, gentle slap from Luke ended her plea and sent a tremor through her, whether fear or thrill she didn't know for sure. She turned back to look at him, saw his pointy beard, and she knew.

"It's you! From the car! You gave me a ride, didn't you? Not the first time but the second time!"

He laughed and said, "I told you I'd be back. Well, I'm back."

"You never said that! What are you talking about?"

"No, not in the car—you're right about that much. Now, I really have you. I love that you're such a tease. What a flirt you were out on the sidewalk."

Lin stared at his face and felt a cold fear thrown in with the thrill, prompting her to look for her mayhem, but she couldn't find it. She felt her knees weaken again at being so helpless. She was close to naked in a hotel suite full of men that not only wanted her—they were impatient and angry too.

And Luke . . . something wasn't right about him.

"I was just saying—"

He spun her around and covered her mouth, and Lin felt his hand rough over her lips as he stifled her words.

"Nobody paid you to talk unless you're saying something sexy. You got that?"

She fought to squirm herself out of his grip. A spike of electricity shot through her when his hold on her tightened, and she felt her back against his chest.

"Oh, that's kind of fun. Yeah, keep fighting. You sure are a fighter."

Looking above his fingers at the closed curtains above the tub, she thought of searching for the black spot to take her home for the last time, never to return.

Instead, she wiggled her arms to confirm that they were tied behind her, and she tried again to turn her head, but Luke was far too strong. All he did was tighten his grip. With her heart pounding a steady beat, just the way she liked it, she made an attempt at ordering him to let her go, and all she could offer was a loud groan.

"That's good! Just remember: we're doing exactly what you said you wanted. Every bit of it, including this."

She didn't expect a red and black bandana to replace his hand, and she felt him work it tight into her mouth, turning the beginning of her protest into garbled gibberish, and he began tying it behind her head.

Knowing it was likely useless, she struggled to free her wrists while trying to turn her head. But both men were far too strong. She'd only caused the edge of the belt to scrape over her skin, and Luke was forced to give her a knot tighter than if she'd have accepted it.

Yeah, she thought with her heart beating hard, I probably did ask for this.

She felt like laughing herself at the muffled whimpering that escaped when she tried to speak. When both men laughed at her, she tried again, more loudly, causing more laughter.

Yep, I'm sure I asked for this, she realized. What else did that dark corner of my imagination plan for me?

When Luke spun her around and held her by her shoulders, all she could do was look into his eyes.

"I like you way better like this. You still look hot as hell, but you're not such a smartass anymore."

Lin felt her heart pounding as she stood on weak legs and kept quiet by his bandana. His serious look receded for a small smile.

"You like it better, too, don't you? You like being gagged, Honey?"

She felt her knees getting weaker, and before she could think about finding a spot to help her leave forever, she knew that it was true, gave up on her escape, and nodded her head.

"Of course, you do. Never would have guessed that. But don't worry: we'll get that out of the way when the time comes. Bet you'll like that too."

She saw that he waited for an answer, and though she saw something dark waiting for her on the wall behind him, she still nodded.

Not far enough yet, she thought. I need to at least get out into the crowd, and long before I'm in any real danger, I'll head right back home.

"Yeah, I'm sure you'll like that. Mack, hold onto her."

Mack stood behind her and grabbed her upper arms, and when she tested her strength against his, all that happened was that he held them even tighter.

"Nice," said Luke as he viewed her breasts straining against the thin white cloth. "Even better than I thought."

He looked back up and brushed a few stray hairs off of her shoulders to join the rest laying on her back. She stared and wondered how a stranger in a world crafted by her intent could seem familiar. It had to be from more than just having taken a ride from him.

"No wonder you like showing them off every chance you get," he said with a laugh. "You ready?"

Lin nodded twice and glanced past him at the tiny dark smudge on the wall. It rested there, and when it seemed like it might be about to rush at her, she looked away from it enough that her eyes rested on the champagne bottle still waiting next to her glass on the counter.

Oh, that sure does look good, she thought. If I weren't bound and gagged, I'd pour myself a full glass, maybe pose with it in my hand for them, or maybe I could drink right out of the bottle—I could sure make that fun to watch—then maybe I'd—

"Alright, come on," Mack said while still holding her arms. "Time to feed you to the animals."

Lin felt her heart spike, and she took hurried steps to keep her balance on her tall heels as they led her out into the dim room. She saw that the other men weren't just in the bedroom or even just in the adjoining suite. They were everywhere.

Hoots and whistles, yelling and laughter greeted her as they paraded her through the crowd. She felt hands grabbing at her and touching her everywhere, pulling at her blouse and lifting it up. She got spanked more than a few times, and the pinches made her try to twist out of their grasp.

Okay, I could do without the pinching, she thought, and I should probably think about leaving. But there's nothing wrong with the rest of it. What a thrill to be driving them all crazy, all those eager strangers in a darkened hotel room. It's just what I wanted: about to be naked, completely helpless, and kind of drunk too. Already, I can barely remember being a bird. No room full of men would ever treat a bird this way!

Luke led the way into the center of the room, and she looked around to see strangers three and four deep, all pointing at her, or laughing, or looking at her in silence, some with eyes that gave her a chill.

But the room was too warm for chills, she knew, and there was no turning back. She had no power to destroy them, or start a storm, or make one of them sprout a few extra limbs. She'd have no choice in anything that would happen, at least until she found the black dot that would take her home.

Oh, as long as I don't ignore it, she thought. Not like the one I just saw in the bathroom. Oh no . . . what if that's the only one in the suite? How would I—

She felt a rough shove from Mack, angling her toward the sitting area.

"Come on. Let's set you up for the first round."

First round? she thought. What on Earth is he talking about? Oh, wait—this might not really be Earth anymore!

Mack guided her like a captured prize toward the couch, where Luke had stopped and stood grinning near a large, cushioned ottoman that had been moved to the middle of the room.

What's this? she wondered. Well, whatever is going on, it was my idea. Maybe I'll have to sit on that for a while? Maybe they'll want to take some photos, which would be fun. I hope someone hands me another glass of—

"Hey, quiet, everyone," said Luke, and the room went silent.

Lin saw his eyes focus on hers, and he said, "Remember, this was all your idea. You must have some weird fetish about being helpless, which is a huge surprise to me, and you're damn sure going to be."

More pushing from Mack left her standing close to the ottoman, and Luke stood on the other side.

"Hold her still, Mack," he said as he reached for her blouse with both hands.

While looking into her eyes, he said, "Finally, you tease," and yanked it open, sending a few buttons flying and exposing her breasts.

The room erupted in applause and laughter, and Lin knew that her rapid breaths were adding to the display.

"Yeah, you really should show those off," Luke said with a serious grin and eyes looking back and forth. "You owe it to the world."

Lin groaned through her gag and looked down at the green fabric of the ottoman, searching for a dark spot.

Wait, she told herself. What's the big deal? Isn't this part of the fantasy? Even if I do see that dot, it's too soon. I can leave anytime I want anyway. I *know* I sure don't look like any kind of bird!

Then, Mack began shaking her from side to side, and though there wasn't any laughter, there were plenty of compliments.

Maybe it's time to leave now? she asked herself. No. They're just admiring the view. No harm in that. I do remember liking to stand naked and be admired.

She felt one of Mack's hands let go but only long enough to pull her blouse over her shoulder and down her back. His other hand took care of the other side, causing more whistles and compliments.

"Well, you sure are a sight, aren't you? Even better than I thought. Alright, Sweetheart, on your knees, just the way you said you wanted it."

No, you can't be serious, Lin thought. What the heck are—

She groaned as several hands on each shoulder forced her to her knees. Luke gave the ottoman a kick to press it up against her thighs.

She looked up at him, and he said, "Hey, your idea. But I gotta say, I'm gonna enjoy the hell out of it."

Well, she thought, I'm sure this was my idea too. I think I can imagine where this is going.

Mack still hadn't let her loose, and she felt more hands pulling at her blouse, some playing with her hair, and more than a couple giving her sharp spanks.

"Oh, I forget," Luke said to the crowd. "Do we tie her legs to that thing first? Or does she lose those sexy panties?"

The room erupted in cheers.

No, don't you dare, thought Lin. Where's my mayhem? I'll destroy you faster than you can—

She looked and found nothing but inebriation from the champagne. She remembered that the rooms were soundproofed, and she couldn't scream anyway. It was all going to happen, and from what Luke had been saying, it was all her idea. Every last detail.

He rubbed his chin with one hand while he looked her over as she took deep breaths, and he said, "I can't remember, but I say, let's drop those panties of hers. We'll get her tied down next."

Constant laughter and comments filled the room, and Mack still didn't let go.

Oh God, is this finally really happening to me? Lin thought.

She knew the answer: yes, it was. For her, this was real. The hotel wasn't real and neither were the men, at least not yet. But *she* was doing this. This was going to happen to *her*. For her, it was completely real just as if it were happening in her real world.

When she'd finally decide to get back to her real life, she'd carry these memories with her and know that all of it had really happened to her. Or, more accurately, this is what she'd wanted and offered—none of it was "just happening." No one had made her continue in this world, to take a hot bath and give herself up naked for a suite full of strangers, for whom she was about to do anything they wanted.

Whether it came from Gloriana's meddling or from something inside her, this was her fantasy. And for her, it was entirely real.

Still, should she leave before any of it happened, even if she did want to stay just a short while longer? Would it be so wrong to let it go for just a few minutes, maybe just for Luke? Why not let Luke go first and see what it was like in a fake world?

And who exactly is Luke? she asked herself again as she recalled their intense talk when she stood beside his car in front of the hotel, liking how his eyes scanned every curve and feature that she'd barely concealed in her tight clothing.

She looked down at the soft green fabric of the ottoman and scanned everywhere for the black spot. She knew that it needed to show itself quickly if she would ever find her escape route.

She could find it and just hold it there until she was ready. She knew that she could let things go on for quite a while if she wanted, and only when she was good and ready would that dot kill her.

"Oh, I almost forgot," said Luke, and he gestured to someone behind her. She felt a wide cloth held over her eyes and tied behind her head.

Now, everything was black! How would she ever find the black dot?

"Yeah, that's it: she likes the blindfold too. She likes to feel really helpless. Feeling pretty helpless now, Honey?"

All she did was nod because she did feel even more helpless. The blindfold, she knew, had probably made it impossible to ever find her escape from that hotel world. And she began to wonder if she should feel grateful for that. Did she know that would happen? Is that why her imagination had arranged for her to be blindfolded?

"Okay, you know what's next, Mack."

Lin felt a hard shove on her back, leaning her down toward the ottoman, and she felt her breasts squeeze into the soft fabric.

Yep, she thought, that's no surprise. I knew that was coming.

She heard the door to the hallway open and more voices. One said, "Hell yeah, come on in. Yeah, this is the room."

Well, I guess I'll never find that damn black spot now, she said to herself. That's the way it goes! And how many more just came in just for me? There had to be—

A sharp spank stung her, and a voice said, "Look at that—ain't she a sight? Yeah, go down to the lobby, and tell them all to get up here."

Wasn't I supposed to be going somewhere? Lin asked herself. I'm sure I wanted to, but why would I? Especially if even more are joining the party?

She felt hands holding her waist and heard Luke behind her say, "Pretty thing like you must have a boyfriend too. Imagine if he could see you now."

Oh God, she thought. Jack! How did I forget about Jack? What would he think of me? I could never tell him. He can never know what I'm about to do!

No, it's not enough to just never tell Jack. This can't happen. It's gone too far already!

"Imagine if he could watch you for the next hour or two. Damn, he'd sure be done with you."

Jack wouldn't have lied to me, she screamed to herself. If he says he didn't sleep with Gloriana, then he didn't!

"The best part would be him seeing how much you enjoyed all of it."

It can't end like this! I just want Jack! I want only Jack touching me! And now, if I don't find that damn spot, this is my life, and I'll never see him again. I didn't even say goodbye!

"That's good. Hold her down. And turn her head to the side."

Lin felt hands on her back and pressing her into the soft ottoman. Someone turned her head to the left and pushed it down into the cloth.

"Oh my God, that looks good," said Luke behind her. "I am *so* glad I'm first. Hey, Beautiful, this is exactly how you said you wanted it. Who are we to argue?"

Lin tried to turn her head but couldn't, and she screamed into the bandana stretched through her mouth.

"Yeah, I'm leaving that in for my turn. I've had more than enough of your backtalk."

Lin groaned and tried to get up, but too many hands had her trapped.

"It's cool that you wanted this, too, because this is exactly the way I've wanted it since I first saw you. Admit it: we were made for each other."

Who the hell is Luke? she wondered with her heart pounding. Who in hell is he?

"Now, let's get you ready for a grateful and appreciative crowd. Me first, of course."

She felt his hands on her hips, fingers slipping inside the elastic band.

Lin felt her heart pounding and knew that she was lost in a world of her own creation. A place where she'd soon forget again about Jack and Taylor and Nomad and even Gabriel. There would be no going home.

"This is what you wanted, Beautiful. I think there are about a hundred of us now. Frankly, I'm shocked that you're this cheap and easy."

I want Jack! echoed through her. Only Jack!

With a heart on the verge of bursting inside her, Lin saw something unusual about the darkness. A part of it moved. Or maybe it got darker. Something was there. She didn't know if she was using her eyes, but still, she focused on it.

That odd darkness within the greater darkness gained some strength. It expanded, and the world behind her blindfold grew even darker. Lin hoped with all of her intent that it would race over her in time.

Luke had found a good grip and began pulling the sheer fabric down over her curves.

"Hey, hurry up with that," said a voice.

"Nope, I'm savoring the moment," said Luke.

Lots of yelling. Lots of laughter.

"Oh, that's looking perfect. I am so gonna love this. Lucky me that I found you here."

What? she thought. What is that imaginary madman talking about? Who the hell is—"

Her lungs turned to granite.

Her thoughts scattered like crows.

Her feelings bled out.

If a suite in a hotel in a phony, made-up world still existed, it had fallen silent. There was only the beating of her heart.

Then, it stopped.

Without a thought or feeling, Lin found her intent. In the silence of her death, she found the unbreakable hold that she'd first known on a lonely road in Georgia with an escaped convict strangling the life out of her.

With only the unbreakable hold on her intent, she waited in an eternity of darkness and emptiness.

Until a tiny point of light appeared.

Chapter 33 – I'm Taking Jack

Lin got dressed, stumbled out of her bedroom, and found Gabriel on the couch in the living room. Nomad took up all of the middle, and Lin squeezed in at the other end, where she let out a deep sigh and smiled.

"Well, that was quick. Something good has happened?"

"Yeah, Gabby. Whatever it was, whether something already in me or put there by Gloriana, it's gone. I took it pretty far and found out it's not even close to what I want."

"You no longer feel a need to travel to that world?"

"Oh, I didn't say that. But if I do go back, it won't be for the same reason. I lived that fantasy and took it pretty far. Actually, I just managed to escape before it got serious. If somehow that would have happened—really just another second or two—I think that world would have had me. It would have changed me."

"Even if you could still return to this world?"

"Yeah, even then. It was a turning point, and I chose the right path."

"I'm proud of you, Lin. By my count, you went there six times. If that world wasn't real by the time you left, it would have been soon."

"You're sure right about that. I need to go back only once more to completely close that door. It will kill that stupid fantasy and only reinforce the best one I can imagine."

"Lin, your goals might be good, but that doesn't change the risk. You're willing to take that chance?"

"Yeah, I think it'll be worth it."

"You'd risk being trapped there alone?"

"No, you don't understand. I'm taking Jack."

Gabriel stared with an open mouth. Big brown eyes quizzed Lin before a question was asked.

"You believe you can do that?"

"It's all intent, Gabby. You taught me that. I took Jack with me before, and we became baby birds. I can do the same with this."

Gabriel laughed and said, "You impress me and amaze me so often, Lin. I believe you can do it."

Gabriel's smile vanished.

"But that still doesn't change the risk."

"You still don't understand, Gabby. That world can't change me because I'm not going there to test-drive being a different Lin. It'll just be me. And Jack. That world can't touch us. All we'll do is find ourselves and each other."

"I'm sure you believe that, but—"

"My mind's made up. I mean, my intent's made up."

"When do you plan to try this?"

"As soon as we can."

"Lin, I almost forgot: did you find a window on that flight?"

"Yeah, Gabby. One that wasn't there the last time. How is that possible?"

Gabriel laughed and said, "In a world where almost everything is made up . . . you're really asking?"

She grinned and said, "Okay, never mind that. I didn't see anything unusual through that window anyway. What was I supposed to see?"

"First of all, Lin, are your eyes real when you're there?"

"I guess they're not, right?"

"Correct. Still, you are perceiving something, aren't you?"

"Oh, Gabby, this is too much. I just want to get going with—"

"I understand. Just one more question: did you notice anything unusual, even if not with your eyes? If you did, then you were noticed too."

Lin stared a few seconds, then nodded a couple of times.

"Yeah, I thought I heard something. But I didn't hear anything."

"Good, Lin. No more questions."

She squinted at Gabriel before continuing.

"That's it? You're leaving it at that?"

Gabriel only smiled and shrugged. Lin let out a deep breath and shook her head.

She looked down from Gabriel's eyes when Nomad turned to gaze at her. He stared for a few seconds, barked once softly at the ceiling, then held her gaze and panted.

"Look, even Nomad thinks it's a good idea. He just told Heaven about it. Now, I think he's even laughing about it."

"He is very wise. I plan to see you soon, Lin."

The door from the garage opened, and they heard Jack kick off his boots.

She gave Gabriel a big smile and got up to find Jack.

* * *

"Jack, I have something I—"

"Lin, hold up. I hope you can forget about Gloriana and her stupid mayhem dreams. I'm going to. I feel more sure of something now than I ever have before. I know what I want more than anything."

"Oh yeah, Jack, let's forget all about stupid dreams. Hey, you're not going to—"

"Lin, there's a question I've been meaning to ask you since that time in Allentown, when you healed Ben. Before The Shield hunted you to read the Words of God. Before all those crazy fake worlds you got dragged to and before Taylor started all those storms. Before you became a crow for six weeks. Lin, would you—"

"Jack, stop. I love you, and I love the question you're going to ask too. I only ask that we have that conversation in a different place, not here. What do you say, Jack?"

She smiled and raised her eyebrows twice.

He smiled and said, "Again, with the eyebrows? You know I can't resist that. Fine. Anywhere, Cowgirl. Where are we going?"

"Someplace special. I promise we won't stay long, and I also promise you'll hear the answer you want and that I want."

"Well, then, yeah, let's go. Right now, alright?"

"Yeah, for sure, Jack. Come on."

She took his hand, and they headed down the hallway to the bedroom. Inside, she closed and locked the door.

"Oh, no. It's some kind of magic thing, right?"

"Yeah, Jack. I just want you to play along, okay? It's important to me. And to us."

"You should know by now that I'll do anything for you. Yeah, of course, I'll play along. What are we doing?"

"Just have a seat, and wait till I call you. Then, come and stand over here by the bathroom door. Can you do that, Jack?"

"Am I supposed to understand any of this?"

"Not yet. But you will eventually. Okay?"

"Alright. You know I love you."

"I know, Jack. And I love you. Now, go have a seat."

She smacked his backside, and he left for the upholstered chair in her room.

Inside the small room by herself, she began by feeling the role she'd sought for her fantasy: that of a cheap version of herself, a Lin that would give herself to a room full of strangers. Or just one special stranger.

She'd already worked out the plans, hoping that Jack would agree. The first step was to take off all of her clothes except for her lacy underwear that tied on each side. She brushed back her mane and slipped on her heels. She took a final look in the mirror at all the bare skin and curves that she'd soon give to a man who would seem to be a stranger at first. And at first, he'd feel like a stranger himself, a man who showed up for a cheap but expensive woman in a hotel room.

"Jack," she called through the door. "Okay, come on over by the door."

"Alright, I'm here. What's going on?"

"We'll laugh about it soon."

Lin knew that there was no way to explain it. Best to just go. She engaged her intent with all the power she could muster and pointed it all toward the plush hotel suite and the scenario she'd planned out. She knew that the black dot would appear where she stared at the door, and it quickly covered her and hid every trace of the real world.

It was a short death, and the white light raced toward her. Her life returned but in the luxurious bathroom of a crowded suite in a hotel in a St. Simons that didn't exist.

At least not yet. And she hoped that it wouldn't while she and Jack lived there.

Chapter 34 – Lin's & Jack's Flight

The warm, humid air rose up to meet her as she looked down at the hot bath water still full in the tub. A glance in the mirror confirmed that she was entirely naked except for her heels and underwear, and she saw a playful shine in her eyes. She knew that she was ready for whatever fantasy she'd requested from all of the strangers beyond the locked door. She gave her hair one final brushing and turned toward the white blouse hanging on the door.

Its color reminded her of innocence, and she grinned at the realization that she'd leave that behind, too, not just the shirt.

The hanger bounced on its hook from the insistent pounding.

"Hey, I paid a lot for this. Don't keep me waiting."

A spike of fear mixed with a sweet excitement as it snaked its way through her. His anger seemed to fuel it, boosting the anticipation.

With a quick turn of her head, she looked at the wall above the tub, saw a window with closed curtains, and knew there wasn't time. She turned back to the door.

"I'm almost ready for you and everyone else. I just have no idea how much longer this will—"

"No, I chased them all out. It's just me. You better get moving and make it worth the fortune I paid for this."

Only one man now? Lin thought. Well, maybe that's even better. One determined man would be better than a room full of losers anyway.

Especially if she could provoke him even more.

"Oh, you know . . . I think maybe I changed my mind."

There was one heavy pound on the door, then silence. Lin just had time to check the strings tied in neat bows on each hip, and seconds later, she heard a key turning in the lock.

She began reaching for her blouse, but the door jerked open, shaking the hanger around, and a large, muscular man with wavy brown hair walked in. Her heels were high, but they didn't bring her up to his eye level. And he didn't look to her like a patient man.

While his big brown eyes studied her up and down, Lin took a moment to appreciate the hard muscles obvious beneath his t-shirt and jeans. It surprised her that she liked his cowboy boots too.

He looked into her eyes with a grin and said, "Damn, you do look good, but no way are you getting out of this. You're just for me now."

He grabbed her left wrist and looped something around it. He jerked her other arm out, and she tried to pull it back, but he still tied her wrists together.

"Hey, what the—"

A quick slap that mostly missed the mark silenced her.

"No more talk. I'll tell you what you can do with that pretty mouth of yours."

"I didn't mean to—"

She felt his calloused hand squeeze tight over her mouth.

"Oh, you really can't stop talking, can you? That explains it."

He reached into the back pocket of his jeans and brought out a blue bandana, which he pulled tight through her open mouth and tied behind her head.

"Pretty damn quiet now, aren't you?"

Lin felt her heart beating strong and excitement flowing like electricity. She nodded.

"Damn right."

He turned and jerked on the belt binding her wrists together. Lin took quick steps on her high heels to keep up with him. She wished it had been a wood floor so that he could hear her heels—she knew that he'd like that. But the room was silent, and it was obvious that no one would come to save her if it got too rough.

The man led her like a pet on a leash to a well-padded ottoman near the couch. He turned and looked into her eyes. She knew that she liked his eyes, but he looked kind of crazed, a man with a singular purpose. And that purpose was her.

She took a quick look at the door to the hallway, but she saw no possibility of escape. The danger of being alone and helpless for a stranger that had bought and paid for her and would do whatever he damned well pleased was her only reality.

He snapped the belt forward, forcing her arms out and squeezing her breasts together. She saw that he liked that, but not enough to smile—just enough to become more focused. He dropped the leash and looked down from her eyes, but she kept her arms up, smiling at him and giving him a view that he liked.

She felt his hands rough on her, squeezing and fondling. He continued with his left hand while he untied her restraint with his right. After he'd freed her, he spun her around and wrestled her arms behind her. Lin felt her heart beating a happy rhythm as the stranger retied her wrists.

"That's a mighty fine ass you got. They said you like being helpless? Good, that's what you're getting. Not my first choice, but it'll suit me just fine."

He grabbed her upper arms and forced her closer to the ottoman. She couldn't fight the strong push he gave to her shoulders, forcing her to her knees on the soft rug.

"Get those knees apart. Do it."

Lin obeyed and soon felt tight straps holding her thighs to the legs of the ottoman.

"That's a good start. You're a cheap one, aren't you? You were going to do this for all of them? That's what you wanted?"

Lin's heart raced at feeling herself so helpless and exposed, powerless to stop him from doing anything at all to her. And since she knew that there was no point in lying, she managed to say, "Mm-hmm . . ."

"No complaints from me. You do look damn good like that. Helpless suits you."

She felt him untying the bandana that kept her quiet, and he tossed that aside before bending her forward onto the soft fabric. With one of his hands on her back and holding her down, Lin waited for what she suspected would come next.

And still, the sharp spank made her squirm and want another. She waited for the next, but it didn't happen. There was a long moment of silence.

"Wait a minute," she heard the man say.

Another lengthy pause.

"Get up."

One strong hand took hold of her arm and lifted her back up onto her knees.

What's he up to now? she thought. Did he think up something even more degrading?

But all she felt was him pulling her hair back over her shoulders and fluffing it back.

"That's nice," she heard herself saying. "You like my hair?"

"Yeah. Your hair, it's . . ."

Using both hands, he pulled it all back and let it drop.

She looked down when she felt the straps around her thighs being loosened and removed. Then, he held both of her arms and helped her all the way up onto her heels. He spun her around to face him, then he pulled her in close until her breasts were squeezed into his hard chest.

While looking into her eyes, he reached around her with both hands and freed her wrists.

Lin held the gaze of the stranger who had purchased her, who could do whatever he wanted with her in a hotel room that didn't exist. And all he did was look into her eyes. With eyes that reminded her of someone from another life.

She watched him shake his head slowly a couple of times and start to speak, only to stop and look into her eyes a few more seconds. Then, he touched her cheek.

I don't know what kind of game this is, she thought, but it's a pretty nice one.

She gasped when he lifted her up into his arms like she weighed nothing at all. He held her there in silence, still looking like he had something to say but unable to find the words.

His steps were strong and steady as he carried her into the bedroom and kicked the door closed. To Lin, the blankets felt cool and soft when he lay her down on them, and again, he touched only her cheek, causing her heart to pound more than maybe anything else he could have done.

He kicked off his boots and dropped his shirt on the dresser, showing lean muscles that appeared to have come from hard work and not a gym. He lay beside her, both on their sides and facing each other, and held her face in both of his hands.

Lin was sure that she knew him from somewhere.

But how could she? she wondered. He was a stranger. Nothing more.

Then, he kissed her with his rough hands still on her cheeks. It was an easy kiss, just brushing their lips together. But something about the man made Lin want to part her lips, and when she did, he did the same. She reached around his waist, and he shifted around so that she could get her other arm under him.

She almost said a name out loud.

He pulled back, and Lin saw his big brown eyes looking into hers. She felt she was melting all over the bed at seeing a hint of a wet sheen over them. And when he spoke, she felt her eyes give up their own tears.

"Lin?"

Her heart pounded inside her, and she knew that she had something to say, but she didn't know what it would be.

"Jack? Is that you?"

"It's me. It's really you?"

"Yeah, Jack, it's really me!"

"What are we doing here? This is where you wanted us to go?"

"Yeah, Jack, and we found each other here. That's what I wanted more than anything. I can't even explain to you how important this is to me!"

He kissed her again, a long and deep kiss, before pulling back and still holding her face in both hands.

"We came here for a reason, Jack. Do you remember?"

She saw his eyes moisten more, and they showed just a hint of a smile when he nodded.

He never let go when he said, "Lin, I want nothing more in life than to spend the rest of it with you. I know you have unimaginable magical powers, and you probably don't need me, but—"

"I need you. I will always need you, Jack."

He cleared his throat, and one small tear escaped to race down his cheek without leaving a trace.

"I love you, Lin Finity, and want nothing more than for us to be married. Will you marry me, Lin?"

Lin smiled and nodded her head gently in his strong hands, and though she wanted to savor the moment, she knew that her answer couldn't wait.

"Yes. Yes, Jack, I will marry you!"

The wetness of his eyes collected into another tear that followed the first one's path toward the bed. She felt her heart racing more than any imaginary world or fantasy could muster as she smiled back at him. She made no effort to control her own tears.

"God, Lin, I can't believe it. I've wanted to ask you for so long. You mean it? We're really getting married?"

"Yeah, Cowboy Jack. We're getting married!"

"My Cowgirl," he said before he pulled her in for a long hug.

Still wrapped up in his embrace, Lin felt a sharp alarm in her heart and knew that they had to return. She'd accomplished everything she needed from that world. The fantasy had been purged, never to return. There would never again be any notion of giving up her powers. No admiring looks from strangers would ever again mean anything. And when she wanted to be sexy and tempting, offering it all to Jack would always be more than enough.

But it was time to go. She took a look around the room and saw that everything had more detail than she'd noticed before. She'd never thought about it in the previous flights, but it all had had a dreamlike quality to it. No more. It all looked as real as the real world she knew that they needed to rejoin. Right away.

With Jack's body warm against hers, she scanned the far wall, looking for a black dot, or a spot, or anything at all that could race toward her and kill her.

Nothing appeared.

She felt Jack's hand at the small of her back and pulling her closer.

"Oh, Jack, just hold me, okay?"

"You feel so good, Lin. And this room, wherever it is, sure is nice. Why don't we—"

"Jack, I want to. How about as soon as we get back, okay? I need to concentrate."

She felt his arm slip under her, and he held her tightly with both hands.

"Jack, no. Not now, okay?"

She kept staring at the wall, even as her feelings were telling her to give in, to let them both celebrate their plan. For a moment, she forgot what she sought on that empty wall.

He reached for the neat bow on her hip that held the tiny garment together. He found one of the strings and gave it a pull. Lin felt the cloth fall away to the front and back of her.

"Jack . . ."

His hand was now on her uncovered bottom, which he rubbed and squeezed as he began to kiss and nibble on her ear.

"That sure does feel good, Jack, but—"

He rolled onto his back, and his strong arms pulled her up on top of him. Before she could protest, he'd covered her lips with a kiss, and she felt his left hand untying the bow on her other hip. Lost in his deep kiss, she felt him pull the thin cloth between her thighs from behind until she was free of it.

She tried to back away from his kiss, but while his right hand held the part of her that he'd just uncovered, his left hand held the back of her head.

Oh no, she thought, is this some lingering part of the fantasy? He's too strong, and I can't stop him!

Without remembering how he'd undressed himself, she felt him hot and ready beneath her, and she couldn't focus on anything else. He continued to kiss her, and she cooperated with his moving and shifting until he found her. Only then did he release her, and she pulled her face away enough to speak.

She realized that, without her powers, she really couldn't stop him, and in some ways, she didn't want to.

"Oh, Cowboy, this is amazing. Even more than usual."

"Because in our hearts, we're already married. I bet that's it, right?"

"Yeah, Jack, that must be it," she said and wondered if it had more to do with the world they occupied, that soft bed in a hotel that didn't exist, in a fake version of St. Simons Island, a place she remembered with a streak of fear was becoming more real every second. They had to return!

I need to find that black dot, she thought, before it's too late!

She tried to look at the wall above the headboard and felt the first tingles of Jack's steady motions jumping all through her.

I'll close my eyes for just a second, she thought, and she felt his lips again pressed into hers.

He held her by her hips, and all she could think about was the rhythmic motions that she'd begun above him, bringing him closer to ecstasy with her, together, in that quiet hotel room, in a luxurious bed, in a hotel that—

Stop! she told herself. Open your eyes! Find that black dot!

She pulled away from his kiss, struggled to not look into his big brown eyes, and looked instead at his forehead. It looked at first like it might be a small freckle, one that she'd never noticed before, and it doubled in size as she watched.

The first big wave of pleasure was so close that she wanted only to lose herself to it. She fought to keep staring.

All at once, much sooner and much more overpowering than she would have guessed, a monstrous wave of rapture broke loose just as Jack's freckle grew so large that it covered her, and him, and the room, and the entire fake world.

Her last thought was about making that jump—dying—while in the throes of the ecstasy they were giving each other. Was that a good idea?

It was too late. Neither could be turned back, and each of them buried her.

No feelings of pleasure remained after her breaths ground to a halt. She couldn't feel anything except that Jack was still with her. She couldn't think a single thought about it, though.

The last trace of her life in that world, her heartbeat, vanished as if it had never existed.

Lin found her intent and held it more tightly than ever. She had nothing else, nothing but a thoughtless certainty that centuries could have been whistling past as she held Jack and her intent in an endless emptiness.

Until a minuscule white point appeared against the darkness.

She latched onto it and sensed it growing, approaching them, and finally, it covered them completely. Her heart began, her thoughts and feelings started to return one by one, and she took a deep breath and waited for every part of her life to resume.

* * *

The first thing Lin noted was that Jack didn't feel as warm beneath her as he had before. He felt different somehow, but he still felt comfortable. She could tell her head was resting on its side, and she knew that she'd soon feel him kissing her neck and ear.

Before being able to feel his lips on her, she had the unmistakable sensation of no longer sitting on his lap. Some control had returned to her legs, and she tried to rise up, even just once, like she'd been doing so eagerly before she'd taken them home.

But it didn't work. She found that she still didn't have enough ability to move her legs.

She fought to hurry the process, to regain all of her life, but it had its own pace, and she could find no way to speed it up.

She heard a man's voice and knew that it must be Jack. It had worked! She'd brought them home! But she couldn't understand what he was saying.

And his kiss felt different against her cheek.

And she believed she'd opened her eyes, but the room was too dark to see anything.

And her arms were behind her. Was Jack holding them there?

She tried again to move her legs and felt them held in place.

Then, she felt hands on her back and head, holding her down.

And two hands on her bottom, squeezing roughly.

Then loud laughter, but not from Jack. Many strange voices talking and laughing. Far too many to count. Through the din, she heard Jack's panicked voice.

"Lin! Good God, what the hell are you doing?"

"Hey, this is what she wanted," said Luke. "She sure is cheap and easy, isn't she? Get in line like the rest of them."

"Lin?"

Lin couldn't answer. She felt only her restraints, knew that she was naked and helpless without any powers, and she knew what else she was only moments away from feeling. And this time, Jack was there watching!

In less than a heartbeat, she focused on a point that she knew had to be waiting somewhere in the depths of night inside her closed and blindfolded eyes. She couldn't wait any longer and prayed a deeper darkness that she couldn't see would soon cover her and kill her.

It did. She died and found herself alone in a vast emptiness with Jack only along for the ride.

*   *   *

A bright streak of white rushed at her and brought her to life. As her heart pounded and she took a deep breath, the warm bath water welcomed her, and she stretched out her legs, with hot jets teasing her on all sides.

Then, her heart jumped as she heard Jack's frantic voice and angry pounding on the locked door.

"Lin, we have to get out of here! There's no time for a bath!"

"Out of the way. Mack, go get that key. I'll drag her out of there dripping wet if I have to."

She turned to look at the door, which was shaking from the violent pounding.

"Lin, we need to—"

"Actually, I'd like her dripping wet!"

"Lin!"

Lin died. She'd found a dark smudge on the tile wall, and it killed her. The bathwater drained away, the pounding on the door ceased, and Jack went mute. But still, she felt his presence with her as she held her intent in silence and darkness.

*   *   *

After what could have been centuries, a shining light caught Lin's attention, and she couldn't look away. It charged at her, devoured her, and brought her back to life.

She took a deep breath and opened her eyes. Only a peephole appeared, and she reached out with both hands against the door to steady herself.

"Lin, what the hell is *that?*"

She turned to see a nightmare version of a man writhing on the floor of the hallway, sprouting new arms every second. His screams echoed down the hall as lights flashed and sirens howled.

"Lin? Did you do that to him?"

She looked back at the peephole and intended for it to kill her. It surprised her, but only for a moment, that she'd found what she needed exactly where she'd intended to find it. An empty eternity enveloped her and brought her life to an end. Her final thought was that she still held Jack's hand.

In absolute stillness and quiet, Lin clung to her intent.

* * *

The moment she took her next breath, she was staring at closed elevator doors. She turned briefly to see that Jack was off to one side, his mouth open and ready to scream, and other men stood all around them.

Before Jack could make a sound, she focused again on the elevator doors and easily found her intent, stopping time. Everything froze, even the storms raging against the tall glass windows in the lounge. She stared and quickly located a small speck of blackness against the plain paint just where she'd wanted it to appear, and she welcomed the death that it brought her.

* * *

Before inhaling the warm ocean air, Lin heard the sports car's engine purring and felt Jack's hand in hers. She opened her eyes and saw a sneer on the man's face as he looked up at her from the driver's seat.

And in that moment, she knew that she was again in control. She knew that she could find the home that she and Jack both wanted.

Then, she remembered the odd things the man had said to her in the suite.

"Yeah," he said, "I'm leaving too. It's not safe for anyone here for much longer!"

"What? How can you even talk about that?"

He pushed his sunglasses up, flashed a polished smile, reached for a travel mug resting in the console, and took a long drink.

"Oh, I needed that. I always do. See ya!"

He drove off, and Lin turned to Jack.

"Lin, I . . . what is . . . I mean—"

"We're leaving this all behind. Are you ready to go home, Jack? I know I am."

"Yeah. God yeah, Lin. Let's go home, alright?"

"We're almost there, Cowboy. Hang on!"

Lin said goodbye to a world that she vowed she'd never intend into existence again. She died from a greasy spot on the street, and she held her intent with a speechless and frozen Jack close by her side.

Chapter 35 – Guess Who!

A racing white dot overwhelmed her, bringing a welcome world, and Lin took a deep breath and opened her closet door. A thick tear began a warm path down her cheek at the sight of Jack down on one knee. He smiled and shook his head.

"What did we just do? All I remember, really, is holding you and asking you to marry me. Did anything else happen?"

"No, Jack, that was the only point of the trip. Oh God, it's good to be back, though. You really don't remember anything else?"

"No. What else was there?"

"Nothing important, that's for sure."

"Did you say yes?"

"Of course, I did! Since you don't remember, though, maybe you should ask me again."

She smiled and raised her eyebrows twice.

Jack laughed and said, "Alright, I will, and I don't dare wait another second because I'm not sure where we might end up."

He reached into his pocket and held out a sparkling ring.

"Will you make me the happiest man ever and marry me?"

"Yes, Jack. Oh yeah, I sure will, Cowboy!"

"God, I really am the happiest man ever! Let's not wait. Let's go—"

A blaring horn from outside shattered the quiet of the bedroom. Lin shrugged and helped Jack to his feet, and together, they parted the curtains. A red convertible had pulled into the driveway, and a man with a big smile and a pointy beard, wearing a black jacket with a clean white shirt, stood on the driver's seat with his arms straight out to each side. In one hand, he held a martini glass, despite the frigid air of

Pennsylvania in January, and his other hand waved around a red and black bandana.

"Guess who!"

* * *

"Who the hell is that? Do you know him? Why is he—"

"Oh, Jack, that's not possible!"

"What's not—"

"Where's Gabby? We have to find Gabby!"

She grabbed his hand, dragged him away from the window, and took him into the living room, where Gabriel sat on the couch with Nomad, both entranced by a loud cartoon.

"Gabby, did you hear that?" Lin said between quick, shallow breaths.

"I heard some kind of horn, but I thought it came from that boat that the penguin is piloting. He's lost somewhere out on an ocean and trying to find someplace with ice and snow and cookies and—"

"Gabby, no, it's not from the cartoon! There's a guy that doesn't exist out on the driveway!"

"What do you mean, he doesn't exist?" said Jack. "I saw him. You saw him. He's got a pretty nice car too."

She continued to look only at Gabriel and said, "Just look, okay? That's a nasty stranger from a world I made up. He can't be here!"

Gabriel opened the front door and stood gazing at the grinning man in the red convertible.

"Yet, here he is."

Nomad slammed his heavy paws on the windowsill. His bushy tail pointed at the ceiling as he growled continuously, stopping only to take in more air.

Jack looked over Gabriel's shoulder, but Lin left them to sit on the couch, and she wrapped herself in a blanket over her shoulders and held it close up under her chin.

"I told you I'd be back. Found a way to keep this slick car too."

"He's back?" said Jack. "Back from where? That fake world?"

"Where's my darling Anna Andreyevna Kelgina and that hot daughter of hers? I really need *both* of them working as a team. Know what I mean? Yeah, that's *exactly* what I mean!"

Jack flinched when he glanced at Lin on the couch—her eyes had lit up like two green volcanoes. He looked again over Gabriel's shoulder.

"God, I've missed drinking!"

He finished his glass and extended the bandana toward the house.

"I found a way to keep this too! How lucky is that, huh?"

Gabriel turned toward Lin but remained in the open doorway. Jack joined Nomad at the window, and despite the dog's controlled rage, he still rested his hand on the big dog's head.

"I know, Nomad. I feel the same way."

"Tell me again how many times you visited that world, Lin?" said Gabriel.

"Too many times!"

"Yes, that's right. I thought your biggest risk would be that the flight would trap you there forever."

"That might have been better! Gabby, tell me that's not who I think it is."

"I have never lied to you, Lin, and I won't start now. Yes, that's Lancaster Wolfe, and as I recall, he looks the same as he did last time."

Lin pulled the blanket up over her head, and only her shining eyes were visible.

"That can't be," said Jack. "I thought you both said he was dead."

"Only scattered. He, whatever he is, can't be killed."

"Can you scatter him again?"

"Not unless he attacks us. I can't interfere until he behaves as a demon. He can be as obnoxious as he wants."

"I have no such rules," said Lin. "I'll kill him."

"He hasn't threatened you, and he certainly hasn't endangered you yet, Lin. Free will, remember? Not good to act out of anger or vengeance?"

The blankets shook, and Lin's green light didn't fade.

"How is any of this even possible?"

"It's all about the magic, Jack. Somehow, Wolfe invaded Lin's flights to forever, and when she returned, he found a way to tag along."

"Great," said Jack. "Hey, Lin, what's with the bandana? What the hell is he talking about? And why do I feel like I should remember?"

She didn't answer. But she did engage her intent, and in no time, she felt her spinning mayhem ready to rip loose. She thought of Wolfe's neck, but a quick look at Gabriel frozen in her living room made her reconsider. Still, she turned her racing hands to face forward and sent out four lightning-fast and razor-thin disks before letting time resume.

"Hey, did you do that?" Jack said after turning toward Lin. "That bandana just got shredded. He's holding just this thin strip now."

Lin didn't answer that question either, and Gabriel said, "Good, Lin. I'm glad you chose a better path."

Wolfe's voice carried into the living room, which had grown colder from the January Pennsylvania air spilling in.

"I hope that wasn't you, Gabriel. You know you can't interfere with me."

Gabriel laughed and said, "Lin won't need my help. And if she does, I can do more than just scatter you. You won't return again."

"Huh," said Wolfe. "That doesn't sound good," and he poured himself another drink.

"What else can you do?" said Lin.

"Let's not worry about that now. The important thing is—"

"Hey, Lin! Tell me what kind of furniture you have in there. If I know you, which I think I do, you have something soft and comfy, maybe about this high,"—he held a hand near his knee—"something with solid legs, and—"

The drink in his hand split in two, and the car divided into four thick slices, the cut metal, ripped plastic, and shattered glass crunching down into a heap with air leaking from the tires, and gas and oil flowed down the driveway toward the street.

Wolfe stumbled and fell into the back seat, holding the base and smoothly-cut stem of his glass high as his legs stuck straight up over the seats.

Gabriel turned to Lin and said, "I'm proud of you, Lin. You could have killed him, but you—"

"What? That didn't kill him? He should be in pieces! Just like those damn cats!"

Gabriel held Lin's gaze with a slowly shaking head.

"Oh, Lin. He was only talking. How could that warrant such a reprisal?"

"How did that not kill him?"

"I don't know, but it is troubling."

"At least it's just him this time."

"We'll have to see. I think he'll gather an army."

"Regular men? Or—"

"Both."

"I don't think I'm strong enough. I'd need my own army."

"He seems to want vengeance."

"Oh, Gabby, he wants a lot more than that," she said with a humorless chuckle.

"I don't get it," said Jack. "What's the deal with furniture? What else does he want?"

"He's insane, Jack, and soon he's going to be—"

She stopped herself and pulled the blanket down to her shoulders. After holding her hair away from one ear, she turned her head, and only Nomad's growling filled the otherwise quiet room until he stopped and turned toward Lin.

Jack and Gabriel stared, and Lin said, "Gabby, I don't hear anything, but I hear it again."

Jack frowned and looked all around the room, then at Lin's blazing green eyes, then back at Gabriel. Lin stared at Gabriel and waited too.

Gabriel smiled and said, "Good, Lin. Soon, you will command the Gold."

Enjoy The Story?

Thank you for reading! Please consider leaving a review and/or a rating at your favorite bookseller or with your favorite book club. Help your fellow readers meet Lin Finity!

For more about Edward Allen Karr and his books, visit:

www.LakesideLetters.com

And follow him at:

Facebook: EdwardAllenKarr

Instagram: Edward_Allen_Karr

About The Author

Edward Allen Karr was born, raised, and continues to reside in Ohio, USA. His adult life has followed a meandering path, ranging from working an automotive assembly line to designing space flight hardware. And through all of it, he's seen that life is a captivating and ultimately unexplainable endeavor. His writing seeks to add a splash of wonder to a world already awash in it.

* * *

Coming next, a novel parallel in time with *Flights To Forever*.

Tayo Tersoo And The Hunter Of Souls
Fringes Of Infinity Book Five

"I must pursue something that hunts in a place without life. And when I find it—if I can find it—even though it's not alive, I must find a way to kill it? Is that all?" ~Tayo Tersoo, from *Lin Finity And The Islands Of Time*

Tayo Tersoo, a man pure of heart, dedicated, and very focused, was asked by Lin Finity to combat an entity that she and Gloriana had trapped and brought back from the Godless spaces between the Islands of Time. They call it a Hunter because it hunts souls in those empty spaces, bringing death to the living and chaos to everything else.

What Tayo did not know when he accepted Lin's task was that the entity, the Hunter of Souls, would invade him physically and from there, launch horrific attacks on him and those around him. Is his heart pure enough? How dedicated is he? If he loses his focus and can't keep the Hunter contained, it will roam the Earth, slaughtering wholesale.

"I do not mean these walls," Gabriel said while pointing all around the room and looking from face to face, then pointing down at Tayo, on the floor and losing his mind. "*He* is the wall." ~From the time-matched novel: *Lin Finity And The Flights To Forever* (Book Four)

*　　*　　*

Then, Lin Finity returns for more magic, romance, and intrigue in:

Lin Finity And The Torrents Of Gold
Fringes Of Infinity Book Six

www.LakesideLetters.com